Sanctuary Deceived

WITSEC Town Series
Book 4

Lisa Phillips

Cover art by Blue Azalea Designs
Photos from Shutterstock

Also By Lisa Phillips

Love Inspired Suspense

Double Agent

Star Witness

Manhunt

Easy Prey

Sudden Recall (March 2016)

Dead End (August 2016)

Denver FBI

Target (A prequel story)

Bait

WITSEC Town Series

Sanctuary Lost (Bk 1)

Sanctuary Buried (Bk 2)

Sanctuary Hidden (Bk 2.5, part of the Team Love on the Run anthology #1)

Sanctuary Breached (Bk 3)

Sanctuary Deceived (Bk 4)

Look for Sanctuary Forever – Book 5 – Coming this summer!

Prologue

From the book, SANCTUARY BREACHED

Through a haze of pain, Bolton understood they had carried him upstairs. The whomp of the helicopter's rotors grew louder, and then he saw them. Bolton gritted his teeth as they slid him inside.

"Bolton." Remy came to sit beside him. Something was wrong with her face.

Nadia Marie was on his other side, biting her lip. He grabbed her hand. "Did John authorize your leaving Sanctuary?"

She shook her head. "This is an emergency. You know that."

Remy piped up. "John is being stitched up. That horrible SEAL who betrayed Sam and killed his team stabbed John in the chest." There was an edge to her voice. Either she was more worried about him than ever, or something more was wrong.

Bolton tried to sit up. Remy and Nadia both pushed back against his shoulders. "Don't get up." Remy started to turn him. "I'll give you another shot."

He heard a plastic latch click and a packet being ripped open. There was a burn in his low back, and within seconds, numbness spread through the area. "Thanks, Rem."

She smiled, but there was none of her usual pragmatic manner in it. She was really worried.

"Help me up."

Neither said anything. They shared a look but helped him to sit. If he kept straight and moved slow he should be okay. He wasn't sure he'd exactly be able to walk if it came down to it, but it was possible. Anything was possible. He of all people knew that. When God had turned his life down a sharp detour, he'd learned what miracles were. And even through all he'd lost, Bolton could see the good.

Until they found out who he really was. Then his miracle would be finished.

He glanced at the pilot, his beanie pulled low and earphones pushed off the ear closest to them so he could hear.

The medical kit Remy was using. A silver suitcase.

His head whipped around to her.

Nadia said, "What?"

Bolton ignored her. Until Remy lifted her eyes and gave him a tiny nod. Bolton said, "Nothing. Just a twinge in my back."

Remy patted his shoulder. "That's to be expected. As soon as we get to a medical facility I'll contact my colleague, and we'll find out about that experimental treatment I was researching." Her voice quavered.

Bolton glanced at the pilot once more. When he looked back at Remy, she nodded.

If that was Tommy, there wasn't much Bolton could do considering the man was trained. Bolton had as much if not more skill in hand-to-hand when he wasn't suffering from a detrimental spinal injury that was going to leave him irreparably paralyzed if he so much as twitched at this point.

If that experimental procedure even remotely worked he was going to high-tail it back to Sanctuary as soon as he could to repay Andy the favor. Although he wasn't going to use a chair. And Andy was going to see this coming.

Nadia Marie glanced between them. "Experimental procedure?"

Remy explained the idea, while Bolton lay helpless. There was nothing in his general vicinity.

The helicopter dipped on a wind current.

Nadia Marie's eyes caught his. "Seriously?"

Bolton shrugged with his face—which is what he had to do, since he couldn't move his torso. "The alternative is living paralyzed."

"It's hardly a death sentence."

He looked away. She was right, but it wasn't like he had to accept it. This was his life they were talking about. As much as he might want her to be a part of it—and she seemed to think that was an option—at some point he was going to have to tell her the truth.

The helicopter began to descend.

Bolton reached under the collar of his T-shirt and pulled out the delicate gold chain. He twisted it so the clasp was at the front and looked at Nadia. "Take this off me."

He'd had it constructed years ago, for someone very close to him. It was a distinctly feminine piece of jewelry, and that fact did not escape Nadia.

Bolton didn't explain.

When she had a right to know, he would tell her.

The helicopter bumped the ground once and then settled. Bolton handed the chain to Remy. "Put this in your pocket. Don't lose it."

The pilot got up and turned to them. "Okay, folks. End of the line."

Nadia looked out the window. "We're in the middle of nowhere."

Bolton pulled her down as Tommy brought up the gun. She screamed. Remy whimpered, and Bolton held up one hand. "No one has to die."

Tommy grabbed the suitcase and pointed the gun at Remy. This was what he'd figured would happen. Bolton did his best to look helpless—and like Nadia was attached to him. He didn't want her being taken as collateral damage. He'd need her to help him to a phone.

Tommy pointed the gun at the door. "Outside."

Remy glanced at Bolton long enough for him to nod. She pulled on the door handle, and Tommy followed her out.

Bolton couldn't see them from that angle, and he couldn't twist to get a view without doing damage. Nadia's eyes were on the door. After a few seconds, tension bled from her face. "He looked back. I thought he was going to kill us."

"He didn't."

"I don't know why. We've seen his face."

Bolton didn't know if he could answer that question. "He has what he wanted. What he came to Sanctuary for."

Had it been him, Bolton would have killed them for sure.

"I suppose." She bit her lip. "I guess God knew we didn't need this day to get any worse."

He smiled. "You'll have to help me. We need to find a phone, and who knows how many miles it is to the nearest one."

Nadia blinked. "Oh…okay."

She helped him to the edge of the chopper in time to see a highway thirty feet from them. A van had pulled over. Remy got in, followed by Tommy. The SEAL looked back and waved.

"Help me get out." He didn't like this. Sure, they had no phones and he was injured, and they had no way of knowing where he was taking Remy. That Tommy knew of, at least.

Still…

"Hurry."

He crawled to the edge, and she helped hold up his weight as they made their way across grass. Ten steps. Twelve.

"Faster."

The helicopter exploded behind them.

Chapter 1

The fireball rushed toward the clouds. The wave of flames roiled and turned black, lacing the air with smoke. Bolton Farrera shielded his eyes as pain screamed from his low spine down to his knees. Smoke billowed from the wreckage of the helicopter that he'd barely crawled out of before it exploded.

Not good.

He turned his head one way and then the other. Nadia Marie lay on her side, facing away from him. *Nadia.* She looked a little singed but otherwise okay, except for the fact she was unconscious. Sun shone on her hair and made the brown strands lighten. She was out of reach.

Same old story. The miracle he could never claim.

Bolton lay back on the grass and tried to push the pain to a corner of his mind. He had to get help, get to a phone, something. He needed Nadia to wake up. He needed to be able to walk.

Truck tires squealed. A heavy door slammed, and a man ran over, keys jingling. White cowboy hat and the face of someone's grandpa, complete with gray stubble.

His knees popped, but he hit the grass beside Bolton. "Are you okay?" Grandpa-guy unclipped a cell phone from his belt and touched the screen. "I'll call the sheriff."

Bolton grabbed the phone.

The man sputtered. "Hey!"

Bolton fisted his right hand and clocked Grandpa in the jaw. The old man fell back in a heap, out cold. Bolton dialed, praying the number still worked after so many years.

"Pablo's Pizza."

"It's Bolton Farrera. Tell Ben I activated Thea's necklace. He'll be able to use it to find Remy."

"Please hold."

Bolton pitched the phone into the flaming wreckage of the helicopter. No trace. He couldn't afford to let anyone find him and Nadia—at least not until he wanted them to.

He'd activated the necklace to save Remy, but it wouldn't escape the notice of whoever was left hunting him. And he knew Dante was still breathing. That he still hated Bolton with everything in him.

Remy's life.

His life.

Bolton would do everything he could to keep himself and Nadia under the radar of whoever cared to look.

He didn't try to sit up but shifted and reached for Nadia Marie. Bolton gave her shoulder a gentle shake. They had only each other now. They weren't in Sanctuary anymore, protected by the US Marshals Service in what was their first and only witness protection town. In Sanctuary every resident had a price on their head, and yet they lived in safety because of the strictures placed on them.

He glanced at her again. It made his heart squeeze every time.

He knew exactly why she'd gotten in that helicopter: him. Her feelings weren't hard to figure out, and he'd been floored that she'd feel that way about him. But that was Sanctuary. Out here, this was the real world, and she didn't know who he was. Only who he'd been in witness protection.

Nadia Marie moaned and shifted.

Flashing blue and red lights. Bolton lifted his head. A cop car.

"Nadia?" He shoved at her shoulder and tried to sit up. It hurt, and he had to come up without bending his spine too much. He probably looked like the vampire, Lestat, emerging from his slumber. Sweat beaded on his forehead, but that would help his story so he didn't wipe it away.

Bolton shifted closer to her.

The sheriff strode over, and for a second Bolton thought it was John Mason. Except Sheriff Mason was a marshal, not an elected official. John wore jeans, unlike the beige sheriff's uniform this man wore. The local law surveyed the unconscious grandpa, the rousing woman, Bolton, and the helicopter wreckage. His gaze came back to Bolton. "This is going to be good. I can tell."

Bolton had been charming cops since he'd boosted that car on his fourteenth birthday. "It's been a rough day."

"I can tell that, too."

"You wanna know the kicker?"

The sheriff motioned to the grandpa. "Besides why my friend here looks like he got punched in the jaw?"

Yep.

"My wheelchair was on that chopper."

The sheriff's head actually jerked. *Surprise.* "Ambulance is on its way. You can't walk at all?"

He didn't have a wheelchair, but he needed one now. Bolton glanced down at his singed chambray shirt, new black Wranglers, and black boots. "Don't suppose my hat is around here somewhere?"

The sheriff stepped past him and retrieved the black Stetson Bolton had worn every day for years. The hat fit the clothes, and the sheriff would put the two together and decide for himself the kind of man Bolton was. Whether that would be true or not. Bolton had to keep Nadia Marie safe until she could figure out her next move, but Bolton didn't have that luxury.

The threat was real.

Nadia Marie's eyes flickered, and she groaned.

"Marie." Bolton reached for her, ran his hand down the back of her head. Not how he'd dreamed of touching her for so long. "You okay, Marie?"

She blinked. Frowned at him but must have seen it in his face, because she played along. "You know I hate when you call me by my given name."

"Great." The sheriff crouched. "This is Marie, and you are?"

Bolton stuck out his hand. "Steven Jones." John Smith was a little too obvious. "Marie is my wife."

The sheriff checked Grandpa's pulse. "And what happened to my friend here?"

"It was a reflex, I'm sorry to say. He rushed at me, and I didn't realize until too late that it was innocent. He thought we were hurt. But the helicopter had just exploded, and I was on edge. Sorry to say I hit him." Bolton tried to look like he felt guilty.

Nadia Marie climbed to her feet. "You need help, honey?"

The endearment sliced through him like a razor blade. Thea had called him honey. Right before she'd stabbed him in the back.

Bolton nodded. It was possible he might have been able to take a few steps, but the sheriff would see him as less of a threat this way. The ambulance showed up, and they loaded Bolton onto a stretcher. He didn't like lying there, but it was the fastest way out. The grandpa-rancher likely wouldn't buy it when the sheriff told him Bolton had said the punch was an accident. But by then they'd hopefully be long gone.

No wheelchair materialized at the small hospital. Instead, they transferred him to a bed. Did they think they were going to run tests on him? When the nurse came over, he grabbed Nadia Marie's hand and pulled her to sit by him on the bed. He surveyed her face. "Are you okay? You didn't fall funny or hit your head?"

She started to shake her head, but he gently squeezed the back of her neck. "Actually, I do feel sort of dizzy."

"I'll go tell the doctor." The nurse ran out.

Finally, they were alone.

"Nad—"

"What was that?" She got off the bed and moved so he couldn't reach her. "You're lying to them. You didn't really punch that old man, did you?"

Bolton didn't answer that. "We have no ID's, no money. No phones. We have nothing but the clothes we're wearing and I'm injured."

She touched a hand to her forehead, and then ran both hands through her long hair. "Why do we have to lie about who we are?"

"Maybe because we're in witness protection?"

"You don't have to talk to me like that." She shot him a look. "The sheriff can call the closest Marshals office. They can contact Grant Mason. He's the director of the whole Marshals Service! He'll send someone to get us."

Bolton shook his head. She was going to freak out and expose them both. "We have to get safe first. It's too risky to do that right now—from here."

"We have to call someone, first!"

Bolton moved his legs off the left side of the bed so his back was to her, and he lifted the back of his shirt. "This is what happened the last time I called for help."

He knew what she saw. Angry redness. Scar tissue from the burns surrounding an injury that cut across his spine. She might have even touched the tips of her fingers to it, but he couldn't feel anything. The whole area was void of sensation. His spine was a ticking time bomb. One he was supposed to have gotten fixed tomorrow.

The helicopter should have taken them away from the wreckage of town, toward a military hospital where he could have received the medical treatment he badly needed. Experimental surgery from some cutting edge doctor.

Bolton lowered his shirt.

"What do we do?"

He waved her around to his side of the bed. She looked so lost it made him want to reach for her again. But that wasn't going to solve anything. Whatever feelings he might have had for her, those were things the Bolton who was in Sanctuary had allowed himself to have. Now that he was out of the protection of their town, it was impossible.

His testimony had put Dante Alvarez in federal prison, and the minute Bolton surfaced, he'd be hunted. It was a given. The man would hunt him until Bolton either disappeared, or Dante killed him. The only advantage he had was that Dante would be looking for one guy, not a man in a wheelchair, travelling with a woman. But the man still had plenty of friends, ones who would shoot first and check Bolton's ID after.

It was only a matter of time before someone showed up with intent to kill.

**

Nadia stared at him. Her body ached where she'd landed on the hard ground. She could barely make sense of any of this, let alone figure out Bolton's plan. It was like he was playing a part. Surely they could call someone, couldn't they? "We need a phone."

Bolton shrugged. "Do you know the number to John's satellite phone?"

The Sanctuary sheriff was her best friend's husband, and the only person in town with a phone that dialed outside town. The rest only worked internally. And the only way for the residents to communicate with the outside world was during the one hour of internet access they got each week at the library.

Antiquated, but necessary for their protection. Nadia had seen commercials for fancy cell phones and iPads on TV and online, but she'd never actually seen one in person. She'd been in Sanctuary twelve years next month. Bolton had been there before her. Neither of them had ever talked about what put them in witness protection. It wasn't done. Every single resident was there to start a new life and leave their past behind. The cost of that life was some of the freedoms people enjoyed. But it was worth it, given the alternative was death.

Nadia sighed. "Of course I don't have the number to John's satellite phone. What about a computer? Maybe I could log on to my email from here and send them a message?"

"We have to be careful. We can't let anyone find out who we are."

"That's why you gave the sheriff fake names?"

Bolton lifted his chin. "If he hadn't shown up, I'd have stolen that rancher's truck, and we'd be two towns away by now."

"But this is where the helicopter exploded," she said. "They'll come looking for us, to help us."

"Everyone will be busy tracking down Tommy and getting Remy back. We have to hang tight. But not here. The good guys aren't the only ones who'll be looking for us."

She'd forgotten about Remy. *Lord, protect her.* Nadia's faith had been born as part of her new life in Sanctuary, and now it meant more to her than anything. God was the one who would protect Remy. Nadia's brother, Shadrach, had been a marine. He would find Remy, and Ben Mason would help him.

When they found her they would deal with Tommy. The rogue SEAL wouldn't get away with nearly destroying Sanctuary and then kidnapping Remy. Leaving Bolton and Nadia Marie for dead. They'd get Remy back. They were experts at saving people, particularly witnesses they were charged with protecting.

"Tell me about that necklace you gave Remy."

Bolton stared for a second then nodded. "It had a GPS tracker in it. It was the only way I could think of that Ben and Shadrach would be able to find her."

"And you just happened to have it on you?"

"Yes." His voice didn't invite any argument. Was she supposed to be grateful he'd told her that much? He'd barely begun to answer all the questions she had about what on earth was going on here. They needed to get back to Sanctuary. Then Bolton could figure out getting his surgery.

"Shadrach will help Remy. Then he'll be here."

"I'm sorry, Nadia. Your brother won't be here for a while."

Nadia folded her arms. "So we wait here for someone else to come and help us."

There was no procedure for this. It was unprecedented.

"We'll be dead before they get here." He wasn't agitated. He showed no sign of distress. Bolton just sat there, cold as anything, and told her they'd be dead. "The necklace was a tracking device, remember?"

"One that will help them find Remy!"

"And it will also help someone else find us. Unless we get out of here and find somewhere safe to hide."

"Who?" He didn't answer, so she said, "Someone is after you?"

Bolton nodded. "The threat against me is very real. They will come looking." He paused. "What about you? Do we have to worry about someone coming after us, who wants you dead?"

Nadia didn't even know how to answer. Her story was so complicated she barely knew where to start or how to explain the way the story had ended. She took a breath and tried to decide what to say.

The door opened. The sheriff strode in. She preferred John Mason, and the way he'd made Andra—a former assassin—do that melty smile she did now.

The man nodded his greeting. "Well, folks. Got a couple questions for you, and then the doctor will be in to see y'all." He looked at Nadia. "Heard you're feeling dizzy."

"Some." She found a chair, just to keep up the ruse. It was basically lying, and she didn't like doing that. She hadn't done it in a long time. But Bolton evidently thought it was going to keep them alive now.

If Bolton was telling her the truth then maybe it would put the sheriff in danger if they told him who they were. Maybe he had kids, and they would come home from school to find their father had been killed. All because Nadia had un-learned how to lie.

"I'm just glad we're okay." She tried to smile. "It's been a hard week, especially for Steven. We were headed to the city for some tests, you know. Get that little problem of his figured out." She leaned toward the sheriff and whispered, "A little night-time problem."

The sheriff coughed. "Of course."

"Wouldn't you know there was some kind of malfunction, and the bird just got out of control. I can't believe it exploded. There was a full tank of gas in there. And my purse!"

Nadia could have burst out laughing at her own fake-ness. Hopefully she wasn't laying it on too thick, or they'd be sunk. She'd never claimed to be a good actress, though a part in the town play had given her a few pointers. Make it real enough they believe it.

She'd said all those lines about love and devotion on the stage and pretended she'd been saying them to Bolton. But that was months ago now.

The sheriff said, "And…who was flying the helicopter?"

"Me, silly!" She slapped her hand down on his knee then lifted her fingers and gasped. Nadia whipped her head around to Bolton. "My ring!" She explained for the sheriff. "It's too big. I stowed it in my purse so we could drop it at the jewelers before my darling's doctor's appointment." She faked up some tears and moved so her back was to the sheriff.

Bolton reached for her. "It'll be okay, honey. We'll get you a new one."

Nadia nodded for the sheriff but widened her eyes for Bolton. She didn't want to give them away, but there had to be a logical explanation for everything.

Her brother would find Remy, and that was good. Shadrach really liked Remy, and he needed to make her safe. Ben and Grant, John's brothers, would bring Tommy down. Everything would be fine—except for them.

Lord, what do we do?

Chapter 2

The sheriff cleared his throat. Nadia shifted on the bed and looked at him like she'd forgotten he was there. Because she was a shallow rich woman with a helicopter pilot's license. Were they different from a regular pilot's license? A rich woman whose cowboy husband had "night-time" problems. She nearly groaned aloud.

"Just a couple more questions." He glanced at Bolton. "Any idea about a cell phone? The rancher you hit said he pulled it out, and you grabbed it."

Bolton had a cell phone?

"No idea. I was so out of it, just coming around. I didn't know what I was doing. That's why I hit him." Bolton paused. "I'm real sorry about that. Will you convey that to your friend? The pain, you see. It's real bad. I wasn't thinking."

The sheriff nodded slowly.

"Anything else?" Not that Nadia was eager for more questions. She just wanted to be alone again with Bolton so they could talk about what they were going to do.

Warm fingers covered hers. She didn't look at Bolton's hand, just turned hers over and grasped his. He always seemed so strong, even like this. Like there was nothing he couldn't do.

"Actually there is something else," the sheriff said. "I'd like to know how you came to be in this area in a helicopter. You see, there's a whole bunch of strictures about flying around here. We're almost a no-fly-zone except for the military, because of this extremely rare, wild bird. It's endangered. Can't set off fireworks. Kites can't be more than two stories high. Forget about clay pigeon shooting. That's what's gotten me so confused, see. The rancher reported you came from over the mountains. Hills we can't even hike because it's this bird's nesting grounds. Yet you flew right from there."

Nadia was going to have to sell this. It was their job to protect the integrity of the witness protection town of Sanctuary. She shuffled on the bed, and Bolton squeezed her hand. "It was my fault." She turned to him, but his attention was on the sheriff.

"The pain was bad, and getting worse. I couldn't hold it together, so I had Marie fly this way. We both know about the flight restrictions, but I couldn't bear to save a bird and wind up losing my dignity all over the floor of the helicopter."

"So you were going to…what? Set down and find a bathroom?"

"Right," Bolton said. She could hear the edge in his voice. Served him right. It was his idea to lie, so why not make the lie that he was going to wet himself. "That was when the helicopter began to malfunction, and we had to set her down. Turned out it was catastrophic, and we barely got out before it exploded."

Some of that was true, but this sheriff didn't need to know about the rogue SEAL or the town of Sanctuary. He wouldn't have believed it anyway.

Bolton shifted and cried out. Was that a lie, too? She'd seen it for herself, and whatever the problem it was surely serious enough he was probably in pain like that. How was she supposed to help him? She didn't have a medical degree like Remy. Nadia was a retired artist who cut and colored hair. Everyone wanted to cover their gray these days. Her small life of work and working out at the town gym, then church. Her friends. None of it had equipped her for this.

Okay, Lord. I guess this is where You come in.

He'd placed Nadia here with Bolton, and she knew He would give her the tools she needed to help him in whatever way Bolton needed help.

And not just because she had been in love with the rancher for years.

**

Pedro swiveled in his chair. The glow of the computer screens was the only light in the room, and it turned Alfie's face an eerie blue-white color.

"You aren't going to believe this. I got something."

Alfie didn't respond. He was chatting with some gal online.

"Alfie."

Alfie sat back in his chair. "Finally. She's buying the plane ticket with her dad's credit card."

Whatever. "The necklace was activated."

"What?"

"The necklace. The one Dante wanted us to monitor."

"Dude, that was years ago." Alfie shook his head.

"Yeah, but its online *now*."

"So make the call. If you want."

Pedro reached for his iPhone but hesitated. "You don't think I should?"

Alfie shrugged. "I'm just saying. It's been years, and your cousin is probably dead in prison by now. We have too much going on with Tank, and that business you have with that crooked DEA agent. We're in hot demand."

Like Pedro wouldn't know if his own cousin was dead or not? He couldn't wait for the day he was free of Dante. "If he's not dead this week and he finds out it came online and we didn't say anything?"

There was an edge of fear in his eyes. "Maybe we don't care. Maybe we ignore it."

"Maybe you shut up and get back to work." Pedro didn't plan to die over a stupid necklace that probably didn't mean anything anyway.

He picked up the phone.

**

"I can't believe you lied to a pastor." Nadia pulled an extra blanket from the closet and hugged it to her chest.

Bolton lay back on the pillows. It had taken some wrangling and a lot of sweet talk, but the sheriff had backed off in lieu of talking with them more the next day. She didn't know what they were going to come up with. The truth wasn't a story they could tell.

He shut his eyes. "As opposed to you lying to a sheriff?"

"That's totally different. The pastor could probably *tell*."

"If he could, it's only because you're such a bad liar." Bolton's lips twitched.

Nadia was tempted to throw the blanket at him, but he'd probably keep it, and then she would be cold.

"You're the one I was worried about." There it was. That flash of what she'd seen in Sanctuary. The part of Bolton that cared, the part she'd fallen for. He was still in there, and *that* was the man she trusted to keep them both safe now.

"Nadia." The look was gone.

She shook her head. She didn't need to tell him what she was thinking.

Bolton looked exhausted. "We needed space. Time to regroup without having to answer more questions."

"I'm pretty sure you could have found that without telling a man of God that we are *married*."

Bolton opened his eyes and raised one brow. "He wasn't going to leave us alone otherwise."

With Bolton in a wheelchair, the elderly widowed pastor had given them his ground floor bedroom and told them he would be perfectly happy in the guest room upstairs. So for the first time in hours they were alone—and totally exhausted. Bolton had to be in serious pain. The injury on his back had looked bad enough from the outside. She couldn't imagine what the inside felt like.

Nadia dropped into the armchair where she would be spending the night. The weight of the day pushed her down into a slump, still clutching the blanket.

"You okay?"

She didn't open her eyes. "I should be asking you that. This morning we woke up in our home town, and yes it's true all was not well. Tommy was bent on taking over the town, and—" Her voice broke.

"What is it?"

"I just remembered about Hal." Tears leaked from the corners of her eyes. "He was in your house when it collapsed."

Bolton's face softened. "He was killed?"

She nodded.

"I'm sorry, Nadia. I know you were close."

The crusty old biker had been a friend. He'd run Sanctuary's only radio station, and she and Andra, her best friend, had helped him out when he had plans with his 'lady friend.' Whoever she was, the woman was likely grieving hard right now.

"I hope everyone else is okay." She shut her eyes and prayed for her friends—more like family, really.

Bolton's voice was heavy with sleep. "I'm sure they're fine. Probably better than we are, except for Remy."

Nadia pursed her lips and blew out a breath. She heard the concern in his voice that bled through only because he was tired. Would it always be that way, wondering what his feelings were behind the words he said?

Bolton had lied to the sheriff, used a fake name, and drawn her into a ruse that covered the things they couldn't tell anyone. The nondisclosure agreement they'd both signed prevented them from telling anyone who they were, why they were in witness protection, or anything about the town of Sanctuary. But he had used that nondisclosure agreement like armor to protect himself. Just like he used the things he said like armor to cover his true feelings.

Nadia was going to have to work hard if she was going to be able to draw him out. The man had more walls up than Andra, and she'd been a government assassin. With Andra, Nadia had simply loved the woman until she caved and admitted she appreciated it. Was that even going to work with Bolton?

Her eyes drifted shut. Was that… They snapped open. A phone, on the bedside table. She could call… Someone. After she looked up their number.

Her brother. The director of the Marshals—Grant Mason. Or his brother, John Mason, who was the sheriff of Sanctuary. The three men all had phones, and she could tell them where she and Bolton were! She could ask for help to get Bolton to the doctor who was supposed to operate on him!

For the first time since she'd realized Tommy was in the helicopter with them, posing as the pilot, she had hope. Prayer was all she could do for Remy, whom Tommy had taken with him when he'd run off. But now Nadia had a way to help Bolton. A way to get them both out of this.

With a whispered prayer of thanks on her lips, Nadia fell asleep.

Hours later her shoulder was jostled. Nadia swatted away the annoyance.

"Wake up, Nadia."

"Huh?" She opened her eyes. The clock by the bed said *2:13*. "Do you need help?" Maybe he needed to get to the restroom.

He was already in his wheelchair. "Get up. We're leaving."

She couldn't see his face in the dark. "Why? What's going on?"

"We aren't staying here, Nadia. We have to go."

"But—" The phone.

He covered her mouth with his hand. "No more talking. Let's go."

**

Four days later

Shadrach swept out the sheriff's office onto the sidewalk. Nothing but a hick town sheriff with no answers as to where Nadia was. This town was a flea on the dog's back of all the places he'd been in the world. Idaho sucked, except for the fact Remy's favorite author—Heather Woodhaven—lived here. Who wanted to live in a place with one area code for the whole state? It was backward. And there were cows everywhere. Wasn't it supposed to be potatoes?

The door clicked shut behind him, and Shadrach lifted his head. Glanced both ways. Anyone who looked at Shadrach for any time whatsoever would realize fast that he was a marine. The sheriff hadn't seen anything but a threat. He'd dismissed Shadrach's search and only asked him questions. Wanted to know why Shadrach was so interested in those two people.

"Long gone?"

Shadrach nodded. "We're not the only ones to come looking for them, either."

Ben leaned against the car, his arms folded. "The fact that they're gone means they're safe." His voice was measured. Shadrach had seen him in the midst of one of the most stressful times of Shadrach's life, and he'd still been total ice. The man was a mystery that itched at Shadrach to solve.

Ben would never broadcast his feelings the way Shadrach did, but whatever. So he wasn't as good as Ben. That was painfully obvious. Which was the reason why Ben was his boss, and Shadrach had been working for him for about forty-four hours. Tommy was dead. Remy was safe now. All that was left was to find Nadia Marie.

"How did I know," Shadrach said, "that you were going to say that? We have nothing. No leads. No answers. Nada."

Shadrach rubbed his face. The calluses on his hands scratched against the stubble. Even his hair was getting long. He needed a cut and shave, or this spiral of disappearing into someone who was not a soldier anymore wasn't going to quit. It was like the marine in him had started to evaporate.

Then there was Remy, in the hospital and telling everyone she didn't want to see him.

His spotter was dead, his career was over. His twin was gone. He couldn't help Remy after what Tommy did to her. Life had dealt him this hand, and Shadrach had to play it out.

"Remy will heal."

Shadrach studied the small town stores across the street. He didn't want to know how Ben knew what he was thinking. Maybe the man read minds. It would explain a lot. Super-spy with hero powers. That made Shadrach—the sidekick. That couldn't have been the plan.

He shook his head. "Remy didn't want me to touch her." He swallowed. "But she let you do it."

"And if you got over yourself and actually thought about it for a second you would realize why that was."

Shadrach whipped around. "What did you just say?"

"Exactly." Ben looked ready to laugh. "What. I. Am. Talking about."

"You think I need to get over myself?"

"I think you're too caught up in your hurt feelings to realize the reason *why* Remy let me help her on that plane." Ben paused. "You know what Tommy did to her."

The blood. Her clothes. It had been obvious what the rogue SEAL had done.

"That's the reason she didn't want you."

"I was trying to help her!"

Ben shook his head. "She wanted someone she knew but didn't care about. Not the one person she didn't want to see her like that. She wants you to see her as strong. Not broken."

Shadrach shook his head. Why was Ben so certain about something that made absolutely no sense whatsoever? Remy didn't want to see him, and Nadia Marie was gone. He had to figure out his stuff later and instead concentrate on what was within his power to fix.

"So where are we at?" Shadrach ran his hands through his hair. At this point, he would have begged for coffee. But since he'd lived through much worse than a need for caffeine, he kept his mouth shut. "The sheriff didn't tell us anything except that we weren't the first people to ask about Bolton and Nadia Marie, and the helicopter wreckage hasn't even been cleared away yet."

"So they're watching the necklace. Whoever they are," Ben said. "And it pinged on their radar, so they came looking."

"Before we even got here. Now we have no idea who they were or who sent them. Only that they showed up and asked questions."

"It's a lead."

Shadrach wanted to punch someone. He should have brought Dauntless with him, but the dog didn't like to fly if he could avoid it. "It makes more sense that Bolton and Nadia Marie would have stayed here and waited for help. Not that they'd take off in the middle of the night and steal the pastor's car." Shadrach thought for a second. "Bolton must have known that activating the necklace so we could find Remy would bring whoever is looking…right to the source of the signal."

Ben nodded. "Precisely."

The man was testing him? Shadrach liked tests. "Where's the necklace now?"

"Remy still has it."

"And someone is protecting her?"

"Yes. Plus Dauntles is there."

"So when these people who are asking about Bolton and Nadia Marie come to Remy, wanting to know where she got the necklace from so they can find them, what's going to happen?"

Ben smiled. "That's why you need to get over yourself and convince her to keep you around."

Chapter 3

Six Weeks Later

Shadrach tossed the screwdriver back in the tool box and sighed. Six weeks since the sheriff's office. Six weeks of working this problem and they still had nothing, just a name they'd dug up.

Dante Alvarez.

A name and a broken back door. It'd been jimmied open so the assailant could gain entry to Remy's house in the middle of the night. Thankfully Shadrach had been on the couch with his German shepherd, Dauntless, two feet away from him on his dog bed. Neither man nor dog had slept in such cushy accommodations in a long time, and not at all in the years they'd been Marine Force Recon. But those days were over, and Dauntless wasn't the only one moping.

Remy stepped into the room, but didn't say anything. He didn't turn around. They'd gotten her back from Tommy, but two days in the hospital and weeks at home and she still wouldn't even look him in the eye.

Shadrach wondered if they'd ever get back what had been between them before—even if it had been little more than the promise of what could be. Their lives were so different. Remy had multiple degrees, a genius level IQ, and her pick of jobs, many of which were independent government contracts. Yet she chose to work for Ben.

Which made them co-workers.

Shadrach stood. "Door's fixed."

"Thank you." Dauntless' tags jingled. She was petting him. Had she just thanked the dog?

Sure, Dauntless was the one who had bitten the assailant who'd broken into her house before Shadrach detained him. Some no-name thug, low level enough whoever sent him could keep their hands clean. Ben had come and picked the man up to get some answers through whatever interrogation method Ben used—which Shadrach didn't want to know about. *Been there, done that.*

Now they had the boss's name. Except that Dante was in federal prison, with a Grand Canyon size grudge against Bolton Farrera.

"Thank you, as well."

He glanced at her. Remy's big round eyes were like gray-blue marbles. They held him captive until she blinked, and for a moment he was released before she ensnared him once again. Shadrach had never met a woman like her, a woman he couldn't seem to shake off no matter how pointless it felt to hang around.

Her head tipped to the side. "Are you mad at Ben?"

Shadrach looked away from her eyes and took in all of her. She'd ditched the nerd get-up she'd worn in Sanctuary that had fit her hacker persona. Now she was back in the dress pants and knit sweaters she'd worn when he met her. A business woman with a medical degree, who spent her days researching infectious diseases. Until that road had led her to witness protection. The outside was different, but Remy was still that same woman. The one who'd caught his attention when the military had brought them into the same briefing room in Iraq.

Shadrach, on the other hand, wore the same pair of jeans he'd had for two years. They were just about broken in. His sneakers had seen better days, and the Henley was more about staying warm in spring than fashion. They were polar opposites. Remy was more like Shadrach's sister, his twin. Nadia Marie had more style than anyone he'd ever met—she'd probably stolen his share in the womb.

"You are." She sighed. "You're mad at Ben. It was my idea to keep the necklace."

"I know that." When she flinched at his voice, Shadrach pulled out a chair and sat to make himself look smaller. "I know, Rem. That's why I'm here. The necklace was going to draw out whoever is after Bolton, and thanks to this break-in, we're a step closer to finding Bolton and Nadia."

Dante. The man Bolton had testified against, a DEA agent now in federal prison. Something told Shadrach that Ben had already known the answer to that even before the tech guys told them. What Shadrach wanted to know was whether the man who had broken into Remy's house had any information on where Nadia Marie and Bolton were, or if this Dante and his men were as much in the dark as they were. Shadrach would know if something happened to his twin, but he still wanted to see she was okay with his own eyes.

He gave Remy a small smile. "You could have given the necklace to Ben. Been rid of it. Keeping the necklace was a bold move. Brave."

Remy touched her red hair with a shaky hand and swiped it back from her face. It hung in loose curls that fell over her shoulders. "I needed to do something strong, even if I didn't feel that way." She returned his smile. "Thank you for being here. I don't think I could have done it if you weren't."

Shadrach got up slowly. "Anytime, Remy. Every time." He stepped closer to her. The more he did it, the more she would get used to him being close and feeling comfort instead of the violation Tommy inflicted on her.

With Remy was where he wanted to be. Where he'd always wanted to be.

He started to move closer.

Her smile shook. "I should get some work done before the whole day is wasted." Remy was out of the room before Dauntless could even raise his head from the kitchen floor.

Shadrach gave him the command to guard, and headed out the back door. He needed a run.

**

Downtown Seattle, WA

"Darling! You, my dear, are a true *artiste*!"

Nadia blinked. The customer stared at her in the mirror, and her boss, Melanie Schaffer—of the Boston Schaffers—grabbed her face. She kissed Nadia on both cheeks and tugged on the ends of her chin-length hair. "I knew I did right, hiring you."

Nadia returned the woman's bleached smile. An artist? Melanie didn't know how right she was, even with that painting hanging on the wall in the foyer. It was one of Nadia's favorites of all the work she'd done.

The customer ripped off the cape and stood, like a ballerina coming out of a bow. "You said she was good, Melanie. You were right."

"Of course I am!"

The two wandered off to the front counter. Nadia cleared away her scissors, the comb she'd used, and unplugged the curling wand. Familiar smells of hair products and dye saturated the air. This was one of the few moments of peace she had through the day before she went back to the tiny ground floor apartment that was more depressing than the man she shared it with.

Nadia grabbed the broom and started to sweep up the hair. She didn't understand him.

"You look like a fly could knock you over."

She smiled but didn't look up. Between work, extra shifts, and helping Bolton at home, exhaustion had set in about a month before. Makeup helped, but it didn't fully disguise the dark circles and lines she now had on her face.

Nate, who stood waiting for her to rise to his bait, had a station beside hers. His specialty being the charming of little old ladies who left fat tips. The salon was high end, catering to the wives of bankers, football players, and local millionaires. Nadia was beyond grateful Melanie had given her a shot, even when Nadia had asked for some money up front to buy a couple of outfits for her first week of work.

"How does lunch at Pasquale's sound?"

Like heaven. But Nadia couldn't afford heaven. Not when Bolton had found a surgeon to perform the procedure—an experimental and risky surgery—that would hopefully allow him to have full mobility for the rest of his life. They almost had enough money to pay for it.

As soon as the procedure was done, Bolton wouldn't need her anymore. Then Nadia would find a way home.

Six weeks of hiding from the man who wanted Bolton dead. They'd either done an excellent job of staying out of sight, or the man who hated him just wasn't coming.

It was time for Nadia to face the fact Bolton wasn't going to let her in, and there was no way to draw him out. She wanted to know what his plans were for after the surgery, but the man wouldn't even share where he was getting the cash he came home with every day. He was saving, like her, but what work he did was a mystery.

"Right. You're probably having lunch with that boyfriend of yours." Nate paused. "It's the wheelchair, isn't it?"

Nadia held the broom handle in front of her and looked at him.

"Okay, so it's not. But seriously, why are you with him?" Nate waited again. It was his thing—pause long enough for thoughts to begin to gather and then cut them off. "Does he make you happy?"

"It's complicated."

"Girl." Nate hopped off the chair and sauntered over. Women young and old drooled over the slender man and his baby face. Nadia just rolled her eyes. "It's *always* complicated."

To his credit, he didn't seem concerned that she didn't respond to him the way everyone else did.

"It won't last much longer," she said. "He's having surgery. When he's healthy again, I'm going to go find my life."

"Girl..."

Nadia grabbed the sandwich she'd packed that morning and went to the break room. A sandwich Bolton had made. Every morning she had to work, there was a fresh sandwich in the fridge for her to take with her. But she didn't want to talk about it anymore. Even if Nate cared for real, Bolton was too much of a mystery. One she couldn't figure out.

The salon was quiet when she preferred busy days. They kept her mind from the fact Bolton hadn't talked to her in weeks. Not really. When it was quiet her thoughts drifted back to that small town hospital. The sheriff's uncomfortable questions, and disappearing from town in the middle of the night in a stolen car. Hiding for weeks, no phones, using only cash from odd jobs. No record of who they were, no licenses. A nasty apartment, but one they could lease under false names from a man who accepted cash rent and didn't ask questions.

She'd been Marie since the helicopter exploded. A semblance of who she was that she'd been able to retain even through all this. Though Bolton had bought awful box color and made her cut her hair to disguise her appearance, while he wheeled around in a ball cap to hide his face. Two weeks after the helicopter, they'd driven into Seattle. The first thing Nate had done when they'd met was fix her hair for free. Nadia had been so happy she'd nearly cried—she'd felt like herself again. Almost.

Dante will find us, and he'll make us beg for death before he kills us.

Both of them had diminished in the weeks since, always looking over their shoulders. She would wake in the middle of the night to hear Bolton moaning on the floor across the room from her. In the midst of his own bad dream. Still, he wouldn't open up. The man she had thought she'd had feelings for was gone, and Nadia didn't know how to get him back.

We have to do this. It's not for much longer, and then I'll be back on my feet.

But what would come after that?

Shadrach had to be crazy with worry. Who knew what Ben or his brother thought about her disappearance? Or the sheriff. Andra. Nadia's heart ached for her friends. Her town. Her church.

Part of her didn't want to believe her life in Sanctuary was over, but the rules stated that once a person left they could never go back. Children who grew up in Sanctuary could leave for college but could never return. Anyone who left the safety of the ring of mountains that protected their town from the rest of the world opened themselves up to danger. Stepping outside was hard enough, given no roads led into town. The only way out was by helicopter or small plane, like the ones the military used to deliver the mail once a week. Now she was out. But not by choice. Nadia hurt—the ache to go back was so strong.

Melanie walked in, shut the door, and sat down at Nadia's table.

"Melanie." Nadia swiped crumbs into her hand and discarded them in the trash with her balled up plastic wrap.

"Marie. How are you doing?"

Nadia sighed and sat back at the table. Melanie wasn't going to let her go back to work if she thought something was wrong. The woman understood the nuances of people's moods, but she was also a shrewd business woman when she needed to be. Nadia had seen her diffuse a trophy wife's claim her hair had been ruined, to such an extent the woman had left smiling ten minutes later. Nadia knew she was Melanie's good deed for the year. The pity-hire. But she wouldn't be there unless she could also do great work.

"I'm fine, thank you."

Melanie sat straight in her chair, her posture that of a career model or dancer. "I don't believe you."

Nadia opened her mouth.

"I've been wondering for a while now how to say this, and I've decided to just come out and tell you." Melanie leaned forward. "I know."

"You…know?"

"I figured it out a couple of days after you started working here."

"You know I'll always be so grateful to you for taking a chance on me."

Melanie patted Nadia's hand. "I know, dear. Do you remember me commenting on the painting above the front desk? It's my favorite. I've redecorated the salon four times and never once changed that painting for a newer one."

Nadia swallowed. Melanie did know.

"I like to keep abreast of what's happening in the art world, and so I was astounded to hear that the painter of that very piece had been involved in dealings of forgery and murder."

Melanie didn't blink.

"A young woman, very young at the time. Flamboyant, a woman of the world who adored style. I would have given my fortune for her to walk in my shop and allow me to work on her hair."

Nadia felt the smile curl the edges of her mouth.

Melanie lifted her phone so that Nadia could see the screen. The picture was from years ago, right after her first gallery showing. She'd been impulsive, idealistic, and ecstatic at the sudden influx of money. A starving artist no more, only her brother had been able to pull her back from total indulgence.

But it wasn't the picture that arrested her. Nadia had wanted to get her hands on a phone for weeks. There were no payphones, not anymore. She wasn't allowed to tie up the desk phone with personal calls, and she had yet to ask someone if she could borrow their cell. If she could get on a computer, she could find the number for the Marshals' office in D.C.

With access to a phone, she could reach out to someone who knew who she was. Someone who could help her.

Melanie set the phone down. "I refuse to believe that woman—you—are satisfied with this life you lead now. You were a true artist, and you do great work here. Don't get me wrong." She leaned forward. "But, whoever you are now. It isn't you."

Nadia nodded. That was the only concession she gave the woman, and it was purely out of respect.

"Is it this man of yours?"

Nadia nodded.

"Is he hurting you?"

"No."

"Are you safe?"

Nadia shook her head. "No."

Melanie sighed. "What can I do for you?"

"You're already doing it."

"I don't believe that. It's like he has this hold on you, and you can't escape, but you can. Gather your things and walk away from him."

"We're safer together than we would be apart." They were his words, but Nadia believed them more than anything else he'd said to her. "Part of it is that he needs my help with mobility, and part of it is…"

"You love him?"

Nadia wanted to cry, she'd held her feelings in so long. "I have for years, and it hasn't turned out the way I'd hoped but I don't believe that what I should be doing is walking away. He…he needs me now, maybe more than ever."

"Oh, hon."

"He needs me, but he doesn't love me." It was fine. It had to be fine. Now that he'd found a surgeon, the clock was ticking. Then they would be over for good.

Melanie touched her hand.

"I didn't know who he was, not really." She still didn't, but there were some big clues. Bolton Farrera had never been a DEA agent, despite the rumor that had been so prevalent in Sanctuary. Nadia was almost convinced that, if anything, he'd actually been the one the DEA was hunting. "I know more now. Enough. He doesn't do anything a person in love does."

"That isn't what your life should have been, Nadia."

The sound of her own name brought tears to her eyes. Nadia Marie squeezed them shut. "I can't tell you what happened between that picture and when I showed up here. Please don't ask me about it."

The part of her that created masterpieces on canvas was dead. She had been allowed to paint in Sanctuary, she'd just never done it. She'd lost faith in herself and in her ability to craft anything more than an attractive haircut. In a lot of ways, it felt like Bolton was also losing faith. In himself. In the world. Maybe even in her as well. All he ever talked about—when he did speak—was Dante, and how he was so sure the man was coming for them. One step behind. Forever at their backs.

"What do you need?"

Nadia Marie thought about Melanie's question. Was it the time now for her to make a move, to try and get her life back?

She looked at the clock. There was time before she got off, before Bolton showed up in the van to pick her up. He was keeping the broken-down vehicle going when by all rights it should have been scrapped years ago. The man had mechanical skills—maybe that was what he was doing for work. But how could he work on cars when he could barely move?

"Can I use your computer and the phone in your office?"

"Yes, hon. Of course." Perhaps she saw the hope in Nadia's eyes, but whatever it was it convinced her to allow Nadia to do something no other employee was allowed to do. Nadia followed her boss into the manager's office. Melanie logged the computer on and then walked to the door. "I'll close this, but come and get me if you need anything."

Nadia sat at the desk, opened the search engine and found the website for the US Marshals. She snapped up the phone and dialed the number. When a receptionist answered, Nadia said, "Grant Mason, please. It's very important."

The director would be able to help her. He was the one who offered witnesses the opportunity to start over in Sanctuary, and his brother was the sheriff of the town.

"I'm sorry. Grant Mason retired. He no longer works here."

Grant wasn't the director of the marshals anymore? The phone fell from her hand and dropped on the desk.

She typed in the website for her email provider, the one assigned to her by the US Marshals.

Page Not Found.

She tried again and got the same message. Nadia ran her hands down her face. What was going on? She didn't know her brother's cell phone number—she'd had no reason to have it, given she couldn't call from Sanctuary. Only email. She'd been cut off living there, and now that she lived in the real world she was still cut off from any semblance of help.

Bolton knew how to stay under the radar. It was how they'd stayed alive this long. But she wasn't going to rely on him to protect her—that was up to Nadia.

The only other person she knew of that might be able to help somehow was the one person she never thought she'd speak to ever again. Her mom. Nadia lifted the phone, dialed her childhood phone number, and prayed it would work.

It rang.

The door swung open, and Bolton wheeled in, his eyes dark. "Time to go."

Chapter 4

Bolton swam to the surface of consciousness. He sucked in a deep breath, coughed it out, and cracked open gritty eyes. In that split second between dream and reality he could still feel the heat of the flames. Dante's gun at his back. The boom as he pulled the trigger and fired that round into Bolton to secure his death. But this time Bolton didn't move.

And Dante wasn't here.

Bolton lay in a hospital bed. An IV bag dripped into his arm on one side and a monitor beeped on the other. All debris from the surgery had been cleaned away. Plastic hung from the walls of the three-car garage where the procedure had taken place. Plastic covered the floor. Plastic covered the door.

Pain had been with him every minute for weeks now. To wake up with nothing but a warm, numb sensation in his body made him want to leap from the bed just because it might be possible.

He fisted his hand.

He'd told the doctor he didn't want any pain medication. That was a road Bolton had no intention of travelling down. Anesthetic was one thing, morphine was a whole different animal—one that liked to take up residence in Bolton's life like a stray dog. That demanded to be fed and fed until there was nothing left of Bolton's life but where he could get more. Being an addict wasn't something he was prepared to allow to happen again, and he certainly had no intention of explaining any of that to Nadia.

Though it would probably settle her if he did tell her the reason he'd been so grumpy the past few weeks: his pain level. And that there was nothing he was prepared to do about it. Among other things. He wasn't an easy man to live with. There were others who'd learned the same thing. She was on edge, ready to quit trusting him, if that phone call she'd almost made was anything to go by. But everything he'd done was to keep both of them alive. One day she would realize that.

Plastic swished, and the doctor strode in. Mid-thirties, a little younger than Bolton. Styled hair and pristine clothes, he charged more than twice what Bolton had expected to pay. But it had been a tricky, experimental procedure that essentially shored up four vertebrae ready to crumble into nothingness. The muscles back there were another story. As was the gnarled skin the doctor had wanted more money to do a graft on.

The doctor smiled. "Everything is looking good."

Which probably meant he'd counted the money, and it was all there.

"Where's Nadia?" His voice cracked, and he cleared his throat. Started to sit up. The doctor pushed the pillows down behind his lower back, and Bolton eased back onto them.

"I thought her name was Marie?"

Bolton just glared, even though it was his mistake. Her name had slipped out. "Whatever. Where is she?"

The doctor sneered. "She's pretty hot, whatever her name is."

Bolton's insides turned to ice. "You touch her, and I'll kill you."

The doctor laughed, but it rang false. He probably thought Bolton would do it. So long as the man didn't put his manicured digits on Nadia, then Bolton wouldn't have to keep his word.

"Couple hours the IV will be done. You'll feel each incision in all its perfect glory as per your instructions." Cripes, this guy liked the sound of his own voice. "The polymer should have hardened by then, and you'll be able to start walking around. Though take it slow. There's a lot of swelling, and moving will jar the adhesive. It won't heal right."

Bolton nodded.

"Your girlfriend is getting some air. I'll let her know you're awake." The doctor didn't leave. "Take it easy, let your body adjust to the surgery, and give it the time it needs to heal. If you do that, a full recovery can be expected."

Another nod.

That was all he wanted. To be upright and fighting. Then it would be time to turn the tables on Dante once and for all. Bolton's testimony had bought him the time he'd needed to heal while he lived in Sanctuary. Now was the time to gather arms and fight. Otherwise he would never be free of Dante. There was nothing Bolton wanted in all the world the way he wanted Dante to know what payback felt like. It burned in him with every waking moment until there was nothing else, not even what was right in front of him.

No matter how much he might wish things were different.

The doctor was gone. Bolton took a breath, longing to see Nadia. To know she was safe and make sure she'd eaten. The woman would get so focused on all the stress, she'd forget and he'd have to remind her.

The plastic rustled. Bolton opened his mouth to ask the doctor what he wanted, but it wasn't him.

This man he'd never met before.

"Who are you?"

"So it's true." Dark features, dark stubble, the man had a heavy Hispanic accent. "Dante sends his regards." The man lifted a gun.

Bolton dove left before the first shot went off. He rolled and landed on the floor on one knee. He grabbed the gun he'd stashed between the mattress and the bed and lifted his body up like dead weight. Squeezed off two shots. The man grunted. Bolton crawled to the end of the bed and peered around. He'd dropped the gun and now clutched his shoulder.

Bolton moved forward without straightening. He was never going to heal if he was dead.

Before the man could regain his gun, Bolton pointed his piece in the man's face. "Where is Dante?"

Cold air brushed the skin on his body save for the boxers he wore. The doctor had left him that dignity at least. The rest of him was a bruised and bloody mess, and the spot where the IV had ripped out was open. Bolton pressed it against the bandages wrapped around his middle.

The man grinned bloody teeth. "Kill me. That's better than what he'll do to me for failing."

Bolton wanted to laugh. "Guess he didn't tell you who I am." He pressed the gun to the man's throat. A round would pass through his mouth and pop out the top of his head. Bolton had seen it before.

"Let me guess," Bolton said. "He called you, told you he'd give you half up front—left in your mailbox—and the rest will be delivered when I'm dead."

"So what?"

"He won't pay the second half. He'll send someone to kill you. Then he'll take everything you have so whatever family you have is left with nothing. Unless he wants them, too." Bolton let that sink in. "Now tell me where I can find him."

"All I have is a number." He motioned with his hairy chin to his jacket pocket. "There's only one problem."

"What's that?"

"You're a cripple. And he sent me to *kill you.*" His hands snapped up, grabbed Bolton's forearm and twisted.

Bolton cried out, tried to keep his hold on the gun. It fired. Bolton fought the man's grasp, lifted his free hand, and punched him in the jaw. It was his weak hand, and he was losing strength. The man barely flinched.

Bolton renewed his attack. He punched as the man continued to twist Bolton's arm. It felt like the bone was about to fracture as every tendon in his wrist tore. His fingers contracted in a spasm, and the gun fell onto the floor between them.

"Bolton! Bolton, are you in there?" Nadia's desperate voice preceded the swish of the curtain. He didn't turn his head but continued to grapple with the man. "The doctor—" She gasped.

The man roared.

Nadia snapped up the man's gun and pressed it to his forehead. "Let go of him."

He released Bolton's arm. Bolton scrambled to his feet. It was strange, being upright after weeks in a wheelchair. He could collapse at any second, but he pulled Nadia back two steps with him as she released a breathy exhale. "The doctor is in the kitchen. He's dead."

"This guy probably killed him on his way in." Bolton motioned to him. Defeat. Dead eyes.

"What are we going to do with him?"

"Give me the gun, and go find the doctor's keys. We'll need his car." He heard the edge in his voice, so foreign to her. But she didn't know anything about his world. Nadia didn't understand who he was or the things that had happened that made him this way. The man he'd been in Sanctuary was a white-washed version of Bolton Farrera, one who lived in a town that was no more than a cushy jail cell. One he'd imposed on himself.

He'd woken up every day in that town, wondering if that would be the day he would leave to get his revenge on Dante.

He heard the hesitation in her steps. "Bolton."

"The gun, Nadia. Now."

She placed it in his outstretched hand. The one he could still lift. Who knew how he would defeat Dante with one working hand and a healing back, but Bolton would find a way. His whole life had been leading to this, and now it was here.

"What are you going to do to him?"

"He can't follow us," Bolton said. "We already have giant targets on our backs. They found us here, where no one should have. I'm not messing around, Nadia. Go. I'll deal with this."

The man's gaze flicked over Bolton's shoulder. While he watched Nadia leave, Bolton marveled. He was actually standing. His body was a smorgasbord of aches and pains, and some abstract numbness. But his feet were planted, and he wasn't going down.

The surgery worked.

The door shut behind her, and he lifted the gun. "Give me your phone."

"You're going to kill me?"

"I won't need to. Not when Dante finds out you failed."

**

Bang. Nadia jumped and glanced back toward the garage. The keys were in a bronze dish on an end table, in a hall that led to the garage. She grabbed them. The house was giant and expensive, just the kind she'd always thought she would live in. Except for the blood in the kitchen, surrounding the body. Doctor Martin Palkin was dead. A nice man killed because she and Bolton were there.

"Nadia."

She jerked and spun around. Her voice came out a breathy whisper, "You're standing." This was what they'd been working toward. What she'd wanted for him since they had left Sanctuary in that helicopter.

"Not for long. Let's move." He strode to her and grabbed the keys. "The fire will spread quickly.

His arm wrapped around her shoulders, and Nadia grunted at the weight he transferred to her. He wasn't as able-bodied as he was making out. "Fire?"

He said nothing, but the distant odor of smoke hit her nostrils. Nadia glanced back, over his shoulder. Flames. "Did you kill that man?"

Bolton shook his head. "I was content to send Dante a message, but his friend grabbed the gun. He killed himself."

"So you set the house on fire?" Was she supposed to understand what was happening?

He shoved the front door open, and they raced to the drive, where the doctor's Mustang was parked. "The police will have debris to sift through, which means Dante and his men won't find us so fast if that's where they're getting their information. We can take the doctor's car, but only to leave a false trail. We'll need a new vehicle."

"Where are we going?" She held the door open while he got in the driver's seat.

"To get something that will buy our way out of this."

He pulled the door shut and fired up the Mustang. Nadia ran for the passenger side. Did she even want to ask about the man? He couldn't be burning alive, could he? Bolton wouldn't do that, whoever he had been before Sanctuary.

He'd committed numerous felonies since the helicopter had exploded. He claimed the police were the ones they were running from, but his assertions that it was all for her—to keep them safe—rang in her head. He had seemed so much like everything she'd ever wanted in Sanctuary. Now that they were in the real world, Bolton was so much different.

"Buckle up."

Jolted from her thoughts, Nadia clipped in. Bolton sped away then parked at the far end of a store, and they walked three blocks. He hot-wired a car no one would ever report stolen because it wasn't worth that much money. Nadia felt as though she was swimming beside him. If this carried on, she was going to lose her strength. And then she would drown.

The stolen car revved. Bolton leaned across the passenger seat to where she still stood in the alleyway. "Get in."

She stepped back.

"Nadia, get in."

He shouldn't lean like that, or stretch his back. He was going to hurt himself.

Bolton grimaced and climbed out of the car. "I shouldn't even be out of bed. I'm not asking, Nadia. I'm telling you. *Get in the car.*"

"Don't talk to me like that." The words came out as a whisper while something in Nadia caught fire like that house—from one tiny flame to a conflagration that engulfed her.

He tugged on her arm. Nadia yanked it from his grip. "Don't touch me."

"You want to do this now? What if someone sees us? We have to *go.*"

"Where? I want to go back to Sanctuary, Bolton." She lifted her hands and let them fall back to her sides. "When is that going to happen?"

"Please, say my name louder so people can hear you." His eyes had darkened until it was like night enveloped them, and he leaned closer to speak right in her face. "Wake up. You're never going back, Nadia. Sanctuary is over, and so are our lives there."

Nadia was shaking her head before he even finished. "No, I don't believe that. I have to be able to go back. Everything I have is there. My life, my friends."

"Your brother?"

"I knew the price I'd have to pay when I chose Sanctuary. I knew it meant I would never see Shadrach, ever again. So we wrote to each other. Then he showed up in town, and it was a gift. But it isn't my life." He reached for her again, and she backed up. "I have to be *there*. Not here."

"What is your danger?"

She flinched.

Bolton grasped both of her elbows. "Nadia, why were you in Sanctuary? I asked before, and I'm still waiting for you to tell me."

"They won't come after me."

"You were sent to Sanctuary. There has to be a reason why you couldn't live out here. Why you were put in witness protection?"

It was time to tell him. "There's no threat. Not to me. It's over."

Bolton's head jerked back. "You're in no danger at all?"

"It was over years ago when Manuel died in prison."

"I'm confused. Why were you living there if no one is trying to kill you now?"

"Where else would I go?"

He frowned. "You could have gotten out."

"I didn't want to."

Bolton blanched. He pushed her into the car, one hand on her head, and then shut the door. When he got in, he turned to her. Said nothing.

She didn't know what to make of that look. "What?"

"Every day I was stuck in that town I wished I could get out." They'd been friends in Sanctuary—it had even been moving toward more than that. "I hated every second of it."

"But…your friends." Matthias would be crushed if he heard this.

"Sure, I'll miss them. But that rancher wasn't me." He started the car. "This is me."

Bolton peeled out of the alley with one hand on the wheel and the other—the one that man had twisted—in his lap. He gunned it down the street until the car caught up with how fast he wanted to go. "There are bad people hunting me. Powerful people with some serious connections. This isn't some mishap. They are trying to kill us, and they will if we don't kill them first."

"So I'm supposed to…what? Live on the run with you the rest of my life." How she felt was made plain by those words, and Nadia didn't miss Bolton's reaction. "Or you drop me off and I walk away, find some kind of life for myself. Is that it?" She waved at the window. "Maybe you should let me out here."

"Is that what you want?"

Nadia let the question hang between them. She stared out the window and blinked back tears. He could never know that the biggest part of why she'd stayed in Sanctuary was him. Or that her feelings had been enough to convince her that life in that town, with no possibility of ever leaving, was worth not seeing her mother or brother ever again.

They pulled onto the street where she worked.

"Dante knows there's a woman with me. It won't be long before he figures out it's you. I'm sorry to say it, but you're stuck with me until I know you're safe."

The salon came into view.

Bolton sighed. "I know that's not what you—"

She grabbed his arm. "Pull over."

Bolton gritted his teeth. "Easy."

She'd hurt him. "Sorry."

But he did as she'd said.

The front window of the salon had been smashed. Police milled around, blue and red lights flashing bright enough to make the whole street strobe like a night light. EMTs wheeled someone out through the front door. A woman.

Nadia gasped. "Melanie."

She grabbed for the door handle, but before she could get out, Bolton gunned the engine and they were off again. "What did you do that for? I need to find out what happened to her. Now we can't know unless we go to the hospital later." He was going to disagree. "We should go to the hospital later."

"We aren't going to do that." Bolton's lips pressed into a thin line. "We're on the run, Nadia. We have no help, nothing but the two of us against an army of men trying to kill us."

"Unless we kill them first." She shot back.

"Exactly."

"I wasn't agreeing with you." Nadia shifted in her seat. "Am I supposed to be okay with this? Because I'm not. I nearly died the last time I was on the run from a man trying to kill me. Now he's dead, and Shadrach isn't here to help fix my problem this time."

Bolton's lips twitched. "Your brother killed him?"

"Manuel died in prison. I told you that. Shadrach protected me." Unlike what Bolton was doing. "That's not the point. The point is that we need *help*."

"No one's going to help us."

"We have to try. We have to ask. That's why I called the marshals' office, but they said Grant doesn't work there anymore."

"He retired."

"What? How do you know that?"

"It was in the newspaper, Nadia." He tapped the steering wheel. "Do you realize what you did?"

Nadia shrugged. "What? What did I do?"

"You exposed us."

This wasn't her fault. She wasn't the one who'd hurt Melanie. "I've been along for the ride this whole time. Doing what you asked because what other choice do I have?" She was done.

"You know I'd change that if I could."

Because he didn't want her there with him? Nadia folded her arms. She'd only been trying to help, and he didn't even want her around. She should have been at the hospital with him, there when he woke up from surgery and then on her way back to Sanctuary. Instead the helicopter had exploded, and all this happened.

"Your phone call to the marshals is what did this." From the corner of her eye, he glanced at her, then said, "You're the reason Dante's man found us at the doctor's house. The reason he sent that man to kill us. The reason the doctor is dead, and why your boss is hurt."

"I didn't—"

"You don't get how serious this is, Nadia. You never have."

"You think I don't get being in danger?"

"Sure, some artsy guy was trying to kill you for messing up his hair or whatever." Bolton huffed. "This is an army of men. You don't want to know what they'll do to you before they kill you."

Bolton hit the brake pedal.

"What is it?" She peered out. All she could see was a mess of lights.

"It's a road block. They're trying to catch us."

Chapter 5

Sanctuary

John Mason, sheriff of the WITSEC town of Sanctuary, sat back in his chair and sipped his coffee. He'd long since gotten over the need to get up and be out and about in the morning. This was the season where he could read the paper and enjoy his third cup. Years of field work as a marshal had ingrained in him a rush of adrenaline. But these days he was married, and his son was happy with their new life. John had a car in a town of pedestrians—a town of almost two hundred protected witnesses who lived peaceably…for the most part.

He set the coffee down and turned the page of the week-old newspaper that had been delivered the day before. Sure he could get news in real-time on the internet, but there was nothing like the feel of newspaper in his hands.

Nothing.

No word on Bolton or Nadia Marie. They were out in the world—two residents he was supposed to be protecting—and he was stuck within the ring of mountains that hid Sanctuary from the outside, trusting his brothers to keep his own people safe.

Ben, the international man of mystery. John still wanted to know what Ben had done to the mayor of Sanctuary to make the old man mad enough to demand John arrest Ben the last time he had been there. But Ben had slipped away. His brother was better put to use applying his skills and substantial resources to finding Bolton and Nadia Marie. From their last conversation he was getting somewhere. Ben never shared, and he always hid stuff up his sleeve. But so long as they were found and returned to safety, Ben could utilize whatever methods he wanted.

Footsteps pounded down from the apartment upstairs, and Pat raced in. The eleven year old still hadn't lost all of that little-kid exuberance, something John's brother, Nate—who'd been the Dolphin's quarterback—never lost in his life. Though at times Pat showed Ben's more quiet, watchful way of observing things. John had also been forced to contemplate the idea his son might have a girlfriend. There were clues. Ones they were going to talk about when they went fishing at the lake Saturday morning.

It was more of a pond, but after an explosive device had taken out half the hill and most of the ranch, leaving a big hole, what else was there to do except fill it with water and spend ten percent of the year's budget stocking it with rainbow trout?

"Dad, Andra's going to walk me to school."

"Okay." John hugged his son, who raced to the door, while Andra stepped into the room from upstairs. Her cheeks were flushed, and her hairline was damp.

"Didn't go so well this morning?"

"The walk will do me good, and I'll leave the door open so it doesn't smell like coffee in here when I get back. That okay?"

"It's not coffee," John said. "That's my new cologne. Eau de Java."

Andra cracked a smile.

"There you are."

"Yeah, yeah. Morning sickness is not my friend."

He pulled her into his arms and kissed her forehead. Pat's mother hadn't suffered any morning sickness when she'd been pregnant with him, but John didn't think Andra wanted that tidbit of information about a woman she'd never met and still managed to dislike.

He could feel the bump under her sweater and smiled, his lips still against her forehead. They'd have to start thinking about cribs and nursery colors soon. He'd have to wear a tool belt, and Andra would watch him with those dark eyes, and then—

"Can we go already?" Pat rolled his eyes. "You guys are gross. Get a room."

John chuckled. "Pretty sure I have one upstairs."

Andra smiled. "Let's revisit that, later."

"Deal."

Her shoulders shook, and he felt the amusement deep in his chest as his son disappeared through the door. "Will I ever get over him being so big?"

"No." Andra leaned back. "But he'll have a little brother on his heels, so you can marvel that this one is so small."

John smiled and leaned in for a kiss.

"Eau de Java." She looked green.

John's satellite phone rang. He leaned far enough back he could see the screen without letting her go. "It's Grant."

"Don't just talk business. Actually ask him if he's okay."

John nodded. He said bye to his wife and then grabbed the phone from the desk. "Did you ever give up coffee when Genevieve was pregnant?"

"Dude that was like twenty years ago. I can barely remember the girls being in middle school at this point. Now I'm forking out college tuition like it's going out of style." He grumbled, but John knew how much Grant loved those girls. Divorce was just hard, and Grant's had been final a few months ago.

"So what's up?"

Grant had "retired" from the US Marshals, while John—as the sheriff of their witness protection town—was technically still a deputy inspector. Though the town was now managed by a private consortium of investors and no longer subject to federal oversight, John had kept his job. Grant, however, served as some kind of freelance liaison between the government connections he'd retained—basically everyone in D.C.—and Ben's company. Which meant Grant was now a domestic man of mystery. John didn't even want to know.

"Couple things. But first, you should know about Remy." Grant filled him in on the man who'd broken into her house. "We were right, it's Dante. We think they might be in Seattle. Shadrach and Ben are both headed there now."

John blew out a breath. "I don't like being benched on this one. Not with a DEA agent after them. Every corrupt federal agent and cop in the country is going to get a BOLO to keep their eyes peeled, with Nadia and Bolton's descriptions on it."

But he couldn't help. John had people to protect here. The safeguards kept Sanctuary protected, and they were in a lull. While John was used to the problems being here, what he wasn't used to was being removed from a problem that was *out there*. Especially when his wife's best friend and a man he called friend were both in danger.

"It gets worse," Grant said. "Dante escaped from federal prison a week ago. He's in the wind, probably has an army of friends helping him stay in the shadows."

"That wasn't in the paper."

"The feds are keeping it under wraps. They don't want the press coverage. They just want to get him back in prison and avoid a PR nightmare."

"Nadia had better not get caught in the crossfire," John said. "Anything else?"

"The marshal over Bolton's case was found dead in his house. Beaten badly, we think they interrogated him for information. Maybe they thought he's been in contact with Bolton. Maybe he is. We'll probably never know."

John sighed. "Right." Someone had to be helping the couple, given how effectively they'd slipped from everyone's reach. But if it kept them safe, John didn't care who it was.

"Then the other thing."

"There's more?"

Grant coughed a laugh. "Brother, there's always more." While John smiled to his empty office, Grant said, "I got a call from the marshal who was Hal's contact, a million years ago when he signed his memorandum of understanding and first entered the witness protection program."

Hal? A wave of grief hit John. The older biker had been a figurehead in this town, as much as he hadn't wanted that notoriety, up until Tommy's bomb left him dead. John squeezed his eyes shut. They'd buried Hal in town, not even knowing who his family was in order to inform them of his passing.

"It was totally out of the blue, this call. The man is like eighty-six. Hal was sixty-seven. Did you know he was the first person to live in Sanctuary? I didn't even know that."

John shook his head. "How do you know this now? You're not even a marshal anymore."

"Thanks for reminding me." Grant's voice was sardonic. "The congressional committee was disbanded, but the marshals kept me on as a liaison. The new director of the marshals was read in to the concept of a witness protection town, and now we go from there. Anyone who agrees to live in Sanctuary will testify, and afterwards, will step out from under the cover of the marshals' service and enter private witness protection."

John wasn't worried about new enrollees. He had enough going on with the nearly two hundred residents currently living in town. And nothing would change for them, except funding would be better. Maybe they'd even be able to rebuild some of the houses so people didn't have to live in forty-year-old government housing that had been patched up over and over.

"So, Hal's case inspector?"

"Yep," Grant said. "I can barely believe what he told me. I thought I knew every resident of Sanctuary, even the ones who moved there before I became director."

"Or before you went to junior high."

Grant laughed. "True. This guy's story is unreal. Get this, Hal had a long-standing relationship with a woman in town."

"I know about his 'lady friend.'" Though that was all John knew. No one could identify her, and she hadn't stepped forward.

"Did you know they had a daughter?"

"What?"

"And she lives in Sanctuary. One of your born-and-bred residents. The librarian—Gemma Freeman."

John nearly stopped breathing. "Hal's lady friend was *Janice*?"

"That was my reaction. Can you imagine, the biker and the hippy?"

"Not to mention they're both older than dirt."

Grant laughed out loud. He took a breath and groaned. "She has to be grieving, and no one even knows why."

John's heart turned over. Hal was gone. Why did it hit him like new every time? "I'll go see her. Find out why Gemma doesn't know that Hal was her father." He'd seen her, and she wasn't acting like a woman whose father had just died.

"I actually might know the answer to that," Grant said. "I'll send you the file Hal's case inspector sent me. But you won't believe half of what it says."

Ten minutes later John's iPad had finally downloaded the ginormous file. He swiped through the pages, and his eyebrows rose. These were the first documents ever to contain the name Sanctuary. Written forty years ago, they detailed the birth of the town he now called home. A town that had been established purely for the protection of one man.

Hal Leonard.

The older man John respected. The biker who refused to play anything but sixties and seventies rock on his radio station.

A man, it turned out, that none of them had really known.

**

Nadia gripped the door handle as Bolton slammed on the gas and the car fishtailed. She exhaled a long, slow breath trying to calm her heart rate. Those days of running, hiding—of being scared—were supposed to be over. And yet here she was, running again. Only now they seemed to be running from the police.

Bolton's hands gripped the wheel. His attention was fully on the road, the traffic. Did he even remember she was still here?

"We should have stopped to talk to the cops. We could have told them about that man at the doctor's house and how he tried to kill you." The police could help them figure this out.

Bolton hit the brakes. He yanked the wheel to the right and parked—badly—at the curb. "The police aren't going to help us."

"Uh…that's what they do."

Bolton snorted. "Not with people like me."

"What does that even mean? You aren't different than anyone else."

"No?"

There it was. Again. That feeling there was this huge thing she was missing. And because she didn't know it, Bolton was treating her like a child. Sheltering her, like the world was this great evil out to get them, and they couldn't trust anyone. But Nadia hadn't made it this far without knowing precisely who her allies were. There were plenty of people she could call—if she could get their phone numbers.

"We aren't going to the police. You think they set up road blocks for people they just want to 'chat' with?"

"How do you know those were for us?"

He glanced at her, one eyebrow raised over his hard eyes.

"It's just a question. You don't have to make me feel stupid."

Bolton sighed. He pulled back onto the road, and they were driving again. "That's not what I'm trying to do, Nadia. I'm keeping us safe."

"Because there's this great threat, and yet you can't seem to explain to me why phones are off limits. Or why the police want to catch us."

"Because Dante set them on us."

"And a man in federal prison can command the police in that way? That makes no sense, Bolton."

"He probably leaked enough information to make them think I'm Dante, so they're on our tail. When they catch up with us, he'll snap the trap closed. The police won't know what happened, and we'll be too dead to care. They'll paint us as the bad guys."

Nadia glanced out the window. She'd hated Manuel for what he'd done to her, trying to frame her for his illegal art deals and then trying to kill her so that he could get away with it. There had been enough evidence of things she'd done that it had made his assertion credible. Nadia had been sunk, until she'd turned herself in to the FBI with a flash drive from Manuel's computer and told them the truth.

They'd offered her immunity for her small crimes in exchange for bringing down Manuel's entire operation. Now Manuel was dead, Nadia had found everything she'd ever wanted in Sanctuary, and there was no going back. This was who she was, and it was where she needed to be again. And would have been, maybe even weeks ago, were it not for Bolton.

She sighed. "Where are we going?" He drove like he had a plan but not anywhere near their apartment. "I don't suppose we're headed in a roundabout way to pick up our clothes." Her bible.

Their apartment had basically no furniture. They'd bought an old TV from a pawn shop and both slept on sleeping bags on the floor of the one room. It had been a sad existence, but a cheap one. Now that Bolton could walk, it made it worth it.

He didn't answer her about where they were headed, so she said, "How is your back?"

"The anesthetic is wearing off."

Which meant grumpy Bolton would reappear, the Bolton who didn't want to take pain medication despite the fact he snapped at her every time she tried to help.

Nadia tried to remember why she wanted to be around him in the first place. Sanctuary had been in chaos. Bolton's home had been destroyed. Tommy had been caught, and Bolton's need for surgery had become imperative since a town resident slammed him on the back with a metal folding chair.

Nadia had wanted to be there when he had the surgery. She'd thought he wanted the same thing, so she'd convinced the sheriff to let her ride along in the helicopter with a special dispensation, given the circumstances.

Maybe Bolton had planned to get out of town for the surgery…and then disappear. In which case, he hadn't wanted her there at all. Because he'd never intended to come back.

Bolton reached over and flipped on the radio. Apparently he didn't even want to talk to her now.

Nadia blinked back tears. How had her life come to this?

"Police are on the lookout for a man in his late thirties with dark coloring, possibly of Middle Eastern descent, concerning the murder of two men, one a local doctor and the other who is believed to be a confidential informant for the Drug Enforcement Administration. The man is six-four, said to walk with a limp, and is wearing a black hoodie. He should be considered armed and extremely danger—"

Bolton snapped off the radio. "That's why we're not going to the police. I'll end up doing life for a double homicide while Dante's sentence is revoked and he sips mai-tai's on some tropical island."

And what about her? "They didn't mention me on the broadcast."

"That's a good thing. It means we've kept you under the radar." Bolton pulled up at a stop light. "I don't think I even want to know what that look on your face means."

He took a right and headed for the highway. Nadia hadn't been out of Seattle since the day they arrived, but apparently Bolton knew every street and exactly how to get wherever he wanted to go. Five miles later traffic slowed, and they faced another set of flashing lights.

Bolton slammed the wheel with the heel of his hand. "Roadblock."

"So we're trapped?"

"They want us in the city so they can hunt us down. If we leave then we're in the wind, but we have an advantage Dante doesn't know about."

Nadia shook her head. "What?"

"You. Dante doesn't know I'm with you, and his men aren't looking for a couple. The cops aren't looking for a couple. They're looking for a lone man, and you're enough to distract them away from me."

Nadia didn't know whether to be flattered or not. "What's with the Middle Eastern thing? Does Dante know something I don't? I mean, your last name is Farrera. I thought you were Hispanic… Farrera isn't your name, is it?"

"Actually Bolton Farrera was the name my parents gave me when they moved here, from Albania. It's probably the most honest thing I have that's still mine, even though it isn't even my birth name. They purposely gave me an American name, but one that could be either Hispanic or even Italian. Add to that the American accent, and it made me blend in better."

"Why did you need to blend in?"

"We need to figure out a way out of town." He scanned the area, both sides of the road.

Nadia studied his face. Had she ever really looked at him? Sure, she'd gazed. But that wasn't what she was doing now. This was the moment the maze dead-ended, and the only way out was to back-track halfway to the entrance in order to figure out where the center was. Did Bolton even have a center? If he did, he'd probably never show it to her. Maybe she could get back to Sanctuary, but she'd have to live the rest of her life never knowing what could have been with Bolton.

His gaze snagged on hers. "You're doing that face thing again."

"You want me to be happy? I don't think I can fake that." Nadia sighed. "I'm just facing the fact that nothing is going to work out the way I thought it would." Nadia swallowed against the lump in her throat. "After I help you, I need to get back to Sanctuary. But I don't know how that's possible now. If Grant Mason isn't in charge of witness protection, then who is going to help me?" Nadia swiped at the tears trailing down her cheeks.

Bolton muttered and pulled out of traffic. "We have to get out of here, Nadia. We don't have time for this." He shoved the car in park, opened the door, and grabbed her hand. Bolton pulled her down the embankment.

"Hey!"

Nadia glanced back. A cop pointed at them. Four uniformed officers ran toward her and Bolton.

"Run!" Bolton dragged her along. She could have argued she was fitter than he was, but the pace he set was punishing. It had to hurt. He pulled out a cell phone and dialed with one hand.

"You have a—"

He'd had a phone this whole time, all the while telling her she shouldn't even go near one?

Bolton's voice was breathy, his teeth gritted together. "Because they're after us, Ben. This isn't working."

Chapter 6

Twenty Years Ago

Bolton lifted his chin and faced down his boss.

The old man huffed. "I'll slap your little teenage face if you say one word. Those girls won't think you're such hot stuff after that." Anton shoved him away. "Take out the trash like I told you to."

Bolton strode past the other two guys who worked at Anton's garage, with their smirks. They got to actually work on cars. He grabbed the trash bag and hefted it outside. The door hit him in the back when he stopped. Rain poured down on Baltimore, a torrent that put a six inch deep puddle between him and the Dumpster.

He hurled the bag at the opening and watched the thing split open to deposit the trash inside. At least it hadn't landed on the street this time.

Bolton turned back to the garage and saw Anton's car pull out with Yuri and his cousin inside. Apparently he was the one to lock up tonight. Bolton went back inside and strode to where his bike had been shoved in the corner. It didn't run yet, hadn't since he'd hauled it out of a pile of car parts at the junk yard and started tinkering with it. Anton and the two goons who worked for him thought the whole thing was hilarious, but they gave him their old tools, and Bolton ignored their jibes.

As he sat beside the bike and got to work on it, the world bled away. It always did. Life didn't matter anymore, not his family, not school and how much he hated it, or how the year until graduation and freedom felt like an eternity. It was like that when he drew, too. Mostly bikes—ones he saw in magazines—and ideas for how he wanted this one to turn out. He had sketch pads full of them between his mattress and the bedframe.

The man who entered did so in virtual silence. But not silent enough.

Bolton didn't turn. "The boss isn't here. Unless it's me you want to kill. Though I don't know why you would. I don't have any cash."

"I'm not here to kill you."

Bolton turned. The man was clean-shaven. That was new. Usually guys who came in the garage were drab in their overcoats and thick beards. This guy had a nice shirt, nice jeans. He looked like some kind of downtown office worker like the ones who sometimes dropped off their BMWs or Lexus's. In his twenties, probably.

"And I'm not here to see Anton. I actually wanted to speak with you."

He sounded proper, but the weird ones always did. Bolton stood, the wrench still in his hand. His father had laid into him enough that Bolton knew how to give back if he had to—if it meant the difference between being this guy's sick toy and getting away.

"Whoa. You could do some damage with that thing." The man smiled, and it was nice enough. Bolton didn't detect anything sinister. "I'm Ben Mason."

Late twenties, Bolton figured. Though maybe he was younger, and he just looked older because of those eyes. People always said that about Bolton, too. "What do you want?"

"Your help."

"I'm not interested." Bolton wanted to get back to work on his bike, but he didn't turn around. This was not the kind of man to give your back to.

"Hear me out. I'll make it worth your while." Ben Mason pulled a hundred from the front pocket of his shirt.

Bolton took the money. He wasn't going to pretend he didn't need it.

"Anton is a bad man, but I'm guessing you already know that."

"What if I do?" Bolton wasn't exactly lily white, not when he had a couple of charges on his juvie record already.

"Men like Anton, they don't do their work in the light of day. Sometimes it's hard to catch them in the act. To bring justice, even though they've hurt so many people. It's my job to bring down Anton and everyone he works with. That's what I'm getting paid for."

Bolton stared. It was a rare man who spoke the truth with no preamble. He could have lied. Easily. But he hadn't. He'd given Bolton the respect of being upfront.

"He's my uncle. You gonna take me down, too?" Bolton watched for a reaction. That was when he knew the man had done his homework. He knew about Bolton's connection to Anton.

"I'm not talking about killing him. I'm talking about him going to jail for a very long time."

Bolton snorted. "Like that'll stop him." Anton's reach spread across the city, if not further.

"Maybe I want to know more about that."

"You think I'm going to betray him when I know he'll kill me if he even *thinks* it was me who talked to you?"

Ben Mason studied Bolton for a second, then said, "Uncles who reign terror on everyone they know are something of a specialty of mine."

"What about fathers?" The question was out before Bolton could even stop it. He shifted, started to move away.

"I can help with that, too."

Bolton shrugged.

"I've seen your drawings."

Bolton's head whipped around to the man. He'd gotten inside Bolton's bedroom?

"A week ago, at the library."

"Guess I know where that notepad went." He'd gone to the bathroom and forgotten it, come back and found it was gone. "So, aside from some kind of creepy stalker and a glorified family counselor, what else do you do?"

Ben Mason cracked a smile. "What you can do with a pencil and whatever image is in your head of a motorcycle is a beautiful thing. You want to restore bikes, maybe even make a few of your own? You have enough talent you could set yourself up for life. But that's for tomorrow. Right now this is what I see." Ben paused. "You're a good kid. And you're not like them."

"I wasn't supposed to be like them, that was the point." Assimilating into the culture was the name of the game. "But if you mean I have a conscience, that's not a real good thing. Not so far."

"Your life can be whatever you make of it. That's up to you."

"My life?" Bolton barked a laugh. "Now I know you're crazy. Not sure how a bunch of sketches translates into millionaire."

"Okay, then. We deal with the immediate, and then we worry about the rest later. Ten grand, you get me what I need on Anton."

Ten grand would get his bike up and running in a week. Bolton would have what he needed to get out of Baltimore the minute he graduated. Anton wouldn't even be able to find him.

Bolton lifted his chin. "What do you need to know?"

**

Present day

Ben slipped the phone into his pocket and strode back into the one bedroom apartment Bolton and Nadia Marie had shared for weeks. *This isn't working.* Bolton had to hold on. He had to handle Nadia Marie, or Dante was going to find them faster than Ben could hide their every move. That phone call she'd made, asking for Grant, had cost them.

Shadrach looked up from a pile of mail he was searching through. "Everything okay?"

Ben nodded. "It will be."

"Daire?"

Ben shook his head. "Daire's on vacation right now. He had some personal stuff to take care of."

"He gets vacation? Nothing about days off in your employee handbook."

Like Ben actually had one of those. "It's meritorious."

Shadrach snorted and went back to the pile of junk mail, all there was in the living room except for two old dining table chairs that sat across from the tiny, ancient TV. Ben strode to the bedrooms. Bedrolls, two sleeping bags on the floor in the bedroom. Almost no other belongings, since they probably didn't want anything personal they'd have to leave behind.

Okay, so most of it had been Ben's plan, but Bolton had followed it well. Between the two of them they'd agreed this was the best course of action to keep Bolton from being found by Dante until the right moment, and in the meantime keep Nadia Marie out of it. Yeah, it bothered him that they'd had to use Nadia Marie for Bolton's cover, but when she knew, she would understand.

Things were working well so far, as long as they could stay out of the police's clutches long enough to get to the safe house Ben had set up.

It was a dance, juggling who knew what and predicting precisely how people were going to react. But it was also Ben's job. And he was good at it. Bolton had helped him take down Anton Sabrowsky, who'd been smuggling arms in from overseas. Anton and his brother—Bolton's father—had been the US end of an international crime family that originated in Albania. Ben had turned the tide of war with the help of one teenage boy, and the kid hadn't even known the extent of how helpful he had been. All he knew was that Ben had funded the beginnings of Bolton's adulthood. A beginning from which the kid had managed to build an empire.

One that Ben had found it necessary to dismantle.

Who knew?

But the kid had done the right thing one more time, testifying against Dante, even if it was only to escape a lengthy prison sentence himself.

The only wildcard in this operation was Shadrach, or more to the point, what Shadrach was going to do when he found out that Ben had known all along where his sister was, and the fact he'd said nothing about it.

Ben strode back to the living room. "There's nothing here. Let's head out."

"Sure." Shadrach stood, holding one book.

"What's that?"

Ben's employee shrugged off the question. "Nadia's bible. That's all." Shadrach glanced around. "I can't believe they were here for *weeks*, and she didn't even try to call me. Just Grant."

He was keeping something more to himself, but Ben let it go. It wasn't like there was a whole lot of truth between them in the first place. Ben had hired him, and Shadrach's skills were substantial. Not to mention that dog of his protecting Remy. Shadrach would make a good addition to the team, but the manner in which Ben was keeping Bolton and Nadia safe would likely make the man quit. If he didn't beat the tar out of Ben first.

Still, when Shadrach walked away, his sister would be alive.

Ben's watch vibrated. It was more an extension of his phone than a watch, but he swiped the screen until he'd read the entire update from his receptionist. Assistant. Accountant. Kenna did it all, but right now she was fielding calls from federal agencies wanting to know why he was in Seattle, given the timing coincided with the escape of a federal prisoner and a man the police were hunting.

Dante. Loose in the world.

The feds were keeping it under wraps, calling it "need to know." No press. No public. Just an internal investigation into how on earth a former DEA agent gone bad had escaped from prison. Ben couldn't claim he wasn't involved much longer before it would become clear he had stakes in this. They just needed to find and re-capture Dante before Ben had to intervene.

Shadrach headed out the door first and down the sidewalk to the truck. The former marine turned back. "What I want to know is why they were at that doctor's house in the first place. You think Bolton's back is getting worse or something?"

"Kenna said that doctor had written a paper on a type of polymer that could be used to treat a very specific kind of spinal injury."

Shadrach reached the car and turned back. "So Bolton had the surgery? He's walking?"

"We have to assume that's a possibility."

"Then at some point during or after, a man came in and killed the doctor then tried to kill them?"

Ben nodded. "That would be my guess." Shadrach was good at this. He would be a good addition to the team, if he stayed.

"So where was Nadia when all this was going down?"

"Helping him would be my guess."

Ben got in the car.

Shadrach buckled his seatbelt. "You know what I think? I think Bolton has been stringing her along this whole time. They go on the run, save enough money, maybe to pay for the surgery. Barely get out of that alive. Dante is on their tails..."

Ben had sent Bolton plenty of money, but having Nadia work as well had kept her from losing her sanity completely. Bolton had reported back that she was withdrawing into herself day by day, but Ben had counseled him to hold on. Love was a powerful emotion, one that could cause a person to stay the course far beyond where others would have given in.

Ben would know.

**

Bolton's back screamed at him to stop, but he pushed forward. They'd lost the cops across two streams and six miles of dense forest, but maybe it wasn't going to be enough. If they headed the right direction to where Ben wanted him, then soon they would hit a town, and if his picture had been plastered across the TV news, Bolton was going to get spotted fast.

"I still want an answer."

He didn't glance at her, though she raced along beside him. "Just because things are quiet now doesn't mean they're not right behind us. They probably have dogs out now to search for us."

"And you happen to know a lot about being pursued by the law, do you?"

Bolton sat on the tree trunk for a second before he swung his legs over. This couldn't last much longer. "This isn't the old west, and I'm no outlaw. But, yes. I do know a lot about being on the wrong side of the law."

"And yet Dante was the one behind bars. A man with connections in law enforcement so that he has every cop in the vicinity looking for us for whatever reason, when *he* is the one who escaped from prison."

Bolton blew out a breath. He should never have passed on that information Ben had given him. He'd known this was coming. "He was DEA."

"And so they put him in jail? For being a fed."

Bolton ignored the sardonic tone in her voice. "It's complicated, okay? He was investigating me, and he wasn't getting anywhere, so he started planting evidence. Coke shipments that were supposed to be my doing that he just 'happened' to uncover. Pretty incriminating."

Okay, so there was a lot more to it, but he'd have to piece it out, or she'd walk away. Bolton wasn't the kind of man a girl like her took home to Mama.

"And you were innocent?"

Bolton huffed out a breath. "Let's focus, okay? There's no signal here, and we need to head west." He glanced at the sky.

Nadia stopped beside a tree. Her breath came in puffs just like his. She hadn't needed to lose the weight that she'd lost eating on their slim budget, but she had. That was on him, too.

She shot him a look. "And the fact you've had a phone this whole time, and you haven't once let me even touch one because it was 'so dangerous, Nadia. You can't call anyone. No one can help us.' And now you have the audacity to stand there and look at me like you did nothing *wrong*. When there is not one single thing about this that is *right*."

"It'll be over soon, and then you'll be able to go home to your normal life." It was what she wanted. He'd known it for a while now. "You wanted to come with me to get the surgery, but the helicopter ride didn't turn out like either of us expected. I took the opportunity to do what I needed to do, and I'm sorry you had to be part of it, but I did what I had to do in order to keep you safe. And yes, that meant lying to you about the phone. If you'd known I had one, then you would have thought about it and thought about it, until it drove you crazy."

"So you command what's good for me, is that it?"

"In this, yes." She started to argue, so he cut her off. "Ben and I have been working together so that we stayed safe."

"And Shadrach?"

"I don't know if your brother knows, but Ben and I agreed to keep the circle small. Like the two of us, small. So likely your brother doesn't know."

Nadia turned away. "We should keep walking the way your new BFF thinks we should. We're getting close to a road. I hear traffic."

"We're headed to a tiny town, not a road."

She shrugged. "Listen for yourself."

Sure enough, Bolton could hear cars. The police had probably raced around the streets and were now ready to cut them off. He brushed past Nadia. "Let me go first."

"Because I can't take care of myself, or others, so I need you to protect me."

"That's not—" Bolton didn't want to argue. He sighed. His steps got more labored. With each movement, the pain in his back ratcheted up a notch. How long before he collapsed outright and was no help to her whatsoever? "We just have to be on the lookout for cops."

"Yes, we wouldn't want noble and honorable officers of the law to catch us."

Bolton glanced at the sky for a second and pressed on. The edge of the tree line gave good cover, and sure enough, two lanes of traffic crossed each other on their way to wherever their busy lives were taking them.

He turned back to her. "Go up there. Stick out your thumb."

"Me?"

"You're attractive." Understatement. "They'll stop for you."

"And when you walk out of the trees they'll drive away."

Bolton pulled the gun from the front of his waistband. "No, they won't."

Ten minutes later they were riding in the back of a semi among a pile of boxes that shifted with every gear change. Bolton lay stretched on the floor and watched to make sure none of the boxes fell on him, as he tried to relax the muscles in his back.

Nadia had her knees bent, her arms around her legs. Her big, sad eyes trained on him, probably not intending to shovel maximum guilt his way, but it was what it was. She said, "Does it hurt a lot?"

Bolton shut his eyes for a second. Some things he wasn't prepared to lie about.

"I'm sorry you got hurt."

"That's on Dante, not you."

"What happened?"

Bolton looked at her then. It was either that or fall back into the whirlpool of memory. Nothing good existed back there. Especially not when he thought about Nadia, and yes, Sanctuary. There had been good there, in the people. But it never changed who Bolton was or what he needed to do when he got the chance to leave town.

Maybe, in a way, they'd given him the chance he needed. Dante's coming after him and trying to kill him, leaving Bolton with an irreparable—aside from experimental medicine—spinal condition. Andy and that blasted chair he'd hit Bolton in the back with, the one he owed him for. It had all given Bolton the chance to come after Dante and finally finish this once and for all.

Sanctuary had never been a permanent solution. It'd been easy to wonder if Dante had been killed in prison, while Bolton lived his life as a rancher. But now that he knew for sure Dante was alive and well—and out of prison—well, it couldn't be denied that Bolton owed him. Dante just wouldn't like the payment. But that was for later. Right now, Nadia was waiting for an answer to her question.

"Ben took the week off. Had another job."

"Ben Mason?"

"He was in charge of my protection when I was brought into witness protection." Bolton had made it a condition, not about to trust a bunch of marshals he didn't know, even if one of them was Ben's big brother. "But that week he had something going on, so he left a friend of his in charge of my protection detail. That guy is no longer of this world. Ben took care of him after we realized that Dante had bought him."

Bolton took a breath and exhaled. "But it was too late. Dante had sent his army to take down the house. I got caught in the fire, and a shot gun blast to the small of my back virtually decimated my ability to walk. It healed some, but every step walking was a hair trigger away from paralysis."

"How on earth was riding a horse okay?"

Bolton smiled, his eyelids too heavy to open. He loved that horse. "Special saddle and a back brace." Warmth descended over him. The peace that the oblivion of sleep brought.

"And you didn't tell anyone?"

"What was the point? Thea was gone." Bolton's throat stuck. "Javier—"

He couldn't say anything else.

Chapter 7

Thea? Who was Javier? Nadia's heart flipped over as she stared down at Bolton. His face had relaxed in sleep, his features taking on an almost serene appearance. Almost. His eyes danced behind their lids and made Nadia wonder if he dreamed about them. These people Dante had come for and taken. Or killed. People Bolton cared about enough that their absence had left him distraught.

Maybe Thea and Javier were the destination. Maybe they had been all along, and Nadia Marie was nothing but an unwanted tag along. That stung. She leaned her head against the side of the truck and tried to remember if there had been any indication in Sanctuary that he was only being polite.

No one wanted to think they were being humored. It would suck if that was what this was, but Nadia just hadn't had the impression her feelings were one sided. Bolton had seemed drawn to her. The medical center had exploded, and Bolton had been with her. He'd been hurt, and she'd thought they'd had a moment, but maybe not. Perhaps it'd only been the pain making him vulnerable. He'd certainly needed someone to help him over the past few weeks, and at times he'd clung to her. But those were the early days before he began to pull away.

Because he'd been lying to her?

If it had bothered him, it was an indicator that he had a conscience. That had to count for something. Nadia couldn't claim she had always made the right decisions, not by any stretch, but she wasn't a criminal. And while she didn't think he'd committed any crimes in Sanctuary, he seemed determined to kill the man who had wronged him.

What Nadia needed to do now was help him not commit murder. Arguing with him, hoping he would change his mind, wouldn't work. His history with Dante was imprinted on the fabric of who he was—it was the same with her brother Shadrach and being a marine. Shad would never stop being a marine, and Bolton would never get off this path. It would take nothing less than an act of God to get him to quit, but Nadia had full faith in the Lord that it was possible. And if she could help, all the better.

She needed to pray about this. To take some time and ask the Lord what the next step should be. Then when it came time to move, she would be ready.

For longer than she cared to remember now, Nadia had held on to the hope that one day she and Bolton would be together, that maybe they'd get married and start a family in Sanctuary. Now that man was gone. The man here with her was a stranger, one she wasn't entirely sure she liked.

Nadia didn't know him, and whether or not she wanted to work on being friends didn't matter much. He still needed her help, and she wasn't going anywhere anytime soon. This was a prime opportunity for her to show him something she thought maybe no one had ever shown him before. Her actions would tell him a story, one he'd likely refuse to believe. But then Andra hadn't believed it at first, though when she'd told Andra the full story of the gospel, the woman had understood. She'd realized why Nadia didn't ever give up on her friend and never shied away from loving her, even when Andra told her all that she'd done.

How many people she had killed as an assassin for hire, and for the government.

Nadia couldn't love any other way than the way she was loved by her Heavenly Father. After all, she'd been forgiven of so much. Why wouldn't she then look for ways to pass that gift on to the people around her?

It had changed Sanctuary when the new sheriff arrived, and Andra had been in a place that she could accept his care for her.

Nadia fully believed that miracles were possible. She'd seen them, and she knew it could be this way with Bolton, too, if he would allow it. It would be harder than it ever had been for him to let her in, but Nadia didn't want to give up, because it could cost Bolton his life. His happiness, or even his sanity, when the hatred for Dante consumed him. If it hadn't already done so.

Nadia was fine with hard things. The past few weeks had been some of the hardest of her life, considering how much mental anguish there had been. How much she'd wished that things were different with Bolton. But now it was time for all of that to change.

Bolton had been right about his phone. If she'd known about it, Nadia would have gone crazy. A week later she'd have stolen it.

The flat, rectangle was visible in his pants pocket. Nadia held her breath and slipped it out.

She'd been cut off before she could talk to her mom the last time, forced to hang up because Bolton was there. At least now she knew she'd had the right number.

Nadia tapped her finger silently on the knee of her leggings while it rang, praying her mom was home.

"Nadia?"

"Mom," she breathed, trying to be quiet in the truck.

"I can barely hear you. Shadrach told me you might call." There was a tone, but her mom said, "He told me not to ask any questions, just to give you his number."

Thank you, Lord.

"I'll have to go find it." Her breath came in rhythmic bursts, and it sounded like she was walking. Nadia's mom had always been big. A hearty appetite and a college knee injury kept her weight steady. But she had also always been happy, a product of her natural—okay, hippie—lifestyle. Nadia had chafed against burlap and herbal tea as a teenager, then she'd made so much money with her art she'd barely been able to spend it all before more came in. She'd had a top floor apartment in Manhattan, two blocks from the hottest club in the city.

They'd barely communicated at that point. A relationship that was never perfect had faded into estrangement. There hadn't been anything to say.

It had been a world away from the small town Kentucky commune her mom had moved to after her kids left home, and Nadia had soaked up every second of it. Shoes, clothes, travel, partying. It had been a relentless onslaught of life. Until Manuel decided to start shipping priceless stolen paintings inside the frames with her work. And then he'd pinned it on her, saying she'd descended into the world of black market art.

Nadia had faced Manuel down and stood up for her own honesty. But she hadn't seen her mom since then, which meant that now, as she moved and muttered around the place where she lived, tears sprang into Nadia's eyes.

"Here it is." Her mom sighed. "Seven-oh-three, five-five-five, six—"

Bolton grabbed the phone and sat up in one move. He ended the call and stared at the phone screen, before he cast a furious gaze in her direction.

Did he think she was going to back down or cower?

"Who?" He barked the word at her.

Nadia could give him any number of answers, but she did try not to lie. "My mom."

"Why?"

"She was giving me Shadrach's number. Apparently he thought I'd call her, and he was right."

Bolton stared at her. There was no clock, but the seconds moved by anyway. Just without the ominous ticking.

"What was I supposed to do? You have a phone, and I need help."

"And so you call someone that can lead Dante right to us."

"Why would he think we have anything to do with a hippy commune in Kentucky?" Bolton's head jerked. Guess he hadn't been expecting that. Well, Nadia wasn't going to explain, either. Her family life was none of his business. "Look, it was only one call. No one even knows who I am. I'm sure Dante won't—"

"If we die, it will be your fault."

"What?" She shook her head. "That's crazy. He's not going to find us, not in a truck in the middle of nowhere."

"We're going to a safe house. Though there's a question now over whether Dante will trace the call back to this phone and be able to find us." Bolton touched the screen. The phone chimed and the screen went black.

"How could he know anything about me? My name wasn't anywhere on that news report."

"Do you want to risk it if he does? We have to get away from this place, just like the sheriff and his questions. This is the first place Dante will look—our last known location."

The brakes on the truck engaged, and Bolton shifted around. He moved toward the back door, ready to get down. Nadia could jump, but he had to do it slowly so as not to move anything.

"Sometimes I really don't like you."

He didn't look back. "That's because you're too nice to just plain hate someone. And why not? Hate is pure. It can give you strength, purpose. Clarity of mind."

"I hate that stupid denim jacket. It's ugly. How's that for pure?"

"At least everything I own isn't pink." He said it like it was an abomination.

"Guess we know where we stand." She folded her arms. "Excuse me while I tag along so you can enact your sick plan to get back at Dante. Or were you planning on dumping me off all along? Using me as cover because Dante wasn't looking for a couple where the man was in a wheelchair, and then the minute I became no longer useful you were going to leave me…where? On the side of the road? You were happy enough for me to hitch hike. What if the next trucker who picks me up turns out to be some rapist? Will you even look back when you drive away?" Nadia took a breath. "Did you ever care at all?"

Bolton's expression didn't change, and she knew then that she was right. "It wasn't real, Nadia."

Sanctuary. He was talking about Sanctuary.

The door opened.

**

The trucker locked up, a crusty older man in a stained wool sweater and knit cap who didn't say much except, "Ten minutes." Not that the time mattered to Bolton. They weren't getting back on that truck anyway. It wasn't far to the safe house.

Bolton pushed the aches and the pain to the back of his mind and grabbed Nadia's hand. She trotted to keep up with him as he made his way down the street. It was a truck stop, nothing more. Bolton pictured the map in his mind and traced their route to the town that didn't even have a stop light, just one sign. The vacation rental was on the edge of this tiny Washington town, and no one would think anything about two tourists showing up late at night.

Nadia's fingers were frozen, so he slipped their hands into his coat pocket. Low clouds began to drizzle. The kind of rain where the damp seeped into your bones. Bolton much preferred the east coast—so long as it was south of Orlando. Florida was just about the only decent place to live as far as he was concerned. Too bad he could never go back there.

One day Sanctuary would be a memory, too. The pain of telling Nadia that their time there hadn't meant anything to him would be nothing but a past he had no intention of digging up. The time they'd spent together, and the life he'd lived in one place not on the run from anyone had been nice. Not to mention a friendship with a whole lot of attraction and feelings underneath the surface.

Things with Thea had been explosive. Even the good times were full of sparks, and constantly having to stop at the jewelry store on the way home to make up for whatever he'd said in the heat of the moment.

Nadia was light years away from Thea. She was comfort. She was peace. Nadia had smiled at him, not expecting anything in return. And the older, hopefully wiser, Bolton who had lived through family war had also lived through years of being stabbed in the back and double-crossed. By the time he landed in Sanctuary he'd desperately wanted some peace in his life, so he'd eaten it up not knowing it would tie her to him.

He wanted her here. That was the kicker. Yeah, he'd had every intention of dropping her the minute her life was in serious danger or when she wasn't a help to them staying under Dante's radar. But that didn't meant he'd have been happy to let her go. It would have hurt, watching her walk away. He knew now how badly it would hurt her.

But both of them would have plenty of life left to live in which to heal from it.

"So what do we do when we get to wherever we're going?"

Bolton didn't glance at her. He couldn't look in her eyes anymore. What he was feeling would only get worse, and he didn't know why she persisted in dragging this out. "Wait until Ben gets there."

"Then what?"

Bolton shrugged the shoulder closest to her. "Find out what he wants to do. I can't keep the cops off our backs alone."

"But you want to take down Dante? And get that…whatever thing you were talking about. How is all that going to work if we're running from him? Don't you want to stop and let him catch you so you can kill him and go get your stuff?"

All of a sudden it was conversation, not Bolton's unthinkable plan. The woman made no sense. "I have to do this right. I have to make a plan, set up all the pieces, and draw out Dante without drawing out his men at the same time. One on one is fine, but if he brings his army of DEA agents he paid off, and men he hired to work for him, I won't stand a chance."

"So Ben is going to help you make a plan to murder him."

"He's not my partner in this. Just a sounding board."

"And Ben is fine with you murdering Dante?"

Now there was a loaded question. "Ben is not lily-white."

"None of us are. I heard he beat up the mayor the last time he was in town—which the mayor probably deserved. But normal people don't kill the people who wronged them and walk away from everything they know before the smoke clears. Not without consequences."

"That's why I need a plan. So the consequences will be minimal, and manageable."

Nadia swiped rain from her forehead with her free hand. It was running down the back of Bolton's collar. Her hair was probably soaked. They needed to get inside fast. It wasn't too cold, but they were going to start feeling miserable pretty soon.

She said, "I can't believe I'm even discussing this, but I want to know why you feel like this is your only option. I want to know *you*."

She wanted to be his shrink now? "There isn't much to know. I was one man, and then I was another one in Sanctuary. I don't know if either were real, but I'm figuring out now who I want to be next."

It was probably the most truthful thing he'd ever said to anyone his whole life. Bolton had made money designing and building bikes to the point the business had become its own entity and no longer required much input from him. That was when he sold it. All that cash, people had started coming out of the woodwork, offering him business partnerships he couldn't say no to. His money had tripled, and he'd ventured into some shady places with people who paid extra so there were less questions.

That was when he'd caught Dante's attention.

"That's the craziest thing I've ever heard. *Who you want to be next.*"

Was she serious?

"We are who we are," she said. "We can't just decide to be someone else. Change is one thing, and personal change is hard to maintain unless it's a 'God' thing. I suppose you could fix some things about yourself. But becoming someone new...that's like a chameleon. You're still playing a part, pretending the core of who you are is different so it matches the outside image you show everyone."

Bolton closed his mouth and felt his brow crinkle. Did she really think it was only an act? Nadia was the kind of person who said what she thought, even if it was hard to hear. But could she have the wrong idea this badly? He'd always figured he was able to be the man he wanted to be to suit any situation. Maybe he was a chameleon, if that's what she wanted to call it. It'd been simply what he did in order to make happen what he needed to. The fact she called it "acting" was proof she didn't know Bolton at all. Because there was nothing on the inside, there was only the shell. Dante had taken everything else. Thea. Even Javier, though the kid hadn't been able to help it.

That was why Bolton had to do this. Why he'd thought of nothing else for years but finally getting his revenge. Payback. Whatever he called it, didn't matter. It was what it was and not even a sweet woman with a knack for loving hard people could change that.

"Could we maybe factor some food into this equation?"

"Sure." He hadn't eaten since the surgery and didn't know when Nadia had, either. She was probably as hungry as he was. "Ben stocked the house."

"And he knew where we'd be?" They stopped at a corner, and she looked both ways at the deserted cross street, the dark houses, and street lamps.

Bolton tugged her to the right. "We're not more than a hundred miles out of Seattle. He had a general area and stuck to that, laid a few contingency plans. This is only one of them."

There wasn't anyone in the world Bolton trusted the way he trusted Ben Mason. Despite the deal he'd made with Ben all those years ago, he considered the man a friend. If Bolton had any of those outside Sanctuary.

Nadia cleared her throat. "Do you think Dante would hurt my mom?"

Did she really want him to say it out loud?

"Maybe I could call her again, warn her that someone might be coming to the commune to hurt her. They don't have weapons. They don't believe in violence."

"Dante does. Words of peace won't help them much if he wants information. He'll find us, and he'll use your mom—or anyone else—to do it."

"Can I call her?"

"Ben will already know you made that call. He monitors the phone." He squeezed her hand. "Don't worry."

Yeah, so there was plenty to worry about—like how that man had found them and killed the doctor. But he had to say it. He had to tell her something.

Bolton strode with her down the drive of a single-story with the living room light on behind the curtains. It was on a timer, Ben had told him. The key was under a plant pot on the back porch, but it only unlocked the side door into the garage. The interior door had a coded panel. Bolton entered the numbers Ben had programmed and went in first.

He cleared the house the way Ben had taught him and then slumped down onto the couch. Bolton closed his eyes. He should get them both coffee and food, but he didn't think he could get up. He should make her a sandwich.

"Can I use your phone?"

Bolton got up and handed it to her. "Grilled cheese?"

She smiled, like a beam of sun between the clouds. "Yes."

"I know you don't want to admit it" —he grinned— "but I'm pretty sure you're going to miss me."

The sound of her footsteps moved away. Bolton didn't doubt that he would miss her when they parted ways, and yet they'd shared only a couple of stolen kisses. He barely knew what to make of this whole thing. All he wanted to know was that Dante understood how Bolton felt about everything that'd happened. Nadia Marie was a complication he hadn't asked for.

"Uh…your phone is going crazy." She strode back in and held it out.

Six missed calls. Bolton played the voicemail, put it on speaker, and held it out.

"I know you're there, little girl."

His blood froze. "*Dante.*"

Nadia covered her mouth with her hand.

"Your precious momma will be fine. Maybe. But only if you bring Bolton to the steps of Portland City Hall by midnight two days from now. Or you could kill him yourself. Either way works for me." Dante paused. "Otherwise…"

Gunshots rang out. People screamed.

Nadia paled. "Mom."

"Time's running out."

Chapter 8

Sanctuary

"I'm looking for a book on George Washington."

Gemma waved the kid toward the back left corner of the library. "Four rows back, halfway down. Look for the covers with faces of old dudes."

"Sweet." The kid wandered out of sight.

Aside from him, Gemma was alone in the library. She had been most of the day which was the only reason she hadn't closed the place altogether. Not that she'd done any work. John was supposed to have told her what her next genre was. She couldn't be a known writer, but she could put books out. If she changed genres and pen names often enough that people couldn't follow her for more than two years before she became someone else, she could be an author. Such was the power of self-publishing these days. It would never have been possible until a few years ago. But what good were books when her whole world had fallen apart?

John's words still echoed in her ears. *Hal was your father.*

Gemma didn't even know where to start. She'd lived her whole life in a witness protection town with a man who was her father, and no one had ever thought to mention that fact? She'd figured her mother got pregnant before she elected to go into witness protection. Not that the aging biker who ran the radio station was her dad.

Now she couldn't even talk to him because he'd died when that bomb destroyed Bolton's house.

Gemma swiped the tears from her face. She'd cried at Hal's funeral. She'd liked him. They'd had a hilarious conversation about tuna at the grocery store that one time. But she'd never thought he might be her father. The worst part of that conversation had been John Mason's face when he realized she really, seriously, didn't even *know*. He'd been all about inheritance, and Hal's last wishes.

How about, "Hey, Gemma. He was your dad."

The kid came back with his tome, and she checked it out while he looked at her like she'd sprouted two heads. Poor boy was going to have to up his game around emotional women or he'd grow up to be one of those guys who freaked out and tried to fix everything just to get the crying to stop.

After he left, Gemma picked up the phone. Again. It rang four times and then went to voicemail, the kind where it played on speaker through the house because everyone had those ancient machines. Gemma was kind of surprised they didn't still have rotary dial phones.

"I know you're there, Mom. I know you can hear me. Eventually you're going to have to pick up and explain to me how in the you-know-what Hal Leonard could possibly be my father. Did you know he left me the radio station in his will? I'm a writer. I run a library. What am I going to do with a radio station for goodness sakes…"

Gemma dissolved into hiccupping sobs. She slammed the phone down and put both palms on her desk, trying to get control.

**

Nadia took the two steps to the coffee table, snapped up the gun, and pointed it at Bolton.

"Nadia, what—" He moved toward her, his gait stiff.

Nadia backed up two steps. "What do you expect?" Her thoughts had crystalized in perfect clarity. "Dante has my mother. He wants to trade her for *you*."

Bolton couldn't possibly think things were going to go on like they had. Not now. "You're going to get her back for me."

Bolton didn't stand. "He'll kill all of us. This isn't going to be a peaceful exchange. Let's call Ben, find out what's happening."

She didn't move. "You're going to get her back."

His face softened. "Lower the gun, and we'll talk about this, okay? We'll figure it out."

He couldn't think being nice would help him. Not now. "Dante wants you. What is there to figure out?"

"Nadia—"

"No! You've been lying to me—to everyone—since the helicopter crashed. Now I'm going to set things right. You're not going to leave me here and take off. You're not going to let my mom die. I won't let you do it!" She gasped for breath.

Bolton's eyes darkened. Before she knew what was happening he had the gun in his hand. He did something with it then put it on the table in two parts. "Nobody is shooting anybody, and nobody is leaving."

"I need to call Ben. Grant. My brother. Someone. There's no one here who can help me, and now my mom is going to die..."

"Because of me."

"What?"

He shrugged. "That's what you were going to say. Because of me."

She motioned to the phone with a wave of her hand. "Call Dante back and tell him you'll turn yourself in, and he needs to let my mom go."

Bolton shook his head. "I'd let you turn me in yourself if I thought it would save her life. Dante will kill her no matter what."

"So she's dead already, and we're standing here not doing anything?" Her mom's life was in the balance, and Bolton could do something about it. Nadia took two steps back. "You can't keep me here. If you're not going to help, I'll go there myself. There has to be something Dante wants that I have."

She realized what that sounded like, but who cared. She didn't see eye to eye with her mom, but she didn't want her dead, either.

Bolton roared, "You don't go near him!"

"Like you even care," she yelled back. "You don't even want me around."

She wasn't *that* kind of girl, especially with a crazy criminal. She wasn't going to barter herself. But Bolton didn't know that.

"I never said I didn't want you around."

"It wasn't real," she mimicked. "You can leave."

Bolton sighed.

"This is the life you want?"

He didn't move. "It's the life I know."

"Sorry I'm such an inconvenience. Guess I was mistaken." Nadia walked to the hall and grabbed her jacket. It felt like she'd been wearing the thing for days. She hadn't had a shower, and she badly needed a change of clothes, but she pushed aside those needs and pulled it on.

Nadia lifted her hands to sweep her hair out of the back of the collar and encountered the shorn strands of her short style.

Tears pricked her eyes.

"Why are you crying?"

He knew it wasn't about her mom. He knew.

Still, Nadia shot him a look. "You don't have the right to ask me that anymore."

To his credit, he looked like she'd killed his cat. He walked to her, unable to hide how painful it was to move. Maybe that was all he felt—the pain in his back. Maybe that look had nothing to do with her.

"Nadia." His voice had softened. He touched her cheek. "Please let me at least try and figure this out." He moved so close she felt the words against her lips. "Nadia." It sounded so desperate.

Why couldn't she just leave? She should be walking away. Instead his nose touched the side of hers, and she closed her eyes.

God, I have to go.

The door hit her in the back. She jumped away and spun as two men walked in.

"Nadia!" Shadrach pushed Ben Mason aside and grabbed her into a hug. He leaned back just as fast and glared at Bolton. "What did you do to her?" He shifted again. "Are you hurt? Don't worry about Mom, okay? If I have to, I'll take Bolton myself and swap him for her."

"You can try." Bolton's voice didn't invite argument.

Shadrach shot him a look, but Nadia was crying. She took a breath and tried to get a handle on her emotions. What was wrong with her? She should be out the door already.

Ben looked over her face and then nodded. He had a weird smudge on his eye, like someone had hit him. He turned to Bolton. "Let's go talk."

Bolton looked like he wanted to argue, but he limped to the living room.

Nadia turned back to her brother. "Where's Dauntless?"

"Watching Remy."

"Is she okay?"

Shadrach actually smiled, even though he was talking about being separated from his dog. Evidently there really was something going on between him and the doctor/genius/hacker who had lived in Sanctuary until Tommy kidnapped her.

Shadrach's smile never looked like a real smile to anyone else, but she'd figured out when they were fourteen that it was how he showed he was happy. "She's doing better."

He filled her in on Tommy's plan, the airplane, and what he'd done to Remy.

"No," she breathed.

"She's healing."

Nadia nodded. "We have to get Mom back." She didn't want to tell him that it was her fault their mom was being targeted, that she could even be killed because of Nadia.

"Ben cloned the phone that Bolton has, the one you used. He played me Dante's message. Up until then I didn't know that Ben knew where you were, or that you were fine." Shadrach pressed his lips in a thin line then said, "That's why he's getting a black eye. I punched him. Apparently it's part of the training process when you go to work for him. People usually punch him at least three times before they get off probation, so I still have two to go."

"You didn't know?"

He shook his head. "I knew you weren't dead, and that you weren't hurt badly. Those I would have known. But nothing aside from that. Ben didn't tell me anything." He set his hands on her shoulders, and Nadia grabbed his forearms. She'd always known when he'd been hurt in the marines. It had always been that way.

He went on. "Listen, we're still looking into what happened in Kentucky. The reports are sketchy, and we can't get ahold of the sheriff there. Don't assume Dante has Mom, not until we get word for sure. There were shots on the line, right?"

She nodded.

"We think he jumped the gun, made the call before he secured the compound."

"So he might not have mom?"

"We just don't know at this point, okay?" He paused. "How are you?"

She didn't want to answer that. Too much had happened since they'd last seen each other. Bolton was…she didn't even know what Bolton was. She'd seriously liked the man and had even thought that it might develop into something more, but no. "It's hard to believe I was so wrong."

She caught him up on what had happened to her.

Shadrach pushed out a breath. "I suppose I should be grateful you're alive, but I'd rather shoot him."

"I need to know Mom is safe before I go back to Sanctuary."

Shadrach ran a hand down his face. "We have two days until Dante's deadline to figure out what happened in Kentucky and make a plan."

Nadia nodded. "I'm glad you're here."

His face softened. "Me, too. We'll figure out how to help mom. Don't worry. Ben has resources you won't even believe."

She tried not to worry, but evidently her present to her mom for not talking to her for years was to bring a killer and his army into her life.

"I should pray for Mom, but I can barely think of what to say."

Shadrach shifted. "Don't look at me. I don't know how to do that."

Nadia grabbed his hand and mangled a request to God that her mom was safe, that Dante wasn't going to get his way in this. She said a couple of things without thinking it through and then muttered "Amen." It wasn't perfect, but it didn't have to be. She had wanted the chance to explain more to her brother about her faith and what it meant to her. Praying together was one better. *Thank you, Lord.* She wanted Bolton to believe, just as she wanted Shadrach to believe. They were both observers in her life, the same way she was an observer in theirs.

And her actions and reactions spoke volumes.

Help me to trust You, Lord. Help them to see the comfort and hope You give me.

Nadia opened her eyes. "Thank you."

"Sure." Shadrach shrugged like he didn't know what else to do.

Nadia hugged him again. "I need to do something, so let's make dinner."

**

Bolton sat on the patio chair without wincing. Which he should have won a prize for.

"That bad, huh?"

Ben had always been able to tell when something was up. "Just tell me that Thea and Javier are still safe. That's all that matters at this point."

Ben let that linger in the air. They both knew precisely what was going on with Nadia Marie and exactly how Bolton had screwed that up—even if there had only been a dream of what could be and nothing more.

Bolton said, "She's the one who called her mom and put her in danger."

"And it's your job to inform her of that fact?"

Bolton looked away, at the dark of the yard beyond the patio. Nothing but black for him to stare into, the way his life had always been. Were it not for the sparks of light—Thea, at least at the beginning, what he'd had of Javier, and yes, Nadia, too—he'd have thought he was blind a long time ago.

"You made the right decision going up against Dante. We knew what it was going to cost us. That wasn't a surprise."

"Us?" Bolton shook his head.

"I've paid plenty."

He glanced at Ben, trying to read what might be behind those words. As usual, Ben gave nothing away. But Bolton had known him long enough to have learned that the man hid a world behind what he showed people. Bolton had plenty of secrets, but Ben was more like a void. Until you dug deep and realized he cared deeply, but also compartmentalized his entire life.

"You didn't answer about Thea and Javier."

"When the simple fact of contacting them will put them in danger, it's difficult to check up on them."

"So they could be dead, and I'd never know."

"That's not what I said." Ben settled on the chair beside Bolton and stretched out his right leg so that it was straight. Bolton had seen the limp, but that'd been a good six years ago before he went to Sanctuary. "I get updates. The last was a week ago. I initiated a request this morning for more up to date information."

That was it. Bolton's whole world consisted of Ben making requests and then emailing Bolton in Sanctuary with "all good" or some such response. All because Dante had nearly killed him and then declared he would never stop trying until Bolton and everyone he cared about was dead.

"So you're headed for the cache?"

Bolton shook his head. "I thought you were the master of stealth and interrogation. You're just going to ask me outright?"

"With you, I've discovered the direct approach is usually better."

"If I head for it and Dante catches me, the cache is gone. I can't risk getting it when the threat is at this level."

"So you take care of Dante and then make a break for it. Use the cache to fund your new life on the run."

"Are you going to come after me?"

Ben blew out a breath. "I'd like to tell you I wouldn't have to. But what's in that cache might be too valuable to let fall into the wrong hands."

"That's why I'm nowhere near it. But I will be at some point, and then I'll disappear. Then the big bad Ben Mason will no doubt add me to some government watch list. Thirty years from now some retired CIA agent will find me sweeping the floor in a cantina and have to decide whether or not it's worth it to him to rush the rest of his drink just for the sake of capturing me."

Ben chuckled. "I suppose that's one way it could go down. Is that really what you want out of your life, sweeping a floor?"

"Sounds great to me. Break up a few bar fights so I don't get rusty, go home to my beach-front shack and sleep to the sound of the waves." Bolton paused. "Do you know I haven't heard the ocean in *years*? I can barely remember what it sounds like."

"Hot air, and sand everywhere?"

Bolton rubbed his forehead. "At least tell me you're doing something about Nadia Marie's mother."

"Grant was closest. He's headed there with a team to figure out what's happening." Ben flipped his wrist over and looked at his watch. "Should hear something soon."

"She's probably dead already."

"And you're missing the opportunity to comfort a beautiful woman when she's upset."

Bolton shook his head. "You know why that's not for me. You of all people know why I can't even entertain the idea of a love life. I'll never be free, not out here."

"You weren't free in Sanctuary, and yet you did 'entertain the idea,' as you put it." Ben shrugged one shoulder. "What was the difference there that you're so dead set against Nadia now, when she genuinely needs you?"

"She has her brother. She doesn't need me."

Ben blew out a breath. "Keep telling yourself that and you'll lose any chance you had at happiness. Trust me, I know what it's like to see the thing you want and never get the chance to grasp it for yourself. That's not the life I want for you, Bolton. It never was. You made your own choices, but you were a good kid, and you did the right thing by Dante."

"Because I had no other choice."

Ben got up then. "There's always more than one choice, Bolton."

He went inside, leaving Bolton alone on the patio with nothing but the night and his thoughts. Never a good thing.

Every single decision Bolton had ever made was only so he could be the man he was supposed to be—to live the life he'd always wanted to live. But he hadn't stepped on others to get there. He'd never hurt anyone to get ahead.

He'd only ever made business decisions his rivals weren't been happy with. They knew business was like that. Especially competing in the same market.

His single fix-it-up bike had ballooned into a line of custom builds he'd sold to whoever could afford the price tag. Not a big market, but it was a big payout, and they were worth it. That was when he'd found out Dante was investigating him, because Dante had money in the competition's business.

Enter the feds, and their investigation into Dante. Or so he'd thought.

When Bolton had decided to fight Dante, Bolton had hidden a trunk of money and weapons and a flash drive that belonged to Dante. This was Bolton's out. Everyone needed money if they wanted to fund a new life, and who cared if the money wasn't on the up and up? He'd stolen it from someone who wasn't innocent—not by any stretch.

Nadia didn't understand who Bolton was or why he did the things he did. Ben barely got it, though Bolton figured the man would've made some different decisions given he had three brothers who loved him. Not to mention a mom who loved to stick her nose in their business.

Bolton had no one, and before he'd moved to Sanctuary he'd barely had Thea and Javier.

Not exactly happily ever after material. At least, not the kind Nadia Marie was looking for. If Shadrach knew the half of it he'd probably put a bullet in Bolton's brain.

Bolton wouldn't stop him.

Or blame him.

Nadia could go back to her life in Sanctuary where she'd be happy, without all the pain his life would bring her.

Bolton leaned forward and laid his face in his hands. He'd wanted her on the helicopter with him, had planned to say goodbye at the hospital before he disappeared. It was selfish, but he'd needed her because he'd honestly been scared over the surgery. Now he'd ruined any chance of leaving with any kind of goodwill between them. She would no doubt hate him forever after this, which was pretty much the story of his relationship with Thea.

Nadia was never going to forgive him. Bolton had to stay the course and hope that she managed to get over it with time. Maybe she'd even forget about him once she realized her feelings hadn't been about who he really was. Maybe she'd find someone else in Sanctuary. That pastor guy, Dan Walden, was nice enough. It could go somewhere.

Pain ripped through him that had nothing to do with Bolton's injury.

In thirty or forty years, when it still hurt that he'd walked away from her, Bolton was going to wake up and realize he'd done the wrong thing. But what would be the point of regret when there was no way to change it? What was done, was done.

Nadia hated him.

"Bolton."

At Ben's call he got up and came back inside. Shadrach stood beside his sister. A stack of grilled cheese sandwiches were plated on the counter beside her.

"It's not dinner," Ben said. "Grant called me back. The compound is a mess, four dead. No one knows where the sheriff is, and their mom is missing."

Chapter 9

Nadia walked beside her brother down the airplane stairs. The limp in Bolton's stride had gotten worse through the journey by plane. From a tiny airport fifty miles outside Seattle all the way to Denver, where they'd disembarked the private jet. But that didn't explain why Shadrach glared at him.

A SUV pulled up in front of them, and a man climbed out. He tossed Ben a set of keys and strode to the plane. On the back of the SUV was one of those stickers indicating the family who owned this car had two parents, three girls, and two identical little boys. Nadia climbed in the back seat beside Shadrach and sat on something. A DVD case. She picked it up and it fell open. *Finding Nemo* and *Max and Ruby*. She tossed the case on the floor. The seats smelled like Happy Meals. Ben drove them downtown and parked in an underground garage that was empty except for three older, nondescript cars.

Up the elevator.

The hall was dark until Ben hit a switch. He walked halfway down, and Shadrach nudged her. He motioned to Ben, who opened the door on a junction box. Instead of throwing a breaker, Ben put his hand inside. A blue light scanned from top to bottom, and the door at the end of the hall clicked open.

"Pretty cool, right?" Shadrach was excited, but the usual streak of nerd he hid below the marine persona was subdued.

Shadrach grabbed her hand and squeezed it. Nadia didn't let go as they walked into the office, a drab and completely impersonal space that consisted of a cubical farm with no workers and doors on every wall—all closed. The far end of the room was lit by a single fluorescent light that blinked. Under that light was the only open door.

Ben walked in first, this casual air of lethality evident in him that was almost mirrored in both Bolton and Shadrach.

A woman sat at a computer in the conference room.

"Remy." Shadrach breathed her name like it was a prayer, a fact Nadia made a mental note to ask him about later. Dauntless got up and trotted over to them. He went to Shadrach's left side and sat, so he was almost leaned against her brother's leg. Shadrach reached down. "Good boy, Dauntless."

Nadia Marie scratched the dog on the way past. "Remy!"

Remy smiled, the red-rimmed glasses she'd worn in Sanctuary gone now. "Nadia Marie. It's good to see you."

Nadia leaned back from the hug. "How are you?"

Remy pressed her lips together and nodded. "Better." Nadia smiled. After what Remy had been through, better was good. "You?"

Nadia didn't even know where to start with answering that. She wasn't going to say "fine." Not when it wouldn't be true.

"We're good." Bolton slumped into a chair with a wince. "Mostly."

"You had the surgery!" Remy hopped up and raced to Bolton. She got him to lean forward and lifted the back of his shirt. The doctor was in.

How anyone's brain could hold a medical degree, everything anyone could possibly know about hacking, and the smarts to do genetic research and engineering, was a total mystery to Nadia. But that was Remy.

Nadia glanced at Shadrach, who watched the pair with wary eyes. There was something there. Not quite a longing, but close to it. They had some kind of previously established connection. Remy had lived in Sanctuary, and Shadrach had known her before he showed up there. Nadia didn't know much about them, but it looked sort of like he wanted to punch Bolton, throw Remy over his shoulder, and walk out—which pretty much equaled Shadrach being in love with the woman.

Nadia wondered if Remy even knew how deep his feelings went.

"The doctor did a good job." Remy cleared her throat. "Before he was murdered by that other guy."

Bolton straightened. "Glad you think so, doc."

Remy started to ask him questions, while Ben wandered to another man Nadia hadn't noticed. He sat at the far end of a conference table with a laptop. Ben leaned down, and they had a low conversation she couldn't hear. Shadrach leaned his head close to hers. "That's Will. He's on Ben's staff. Tech support."

Nadia nodded. "And the guy driving the SUV at the airport?"

"Operational support."

Remy clapped. "Let's get started." She sat back at her spot at the conference table and brought up a series of images on a wall screen. "This is what we have so far. A list of Dante's known associates, all of whom we are running down via cell phone GPS to obtain their whereabouts and find out if they're working with the man in question."

Bolton studied the screen of pictures. Nadia didn't recognize them, but most looked like those serial killer or terrorist photos on the news.

He said, "What about current DEA agents that could be sympathetic? Old colleagues he could contact for help?"

Remy clicked her mouse. "That's the next page."

The image switched to four men.

"Bottom right."

Remy glanced at him. "You're sure?"

Bolton nodded.

"Tristan Sanders is only on the list because he was Dante's partner. We have no reason to believe he was dirty other than by association. In fact, we think he had no part in it. Otherwise there'd be more evidence."

"He was in on it."

Ben straightened. "Are you certain?"

"He was there." Bolton looked over at Ben. "Dante was the figurehead, but Sanders was the brains behind it. I actually heard Dante ask him if he agreed they should kill me."

Ben said, "He might be the why of how Dante escaped. Plus he'd be able to pull enough strings he could get the manhunt kept under the radar." Ben blew out a breath. "Tristan Sanders could be the answer to this."

"I'll find him." Remy typed on her computer faster than Nadia had seen anyone do. Within minutes, she said, "Cell phone…puts him in Venice. On Bainbridge Island, just west of Seattle. Which no one here will think is a coincidence."

Shadrach sat on the edge of the table. "So is he there for some unrelated reason, is he doing something for Dante, or is he coordinating what's happening from there? Is Dante coming to him?"

"All good questions," Ben said. "None of which we can answer without going back there and finding out for ourselves."

Nadia glanced around. They'd only just got here, and now they were going back to Seattle?

Bolton nodded. Shadrach had his arms folded. Nadia just stood there. It felt like she'd been teleported into one of Shadrach's military briefings, and she seriously did not belong here. The artist among the warriors. They were all ready to dig in and fight, and all she wanted to do was retreat to Sanctuary where she could pray for her mother.

Here, there was nothing but white noise in her head. She needed Sanctuary's peace. The mountains. Right now she couldn't even concentrate on asking for her mom's protection, let alone figure out what God was doing through this situation. She tried to breathe in peace. To ask for it without words, knowing God heard the cry of her heart. But Nadia couldn't fight through the screaming fear that her mom was already dead.

This was all a total waste of time.

Nadia had killed her.

"Nadia—" Shadrach's voice barely cut through the rush in her ears.

But in front of her was Bolton. He touched his cool palms to her warm cheeks and spoke words she couldn't decipher. He mouthed, "Breathe."

"...panic attack."

Nadia couldn't get air. Bolton's gaze had hers locked on him, unable to see anything else. She tried to shut off the swirl of dark thoughts that had to be a fight for her peace of mind. Never in her life had she experienced fear this acute or an attack from her spiritual enemy this powerful. Nadia sucked in a breath and grabbed Bolton's forearms.

God, help me.

Bolton wrapped his arms around her. The rushing in her ears dissipated, and she heard him mutter comforting words in her ear as he rubbed his hand up and down her back and held her.

When she could catch her breath, she said, "I'm okay." *Thank you, Lord. Give me peace, even still. Be with my mom and help her.* The lump lingered in her throat while she glanced at Shadrach and tried to reassure him with a smile. He didn't look convinced.

Ben came over. "Stay with Shadrach and Remy, okay?"

Nadia nodded, though it hadn't been a request. Ben asked, but he didn't *ask*. He looked at Bolton then motioned to the door with his head. "Let's go get Sanders."

Bolton squeezed her elbows. He followed Ben out the door without a word. Then Shadrach was in front of her. "You want to tell me what that was?"

"I was freaking out."

"I know that. That's not what I'm talking about. I've seen you have anxiety attacks before, but you don't come out of them because some guy gives you a hug. It used to take hours and quiet space."

Behind him, Remy smiled. The small smile of someone who had discovered something.

Nadia looked back at her brother. "Can we not talk about this?" She sighed. "Bolton and—it's complicated. I don't even know what to say about it."

"I'm sorry you got stuck with him, Nadia. But that is not the kind of man you want to fall for." Shadrach didn't look like he was going to back down any time soon. "You don't even know the half of what he's done or what he's capable of. If you stay with him you will never, ever be safe."

"I'm in witness protection. Safe is pretty relative."

Shadrach didn't smile. "You've been in Sanctuary for *years*. The real world might have changed, but people are still as selfish as ever."

She glanced at Remy. "Wow, optimistic isn't he?"

Shadrach groaned. "You need to take me seriously."

"Shadrach—"

"Don't kid yourself that Bolton is willing to do anything unselfish. The man is the epitome of the out-for-himself thug who'll do whatever it takes to land on top."

"Bolton is a rancher." That was how she'd known him, how she'd come to love him. Nadia knew the man inside, despite Bolton's assertions that he wasn't that man. No one could keep up a ruse for *years*. "He isn't a thug, not anymore. And I know it kind of looks like he wants to be one again, but he doesn't realize that revenge isn't going to make him happy."

"It'll make him feel better."

"That isn't true either."

"And you know this?"

Nadia stepped away. She didn't want to talk about that, not right now at least. And definitely not with her brother. They'd been close at one time, but years of estrangement only broken by the occasional letter had put both space and time between them. Life had gone by. Shadrach didn't know everything about her. Not the way that he might have years ago. He didn't know what had come of Nadia's friendship with Andra, or the way faith had molded her into the best version of herself.

God had brought her out of the darkness, and set her in Sanctuary because He'd had a job for her there. Now that she was out in the world, Nadia didn't know what her job was. Aside from helping Bolton. And she was still trying to figure that out.

**

Shadrach watched his sister slump into a chair and shut her eyes. The dissipating adrenaline would leave her exhausted, but there was nowhere here for her to sleep. Ben had only set up the office this morning. If it stayed in Denver more than a month, Ben would add a down-room where they could get some rest.

"Is she okay?" Remy had gone through a serious trauma, and yet she managed to set aside her own recovery to care about Nadia.

Shadrach touched her elbow for a second. When she didn't flinch he stepped an inch closer and smiled. "She will be. She's tough...and stubborn."

"Sounds like someone else I know." Remy smiled. "I think they might even be related."

Shadrach's chest shook, but he made no sound. It was the closest he came to laughter these days. He exhaled and the amusement dissipated the same way Nadia's adrenaline had. "What are you doing here, Rem?"

"Working for Ben." She lifted her chin. "What does it look like?"

The postage-stamp amount of information Shadrach had amassed about women told him to tread carefully. "You're a scientist, and yet you're here hacking for Ben?"

"I'm making a difference. Dante is out there, and he's a threat to both Sanctuary and your sister. Why shouldn't I help if I can?"

Shadrach blew out a breath. "Can't you make a difference in the scientific field? In a lab." Where it was safe, and he didn't have to worry about her every second.

She had to know he didn't want her involved in this. He didn't want her anywhere near Dante or anything that had to do with the man.

This time it was Remy who touched his shoulder. "I need to do this."

Shadrach nodded. "I just want you to be happy."

"You have to let me be happy being who I'm going to be. Even if you think I'd be happier doing something else, it has to be my choice."

"And I have to be okay with it?"

Remy leaned in slowly, tentative. She kissed him on the cheek.

**

Bolton stretched out of the car and narrowly missed getting beaned by the tree branch Ben had parked under. Ben got out the driver's side, and they slammed both doors. "A three hour flight is way not long enough for the amount of sleep I need."

"Sucks for you then, since I doubt you'll get much in the thirty-six hours before Dante's deadline."

"You think I'm going to be anywhere near Portland City Hall when the time comes?"

Ben said, "Guess we'd better find Shadrach and Nadia's mom, then."

Bolton extricated himself from the brush Ben was using to disguise the car on the roadside, and adjusted his ball cap. Yes, if he was honest he'd have to say he did miss his cowboy hat. It had been necessary to lose any identifying marker. He'd worn it for years, though. But that wasn't what was on his mind at the moment.

"You really think Tristan Sanders is holding Nadia Marie and Shadrach's mom here? It's a long way to bring her from Kentucky. The timeline is tight if he kidnapped her and put her on a plane."

Ben shrugged one shoulder and kept walking. "Seattle isn't that much farther west than Portland if you're flying from Kentucky. And Dante needs a way to get around." He pulled out his phone. "Maybe Remy can find out if any of his associates has access to a plane." Ben lifted his wrist and squeezed both sides of his watch. "Check Dante's known associates for an airplane he might be using."

Bolton had seen him use it before, but it always baffled him the leaps technology had made while he'd been ensconced in Sanctuary. "You know, I always thought you were CIA. But you totally have this 'special forces, survivalist' thing going on. I never could pin down what it was that you really did."

"Maybe it's all of it, and none."

Bolton snorted. "Or maybe you just want to act all 'international man of mystery' so you don't have to talk about yourself. Maybe you have trust issues."

"I'm not sure seeing a shrink would help at this point." Ben glanced at the sky. "At least not without a lengthy nondisclosure agreement."

"They're not supposed to break confidentiality. It's a rule."

Ben glanced over his shoulder. "Don't tell me you've been to a shrink."

"It's a witness protection thing. They have to make sure you're sane even though you're doing a totally *in*sane thing that no regular person would do." Bolton caught the look on Ben's face. "Don't give me all that junk about doing the right thing. It's a bunch of baloney. The only reason anyone ever does anything is for themselves."

"Just because you were only out for yourself doesn't mean that's the case for everyone," Ben said. "What about Nadia Marie?"

"What about her?"

"How much do you know about why she was inducted into witness protection or the reason she had to come to Sanctuary? I doubt it was because she was a stylist, and they needed someone to cut hair."

Bolton didn't know the whole story, but there was a reason. "She was an artist. But we don't talk about that in Sanctuary. No one asks anyone else about their life before they got there."

He'd figured the person who targeted her had a wide enough reach that she had to disappear altogether, instead of being relocated to another city as most people were in witness protection. Much the same as himself and the threat Dante presented even from jail. But it could just as easily have been the fact she was well known enough that, even with a new name and a new life, she might still be recognized by someone who knew her in her old life.

"I'm pretty sure my brother and his wife, who used to be an assassin, told each other that stuff."

Manuel died in prison.

Bolton shook his head as he trudged behind Ben through the Venice neighborhood. Two thugs out for an evening stroll. "John and Andra are an anomaly. Her past was plastered all over the Meeting House. Everyone knows she used to be an assassin."

"And yet you refuse to tell anyone who you were."

"You think they want to know they were living with a criminal kingpin?"

Ben glanced back, the corner of his lips curled up.

"Sure, they'll think it's hilarious."

Ben stopped, his face plain enough Bolton thought he might have actually disappointed the man. Ben said, "No one ever put a gun to your head and told you to sell drugs."

Bolton shifted. "You think you know me or anything about my life. But you *don't*."

"I know we could have been friends. I know I gave you what you needed to set up your life, and I know you walked off that path into dark places."

"I didn't have a choice. It was business." Bolton folded his arms. "That's all." Ben wasn't some kind of divine being who directed other people's lives. Bolton had made his own choices.

"Dante doesn't think its business. And I don't think you do, either. Not really. The two of you are in this together, and it's one hundred percent personal."

"Because he deserves to be put down. He got close enough Thea had no choice but to walk away." Bolton took a breath. "Thea knew what I was; she knew what her father did. But she still betrayed the both of us, and her father sold me out. Dante got the dregs of what was left."

"And Javier?"

"My son has nothing to do with this."

Ben stared at him long enough Bolton shrugged. "It's been years. Why cry over what will never be?" He didn't blame Thea for walking away when she was pregnant with his son. He hadn't been able to protect her.

"And yet you persist in going down this path instead of making something new of your life. That's what Sanctuary was. A clean slate. But you're so dead set on retribution you took the first opportunity to destroy everything you had there."

"My father always said, 'why dream for something you'll never have when life is in front of you for the taking.'"

Ben lifted his chin. "My mother says, 'You walk the path the Good Lord put in front of you.'"

"How's that working out?"

Ben turned and started walking. Anyone else probably would have felt guilty, especially knowing the little he knew about Ben's personal life—or lack thereof. But Bolton just followed him to the mansion at the end of the street. Tristan Sander's house.

Ben acted like Bolton wasn't even there. The watch buzzed, and he read aloud the info from Remy. No cars in or out of Bainbridge in hours. No one on the ferry from Seattle—the way they'd gotten there—who matched the description of either Dante, any of his known associates, or Nadia's mom. Ben didn't even acknowledge his existence. Maybe the man did that with everyone he didn't like, but if he did, then it begged the question of how he'd stayed alive this long.

Ben hadn't had his own private company back when they had first met. That had been all official channels and checking in with superiors. Not Bolton's thing, despite the fact he'd done it with Thea's father when they'd partnered up—though a lot more informally.

Night was beginning to blanket the sky in low, black clouds that blocked the stars from view as they stopped and stared at the rear of the house. No fences in this neighborhood. The house was lit from inside, revealing armed guards who walked the grounds.

Bolton studied the house, using the plan he'd made for his own residence in Miami as a basis. There would likely be cameras, more guards on the front side and other security measures. "So how do we get inside to see if they have Nadia's mom?"

"How does a DEA agent manage to have this much home security and no one has called him on it yet?" Ben's teeth flashed in the dark. Apparently he was over his ignoring Bolton thing.

"Good question."

Rustling of branches preceded a low, male voice. "Why don't you ask him?"

Ben shifted. Bolton spun around. Six men, automatic weapons.

Tristan Sanders. "Bolton Farrera."

"Where is the woman Dante took from Kentucky?"

The man shrugged like he had no idea what Bolton was talking about. "Dead, probably. Or she wishes she was." He chuckled. "Take them inside."

Bolton only got half a step before he was hit in the back of the shoulders, and he went down.

Chapter 10

"You should at least think about it."

Nadia stared at Remy. "I know you're a genius and all, but I'm not going back to Sanctuary right now."

"Grant is looking for your mom, Bolton and Ben are taking care of Dante. You said yourself that you wanted to go back to Sanctuary. Why not now?"

Shadrach stepped between them. "Rem—"

"No." Nadia put a hand up to stop Shadrach. "She has the right to say whatever she's going to say. Remy doesn't mean I'm useless, she's just using logic. I'm not helpful here. You could possibly even argue I'm a hindrance. It's just Remy-speak."

Remy glanced between them. "What did I say?"

"Nothing." Nadia sat back down. "It's fine."

Shadrach shook his head. "That's it? Maybe you should get a ride back home if that's what you want."

"I want Mom to be found. Safe, and alive. That's what I want." Nadia shrugged. "If I had a helicopter, too, sure. Maybe I would go home."

Remy reached to the back of her neck and drew something forward. "Whatever you decide I want you to have this. Bolton gave it to me, and it kept me safe."

"Because it has GPS in it. It's also how Dante knew to come after him." He'd explained that to her. But what was the point in Nadia having it? Bolton hadn't given it to her, not when Remy needed it more.

"I know." Remy nodded. "Ben showed me how to turn it off. It's not transmitting until you click the button on the back and activate it."

"And I should take it? I'll be in Sanctuary. Safe. No one needs to find me there. At least no one who doesn't already know where I am."

"Still." Remy set it on the table. "It was Bolton's, and I think you should be the one to take care of it for him."

Sure, that made total sense when he'd jumped—okay, not literally—at the first opportunity to leave her with someone else and go after one of Dante's friends. Nadia sighed but took the necklace. When he got back, she'd give it to him, but for now she slipped it into her pocket. Wearing it would be weird, especially when Remy had only just taken it off.

Shadrach's cell phone rang. He moved his thinking-gaze—whatever that was about—from her, swiped the phone up off the table, and looked at the screen. "It's Grant. I'll put it on speaker."

He laid it back on the table. "Yes, Grant. This is Shadrach. I've got Remy and Nadia here, and Will is listening."

The IT guy was still at the other end of the table, working on…whatever he was working on.

"Nadia." Grant's voice crackled, and he sounded out of breath. "How are you doing?"

"Better." She smiled even though he couldn't see her. She'd always liked the director, even though he didn't work for the marshals anymore. Apparently now he worked for Ben.

"What's up?" Shadrach sounded all business.

"Have you heard from Ben?"

"Not since they got to the house," Remy answered.

"Nothing since then?"

Shadrach shook his head. "No."

Grant said, "I'll try again. Maybe you should call Daire."

"He's on personal leave."

"Okay, don't call Daire."

Shadrach scrubbed his fingers across his hair, a move Nadia had seen most when he'd been studying for big tests at school. Having a twin had meant a built-in study partner, and they'd helped each other survive those cut-throat days of school when they'd been gangly zit-faced teens. Now her brother was handsome, still had his military bearing, and didn't know what to say around the girl he liked.

Shadrach caught her gaze and shot her a question with a flick of his head. He always knew what was on her mind, but she wasn't going to explain thinking he was cute around Remy.

Nadia waved off his concern and said to the phone, "What's the latest with finding my mom? Do you think she's in Seattle?"

"Right now I have no idea," Grant said.

"Me, either." Remy huffed. "Getting information on your mom is like trying to find an invisible needle in a stack of needles. Are you sure she doesn't have a cell phone?"

Nadia nodded. "I'm sure."

"Email? Internet access?"

"I only had the landline number, which she must have brought to the compound with her. Maybe in case I used it one day."

Nadia and her mom hadn't been super close, but it was possible her mom still wanted to talk to her again. "What about the van you were talking about? The one from the witness statement in the police report?"

Remy said, "The compound has no surveillance for me to hack into. I checked any traffic camera in the area, but no van of that description came into town after whatever went down. They must have hit the highway instead, at which point they could've gone anywhere."

"What about an airport?"

Grant answered next. "No private planes have taken off since before the hit on the compound took place. I flew in commercial with the team and caught up, but the police don't want to know who we are or why we're asking questions about a 'bunch of dead hippies.' His words, not mine. They're thinking cult murder-suicide. The investigating detective basically admitted he's not even looking for a van. He doesn't know your mother and refuses to believe anyone's missing. Apparently the sheriff told him that aside from four dead people there's no problem."

That made no sense. Nadia leaned forward. "How can they dismiss it all like that?"

"The compound kept no record of its residents. There's no list of who lived in which room, and right now they have more people accounted for than rooms. The police have no reason to believe anyone is missing, despite what we told them."

"What about...the bodies?" Shadrach set both palms on the table. "Did you check if any of them are mom?"

Nadia knew that catch in his voice. He wanted to be on the ground helping find their mom, but instead, he was babysitting her. Shadrach was her twin, and if anything happened to him it would be something she'd struggle to get past every day for the rest of her life. She needed him to be safe—but Shadrach was the kind of person who put himself in harm's way to help others because it was the right thing to do. He'd always been the translator when Nadia and her mom miscommunicated. He was their middle ground. Shadrach had to be feeling every inch of the possibility of Mom getting hurt and his not being able to do anything about it.

Grant said, "That's my next stop."

"Can I talk to you in private?" Neither her brother nor Remy objected, so Nadia grabbed the phone and took it off speaker as she went out into the sea of unoccupied cubicles. "Grant?"

"I'm here. What did you need, Nadia? If you're worried about your mom there's not much I can say that's going to help. But I am giving everything to finding her, and I know Ben is doing the same."

"I appreciate that." Nadia took a breath. Maybe Remy was right. "What's the procedure for getting me back to Sanctuary?" She'd need to know eventually, at least.

"You want to leave?"

"Shadrach is babysitting me instead of out looking for mom."

"So you want back into town?"

"I know that's against the rules." She sighed. "I left, so I shouldn't be able to get back into town, but it's been my whole life for years. It's my home."

"Nadia," Grant said. "Who told you that you couldn't go back?"

She opened her mouth to answer, but faltered. "Bolton...we left."

"That's on Tommy. Not you, but the crazy SEAL who blew up half the town. No one faults you for leaving in the helicopter, Nadia. You should have been under the military's protection, not left alone and loose in the world to fend for yourselves." He sounded guilty, which made Nadia feel worse for bringing it up.

But a spark of hope lit inside her. "I can go back?"

"Sanctuary doesn't have the same rules anymore. It's no longer a federally operated town. It's owned by a group of private investors who keep it running. WITSEC still sends me people who need the kind of protection Sanctuary provides, but the new director of the Marshals has no idea where the witness protection town is. Only I and a handful of others do."

"I had no idea."

"A lot has changed in the past few weeks. After Tommy found and breached the town, new security measures were enacted. In fact, Ben and I were a hairbreadth from moving everyone to a new, secure location."

"Wow." Nadia sat on the edge of the closest desk.

"We'll have to get a plane that can transport you back to Sanctuary, and Ben took his. Can you sit tight until he gets back?"

"I can do that." Nadia tried to think of another way she could help. "I wish there was something I could do to help with everything. I feel so powerless."

"This isn't like Manuel, even though that was crazy. Dante's reach is far more dangerous. Its best you stay with Shadrach until we can make you safe otherwise."

"Understood."

Grant chuckled. "You've been hanging out with Shadrach, you're learning how to take orders."

She found herself smiling. "Don't count on it."

"I know what it's like to feel powerless when you want to do something to fix the situation. You can take care of yourself, but this isn't your fight. We'll find your mom, and then I'll get you home."

"Okay. Thank you, Grant."

He ended the call. Nadia laid down the phone. Shadrach had seen his twin living a life that could get her in trouble and taken it upon himself to teach her everything he knew about escape and evasion, weapons, combat…and self-defense. That was what they'd called it when Nadia had come up against Manuel's men. Only it hadn't helped—it had made Manuel twice as determined to kill her.

He'd hired a team of ex-military assassins to get rid of her, making nowhere in the world safe to hide. Except Sanctuary.

Grant was right, she could take care of herself. She'd only forgotten because Bolton had needed so badly for her to help him. Her feelings for him had made it so that Nadia could barely think past the need to make sure he wasn't helpless and alone while being hunted by Dante. Now Bolton had had his surgery. He was off doing what he wanted to do.

Shadrach and Grant were going to find her mom.

And Nadia was free to take care of herself. This *was* her fight. Because she wasn't going to let Dante hurt people she cared about.

**

"It belongs to Tristan and Dante." The man pulled his balled fist back and struck Bolton again in the face. "Where is it?"

Bolton turned his head to the side and spat. Of course they wanted what he'd hidden in the stash. Everyone wanted it, apparently.

Blood ran into one eye and left his vision in a haze. His jaw might be broken. He definitely had a couple of loose teeth. "Are you guys DEA, too? Or like that guy I killed in the doctor's house. One of y'all's confidential informants."

His fist slammed into Bolton's chest, forcing the air out. His mouth tasted like copper.

Bolton sucked in a painful breath. "A lapdog, maybe. Dumb muscle paid to hit who they tell you to hit."

The fist hesitated. Not like the guy had a brain, at least not one he was using. The man straightened and turned to his buddy. "This guy is crazy."

Bolton smiled, his mouth laced with blood as they shared a look.

The second man in the pool house with him pulled a gun. Unfortunately for Bolton, he was the only one tied to a chair at present. "How about I put one in each knee? Then he won't be smiling."

Because Bolton didn't have enough problems walking already. He needed to be knee-capped as well.

The muzzle of the gun touched his leg. "Where's the stash?"

"So your bosses can steal it from me?"

"It's theirs. You're the one who stole it."

"Of course that's what they told you," Bolton said. "Doesn't make it true." Bolton had compiled that stash as his out, a rainy day B-plan if anything ever happened to jeopardize his business. And Dante and Tristan thought it was *theirs*? No way. He needed that to start his new life.

"WHERE IS IT?"

Bolton grimaced as spit flew at his face. "Anchorage, Alaska."

"Think you're a comedian, do you—"

The door swung open and Tristan walked in. "I take it you haven't gotten the information yet. Unfortunately we don't have time to wait for you to get it out of him."

Tristan lifted his gun and shot both men.

Where was Ben? They'd been brought to the house together and then separated. Had they killed him? That would be a serious shame. A lot of evil in the world had been held at bay over the years because of what Ben Mason did. Bolton didn't exactly know what capacity he worked in or precisely how he did it, but he did know Ben had done a lot of good in his life—and he could still do a lot more.

Bolton also knew a ten year old boy whose world would be crushed if anything happened to his uncle.

Tristan looked down at him. "Dante has his ways, and I have mine."

Bolton didn't want to know what either of their plans were. Though if he had to guess, it would be that Dante was the one chasing after Bolton and kidnapping people. "Tell him to let the mom go."

Tristan sneered. "Imaginative, I'll give him that. Counting on your girlfriend to break. And she did."

"She's not my girlfriend." What did he mean, she'd broken? What had happened to Nadia?

"Turned you down, I'm guessing." Tristan chuckled. He looked Bolton up and down with a sneer on his face. "I can see why."

"Did you know her twin was a Force Recon sniper? Not a man whose mom you want to mess with." Bolton shrugged without letting Tristan know how much it hurt. "You should probably send Dante a text. Let him know the brother will be on the rampage."

Shadrach wasn't a messy person, but he would take care of business the minute he was freed up to do so. Bolton knew that much about him.

"It's nice to know you care so much about Dante." Tristan grinned. "There something going on I don't know about? You come out of hiding, and all of a sudden Dante is off on one of his grand adventures, shooting up compounds and taking hostages. Determined the girl will trade you for her mom with enough persuasion. Did you know she shot two men?"

Nadia?

"Dante told everyone he could the moment he found out. Headshots, both of them. The cops thought it was a professional hit, but the girl swore up and down it was self-defense. That her brother taught her to shoot. Dante's gonna offer her a job when this is over." Tristan leaned closer. "When he's found our stash and put a bullet in your head."

"Because that's not your style?" Bolton tipped his head to the side. "Everyone else gets their hands dirty, and you collect the paycheck?"

There was no way he'd let Dante get Nadia. No. Way.

"They answer to me. Even Dante."

Dante was a loose cannon Tristan could barely control. He'd had that inkling Tristan was the boss, but Dante left chaos in his wake. He always had.

Bolton figured that was why Tristan had allowed him to take the fall for the whole operation and go to prison.

"So did you break him out, or did he really escape all by himself?"

The muscle beside Tristan's eye twitched. "Once in a while it's necessary to let the dog out of its cage to run loose."

"Except that you have to clean up the mess afterwards. Again."

"Worth it, given the things he can dig up." Tristan leaned closer. "All kinds of buried things."

They were trying to find Thea and Javier. They were going to use Bolton's family to get him to tell them where the stash was. Thea would probably help them just to spite him, but there was no way Javier needed to be involved in this.

Dante likely knew Bolton wouldn't feel too much guilt over letting them shoot Thea, with no intention of telling them where it was. And she would deserve it for everything she'd done to him. But the kid didn't need to lose both parents.

"So what happens now?" He wanted to ask where Ben was, but if they thought he cared at all about the man they would use that to their advantage.

"Now we wait for Dante's next move."

"The meet in Portland?"

Tristan barked a laugh. "Were you planning on being there?"

"Of course not." And neither was Dante by the sound of it. But why the ruse?

"You think he's going to waste time when he can go get the girl himself?"

Bolton strained against the plastic ties that held him to the chair. "Don't you touch her!"

Tristan smiled. "As I thought."

Bolton roared. Now they knew he cared about Nadia. They knew she could be used against him. But they'd better not hurt her, or he was going to kill every single one of them. Bolton had only actually killed three people—men who'd double-crossed and tried to kill him. Such had been the life. But this was a lot more. He was willing to make the exception in this instance. Nadia didn't deserve this, she didn't deserve him and what he'd brought into her life.

That panic attack of hers was still too close to his mind. He'd done that, but he was going to make it right. Bolton would fix this for her.

Tristan strode to the door. At the last second he looked back, "Don't go anywhere."

Then he was gone.

A rustle behind him brought Bolton's head around. Ben stepped in from a back room. "We know what Dante's plan is, then. He's going after Nadia."

"But we're here, and she's in Denver."

Ben crouched and cut the plastic ties. "Shadrach has her. He won't let anything happen. Worry about how we're going to get out of here without being seen first."

"We couldn't even get in without them discovering us. And how did you get free?"

Ben grabbed Bolton's arm and hauled him up. He stuttered, "I-I don't even know that guy. I was out looking for my cat. He got out." Ben smiled. "They didn't even tie me up. We needed to know Tristan's part in this and what Dante's plan is. Now we do."

Bolton stared at him. Of course, why hadn't Bolton thought that getting captured by Tristan was a good plan? "Sure you are."

"Let's go before the guys who were holding me wake up." Ben pulled a phone from the pocket of one of the dead men. "Here we go."

As they ran, Bolton gritted his teeth. Ben dialed and put the phone to his ear. "Yeah, Shadrach. We're good. Where's Nadia? We got word that Dante is coming for her."

Ben barked the word, "What?"

He hit a button on screen and held up the phone as they crossed the grass and raced for some trees. Thankfully it was dark enough, and no one had sounded the alarm yet. Shadrach's voice came over the phone at a low volume. "She said she was going to use the bathroom. But Remy checked. She isn't in there. She's gone."

Bolton's steps faltered. He hit the ground on one knee with his hand in the grass and hissed against the pain.

Someone yelled, "There they are!"

Ben hauled him to his feet, and they ran. A crowd of men poured from every direction.

"Freeze!"

Chapter 11

Sanctuary

The mayor climbed out of the golf cart the driver had parked in front of the library. It galled him to play the part of a much more frail man, but those with strength often overlooked the weak. Even when it was the last thing they should do.

Morning had dawned crisp and fresh, but he wasn't out to admire the scenery. Surprise, surprise, the mountains that surrounded Sanctuary, like castle walls keeping villagers in, looked exactly the same as they had every day since he arrived nearly eight years ago now.

No, he was out of his house for an entirely different reason.

Mayor Collins, or Samuel to those who thought they were close to him, utilized a hitched stride to enter the library. Could he do anything over again, he'd have asked the people who'd sent him to this place to give him a name that wasn't so common. So far in Sanctuary he'd met two others named "Sam." The Navy SEAL didn't live there anymore, having run off into the sunset with the dead president's daughter. The gym owner, Sam Tura, was another story. The man had businesses on both sides of Main Street—a diner and the gym.

The Mayor hadn't had much luck getting close to him. Tura was, evidently, not the kind of man who could be coerced. Or bought. He was about as useful to Collins as a wife had been. Turned out the woman was much more helpful after she'd been murdered.

He should have thought of that first.

The librarian met him at the door and held it open for him. "Mayor Collins, it's so nice to see you."

He could see from her face that wasn't true, but he appreciated her saying it nonetheless. Samuel held out his hand and shook hers, his free hand on top so that it was a two-handed shake. "How are you, dear?"

Gemma blinked. "Oh, fine. Thank you."

"I heard you might have received some bad news recently. I wanted to check in with you myself, to make sure everything was all right. No one is bothering you, are they?"

"No. It's nothing like that, I assure you." Gemma shot him a pleasant smile. "Just some bad news, I'm afraid."

Samuel knew Hal had been her father. If she'd taken possession of his belongings after his death that meant she would likely find exactly what Samuel was looking for. But how could he get her to trust him?

"And your mother?" Samuel asked. "How is she?"

"She's fine." There was a fakeness to it that made Samuel wonder if she was even sure that was the right answer. "I'm going to see her later."

"I'm sure that will make her feel better. She has been out of sorts since the town blew up."

Samuel couldn't believe those Mason brothers had actually allowed a bomb to detonate in *his* town. It was unthinkable, and yet the ranch was in ruins. The town was abuzz about rebuilding Bolton's house. The lake was a nice addition, but why build a house for a man who may never return?

Gemma sniffed. "She has been out of sorts, hasn't she?"

"Why not take off and go see her now?"

"You know what? That's a great idea." Gemma strode to the desk and got her purse. "Will you lock the door after you're done?"

"Of course, dear."

The door whooshed shut behind her, and Samuel Collins stood alone in the library. The minute she was out of sight, he went to the check-out desk where the woman wrote all of those trash novels and started looking for anything related to her father.

His sources were never wrong, and if this panned out the way he thought it might, then it was the answer he'd been looking for. Then, finally, Sanctuary would be nothing but a memory.

**

"I know you want to rush out there and find her, but hang on for a second." Remy tried to grab his arm.

Shadrach spun around. "I have to go get her back, Rem."

"The necklace. Remember?"

He stopped at the open elevator door. "It's a GPS. But she isn't going to turn it on. Dante will find her the same way he found you."

"She doesn't have to turn it on. Once I knew what the necklace was, I rigged it so that I can remotely turn it on and find whoever has it."

Shadrach stepped closer to Remy. "Did you know she was going to leave?"

She tensed but held her ground. "I knew she would go back to Sanctuary eventually. I thought there might be a risk from Dante. That's why I gave it to her. But I didn't know she would leave like this, without saying anything." Remy paused. "She didn't say anything to you, did she?"

"No." Shadrach didn't like this at all. "She didn't let me know."

He glanced at the exit door at the far end of the hall. Where had she gone? Nadia couldn't have thought it was a good idea to go off on her own, not when Dante was out there, and she had no way to get back to Sanctuary. What had she been think... "No."

"What is it?"

Shadrach trotted back to the conference room where Will still sat, typing away. The man was so private Shadrach knew next to nothing about him. The way he just...worked...was so infuriating. Shadrach would atrophy if he sat for that long. Not to mention Dauntless didn't even like the man.

He turned back to Remy. "Activate the necklace. Now."

"It wouldn't kill you to be nice about it." She sat.

"I'm sorry. But if she's doing what I think she's doing then we need to get to her now."

Remy typed. A map of the city opened on her screen. Shadrach tapped the table until the red dot appeared at the center of the screen. Just above... "Thornton National Bank. Why would she be..."

"Dauntless, hier."

Will tossed him a set of keys he caught mid-air, and Shadrach ran for the elevator with the dog right behind him. He hit the elevator button, and Remy stopped to catch her breath. "Why is a bank a big deal?"

"It's where Manuel kept his money."

"Can she access it? Wouldn't the police have seized his assets when Nadia Marie testified and he went to prison?"

"Manuel was Nadia Marie's money manager. The FBI seized what belonged to Manuel, but that wasn't the whole of it. Four million dollars is sitting in a bank account with Nadia Marie's name on the account. When he went to jail she left the money alone, knowing it would only be a trail from him or an associate to the bank, back to her location. She never touched it. It's *her* money."

"She's going to make a withdrawal? She doesn't have ID."

"I don't know how she's going to do it, but Nadia is going to give Dante four million to get our mother back."

**

Nadia Marie placed her hand on the scanner. The green light ran down her palm and registered her fingerprints. *Thank you Lord for fancy technology.* It barely mattered that she didn't have ID or any other proof that she was the named owner of the account.

The machine chimed. *CONFIRMED: Nadia Marie Carleigh.*

She stepped back.

"Okay, then." The bank manager stepped back. Not surprised as such, but he certainly hadn't expected her to be exactly who she said she was. "If you'll take a seat, I'll start the paperwork."

He walked off across the expansive lobby of the bank to his corner office. The sun was setting outside and cast a yellow glow across the room. The tellers looked tired from their long day.

Nadia moved to a cushy armchair, looking like a hobo at a banquet. She'd needed a shower and a fresh set of clothes two days ago. Who knew what her hair looked like? Maybe she should offer Dante three and three quarter million and keep the rest so she could clean up and catch a flight home.

She fingered the necklace. Should she activate it? What would Bolton say when he found out what she was doing? Maybe he wouldn't even care, but she wasn't ready to believe that. He'd been right there in the office when she was freaking out. She was still freaking out, and he was off trying to solve the problem. Men were like that, wading in so they could fix everything.

But someone like Dante didn't want to be solved. He only understood two things: power and money. A corrupt DEA agent just escaped from prison needed the cash to do what he wanted, and it wasn't to hang around where people would find him. Why else would he be flying all over the country to stir up trouble and get to Bolton? Dante probably thought Bolton owed him something.

Nadia had enough money to pay for it.

The bank manager walked over with a tablet like the sheriff had. Nadia had only seen one on the internet, and on TV commercials. Maybe she would get herself one. There was no wireless signal in Sanctuary, but she could use other stuff on it. Everyone needed a calculator once in a while.

"Sign here, please."

Nadia used her finger on the screen to authorize the transaction.

"And the recipient's account number?"

"I'm going to get that for you very soon, but for right now I'd like to make a small withdrawal. Say, five thousand?"

"Certainly, Ms. Carleigh. Although we close in thirty minutes so the...larger transaction may need to be completed tomorrow."

"If I get the account number for you tonight, I'll bring it first thing in the morning." It meant another night of worrying about her mom, but nothing would stop her from finishing this. She'd drawn enough attention to herself that Dante had to be on his way. When he showed up she would offer him the deal.

"Of course." The bank manager scurried off across the polished floor.

Nadia sat again, the weight of the day heavy on her shoulders. Probably the weight of the last two months. Were Bolton and Ben okay? They'd been walking right into the lion's lair. Had they found her mom there? Nadia fingered the necklace some more. She pressed front and back together, clicked the mechanism into itself and activated the tracker.

How fast would he find her?

Hopefully he would come before Shadrach, Remy, Ben, or Bolton figured out what she was doing. When he showed up, she'd convince Dante to accept her transfer and return her mom safe and sound. He needed to leave the rest of them alone then, whether or not he still intended to get Bolton. Nadia wasn't under any illusion she could save him. Not if the man was determined enough. But Bolton had Ben on his side and apparently had for a long time. They were nearly BFF's. If men like that had BFF's. Bolton didn't need her now. She would remove herself—and her mom—from this situation and do what he wanted.

Walk away, and leave Bolton to live his new life the way he wanted her to.

A man crossed the lobby and stood in front of her. Dirty jeans, thick blue jacket. Dark hair, but gray at his temples. The refined features of someone who got their hair cut and face shaved for no less than three hundred dollars but who had fallen on hard times. Or who'd been in prison for years.

"Can I help you?" He probably thought she needed to be escorted from the building.

"Hello, Nadia. Your mother sends her regards."

It was him. Dante. "I guess you caught me."

He leaned down and whispered. "I guess I did."

**

The SUV sped down the interstate toward SEA-TAC airport. Bolton sat beside Ben in the back, both handcuffed. Where Tristan was planning to take them, who knew? Not somewhere public, given Bolton felt like he'd been on the wrong end of a mugging.

Ben hadn't been touched. He looked like an insurance salesman.

The two men in front were more of Tristan's soldiers. Bolton eyed the door, but it was locked. Probably child-locks too so they couldn't get out. Though if he did he would only end up landing on the pavement at fifty miles an hour, and his back already hurt enough.

"Sit tight," Ben whispered.

Bolton glanced aside at him but could read nothing on the man's face. Ben always had something up his sleeves, but these were rolled up. Dante was going after Nadia, and Shadrach didn't even know. There wasn't enough time for Grant to reach them, and Daire was on vacation of all things.

The front passenger turned back and smirked. "They told us you were rolling with Ben Mason. For real. Like that could happen. There was a rumor you guys were buds from way back, but looks like you got this guy instead of 'The Ghost.'" He lifted the wallet in his hand and snorted. "Arthur Wilson. Insurance salesman."

Ben never had his actual, real identification on him. Bolton knew that. He had no digital footprint, and couldn't be traced through bank transactions, email, or phone calls. His entire life was a shell corporation hidden in a shell corporation, so that anyone trying to find him only discovered a trail of activity that led back to a company owned by a company, owned by the trust fund of a deceased billionaire with no heirs. Confusing to anyone trying to find Ben, or trying to figure out who this man was.

Still, evidently "The Ghost" had made some kind of impression on the world.

Bolton turned to him. "It's nice to meet you, Arthur."

The front passenger balked. "You don't even know this guy?"

"Met him on the road outside Tristan's house. He must live nearby."

"We picked up a bystander!" The man bounced in his seat. "This is unbelievable. Tristan is going to freak when he finds out. He'll probably kill us like he killed Stills and Hammer." He stared hard at the driver, who wrung his hands on the wheel.

"Just be cool, okay? Tristan isn't going to shoot us and leave himself with no one but Little Pete. That ain't gonna happen."

"Right." The front passenger exhaled. "He wouldn't do that."

"So where are we going?"

The front passenger jumped and turned at Bolton's question. Apparently neither man had been privy to any conversation that might've happened between Ben and Tristan. Nor were they questioning the fact that this insurance salesman and supposed bystander wasn't upset in the least about men with guns in his neighborhood—or about being taken captive by them. Or that he'd slipped away from whoever had been watching him in time to free Bolton.

The front passenger opened his mouth and was side-swiped by the driver. "Ow!"

"Don't tell him anything. It doesn't matter where we're going."

Bolton shifted in an attempt to relieve the ache in his back. "Did you know Tristan is DEA, and that Dante Alvarez, the DEA agent who escaped from federal prison two weeks ago, was his partner?"

The front passenger couldn't hide it. He hadn't known at least that last part. Until now. "The man is on a rampage Tristan isn't going to be able to contain. He'll probably kill all of us when he gets the chance. I mean, the man is coming for me. There's no doubt he's going to pop off anyone who gets in his way."

The driver snorted. "Why do you think you're going into DEA custody? The feds will keep you contained and alive. At least while Tristan decides what to do with you."

Bolton glanced at Ben, who shut his eyes slowly. He was right, that wasn't good. Though it was a valiant attempt by Tristan to control Dante. If he found Bolton in the DEA's custody there wasn't much he could do without alerting Tristan to it in the process. He was an escaped fugitive who should have been the subject of a nationwide manhunt. Marshals, DEA, FBI, ATF. Cops and sheriffs. Everyone should have been looking for Dante, and yet barely anyone even knew he had escaped.

Tristan was doing okay so far, keeping this quiet. But how long did he have before the situation turned on him? They were all fighting the clock. If Bolton went back to Sanctuary, if he disappeared and Dante never found him—again—what would the man do? Would he leave everyone Bolton cared about alone, or would he never stop coming, never stop looking, until he uncovered Sanctuary and put everyone there in danger?

No, Bolton needed to end Dante once and for all. To take the man down in a way that meant he could never destroy anyone else.

The driver pulled the SUV into a rear entrance at the airport, slowed for the security guard and flashed a badge.

Ben twisted his wrist to see the face of his watch, which flashed. The numbers disappeared and text scrolled across. "It's Will." He looked up and mouthed, "Shadrach located Nadia. He's going to get her."

Bolton nodded. At least that was something. Shadrach would make sure his sister was safe, and Bolton certainly needed one less thing to worry about. Dante was enough for six lifetimes, let alone one lifetime where there were a handful of people—and a whole town—he had to make sure Dante didn't find.

Ben squeezed both sides of his watch and nodded his head in a slow count. He reached forward and touched the passenger's neck. In one zap, the man slumped.

The driver glanced aside. "What—"

Ben touched his neck with the watch.

With a muffled "huh" the man's head hit the window. Ben reached forward and put the car in neutral. They were rolling slowly, but not slow enough this wasn't going to hurt.

Ben leaned across the driver's lap and pulled the door handle. He fell out. Ben climbed in his seat, put the car in drive and hit the gas. He turned the car in a wide circle and headed back out of the airport.

"We need to get on a plane. Why are you leaving? And what was that watch thing?"

"Electric pulse, that's all."

"Your watch gets texts, and is a stun gun?"

Ben glanced aside as he drove and smirked. "Sends voice messages, too."

"Is that why you don't have a cell phone, double-oh-seven?"

Ben made a face. "Can't go on an op with your phone beeping because your mom decides now's a good time to chat. The only people who know where I am are my people. Cell phones give anyone who cares enough to look access to your entire life, everything personal there is to know about you and your precise global location. Tell me why I would want one of those?"

"Because it's easier than finding a payphone." Bolton shifted forward and rummaged for the passenger's phone. "Or stealing from someone. Pull over, will you?"

Ben parked.

With the man's cell in hand, Bolton shoved him out the door then got out and collected their belongings—and a few extra's like that nice Sig the man had been carrying. He got in the front seat and shut the door. "Go."

He set off. "Any other requests, sir?"

Bolton ignored him. "Those guys are going to wake up twice as mad. They'll be trying to find us before Dante does just so they can hit you back for that move."

Ben smirked. "I'll add them to our list of known enemies. Oh wait, there isn't enough paper in the world for that."

"Like you'd compile it anyway. How do you keep track? I'm surprised you can go anywhere in the world without someone there trying to kill you."

"There are a couple of tiny islands. And my mom's house."

"Of course," Bolton smirked. He'd heard some rumors himself about Ben's life. "Your mom."

"Don't go there."

"Why, will you zap me, too?"

"Yes."

Bolton dialed Shadrach's number and waited. "He's not answering."

"Try Remy." Ben rattled the number off the top of his head.

"No answer from her, either."

Ben didn't offer any cute platitudes that involved lying about being sure they were fine. That Nadia was fine. Bolton didn't want to think about the alternative. This was Nadia.

Dante was going to try to take that away from him. From Andra and John, from Pat. From everyone Nadia went to church with and loved. Didn't God have something to say about what was going on? Bolton figured if she loved God as much as he knew she did, then He had to be doing something about her being in danger. Otherwise her faith was pointless.

Okay, God…

He didn't even know what to say.

Chapter 12

Shadrach grabbed the keys and jumped out of the car. He heard the passenger door slam but didn't have to look back to know Remy was right behind him.

"He's still in there."

"Doing what?"

Both of their voices were breathy as they ran across a busy downtown street toward the bank where Nadia had gone. *To make a deal with the devil.* All for the sake of a man who wasn't even with her, because he had gone off to fix his own problem. For some reason, Nadia had it in her head that she could fix this for Bolton.

"Just talking to her, it looks like."

Shadrach ducked into the alley and leaned against the outside wall of the bank. Dauntless sat. Ready. Remy tucked herself right behind him, out of sight, just like he'd told her to. He peered around the corner. Two men stood by a black van parked on the outside. Dante's men.

He turned back. Remy's attention was on the tablet in her hands, the screen a display of the internal camera feed from the bank that she'd hacked into. Nadia, face to face with an escaped federal prisoner who had an axe to grind. He wore a disguise, but it was Dante. If she survived this, it would be a miracle. And if she didn't, neither would Shadrach. He was enough of a man to know that if his twin was killed, it would destroy him. This fight was to save both of their lives.

"I have to get in there before he gets her out."

"What about Dauntless?"

"He stays with you." Shadrach peered around the corner of the wall again. "I'd prefer my rifle and a rooftop, but people in busy cities tend to freak out about snipers shooting people in the middle of the day."

Remy's mouth curled. Shadrach didn't want to decipher what that meant, so he said, "Call 9-1-1. Report a sighting of the fugitive Dante Alvarez."

"You *want* the cops here? They'll flood the place trying to figure out who you're talking about, and you won't be able to get Nadia out without a lot of questions."

"I'm not scared of them." Shadrach grinned. "I'm not Ben Mason."

She frowned. "Then you have your real ID in your wallet?"

"Of course not." Shadrach gave Dauntless the command to guard and set off. He knew the kinds of things Dante had been involved in before Bolton's testimony sent him to prison. He suspected more than was reported officially, but Shadrach couldn't be sure if what he had an inkling of was true. Now wasn't the time to try for proof. When the cops found Dante he would go back to his lifetime prison sentence. Additional charges wouldn't make much difference.

The two men saw him, but didn't make a move. Shadrach's trigger finger itched. Maybe Dauntless should have come inside the bank with him. A service vest wasn't exactly ethical, but the dog performed a service. He kept Shadrach from shooting people who annoyed him.

The heavy door opened with a rush of air-conditioned breeze. Dante reached out and pulled Nadia to her feet. To her credit, she didn't look ruffled. Had she already presented him her deal to get Dante to back off of Bolton for good? If she had, Dante seemed in the mood for a different kind of deal.

Shadrach glanced at the security guard to give him a signal that something was happening, but the man only stirred his coffee with a short red straw. He lifted the Styrofoam cup to his lips and winced. Too hot.

Shadrach could have rolled his eyes. Instead, he reached to the back of his waistband and fingered his gun. Just in case.

Nadia's eyes locked with his. The action was enough to get Dante to turn his direction and place Shadrach's sister in front of him.

"Let go of my sister."

Dante's face was lined, a man who had seen much and done more. Shadrach didn't care about any of that. He was a simple guy, and he wasn't going to apologize. One corner of Dante's mouth curled up. "Guess I know why Bolton sent you."

They faced off, six feet from each other.

"Let her go now, and I won't shoot you."

The security guard set his cup down and started their way. "Something wrong, fella's?" At least he had some kind of instinct for this gig.

Shadrach held up a hand. "This guy is going to let my sister go, and she and I are going to walk out of here. No harm, no foul."

The security guard turned to Nadia. "What's your decision, little lady?"

Shadrach saw the war on her face. She didn't want to go with Dante, but she did want to finish the transaction. She still thought she could do this, instead of comprehending the simple fact it was a fool's errand. Dante would probably take the money and then kill her—and that was the best case scenario.

Dante lifted his gun and rested the heel of his hand on Nadia's shoulder, so that the weapon would fire right beside her face.

Shadrach's gun was aimed at the spot between Dante's eyes. A place Shadrach would dearly love to embed a .9mm round from his Glock.

"Now, now..." the security guard began. He didn't even have a decent weapon. Dante would shoot him before he drew that stun gun.

Police sirens sounded in the distance.

"This is the end of the line, Dante."

Dante laughed and glanced aside at the security guard. "Perhaps your eyesight is poor, old man, but let me enlighten you. This is the man who killed President Sheraton."

Shadrach didn't wait for the security guard to try and figure that one out. Evidently Nadia didn't intend to either. It was her that said, "That was disproved."

Shadrach didn't care what people thought of him, but it was sweet of his sister to come to his defense. "Dante, give it up. The cops will swarm this place in under a minute. All that's left for you is to go back to jail."

The door swished, and Dante's men entered.

The man's gaze flicked aside for a split second. "Take care of the cops."

The door swished again.

"I'm not going to let you take my sister anywhere."

Dante clenched his teeth together. "You deserve it for what your mother did to me." He shifted the gun and motioned to a wicked gash on his face that hadn't been treated.

Ah, so his mom had done some damage.

"Pulled some old-man revolver. Shot up my men and then ran off with the sheriff." Dante let out a bark of frustration.

"Good for her." Shadrach grinned. "Who do you think taught her how to shoot?"

"An eye for an eye."

They both fired, Shadrach a split second after Dante's bullet left his gun and before the bullet slammed into his vest. The impact forced him backward, and his shot went high. His back hit the floor, and all he saw was ceiling.

Two rounds. The security guard hit the floor.

Shadrach lifted his head, gun already up. He returned fire as Dante dragged Nadia Marie toward the back of the bank. Fire exit.

Every breath burned like fire in his lungs. *Broken rib.* True to form, the thin veneer over Shadrach's luck had cracked at precisely the moment he needed it to remain intact. *Figures.* He forced his body to move and managed to get up. He stumbled to the back as the police ran in.

"Denver PD, nobody move!"

Shadrach kept going. The hallway. The EXIT sign above the door had been flung open, the siren blaring. He raced toward it. Dante had to have another vehicle back there, or he planned to steal a car. Either way he had Shadrach's sister, and Shadrach had to try and stop the man.

The device on his wrist vibrated to signal an incoming call. Shadrach pulled his cell from the back pocket of his jeans. *Unknown Number.*

He answered. "Please be someone helpful…"

"It's Bolton."

"Hopefully you're having a better afternoon than I am." Shadrach slammed into the wall by the door, his legs about to buckle. He needed to breathe, but it *hurt.*

"What's going on?"

He peered out. No sign of anyone.

Shadrach lifted his weapon and scanned as he emerged from the building into a rear parking lot. "Dante was way ahead of us. When Remy activated the necklace to find Nadia, Dante was already in Denver. He beat us to the bank, and it doesn't look like he's interested in Nadia's money to settle this. Looks a whole lot more like he's just interested in Nadia." Shadrach sucked in a breath.

"She tried to…what?" Bolton's voice was low and lethal.

"He piled her in his car and took off."

"She tried to save me." Bolton's voice was distant, and then came back louder. "Ben and I will head back, but it's going to take a few hours."

Shadrach sucked in a breath and stared at the empty street where his sister had been. He'd failed again, just as he had when Remy was hurt, and there had been nothing he could do to fix it.

"She'll be dead before you get here."

**

Nadia couldn't move. The effects of the stun gun had worn off and left her jittery but unable to get any kind of relief. She cracked her eyes open. The fluorescent overhead washed everything in bright white. Still couldn't move.

She looked down at her hands. Plastic flex-cuffs held them to the arms of the metal chair. Her feet were tied the same, so that she was completely immobilized.

She shut her eyes again, and prayed for some dream that would be better than this nightmare. But when she reached for relief, all Nadia saw was the flash of gun fire as her brother fell down. Was he dead? No, she would know if he were. They were twins. She'd have felt it. Still, this heaviness in her chest had to come from somewhere.

Whatever way she spun it, Nadia was alone.

The room was empty, a bland-walled room with concrete floor that smelled like old dust. An office. A freezing one—she could see her breath when she exhaled, though the air didn't feel too cold on her skin. A storage unit, maybe. Did it matter? Probably the only significance to this room was that it would be the crime scene where her mutilated body was found.

Tears streamed down her face. Probably her nose ran, too. Nadia wasn't too proud to fight the tide of what was happening to her. Maybe her snot would freeze with Dante's fingerprint in it.

You might have to help me out with this one. She could barely cogitate a decent thought, but God knew what she was trying to say. *This wasn't the plan. I was supposed to be helping Bolton. Apparently paying Dante off was not Your idea, just mine. It didn't work. Or maybe I was always supposed to arrive at this moment.*

God didn't cause bad things to happen, but He did use man's actions—good or bad—to fulfill His purposes. If He had brought her here or if Nadia had landed herself here because she hadn't listened when the Lord had tried to tell her that paying off Dante was an awful idea, it didn't much matter.

Either way, God had always known that she would wind up here, tied to a chair and waiting for a madman. Wondering if her brother was even alive.

Help me know what to say. How to answer them. Protect me. Protect Bolton, and Ben and Shadrach, Remy. Everyone helping to find me. Help them find me.

Nadia sniffed. It had been a solid plan, but it wasn't the first time in her life she'd done what she thought was right, and it had turned out badly. Go figure. Maybe she hadn't been changed, made new, as much as she'd thought. Maybe God still had a lot of work to do on her.

She prayed there would be time enough for Him to do that.

As the minutes ticked by, Nadia racked her brain for something to distract her. A song she could sing. There was plenty of music on her iPod that was in Sanctuary, but she couldn't remember even one song. All she could remember was a song she taught the kids at Sunday school. So she hummed it.

Jesus loves me, this I know…

The door handle turned, and Dante strode in. He stopped two feet in front of her and looked her over. "Hmm."

Nadia's lips didn't open. She might have been able, had she tried. Only it felt like they were being shut on purpose. God had promised an answer in every situation, but maybe this was His doing also. Silence in the face of the enemy.

"I'm not a bad man, though I have been known to do many bad things. But you never have to learn exactly how bad I can be." Dante unbuttoned one sleeve and proceeded to roll it up. "This can be pleasant for both of us." He did the same with the other sleeve and then stretched his arms in front of him and cracked his knuckles.

Dante had grabbed the back of her head in the truck and slammed her forehead into the dash to get her to stop struggling. The stun gun had come later, when they'd arrived here.

Nadia didn't want to know what this man was going to do.

"I only want to know where to find Bolton Farrera."

Nadia didn't move her gaze from his face. After a minute of silence, he spoke again.

"Your boyfriend is a very bad man, Ms. Carleigh. Over the years, he has bought and sold a great deal of illegal merchandise—even women. Bolton Farrera has killed those who got in his way and even partnered with a cartel to bring drugs into this country. Drugs like the ones you were fond of in your younger years.

"It's funny that you have this connection. But your former life and Bolton's are quite different. He has been a force of destruction in this world, while your actions never hurt another soul. You, Ms. Carleigh, created things. Bolton Farrera ruins every single thing he touches."

Dante pulled a photo from his pocket and showed it to her. A woman lay on the ground, dead. Blood matted her hair to her face, and she stared with sightless eyes as though all her dreams had been lost. Stolen.

He let go, and the photo fluttered to the ground.

"Bolton Farrera is not your friend. If you continue to associate with him, you will end up either dead or in jail as a party to his activities."

Nadia shut her eyes.

No wonder he'd never said anything about who he was or the things he had done before he came to Sanctuary. He'd been the worst sort of person. A criminal, a dealer. And while part of what this man had said was right, he didn't know that she had harmed someone with her wild days of parties, alcohol, and recreational drugs. Nadia had harmed herself, and she had pushed away her family. Her friends had walked the moment it became clear that she was in danger.

"I see you aren't disagreeing with me. Perhaps part of you knows that what I say is true."

Part of what he said *was* true. The rest, she couldn't be sure. It didn't ring as completely legitimate. Still, something in her just couldn't manage to argue with him. To deny it, however feebly. Bolton Farrera was a dark person. He had never managed to fully hide that part of himself.

He had strong opinions and wasn't afraid to stand up to people.

He almost reminded her of Ben. Mysterious, with an edge—but ultimately a force for good in the world. Even if the way he went about it was bad.

Or maybe that was the artist in her who wanted to see the best in the people she cared about, and their families. Andra would never have married the sheriff if she'd had reservations about his brother. They'd have talked about it, but Andra never said anything about Ben. In fact, Nadia had almost wondered if they might have met before on some kind of spy mission.

"Tell me where your boyfriend is, and I'll let you go." His voice was hard but had an edge to it. "You will not like the alternative."

Nadia opened her eyes. "I don't know where he is."

"Does he have a phone?"

"I don't know the number."

"Where was the last place you saw him?"

"Denver." He wasn't there now, so what was the harm in telling Dante? It was a big city, after all.

"Where did he go?"

"To find someone called Tristan."

Dante pulled a phone from his pocket and typed for a few seconds. He stowed it in his pants once more. "Has he told you anything about a 'cache'?"

Nadia would have shrugged, but she was tied to a chair. "It's been a crazy few weeks. I can't remember if he said anything."

"Yes, let's talk about that. Before six weeks ago, when the necklace you are currently wearing was first activated, where were you? With Bolton?"

He wanted to know about Sanctuary? Nadia wasn't going to put all those people in danger. Bolton had Ben. He could take care of himself. If half the things this man had said were true, then Bolton deserved to face his enemies. He'd figure out a way to get out of it. Nadia only had to come up with some kind of plausible half-truth.

"I met him six weeks ago. He had the necklace, and I wanted a new life. So I got in his truck, and we headed for Seattle."

It was so flimsy, she probably had a look on her face. Like, *please believe this.* Dante studied her. She wanted to shift in her chair, but she couldn't move.

"Two people, both in witness protection. A helicopter explodes and you have a chance meeting? I think not. And a sheriff's report in a small Idaho mountain town proves you wrong. You showed up there with Bolton Farrera." He leaned closer. "Where did you come from?"

"It's witness protection, I can't tell you. There are rules."

"And I have tools to get around whatever will you possess that keeps you silent. I want answers, and you will give them to me." He pulled his phone out and made a call. "I need the needle."

Nadia stayed frozen in her chair.

"Just a little sodium pentothal to loosen those lips. Nothing to worry about." He smiled. "I'm sure it won't hurt. Too badly." His face contorted into a grimace, and her breath caught in her throat.

Where are you, Shadrach? If he wasn't dead, then he had to be looking for her. These guys knew about the necklace, but Remy could still use it to find her. Right?

The door opened.

Dante was upstaged by a scary guy with long hair. The needle was stuck into the fleshy part of her upper arm. "Now for the truth."

Chapter 13

Nadia's foot hit the bottom step, and her brother emerged from the living room into the foyer of their tiny house. Silent, like always. His limbs were gangly like hers, but he'd dusted off that tendency she had to be uncoordinated. Thankfully she didn't trip on her dress and these shoes.

"You look beautiful, sis."

Nadia smiled. "Thank you, Shadrach." She kissed his cheek and for once he didn't make a face. Two days after their sixteenth birthday and she was going to homecoming! Todd Arnett had actually asked her, and she'd said yes (of course)! She'd filled half her diary in the past week.

"He's a doofus, but I know you like him."

"Shad—"

"If he tries anything I will kill him."

Nadia laughed, but part of her wondered if he might be serious. She and Todd had plans for tonight, and she wasn't going to let her brother ruin it. Shadrach had gotten most of the serious genes. The little that she'd gotten in the womb were about her art. The rest of her life should be fun. She was a teenager, after all. A teenager that art developer had said was, "Going places." Whatever that meant. But he'd given her a check for a series of paintings she'd done the summer before.

A big check she'd cashed. Some of which they were going to spend tonight on some stuff Todd said he could get.

Nadia pushed against the fog of memory, trying to break free of it. She didn't want to re-live the remainder of that night and what had happened. Todd's family still blamed her. So did the parents of the other boy who had been in the car. Like she hadn't broken her arm when they'd hit that tree. It wasn't her fault she hadn't died.

Shadrach hadn't spoken to her for two weeks. He'd sat with her every day, reading thick books and ignoring her, but by her side nonetheless.

"Tell me about Bolton Farrera."

The moment she saw him, Nadia's steps faltered. This wasn't good for her. This new guy, whoever he was, he was not good for her. She'd become a Christian, and part of this new life involved not going after every good looking guy she saw. She was supposed to be new now, and Father Wilson had told her that involved changing her ways—doing her part to honor what God had done for her, even as He helped her do that.

"What is she talking about?"

"I have no idea." His breath was warm on her face. "Where was Bolton?"

Bolton and John were running toward them, sweating as they sprinted up the trail. John didn't look good, his face covered in red marks and bruises.

"Dad!"

"Pat." John hugged his son. "Where's Elma?"

Nadia said, "She's in there. Hal's with her. He needs help."

Bolton gave her a dark look and ran to the cabin.

John crouched. "Stay with Nadia just one more minute." He ran inside.

Nadia tugged Pat to the side of the trail, and they waited. A minute later Bolton came out, hauling Elma by the arm. His grip on her made the muscles in his arm and shoulder flex. He shot her a look. "We're gonna talk about what just happened."

Nadia felt her eyes bug out.

Bolton strode down the path with the crazy teacher as if that one sentence didn't make it sound like there was something between them. How could there be? Since when did Bolton see the need to share his opinion on anything with her? He barely knew her name.

"Where did you live?"

He didn't know? Everyone knew about Sanctuary.

"Where is it?"

"My mountains." She heard the word spoken from afar, underwater maybe. Which was weird, because she was dry.

"Tell me more about this town."

Nadia Marie let Dauntless lead her to the medical center. She'd probably have to tie him up outside if she wanted to go in. Not that she should be looking for Bolton when he was supposed to be dead. Everyone in town likely expected her to be distraught, so if they were going to pull this off she should probably act her part.

Still, she wasn't about to leave Dauntless outside by himself.

It no longer bothered her the town knew. Not the depth of her feelings for the mysterious rancher—they couldn't know that. But it was expected for her to be grief-stricken at Bolton's death. Even though by some silent agreement they'd barely spoken. Something was holding Bolton back from pursuing her. That was all she could figure. She wasn't happy about it, but it wasn't like they didn't have forever ahead of them.

The closer she got to the medical center the more Dauntless strained against his leash. At the front door he ducked his nose to the ground and turned right, making his way around the building to a side door that was a fire exit. He sat. Barked once.

Nadia Marie looked at him. "Was that a question, or a statement?"

Dauntless cocked his head to the side.

"Fine." She tried the door, and it swung out. No alarm sounded. Had someone disabled the bar on the door that triggered the warning noise whenever someone used it?

Dauntless rushed in, nose to the floor.

"Whoa." Nadia Marie was dragged along behind him. "Dauntless, stop." She tried to remember what she was supposed to say. "Uh… Fuss. Dauntless, fuss." But the command to heel didn't mean much when he was determined to find what he was looking for.

He dragged her around the corner, and Bolton stepped into the hall at the far end.

"Nadia. The sheriff said Wilson is at Maria's house." His eyes flicked to the dog, who had sped up. "What are you…"

She and Dauntless got all the way to the door of the storage closet. Dauntless sat and barked once.

"Oh, no." Bolton ripped open the door to the closet.

Before she even got the chance to look inside, he was pushing her. "There's no time. Oh, God. All these people."

Nadia stumbled. Bolton grabbed her around the waist and lifted her, running and bearing her weight. She looked over his shoulder. "Dauntless! Hier!"

The dog raced after them.

They were almost to the end when all the air was sucked out of the hall, pulling Nadia's hair across her face. The fire started at the closet, rushing out toward them like an action-movie bomb exploding in slow motion.

They were going to die.

A thick hand shook her shoulder. Nadia Marie moaned. She blinked and opened her eyes. That woman, she was dead.

"Have you ever seen this woman before? Her name is Thea, and she has a child."

"She's dead." They couldn't see that?

Someone snorted. "Dead people don't always stay that way. Not in this business." He paused. "Does Thea live in Sanctuary?"

"No?"

A figure passed behind the man and left the room.

Nadia shifted and tried to focus. Why were they asking questions? Her head swam, and she lost her hold on the man in the room.

Bolton sat at the table, his wheelchair pulled up so that he could see the cards in front of him. How he played that game for hours and hours was beyond her. There was no skill involved, and she'd figured out there was a reason it was called "Patience."

"You need something?" He didn't look up from his cards.

Nadia Marie turned to the oven and checked on the lasagna he'd put together. "Nope." She didn't need anything. And if she did, he wasn't going to stop playing his game to help her with it. These weeks of working all day, followed by nights with a surly man, too in pain to converse like a human being, were tearing her down. The longer this went on, the smaller Nadia Marie would become. She was going to diminish until there was nothing left.

Behind her, Bolton sighed. So he knew something was wrong. He just didn't want to—or couldn't—do anything about it.

Nadia set her hands on the counter and hung her head to whisper, "Jesus, help me. This is too hard. I'm supposed to be helping him, but I'm not doing anything."

Someone snorted. "Sounds like Bolton got himself one of those Jesus, bible people. Don't tell me he got saved. That would piss me off, but I'll still kill him. I'm already going to hell. Won't make much difference."

The man came back in. "He said you know who to ask."

Dante nodded slowly. He pulled out a phone and made a call. "Yes. We're done here. Give the woman to Earnest and get me Grant Mason."

**

Shadrach tried to stand, but she leaned hard on his shoulder until he sat back down. "I can't help her by sitting here, Remy."

She didn't back down. "You also can't help her without seeing a doctor."

Shadrach pushed down the urge to growl. He didn't like it when Nadia was out in the world, and he had no way to help her. Because she *always* ended up in trouble. Even in Sanctuary she hadn't been totally safe, despite it being a witness protection town.

It was why he'd trained her. Why he'd encouraged her to go to the gym in town and keep up her skills. To know how to protect herself. Too bad her brain had overruled her reflexes, and she'd determined to fix this problem for everyone. He was going to have a serious word with her when they found her—after he hugged her.

He looked at Bolton, stood beside Ben who was asking Will something. Four men in one room, plus one Remy. They should know where his sister was by now. Instead they were "conferring." All because Bolton had entangled Nadia Marie in his business.

Dauntless put his chin on Shadrach's knee and whined.

Shadrach scratched the back of his head. He wasn't going to punch Bolton, as much as he might want to.

Bolton studied the screen on the wall, known locations Dante and Tristan operated from. Places they might have taken Nadia.

What bothered Shadrach was what they would do while they had her.

Remy folded her arms. "If you're not going to see a doctor, then you need to show me the damage the bullet did."

"It hit my vest. Bruised a rib."

"And if the bone is broken?"

He lifted one eyebrow. "You want me to pull up my shirt and show you?"

"I'm a doctor."

"That's it?"

Remy didn't say anything, but she didn't back down. "You think I can't handle it." She leaned down and spoke with her voice low, so only he could hear her. "You're helping me, believe it or not. Wasn't that the point?"

Shadrach dearly wished they were having this conversation at any other time. "Rem—"

"Forget it. You probably have internal bleeding, but if you won't let me help you I guess we'll just let you die."

Shadrach grabbed her hand. He strode from the room with her pattering steps behind him.

"Okay, so you're not dying."

He stopped and turned to her. "I know what broken ribs feel like. This isn't that bad." He lifted the side of his shirt, so she could see what was probably a nasty bruise on his right side at the bottom of his ribs.

Remy stared. She reached out with her fingertips but didn't touch the bruise. She traced the scar that ran down the left side of his abdomen. "That's not from having your appendix out."

"I'm a Marine." He'd lost a lot of brothers, but he'd never really known what the fight was for. Not until he stood with Remy in her kitchen in Sanctuary and discovered what the point of it all was. As much as he'd helped her feel safe the past few weeks, Remy didn't even know how much she had helped him.

"I'll find Nadia Marie for you."

Shadrach touched the sides of Remy's face and leaned down to kiss her forehead. "Thank you."

**

Remy's laptop chimed.

Bolton walked to see what the screen said. *Search Complete.* He called out, "Remy, your computer has done something!"

She walked back in with Shadrach, who looked a whole lot more relaxed than he had five minutes before. Bolton didn't even want to know what they'd been talking about in the hall. With Ben and his computer guy, Will, it was all about checking angles. Contacting sources. Garnering information on Dante that might give them a lead. It was painfully exhausting to watch and know there was nothing he could do.

All of Bolton's old contacts had either expired because it had been too long, or they were the unsavory kind who might request a meet for the sole purpose of shooting Bolton when he got there.

There was only one possibility left. Could he go there?

Remy sat, eyes on her screen. "Okay, I figured as much."

Shadrach stood behind her, his gaze over her shoulder. "Is that her location?"

"It's the last place the necklace transmitted from. I'm guessing Dante knew what it was and destroyed it so we wouldn't be able to find her."

"Great," Bolton didn't bother to try and hide his sarcasm.

Remy shot him a look. "That's why I added a secondary tracer to the clasp. If they smashed the locket, it should still transmit." She typed on her keyboard. "It's intermittent, but I'm getting a signal."

"Let's move."

Shadrach was out the door before Bolton could finish processing the fact they had a location where Dante was holding Nadia Marie. He took a step and pain shot from his back, down the back of his right leg. Halfway down he caught himself with a hand on the table and managed to not hit the floor.

"Whoa." Remy grabbed him under the arms. "You okay?"

"I'm good." The pain had already dissipated. Bolton got his feet back under him and straightened.

"Let's go." Ben strode out without looking his way.

Bolton lifted his chin to Remy and followed. Her sputtered words followed him, the beginnings of him needing to stay and rest, maybe sit this one out. Whatever it was, he didn't want to hear it. Bolton just wanted to get on with his life, however long it would last. That's how it had to be for a man who'd seen and done everything he had. Not always on the right side of the law, and not always on the wrong side of the law, there wasn't much in this life he couldn't lay claim to. But he'd never been responsible for the death of a woman. Not yet. And Bolton had no intention of allowing that to ever come to pass.

He stepped into the elevator where Shadrach held the door open. Ben lifted his chin, and Bolton answered the question by doing the same. He was good to go. And even if he wasn't, Bolton would not have let anything stop him from going with them to confront Dante and get Nadia Marie back.

Shadrach didn't need to tell him aloud that this was his fault. Bolton saw the accusation written on the former Marine's face. Not a man he wanted to get on the bad side of. Especially not with that dog of his.

Bolton wasn't going to lie and say the dog didn't freak him out at least a little.

Ben drove, being the only one not currently injured. Bolton claimed the front seat so he didn't end up with the dog beside him, just animal breath in his ear.

When they pulled into the business complex there were few cars. A couple of loading bays, offices, industrial spaces, and the office of an oral surgeon.

Bolton checked his gun while Ben parked. Then he pulled his ball cap from the dash and set it on his head. "I'm good to go." His wrist hurt about as much as his back, but this was Nadia. They'd get her back.

"Me too," Shadrach said from the back.

Ben pulled out a phone, and Bolton gaped. "What about your precise global location?"

"It's a burner," Ben said. "Will gives me one when I need to make a call. When we're done, I dump the phone, and next time I need one Will gives me a new one."

Ben didn't wait for Bolton to say anything else, he dialed on the phone and then inserted an earpiece in his ear. "Go ahead."

Bolton got out the car and clicked his own earpiece, so he could hear the call between Will and Ben the same way Shadrach would be able to.

Will's voice came through loud and clear. "Exits are clear. No one's come in or out in the last twenty minutes."

So either they were still in there with Nadia, or Dante had cleared out before they located the building, and Bolton was too late.

"I'll take south," Ben said. "Bolton take the north entrance. Shad, west side, there's a fire door."

"Got it."

"Roger," Shadrach trotted off around the corner.

Bolton readied his weapon and made for his spot, a set of double doors that were the main entrance. There was no hiding, not while Dante was out. Not when Nadia Marie's life was at stake. He might as well lead the way in the front door.

Inside was quiet but for the swish of the door shutting behind him. No sounds of people inside, machines working, or phones ringing, nothing that might indicate a sign of life. Dante had chosen well when he picked this spot. No cameras in the parking lot. An older building with bad security and a layout that consisted of nothing but blind corners and loops that set him back where he'd been a minute before.

Was Dante even here?

Bolton was less and less sure this was where they'd held Nadia Marie with every door he opened down the hallway. Nothing but empty rooms and storage closets that had been cleaned out. He sighed. "No sign of them so far."

"Me, either," Shadrach said. "Dauntless has nothing. I think they might have cleared out before we got here. If they were ever here."

Bolton opened the next door. A single chair and four discarded zip-ties and the necklace. "I found something."

He knelt and picked up one of the plastic ties. Cut, not broken. The necklace—their only way to find her—broken.

Shadrach raced in the door. "What is it?" His dog went straight to the chair, sniffed and sat down. He barked once. "Nadia was here."

Bolton nodded. "Did they know we were coming?" He scanned the room, looking for something out of place. Dauntless watched him. It was unlike Dante to clear out of a place without leaving a nasty surprise for whoever found it.

"Found it." The words came through his earpiece.

Bolton stood. "What is it, Ben?"

"Building's wired to blow. We must have started the timer when we breached. Forty-five seconds left."

"Time to go." Shadrach called Dauntless and headed to the door.

Bolton turned back to the chair. She'd been here. Not long ago Nadia had been here in this building, tied to a chair. Had they questioned her? Dante could have just stuck around and waited for him if he'd wanted to know where Bolton was.

But he'd taken her, and gone someplace else.

"Let's go!" Shadrach grabbed his arm and hauled him out. Bolton ran with him to the exit, seconds before the entire building exploded. The blast threw him into the air, and he landed with a thump on his back.

"Was that necessary?" Shadrach's question reached Bolton's ears as a muffled blur, but he read the man's lips to fill in the gaps. Dauntless licked Shad's face, and he pushed the dog away.

Dante wasn't worried about "necessary." He only wanted maximum damage, and the complete destruction of anyone or anything connected to him. Bolton had learned that the hard way, and it was the reason his back screamed the way it did just then.

"Ben? Shadrach? Bolton? Anyone?" Will's voice penetrated the rush in his ears.

"We're okay."

Bolton looked around for the source of Ben's voice. Leaned against the car, one foot crossed over the other, and his arms folded. Ben looked perturbed.

Bolton gritted his teeth and clambered to his feet. *Ouch.* He brushed off his pants and looked back at the smoldering wreckage of the building. Emergency services would be there soon and didn't need to find the three of them.

This was all he needed. With no Dante and no more leads they'd never be able to find Nadia. Shadrach was probably right that she would be killed before they found her.

"Head back to the office," Will said. "Got word of some chatter. I think Grant might be in danger."

Chapter 14

Sanctuary

Gemma strode into the radio station. Her steps faltered. All bravado bled from her as she looked around. It smelled like him. Nearly three decades she'd lived in town with Hal Leonard, and only now that he was dead did she discover he was her father? She wanted to scream. To throw a tantrum like an unruly child at the unfairness of it all.

"Why didn't you tell me?" She asked the question of the empty foyer.

No answer. Like her mom had given her—nothing but a bunch of nothing. Thank you very much. Her mom had only cried harder, unintelligible words she couldn't decipher. A great way to tell Gemma absolutely nothing. So Gemma had gone through her dresser to try and find some evidence that she was the child of Janice Freeman and Hal Leonard, and the reason why neither had ever told her that Hal was her father.

The radio station had been Hal's whole life. He'd played only 60's and 70's rock, adamantly refusing to play anything else until people quit asking. She'd always wondered why that was, even while she admired his ability to stick to his guns.

Gemma walked the hall to the broadcast room. The desk of ancient equipment didn't surprise her, though it looked like the set of a seventies space movie about the year two-thousand. No wonder he didn't play any modern songs. His equipment probably didn't recognize the first thing about a CD, let alone an MP3.

She turned in a circle. No one had played a song on the airwaves since Hal's death. There were people in town who'd helped him broadcast when he needed a break from the job. So where were they, and why weren't they playing Hal's favorite tunes in his honor?

It was almost as though, without the music, no one knew the first thing about Hal. Which meant Gemma had nothing to go on if she wanted to find out who her dad had been.

She'd asked her mom and got nothing. She'd gone back and asked the sheriff, and he'd just given her back a passel of questions. How could she know whether she wanted to open the can of worms unless she knew what was in there? Gemma hadn't written any new words on her novel-in-progress since the sheriff came to the library. There was no inspiration, only the burning desire to solve the mystery of who her father was.

Gemma rifled through the papers on the desk and looked in the drawers of the file cabinet. There wasn't much besides a schedule of residents' birthdays to announce on the radio and an old newscast script about a birth. That kid was five now.

Maybe Hal's house would yield more results. But by all accounts he'd essentially lived here. She wasn't sure she even knew where his house was.

Gemma branched out to looking under drawers and behind furniture, trying to remember every mystery novel she'd ever read—or written herself—and where the hidden thing had been discovered. Then she ran her hands along the wainscoting on the walls. Hidden safe or not, she felt pretty ridiculous. He'd been a simple man, an aging biker. He probably didn't have anything hid—

The wall gave under her fingers. A section six inches tall and three inches wide and about hip height off the floor popped out like it was on a tiny hinge.

Inside was a handle.

Gemma pulled the handle and the section of wall in front of her popped out, opening a door in the middle of the wall.

She glanced inside.

"Of course there's a secret room."

**

Nadia Marie might not live that life anymore—not for a long time—but she remembered very clearly what a hangover felt like. It hurt to open her eyes. It hurt to try and figure out where she was…a motel room? A camera had been set up on a tripod in the corner of the room. Pointed at where she lay on the bed. Nadia looked down at herself.

She was dressed in a skimpy red nightgown.

So not good.

She shifted around on the bed and pushed away the fog of being unconscious and whatever they'd injected into her. Hands tied to the headboard rail. Nothing on the nightstand she could use to cut the ties. She barely remembered what happened between then and now as they'd stuck her with another needle.

What had Dante said? *Give her to Earnest.* Apparently this was what being given to Earnest meant.

Nadia scooted as close to the headboard as she could. Even as she prayed with all her might that what she suspected was definitely not going to happen, the rail snagged the ties. Nadia moved her fingers over…the point of a nail! She caught again and preceded to saw through the plastic. The nail lit across her wrist, but it couldn't be helped. Nadia steeled herself against the pain.

If Shadrach could survive everything he'd been through as a Marine, being framed for the president's assassination, being blown up in Sanctuary, boarding an aircraft in-flight and rescuing Remy from that crazy Navy SEAL, then she could get out of this room.

If her mom could fight back against Dante, and do it so well that he was forced to retreat, then Nadia could get out of this room.

If her best friend Andra could give up a life as an assassin and marry the most straight-laced person either of them had ever met, Nadia could get out of this—

The door opened.

"Well, well, well."

Nadia flicked her gaze to "Earnest." Twenties, white. Stringy hair and the body Shadrach had before he'd filled out.

Warm liquid ran down the inside of her forearm, but she ignored it and the considerable sting and kept sawing at the plastic.

Eliminate the disadvantages, or use them to your advantage.

There were so many disadvantages to her current situation that she barely knew where to begin. Nadia flicked her hair back with a shake of her head and lifted her chin. "I guess you're Earnest."

"Dante said you'd earn well. He didn't say you were famous."

"You don't look old enough to know who I am."

He flashed a mouth of yellowed teeth. "Age doesn't matter when you have the internet." Nadia could see the outline of a cell phone in the front pocket of his pants.

He had a phone.

"Guess you're ready to get started."

Nadia shifted so he could see the blood on her arm. "Actually, I seem to be having a problem." If she pulled hard enough on the ties, would they snap? *Lord, help me.* This couldn't be His plan. That was supposed to be hope and a future. Right? All of which seemed very distant right then, when she was caught in this spider's web with no way out. Her foolish attempt at helping Bolton fix his problem was over if this didn't work.

He cried out in frustration. "Are you kidding me? You're supposed to be in good condition!"

He didn't come close enough. No, he went to the bathroom instead. Nadia pulled at the ties as hard as she could, praying they would snap. Three seconds later he came back into view, and she was forced to relax. He put the towel around her wrist and squeezed.

Nadia hissed. "This isn't going to work. You can't even see what you're doing."

He groaned and reached behind him to produce clippers. Nadia bent her legs under her as far as she could.

The ties were cut.

Nadia launched from the bed. She wrapped her legs around him and punched. Sure, she could have offered him money to let her go. But where was the satisfaction in that?

He swung the clippers around and slammed them into her upper arm. Nadia cried out and punched again with her other hand. He pulled the clippers free. She wasn't going down like this. Nadia grabbed them and slammed the pointy end into his nose. Two more hits and he was not only dazed, but unconscious.

Nadia shifted down his body and pulled out his phone. She dialed Shadrach's number and pressed *Call.*

A gun cocked. The phone slipped from her bloody fingers and dropped on the floor.

Nadia lifted her head and saw a suited man stood in front of her, pointing a painful and messy death in her face.

"Let me guess," the man spoke in slow, measured words. "He indicated he was Earnest."

"I think you need better help."

"Sadly, hard to come by. Unless you're offering. I have a feeling you'd be a worthy addition to my team."

Nadia would have liked to vomit on the floor, but that would be unladylike. "So what now?"

Two men appeared at the door.

"I had hoped to do this here, but it looks like new accommodations are in order." He lowered the gun and lifted his elbow, indicating she should take it. "Shall we?"

This was by no means a retreat on his part. One wrong step and she'd be shot by this guy, or one of his goons. All that training she'd done didn't matter much unarmed against a bullet travelling more than a thousand miles per hour to hit her between the eyes.

This was not a man you tried to deal with.

"Nadia Marie Carleigh, I presume."

Please, God, let that call have gone through.

Nadia looked around for the wash cloth and picked it up. "I certainly am." She said it as though him thinking otherwise would be an affront.

The phone lay on the floor but face down so she couldn't see if it had connected. *Help.* She held the washcloth over the wound on her arm and couldn't hold back the wince.

"Excellent. I think I'm going to enjoy this, though our acquaintance will be shorter than I'd have liked."

Nadia dredged up something of the young woman she had been and shrugged, determined to play the part and survive until help came. "Whatever, just so long as I get paid."

"Let's talk terms in the car."

She had to go with him, to take his arm and leave the phone on the floor, not knowing if she'd managed to call her brother, if help was coming. And now it would come to a place she had been. Not the place where she was.

**

Shadrach gave Dauntless the command to stay and shut the car door. *Earnest.* He'd heard enough on the call to know what she was up against but not enough to be able to find her.

He readied both guns and walked into the restaurant, one in each hand in plain view. Decorated in gold accents and bold red carpet, it smelled like funky sausage. Shadrach shot the bartender before he could draw that weapon—likely a shotgun—from under the bar. A busty waitress screamed and scurried out of sight. Two goons drew on him. Shadrach shot their kneecaps then held aim on them to make sure they weren't going to fire back at him.

Lazlo Silver pulled the napkin from his collar and stood. Wiped his hands. He discarded the cloth on the table and eyed Shadrach like this was just another day at the office. The Russian boss was built like a boxer, and his biceps bulged from his tailored silk shirt, with short sleeves that showcased his tattoos. His hair was shaved, and his eyes were so dark brown they looked black, as though the stains on his soul couldn't be contained.

"And who are you?"

"Who I am doesn't matter," Shadrach said. "I have one question. You answer it, I leave."

Humor flashed in Lazlo's eyes. "Tell me now why I shouldn't simply kill you."

"Do that, and word is spread that you're drafting plans to make a power play against Earnest."

Lazlo stilled. "What do you want to know?"

"Where to find him."

Lazlo shook his head. "You want to make the short trip to hell, who am I to stop you? It's not like you'll be around to attend your own funeral. Earnest will, however. The last person who crossed him was blown up one more time, after his death. In his own casket. Killed every person in attendance just to send a message."

"Let me worry about my funeral. Just tell me where to find him."

"Whatever reason you have, let it go. I don't like you" —his goons were on the floor, each clutching a shot-out kneecap and moaning— "but I consider it professional courtesy to warn you this is pointless."

"You're that scared of him?"

"In some circles," Lazlo said, "simply to speak his name is death."

He hadn't sounded all that scary on the phone. Nadia had done good, getting them the man's name. The call had been long enough to trace the motel room where she'd been. Even if it had been too late, it was still a lead. One they were all going to push to its limit until they knew how to get Nadia back.

Shadrach lifted both weapons from the goons, to Lazlo himself. An action that typically brought about a death of its own. Or so the newspaper reports led people to believe. "Where can I find him?"

Lazlo blew out a breath and shook his head. "Foolishness begets foolishness. And I will not cross that man. Not for you."

**

Ben clicked the locks on his vehicle and pocketed the keys. This stretch of Chinatown was quiet, and home to a restaurant Ben had wanted to try for a while but felt the need to steer clear of. At least until tonight.

The hostess was a tiny, older lady in a silk print dress and her gray hair in a bun.

Ben said, "I'm meeting someone," in Mandarin and kept walking. While she sputtered behind him, Ben strode through the sea of tables toward the door at the back. There was nothing remarkable about the restaurant, but the wontons were to die for—or so he'd heard—so they did a steady business. It smelled really good, and his stomach rumbled. Maybe he could pick up an order to go on his way out.

The door at the back of the room said *Private*. Ben ignored the stares from people enjoying their fried rice and turned the handle. It was locked from the inside. He drew his Sig and gave the door a swift kick.

The hostess screamed. The sound rose as she ran across the room toward him. Ben pushed the door closed and heard the bang as she slammed into the door, and her scream cut off. Dim hallway, four doors to choose from, but the layout matched the building plans Remy had dug up online.

Halfway down the hall a man emerged from the room at the end.

Ben shot him.

Another man stepped over his body, but Ben shot that guy so that he landed beside his associate.

Ben strode to the room. Four automatic weapons pointed at him, held by suited Chinese men. The old man behind the desk didn't stand, he simply lifted his eyebrows as he studied the man who had just walked into his restaurant and shot his men. "Before I kill you, I confess I wish to know what you want."

Ben nodded. He answered in Mandarin, "Some assistance for the man who got George Seng Mei out of Taiwan."

Two of the men with weapons flinched. There was an intake of breath from one. The old Chinese man simply stared harder. "That was you?"

"It was."

"Then I appear to owe you a debt. One that covers the death of my men."

Ben lifted his gun and held it sideways. "Tranquilizers." He said it in English because he didn't know the Mandarin word.

One of the guns turned his head to the old man and said one word.

The old man nodded.

Ben switched back to Mandarin, "Where can I find Earnest?"

The old man started to shake then laughter spilled from his mouth in a cackle. "You want—" He laughed harder. "Whoever she is, or whatever this is for, it is not worth the mess you will find yourself in when you kick that hornet's nest."

"Nevertheless."

"Even a man of your…skill has no hope to get her back."

"Perhaps additional assistance is required," Ben said. "Concerning that debt…"

"You consider it enough that you saved my brother's life that I would go to war with Earnest?" The old man squinted. "Perhaps I only wanted my brother here so that I could kill him myself?"

"If that was the case, he wouldn't be working at that upscale Cantonese restaurant on Broadway."

The old man made a sound. "Can you believe that? Wants to go straight." He shook his head. "Ungrateful."

Ben didn't comment on that. A man who had been through what George had was entirely at liberty to control his own destiny now that life had been restored to him.

The old man regarded him. After a minute of silence, he said, "Very well. I give you the address and my men will assist you."

The man who'd given him the word for "tranquilizer" whipped his head around to his boss and began to speak in rapid words almost too fast for Ben to keep up.

The boss barked one word, and the man shut up. "Leave your number with the hostess."

Ben gave him a short bow and let himself out.

**

Bolton gripped the phone. It was on the tip of his tongue to pray this would work, but he just couldn't bring himself to be indebted to God. Not yet, at least. Dante had passed Nadia to some guy named "Earnest." Because he was done with her? Bolton didn't want to know what Dante had gotten from her or what passing her to Earnest meant, other than payment.

The call connected. "This is Special Agent Liam Conners."

Bolton waited quietly while the third person on the line, the man he'd called, greeted the agent.

"Liam! This is Terry over at Quantico."

"Terry, how are you?"

Bolton listened to their small talk, tapped his fingers on the edge of the table and tried not to get impatient. This was the way he'd chosen to try and find Nadia and this Earnest person. He was going to have to see it through now that he'd opened that door to his past once again.

"I have on the phone a friend of mine. I've fully vetted him, and he is who he says he is, so there are no worries there. I know you're heading the case on Earnest Wells, and I'd like you to answer any questions my friend might have."

The Liam guy sighed. "You want me to tell him whatever he wants to know."

"He has earned that much from us, Conners. And he's asked that we do him this favor so that he might help us all the more."

"Fine." Special Agent Liam Conners didn't sound like he thought it was fine.

Terry said, "You need anything else, son?"

"No, Terry," Bolton answered. "Thanks. I appreciate your help."

"Okay, I'm hanging up so you two can talk." Terry's end of the line clicked.

"Are you still there?" Bolton figured if he was this "Liam Conners" guy, he'd just hang up and forget all about the call he had no intention of taking.

"Yeah, I'm here." Liam sighed. "Terry is a friend I respect, but all this is sensitive information I'm not sure I should be giving you. I don't know you from the guy at the hot dog stand."

Bolton squeezed his free hand into a fist. "Type this number into your computer." He rattled off a series of numbers he knew by heart and then said, "My name is Bolton Farrera. Earnest Wells kidnapped a friend of mine, and

I need to get her back. If you can help, meet me at the West Side Diner on Central as soon as you can."

Bolton hung up, picked up his coffee, and took a sip. He barely tasted it, the nausea in his stomach eclipsing every other physical sensation. Nadia was in the clutches of a madman. Sure, she'd faced evil in the past, but there was no way he could convince himself that experience was enough to face a man who was what they expected Earnest to be.

Fear crept up into his throat and threatened to choke him.

But he stayed in the diner and waited for Liam Conners.

**

Ben felt his watch vibrate. He lifted his wrist and read the numbers that flashed across the screen, pulled out the burner phone, and dialed the number.

"That you, boss?"

"Yeah, Remy." Ben smiled to himself as he navigated the streets of lower downtown Denver. "What do you have?"

She was quiet for a moment—never good. "That side project I've been working on…"

"What about it?"

"You were right. Though I have no idea why I was looking at all that in the first place since it isn't related to any of your open—"

"Remy."

"I ran Nadia Marie's picture and got a hit. Someone—I'm guessing Earnest—has put her up for sale. Bidding ends at noon tomorrow."

"That's good. It's what we expected, and now we can get to the sale before anyone else and get her back."

"Good? Dante knows all of your faces. He'll have told Earnest."

"We're assuming Dante is too occupied with other things to follow up on what happens to Nadia. Besides, there's someone I can call. A neutral party who can go in and get Nadia out."

"Do you want me to make the call?"

"It's okay," Ben said. Though his stomach churned even thinking about it. "I'll make the arrangements."

He hung up and pulled into a parking space outside the West Side Diner. Ben hung his head and pushed out a breath before he dialed the number.

"Hello?"

Her voice. It was like a punch to the gut.
"It's Ben. I need your help."

Chapter 15

Bolton slid the magazine in the gun and pulled the slide back. So far everything seemed to be going to plan. At least up until the point he contemplated that Earnest was going to *sell* Nadia. Being paralyzed with fear wasn't going to help right now. They'd separated to find both information and allies, but at this point they'd have to take what they could get.

Ben and Shadrach geared up, much the same except Shadrach wore a Yankees hat. Even the dog had a vest on.

FBI Special Agent Liam Conners strode in the door, stowing his phone in his back pocket. "No movement outside since the truck brought the girls in for the sale. My CI is sticking around. He'll call if anyone enters or exits the old theater. The light is green when y'all are ready."

Liam had turned out to be very amenable to what amounted to an illegal takedown of multiple targets who may or may not be people he needed to arrest. Bolton didn't care about charges or admissible evidence, or warrants. All he cared about was getting Nadia back—before or after he put a bullet in Earnest's brain didn't matter much to him. The man had messed with the wrong girl.

Bolton glanced at his new friend. "Something up?"

Liam wiped the frown from his brow. "Can't say I wouldn't feel better with a little more information on exactly who your friends are."

Ben looked over, raised one eyebrow.

Bolton shrugged.

"The chance to take down Earnest certainly sweetened the deal. I've been trying to figure out who he is for months. The man's identity doesn't exist in any database I have access to. Hard to get an arrest warrant on someone who doesn't exist." Liam glanced at each of them. "But I'm the special agent here. Therefore, since no one is willing to list out their work history that means you guys follow my lead."

Ben shifted so slightly it was almost imperceptible. "Or, you hang back. We take point, and you don't risk your ability to go home tonight to your wife and baby."

Liam's stare turned deadly. "And how would you know about my family?"

"You think I don't research the people I work with?" Ben lifted one eyebrow. "Now we should finish gearing up, because we have no idea how many men are in there. It's going to be all hands on deck on this one."

Shadrach made a face. Any other time, Bolton would have laughed, but neither of them cared about the men in there. They only wanted Nadia, while Ben seemed to feel this moral imperative to save everyone innocent in the building and bring down every bad guy.

Ben had been on edge for hours, since he'd told them he called in additional help that they would likely never meet. Someone who would be instrumental in securing the girls and hopefully getting Nadia to them.

Bolton wasn't going to wait for someone else.

He and Shadrach had found a common goal. Bolton wasn't going to take that for granted, not if it meant they'd get her back. He and Shadrach had forged an amendment to the plan wherein they broke off and made a bee line for Nadia. Room by room by room they were going to tear that place apart until they found her. Whether she spoke to him afterwards or not, Bolton would at least know that she was safe.

Ben lifted his chin. "Tensions are high, but we can do this. Secure the men in there, and then call the cops for cleanup."

The door at the end of the room opened. Liam said, "I already called them."

A tactical team walked in, full uniforms, helmets, night scopes, automatic weapons. All of it. The lead man grinned. "Someone call for an off-the-books takedown?"

Liam stuck out his hand. "I appreciate this."

"What else would we do for Johnson's bachelor party?" They all chuckled.

A door on the wall perpendicular to them opened and four suited Chinese men walked in. The tactical team pointed their guns at the same time the Chinese did.

"Guns down," Ben said as he strode to the lead Chinese guy. He looked at Liam. "You're not the only one who has friends with guns, who owe you a favor." He said something in Chinese, and they lowered their weapons.

Liam shrugged. "The more the merrier, I guess." He glanced at the lead Chinese man. "Doesn't mean I won't arrest you next week."

The man replied in Chinese, and his men snickered.

"This isn't about grudges," Liam said. "This is about taking down Earnest once and for all. Destroying his operation. We go in hard, we scoop up whoever's in there, and we secure them."

"In the confusion, the girls will be extricated."

Ben had already explained his contact planned to buy up all of the girls, or just steal them, and then take them to a safe place where they could recover and heal. Transition back to regular society and normal lives. Evidently it was something his contact had done before. The only difference this time was that Nadia would be returned to them.

Liam nodded. "Got your story down?"

Ben produced an innocent face—the same as when they'd been at Tristan's house. "I had no idea officer. My buddies said it would be fun, but then they brought the first girl out, and I realized what this place is. Then gunmen stormed in. They tied everyone up and took the girls. I have no idea who they were. I *swear*." There was a tinge of high school girl in the last word, but other than that it was flawless.

"You're good. I'll give you that," Liam said.

"Of course I am." Ben almost smiled.

"Awesome." Bolton wanted to shake his head. Like Ben would let himself get caught anyway. "Can we just do this?"

They needed to move in, or someone in the room would end up getting shot. A cat fight among armed men wasn't going to end up with anything less than walls covered with blood spatter and uncomfortable questions asked of anyone who was still alive at the end of it.

"Let's move," Shadrach trailed out.

One of the tactical guys stared at him as he did. "Isn't that the guy everyone thought shot the president?"

Liam turned to Bolton. "Interesting company you keep now."

Bolton shrugged. "More interesting than being dead."

**

Shadrach secured his mask. He readied the weapon and then fired the canister of gas into the main auditorium of the small, abandoned theater. Canisters flew into the open room from all four corners and dispersed tear gas into the room.

Shad dropped the weapon and pulled his guns. He strode down the aisle, arms extended out in front of him, firing the second he spotted a gun being pulled by anyone sitting in one of the rows. The sound of his own inhale and exhale echoed in the mask like Darth Vader breathing. It would have been comical if he hadn't already shot out four knee caps, two shoulders, and a gun-hand. When the confusion settled, they started tying everyone up.

Lame. It wasn't like anyone would miss these guys.

Within minutes the room had been secured.

"He's not here." Liam's voice echoed in his earpiece. "Earnest isn't here."

Dante wasn't here, either, by the looks of it. Bolton was out of luck if he wanted to confront the man. What was Dante's plan? He was off now doing something else. But what?

"The girls have been secured." That was Ben. "I've got a couple of goons down back here, and I took care of the other two. She got them out. I'll find Earnest."

"Okay," Liam answer. "Let's clear out."

She?

Shadrach detoured to the back of the stage. Nothing had been left behind. It would be near impossible to prove what had gone on here tonight. Some kind of business, but he doubted the police would be able to figure out what. There was little evidence they'd been here to purchase girls.

One of the tactical guys strode across the backstage area toward him. Shadrach lifted his chin and removed his mask since the gas hadn't reached back here. Once it was off he could hear the moaning from the auditorium.

The man came closer.

"Time to head out, I—"

Gun.

The spark of powder igniting flashed in front of him, and Shadrach hit the floor on his back, pain like a lance in his chest. Armor piercing round.

With his free hand the man lifted the black mask from his face. Long hair, not one of the tactical team. Was it one of Dante's men?

Shadrach clutched his radio with sticky fingers. "I…" He couldn't catch enough breath to speak.

This was how he was going to die? Put down by someone who didn't care about him at all? He'd figured a vendetta owed would be his demise. There were enough people in the world who had a price put on Shadrach's head that one of them would come calling. But this? Not what he'd imagined. Bolton was going to owe him big time. Again.

The man had better not rest until Nadia Marie was found. Then he had to make sure Dauntless was taken care of. Otherwise Shadrach wouldn't let the man rest. Even after he was dead he'd make Bolton's life a misery. Somehow.

The gunman aimed the again, this time at Shadrach's face. He shut his eyes. *So long world.*

"Don't even think about it!" Bolton's voice echoed.

Shadrach's eyes flew open.

The man lifted his gaze beyond where he lay. "The fallout of your actions will be catastrophic. Unless you tell us where the cache is."

"I have nothing for Dante."

A gun fired, and Shadrach blacked out.

**

Nadia Marie sat on a bench seat in the bus station. She wrapped the trench coat tighter around her and eyed anyone who tried to come near. She didn't even want anyone looking at her right now, let alone getting close enough to touch. Exposed, out in the open. She was in public when she'd rather have been alone in private, but at least it was safe here.

The giant clock on the wall had just ticked past two-thirteen in the morning when she heard Dauntless bark. The dog crossed the room in his service vest, skirted a homeless man and ducked under a table to reach her. He sat by her knee, his body weight a comforting push against her leg.

Nadia closed her eyes.

"She doesn't look good." Ben's voice preceded footsteps that stopped several feet from her.

She wanted to scratch the back of Dauntless's neck, but she couldn't let go of the coat. Not just yet. Instead, she opened her eyes.

Bolton and Ben. Where was Shadrach? He should be with his dog.

"He got hurt in the raid," Ben said in answer to her unspoken question. "I'll take you to him whenever you're ready."

Nadia nodded. *Shadrach.* How bad was it?

She couldn't look at Bolton. She couldn't see that look in his eyes or the question on his face. He didn't want to know the details of the past twenty-four hours of her life, and if he was any kind of friend he would realize that and not ask her one question. Freaked out. Scared down to her bones. She hadn't been touched—much—but that didn't mean it hadn't been horrible.

Not even rescue had been a pleasant experience, given it had been undertaken as a purchase—of her. Nadia's "owner" had brought all the girls to a truck and loaded them in. To their confusion, inside had been blankets, snacks, water, clothes. Everything, down to socks and the sneakers she rubbed together now. But she was still frozen to her middle.

She needed coffee, only there had been no time when she was driven a few blocks away and released from the truck. The woman who "purchased" her had given her the coat she'd been wearing and told her where to wait.

"Is she a friend of yours?" Nadia winced at the sound of her own voice. Raspy and brittle, but not broken.

Ben nodded.

Nadia motioned with her head to the envelope on the chair beside her. "She said to give you that."

Ben took the package, slow enough she could track his every movement. She hadn't been raped, although she had figured it would be soon coming. Still, her foray in the world of sex trafficking wasn't going to leave her any time soon.

"She's good at what she does." Ben retreated to a seat across from her. Far enough away she felt some assurance of privacy, but she doubted it was more than an illusion. He could probably hear every word.

Dante had handed her over to lose everything she knew about herself in the process of becoming someone else's property. She never wanted to feel that way again, and at the same time her heart screamed at the thought of those whose whole lives were spent like that. If she had any energy, she'd figure out what to do about it. At least the girls she had been locked up with tonight were free now.

Nadia's eyes slipped shut. She sucked in a breath and forced them open. This wasn't the place to fall asleep.

"You're exhausted." Bolton's voice didn't sound any more whole than hers. Nadia didn't want to know what look was on his face. She couldn't handle his emotions right now, not when hers were on overload.

Bolton settled in the seat beside her but with enough space between them that there was no risk of their touching. "What do you need?" His voice was small, and his fingers twitched like he wanted to move, but he didn't.

So long as he didn't tell her he was sorry, Nadia would be able to keep it together. Besides, it was her fault she'd been in that situation in the first place. Trying to make a deal with Dante had been the stupidest move of her life.

"Nadia?"

That chair. And the room. "He asked me about Sanctuary, and I think I told him where it was. He was looking for a dead woman." She could barely convey what she was trying to say. Her thoughts were garbled in the residue of the drugs and exhaustion. Hunger. Zero adrenaline to give her any kind of energy. She was replete of any and everything she should have been able to fall back on. *Jesus, help me.*

She'd cried out to him so many times. Nearly every minute of every hour she'd called to the Lord to help her, and now here she was. Still needing His help…but safe. Alive. Unharmed. *Thank You.*

As peace settled over her, she opened her eyes. "It made no sense, Bolton. They drugged me. Everything is garbled in my head, I can't even think." She looked around. "Where's Shadrach?"

"Nadia—"

She caught the look on his face and gasped. "Is he dead?"

"No. But he was hurt, badly. Dante showed up at the theater during the raid. He shot Shadrach and tried to shoot me, too. I fired at the same time, and we winged each other."

Her face whipped around, and she scanned him with her gaze.

Bolton pointed to the blood on his ear. Like he needed any more injuries. "Ben showed up, and he ran." He paused. "Live to fight another day, I guess."

"I'm supposed to be clean now. And they shot me up to get answers." She whipped her head around to look at Ben. "They mentioned Grant. I think they're looking for him. Or someone else. Or both." She squeezed her eyes shut. "I don't know."

Ben got up and walked away. His back to them. He pulled out a phone.

"You need to rest."

She looked at him then. Looked right in his eyes, and said, "Who are you, Bolton Farrera? Why does Dante have so many questions? What does he want?"

**

Bolton stared into her dark eyes and nearly broke. He nearly told her everything, but he could barely bring himself to think about what would happen if she knew who he really was. Bolton Farrera was nothing but a coward. A product of his circumstances. Unable to do what he wanted or to live the life he dreamed of.

At every turn he'd been thwarted. Every time he'd gotten close enough to actually believe that a happy, free life was possible something happened. Slam, the door shut on his future. Until he'd hit the point that he stopped dreaming.

And then he'd met Nadia.

Bolton lifted his hand but didn't try to reach for her. He wanted so badly to know if they'd hurt her, but he couldn't bring himself to say that, either. Such a coward.

"Shadrach?"

"Let's go check on him, okay?" He wasn't going to rule out her need to be checked by a doctor. Maybe he'd suggest it, since they would be in the hospital anyway.

Nadia nodded but didn't move. Not even the bright white sneakers on her feet twitched. He didn't think his back could take carrying her, not the way it had been acting up. So Bolton got to his feet. He held out his hand, wishing with all his might that she would take it. A small peace offering. An indication she didn't hate him for what Dante had done to her.

He knew now that she didn't trust him, but if Bolton could bring himself to tell her everything maybe he could earn that back.

Nadia pressed her lips together. She set her soft, cold hand in his and got up.

Bolton lifted her hand and pressed the back of it to his chest. Her big eyes gazed up at him. "I'm glad you're safe, Nadia."

She ducked her head and pressed her forehead against his chest. Her breath hitched, but she didn't cry.

Bolton wrapped his arms around her. Had Bolton ever met anyone as strong as she was?

**

Ben stood in the hall of the hospital floor where Shadrach had been admitted—though, not under his real name. He gripped the phone, trying to figure out where to channel this worry that he'd get a result fastest. "Your name has come up twice now in as many days. Want to tell me why?"

Grant chuckled. "I'm hunting Dante, same as you. That's the assignment you put me on, *boss*. Checking out the mom and finding out where she's gone and what happened. I tracked down the sheriff. Shadrach and Nadia's mom is fine. She's been hiding out with him, freaked out. Apparently they have a relationship, and he kept her hidden to protect her, since Dante waltzed into the compound asking for her by name. So it's all good. How is Nadia?"

"Don't change the subject. I know she called you before she got that wild idea to hit the bank and pay off Dante."

"That was all her. I only told her how strong she is. Strong enough to take care of herself."

"Yeah," Ben scoffed. "That worked out real well."

"I'm sorry, okay?" His older brother sighed. "I didn't know she would do that."

Ben blew out a long breath.

"Want to tell me about that woman Will said saved the day?"

"No."

"A friend of yours, he said. Will looked her up. Didn't find anything except a vague Interpol reference to long, dark hair and a preference for knives."

Ben's lips curled up at the corners, but he kept his voice stern. "This isn't a gossip session. You might be in danger, and you're getting sidetracked. Maybe you're not cut out for field work."

"You want to bench me? I was the director of the marshals for years."

"Desk work."

"You gave me a team. They're good. They'll keep me safe if someone comes after me." Grant paused. "Right guys?"

Muffled laughter reached Ben's ears through the phone line. He'd vetted every one of them, but it was never foolproof. Anyone could be bought with the right amount of money. The "team" Ben assigned to him were there to keep Grant safe, and if anything happened to his brother he'd hunt down every single one of them. "Keep an eye out. Don't let your guard down for one second."

"Any idea what Dante wants?"

"Yeah. Tell me what you know about Thea Farrera."

Silence.

"That means you know something, Grant. You just don't want to tell me."

Grant sighed, long and low. "Excuse me for a second, fellas." A car door slammed, and then Grant said, "Thea Farrera is, for all intents and purposes, dead."

"Because you faked the reports and hid her somewhere. But not Sanctuary."

"Thea didn't want to be anywhere near Bolton. I stashed her in the farthest place I could while still being in the US."

"And where is that?"

"Dante can't know," Grant said. "That's probably why he wants to get at me. He may even have this phone bugged, so I'd better not say over the line until we know for sure we have a secure one."

Which meant Grant was going to use alternative means to contact Will with the information. "Stay safe."

"You too, brother. And if you tell me I'm not cut out for this one more time I'm going to punch your smug face."

"You can try." Ben hung up smiling.

The world was a safer place when the people he cared about weren't the target of some criminal trying to get at him.

Ben let himself into Shadrach's room. Machines beeped, a good sign. The former marine was alive. His sister was safe now. He would recover.

Remy sat with Nadia, holding hands. Bolton leaned against the wall beside the door. Ben went to stand with him. "Any change?"

Bolton shook his head. "He took one to the chest. Armor piercing rounds." And Bolton had killed the man who shot Shadrach.

"The men we caught, they've been taken care of?"

"Liam is combing through the package that woman got you, but it looks like everything he needs to bring down the entire ring of traffickers."

"Good. That was good, you calling in FBI contacts. Liam's help was invaluable."

"Unlike those crazy Chinese dudes."

"So long as we take them down, doesn't it matter?" Ben extremely disliked people who traded off the innocence of others. His watch buzzed. "Will is finding Earnest." He looked at the screen, a new message from Will.

"What about us? We need to figure out what Dante's next move is. I don't like the idea that he traded Nadia to Earnest and then disappeared. Where did he go? And for what?"

Ben turned so his back was to the bed and the two women. "I think he's going after Thea and Javier."

Bolton said, "I have to protect them, but so far that has meant not knowing where they are. And how can Dante find out their location? That has to be why he wants Grant."

"That's why we're keeping Grant safe and working to protect Thea and Javier, too." Ben read off his watch screen. "Have you ever heard of 'Pu'u honua'?"

"What does it mean?"

Ben grinned. "It's the Hawaiian word for Sanctuary."

Chapter 16

Bolton set both coffee cups down on the table and sat. Nadia flexed her fingers and linked them around the cup.

"Still cold?"

She shrugged one shoulder. "I'll be okay."

An announcement was made over the hospital intercom system. The cafeteria was a barren wasteland. Probably everyone had already tried the coffee and then never came back.

She'd broken down, seeing her brother fighting for his life. Surgery had gone well, and they'd repaired the damage to Shadrach's chest where the bullet had punched a hole clear through him. Now it was a waiting game, watching to see how he healed.

Nadia lifted her gaze. "What did Ben say to you in Shad's room?"

Bolton didn't figure she was just making light conversation. She wanted to talk, so he said, "I might have to leave."

"Because Dante wants to know where that woman called Thea is?"

Bolton nodded. Nadia would stay with her brother, until he recovered, and then head back to Sanctuary. Bolton had just gotten her back, and now he needed to go and make sure that Thea and Javier were okay. Protecting them from Dante was the jurisdiction of the US Marshals Service, but it was also on him. He'd put them in the position of needing to be in witness protection in the first place.

"And she's not dead."

"That was faked. The picture they showed you was from the file, evidence. A woman had died and the DNA was switched out so it was believed to be Thea. Grant stashed her in a safe place and told no one so that Dante would think she was dead."

"And now Dante knows she isn't in Idaho. That's why he wanted Grant, isn't it? Because he's the one person who's going to know where she was placed in witness protection." Nadia's smiled evaporated. "So...you're married? Or you were married, at one point?"

This was what she wanted to talk about. Bolton figured she deserved an explanation, but was now really the right time? She'd been through something horrendous, and he still didn't even know the extent of it—though she didn't appear to have been physically harmed.

"I need to know, Bolton. And I figure being drugged, interrogated, and nearly being the true story behind a made-for-TV-movie about my tragic life earns me the right to at least ask. There's a woman out there who meant something to you at one point, and I want to know who she is."

"There's more to it than that, Nadia." Bolton took a sip of his coffee and set the cup on the table. "It isn't just about Thea. This is about me, and who I was. Or maybe who I tried to be. It's about having a son, one I've never even seen—not even a picture."

"What happened?"

"Initially we went into witness protection together. But Dante kept coming. He found us, time and time again, and Thea couldn't handle it. She was pregnant, and I think it messed with her head having a baby inside her and being in so much danger. I don't know. I'd like to say it was my getting hurt that clinched it for her, but I think that was simply the door she saw as her way out. I woke up in the hospital from Dante's latest attack, and she was gone.

"Six months later Grant sent word that she'd had a boy. Javier. Like knowing his name wasn't worse torture than living with the knowledge I would never even see him." He blew out a breath. "I don't know if it was the situation or if she'd never really been in love with me. Either way it was too much for her. I've thought about it a lot over the years. Maybe Thea was more in love with the person I was pretending to be, than with who I was. I wonder if she was ever really happy, or if she was just playing a part the exact same way I was."

Nadia bit her lip. "What do you mean?"

"I was twenty-five. Business was good, but family ties were encroaching. They wanted a piece of what I was doing, and I was supposed to hand over nearly half the rights to a company I'd constructed myself, just because we were related. I was about to cave when the FBI showed up."

"FBI?"

Bolton nodded. "I got a better offer. I sold the business to a friend of mine to free up my time and just worked design on commission. The FBI was investigating a ring of dirty DEA agents, hoping to bring them down discreetly. It looked like the DEA's reach was more widespread than they'd originally thought, so I was tasked with infiltrating their operation. And it worked."

"You worked for the FBI?"

"They actually swore me in at one point, paperwork and everything. Never went to Quantico, never sat at one of those fancy FBI desks. I think I only stepped in a field office once in my life. But yeah, I was...I don't know, not an agent. More like an asset, or an independent contractor." He didn't smile. "I was young, and I made assumptions when I should have asked questions. But it was cool, for a while. Before the sheen of being one of the good guys wore off."

"What happened?"

"It took a few years. Time during which I'd convinced the friend who'd bought the business to partner up with Thea's father to expand. Had a pregnancy scare, got married. I thought we were happy, and I thought I was doing something good. The FBI agents who'd hired me started making...suggestions. Hide this, break in there, little insinuations like 'if this guy disappears, it wouldn't be so bad.' I started to have an inkling they were padding my assignment with side jobs that helped them, so I called Ben. After we renewed our acquaintance he ripped me up one side and down the other for taking on a job like that without calling him. He found a link between the FBI guys who were my handlers and the DEA—specifically Dante and Tristan."

"They were dirty?"

"It wasn't overt. It never is. But there were signs, and Ben had enough proof to go above their heads. The justice department launched an investigation into members of the DEA and FBI. It took two years, living that life pretending to work for a couple of crooked FBI agents, supposedly "investigating" Dante and his partner. A double, double agent. The most we could figure was that they had an arrangement with Dante and Tristan, and they had me looking into everything to make sure they didn't get screwed over. I was their insurance policy that Dante was holding up his end of the bargain."

Nadia shook her head. "Wow."

"They were pretty convincing in their pitch. And the angles they had me running seemed legit. I passed them information about a deal about to go down, suddenly four people turned up dead or a shipment was intercepted. I started to ask questions, but someone trashed one of the shops in the middle of the night and the damage to those bikes was in the millions. So I shut my mouth, called Ben again. If it wasn't for him, I'd probably have been killed."

Or he'd have left the country and made a new life for himself. Bolton certainly wouldn't have put himself in the witness protection town of Sanctuary to hide from Dante.

"I gathered evidence against them, but the FBI agents had double crossed Dante. He killed them one night, so I told Ben where I thought they might be buried. We made a deal with the justice department, and I testified against him with what I knew of Dante's operation. By that time Thea had figured out I was up to something, so I told her. All of it."

Bolton winced, remembering her reaction. The way her face had twisted in rage, and she'd spewed foul words at him. "She couldn't believe I would risk our livelihood—her shopping money—by doing something as stupid as testifying. She wouldn't even talk about witness protection. Refused to even contemplate it, like I was the criminal doing a foul thing and hurting people." He shook his head. "She wanted to leave, but Dante had found out what I was up to, and his army began to wage their war. FBI agents, DEA agents, guns for hire, cartels they'd partnered with. You name them, we were on their hit list."

"Sounds like a harsh life."

"Thea and I couldn't go anywhere without a guard, and they moved us frequently. Usually in the middle of the night. I wasn't sleeping, she was moody. We fought all the time, great screaming matches where picture frames get thrown across the room and furniture gets smashed." He shook his head. "It wasn't pretty, but I think we were just scared kids who couldn't control what was happening. We had no idea what the future would hold, or even if we were going to live to see tomorrow."

"Did you get a divorce?"

"Dante attacked the convoy on the way to the federal courthouse for the first of a series of testimonies I was supposed to do on camera. Thea had stayed behind. When I woke up in the hospital Ben was there, and Grant. Thea left me with divorce papers. Grant said he'd relocated her because she didn't want to stay with me. I testified, and they offered me a new life in Sanctuary."

He sent her a small smile when all he felt was regret. From the beginning he'd taken the wrong path and messed up his life. He'd put his wife in danger, the business he'd wanted to save he'd sold. He'd ended up in Sanctuary, little more than an upscale prison surrounded by impenetrable mountains and people he'd tolerated—okay, a few he'd called friend. But never, not once, had Bolton been the person he'd thought he could be. Never had he lived the life he'd thought up in any kind of dream.

Not once.

"So what now?"

Her question was a simple one, and the answer was anything but. "Dante is going to go after Thea. He's trying to destroy me, and when he's taken out everyone I've ever cared about, then he's going to come after me."

"You're leaving?"

When Ben had told him, Bolton hadn't known whether to laugh or get mad. "You're not going to believe me when I tell you."

She dipped her head to the side. "Tell me what?"

"There's another Sanctuary. In Hawaii." Her jaw dropped. It was so cute Bolton almost laughed. "If Thea didn't hate me so much I might've actually gotten a vacation out of this."

"Yeah, so terrible. I'm sure going to Hawaii will be awful."

He smiled. "You're only saying that because you've been stuck in Idaho for years."

She actually smiled back. "Hey, I like our mountains. But I've got a bone to pick with Grant if there's a Sanctuary in Hawaii, and no one ever told me."

He chuckled.

She frowned at him then. "You told me that you hated Sanctuary."

Bolton nodded, wondering what more she wanted him to share. "I did."

"I want to go back there. It's where my home is."

"I'm glad for you. Knowing what place to call home is a powerful thing." He leaned across the table, closer to her, and laid his hand over hers. "I want that for you, more than I want anything else I want you to be happy. I'm sorry I dragged you through this. I should never have done that, not when I knew what it might do to you. But I was selfish, I wanted someone with me. One day maybe you could find it in your heart to forgive me for what I did."

Bolton wouldn't try and forgive himself. If he could do it all over, he would do the same thing. Grab her hand and run. Get lost in the world together, just the two of them. It had been frustrating and hard, but they'd spent more time together in the past few weeks than they had in years.

He wouldn't trade those quiet moments for anything, even if he'd been on edge and she'd been scared. She'd even been scared of him. But some part of Bolton understood that was reality. He was the kind of man who caused the people he cared about to fear him, to misunderstand what he was attempting to do and walk away because—for some reason—they would never fully know him.

It was simply who he was: a man who, even at his age, didn't really know who he was.

"Bolton—"

"You don't have to say anything, Nadia."

He didn't want her to try to explain what had gone wrong or all the ways he'd ruined whatever tiny thing had been between them. Bolton wasn't blind enough to not know a spark when one ignited in his face. But that had happened with Thea, and it had been way more volatile. With Nadia it felt...fragile, gentle, and in need of care.

Something he didn't have the ability to give.

"As soon as I know Thea is safe, I'll be gone."

"You're still going after that stash?"

Ben cleared his throat. "The two of us need to talk about that."

Bolton shot him a look, stood beside the table like he hadn't just appeared out of nowhere. Couldn't the man tell he'd been having a private conversation with Nadia?

"Now that I know you have brothers, it makes way more sense that you talk to me like I'm your kid brother." Bolton shook his head. "Though it still ticks me off." He stood and faced Ben. "I'm going to do what I need to do, and then I'm gone."

"After we talk about that stash, I might let you." Ben's gaze flicked to Nadia and then back. "Even if you are being an idiot."

"You think I'm giving you my only insurance?" Okay, so he probably would if he didn't need it. But Ben didn't have to assume.

"If your plan is as good as you think, you won't need it. Not if Dante is dead or back in prison for good."

"We'll see."

Bolton touched Nadia's shoulder and walked out. There were way too many variables to promise Ben would get what he wanted. Way too much to go wrong or get mixed around. Bolton had to finish this, and then after that he would be sure of what the future held. A future where he figured out, for the first time in his life, what he wanted to do.

Who he wanted to be.

**

"Everything okay?" Ben wasn't sure he was equipped to help, but he still asked.

Nadia left her coffee untouched and got up. "You really helped him that much?" She shook her head, a small smile on her lips. "Scratch that, of course you did."

Ben felt his own lips curl. "Of course."

"Can I ask you something?" When he nodded, she said, "What will happen to those girls? I mean, they're out, right? She does that, takes them from that life and sets them free?"

Ben nodded. "They have a long road ahead. Sometimes it's hard for them to believe it's over, or that they can truly be free. But she's good at what she does. She'll give them what they need. Schooling, counseling. Fun. Help. Things some of them have never experienced in their entire lives. It's a long road, but she'll get them there."

"Wow. That's an incredibly noble thing."

"Nobility is something people dream up to make themselves feel better. The truth is that none of us can claim to be noble, not if we're honest about who we are."

Nadia leaned closer and peered up into his eyes so that Ben couldn't look away. "That's because you've never been the recipient of someone else's noble action."

"Maybe that's true."

Nadia leaned up and planted a kiss on his cheek. "Tell her I said thank you."

Ben watched her walk away, and at the same time he tried to recall if anyone had ever been noble on his behalf. Perhaps Nadia was right. He expended himself over and over, but had he ever accepted the same from someone else?

He pulled out his phone and sat at the table. Grant didn't even let it finish the first ring before he picked up. "Yep?"

"Busy?"

"Managed to track down an old associate of Bolton's, Thea's father. He had no idea about any stash or where Bolton might have hidden it. Then he pulled a gun on me." Grant paused. "These are some interesting guys you assigned to be my team. They had him on the ground, disabled, within three seconds."

Ben smiled to himself. Grant's "team" were a crew of personal security guys. Men he'd hired to protect his brother under the guise of assisting him in his investigation. Not that Ben didn't trust his brother to keep himself safe. It was more that Ben took zero chances when it came to family.

"So everything is good?" It had better be; Ben was paying enough money. "No sign of Dante?"

"You worry as much as Mom. Whether Dante wants to come and grab me so that I can get Thea for him or not, he was in Denver. He can't be two places at once, and that's a lot of jet fuel to keep darting back and forth across the country."

"He has friends."

"Well so do I. Like this team of mine," Grant's voice turned sardonic. Ben heard Grant say, "One sec, fellas." Then a car door shut. "Told me their last job was protecting a diplomat on a tour of Colombia. Fancy that. Made me wonder if they weren't assigned to do the same with the 'retired' former director of the US Marshals."

"That would be dishonest, doing that and not telling you."

"You've been telling lies your whole life," Grant said. "You're good at it."

"Your girls might be grown, but they still need you." Ben didn't add that the rest of them needed him, too. "Just keep an eye out for Dante, okay? He's going after Thea, and you're the fastest route to her whereabouts."

"But not the *only* one."

"As far as everyone's concerned you are."

Grant huffed. "This is a nasty chess game you're playing with people's lives."

And that was why Ben would never claim to be noble. He saved people, but so often what they needed saving from was themselves. And how did he achieve that? He could put a dent in the evil in the world, but that tide just kept on rolling in. One day it was going to deposit him, battered on some distant beach, to recover while it laid a path of destruction Ben could only watch and do absolutely nothing about.

"Just watch your back, okay?"

**

Grant hung up. He got back in the front passenger seat. "Let's roll."

The driver pulled out of the space and set off down the street faster than Grant would have pushed it. They didn't need to draw a cop's attention, but Grant wasn't in the mood for slow.

"Everything okay?"

The blandly spoken question made Grant shrug. "He said to be careful."

"We always are."

They pulled up to a red light, and Grant turned to the back seat. Something cold touched his neck. A crackling sound preceded the sensation of lightning that whipped through his body. Grant fought against it, but there was no use. The stun gun sapped him of all strength, and he slumped into the seat on the edge of unconsciousness.

"Call Dante. Tell him we're certain Grant Mason knows where Thea is."

Chapter 17

Remy had ducked out for something to eat, so Nadia sat with her brother for a quiet moment. She stared at his pale face, but all she could see was Earnest. Her being shuffled from room to room. Paraded around and pawed at. It wasn't something she wanted to relive, but she'd have to get it out. She'd have preferred it be with Andra, not her brother—even if he was unconscious.

A light tap sounded on the door. A woman walked in. Nadia half expected it to be a nurse, but it wasn't.

"Mom?"

A stout man in jeans and a heavy jacket followed her mom into the room. She glanced between them. Her mom had switched the hippy clothes Nadia was used to for a long striped skirt and whatever shirt she wore under that pea coat.

The woman, an almost exact replica of Nadia's dark hair and dark eyes, gaped. "I didn't know you were here." She swallowed. "They told me Shadrach..." Her eyes filled with tears, and Nadia's vision of her got blurry. "My baby girl. Right here in front of me."

Nadia rounded the end of the bed and strode to her mom, who opened her arms to embrace her. As Nadia settled into her mother's embrace a sob worked its way up to her throat. Love between them had never been the problem. The tension came when they tried to communicate or cohabitate. Not helpful for an unruly teenager and her exasperated mother, but Nadia was an adult now. Perhaps things would be different.

"My baby girl," her mom said again, as she stroked Nadia's back. Who'd have thought what Nadia needed right then was a hug from her mother.

"It's been a long time." *Thank You, Lord.* He had known and blessed her—yet again—in ways she couldn't even have fathomed. Nadia pulled back and wiped her cheeks with the back of her fingers. "I can't believe you're here. That's so crazy. I didn't even know you were coming, but I'm glad."

"I can't believe *you're* here. For years my baby girl has been hidden away from me. Now here you are, a beautiful woman."

Nadia nearly choked. She didn't feel beautiful, not after the last few days. Mothers always saw what they wanted to see in what they had created. What those men the night before would never have seen or even vaguely noticed about her.

"This is Michael. He's the sheriff in Kentucky, where I live."

Nadia tried to look like she wasn't a crazy mess and shook his hand. Refined but strong. Knew how to handle himself and probably took good care of her mom even while he didn't let her get away with anything. "Nadia Marie."

"I've heard a lot about you. I feel, in a way, as though I already know you."

Nadia smiled.

"You ladies have a lot of catching up to do, so I'm going to step out and talk to those gentlemen in the hallway." He planted a soft kiss on Nadia's mother's cheek and then left.

Her mom glanced back to her and smiled. "He's good to me."

"I'm glad, Mom."

"They told me Shadrach had been shot."

Nadia nodded and turned to her brother, lying in the hospital bed hooked up to all those horrible machines and wrapped in so many bandages he looked like a mummy. She pulled the sleeves of her sweater down over her hands. "It cut through his vest and went straight through him, nicked his heart as it tore a hole in his chest. The doctor said he barely made it through surgery."

"And that dog of his?" Her mom made a face.

"A co-worker is watching him."

"And you?" The question was tentative. Nadia tried to figure out what she was asking.

She couldn't tell her mom about Sanctuary. She'd only spilled under the influence of narcotics. The memorandum of understanding she'd signed when she was inducted into the witness protection program was voided if she told anyone the location of Sanctuary or exposed anything about the program—or anyone in it.

Her heart sank in her chest. Would they let her go back now?

"Honey—"

Nadia shook off the thought. "There isn't a lot I can say about it. But I've been happy. I like my life, where I live. I like the people there." She scratched at the skin of her arm. It felt like something crawled between her sweater and her arm.

"Coming down off something?"

Nadia's head jerked. "Excuse me?"

"It was a simple question. It's been years, and I don't know where you've been. Or what you've been doing."

Yeah, it was so simple. "I was kidnapped and injected with something against my will. To get me to talk."

"Did it have anything to do with Shadrach being shot?"

"The same man was behind both."

Her mom settled on the edge of Shadrach's bed. "I guess it was too much to ask that since you're here that meant you were no longer in danger. I guess some things never change."

"None of this was about me. We got caught up in Bolton's thing."

"One of those men in the hall?"

Nadia nodded.

"Both of them are more dangerous and more deadly than my son. Which is saying something, considering my son is Shadrach Carleigh. Let me guess, you had a part in his being accused of shooting the president, too?"

"No. I had nothing to do with that." Nadia scratched at her arm again. "Mom—"

"I think I need some space, if you don't mind." She shifted on the bed and presented Nadia with her back. "I'd like to be alone with my son."

She was going to blame Nadia for this, like it was her finger that had pulled the trigger and shot Shadrach? As though Nadia would ever do something to hurt her brother. He'd been her ally. He'd taught her to be smart and to survive. She'd have been dead a hundred times over if it hadn't been for Shadrach.

Nadia strode to the door and let herself out. She set her hands against the opposite wall of the hall and hung her head.

"Whoa, whoa." Bolton touched her shoulder, and she realized she'd started to cry. "What just happened?"

Nadia cried harder. Her mom's *friend* or whatever ceased his conversation with Ben and frowned at her. She turned away from him. She didn't know him, and she didn't need to take on whatever he would dish out in defense of her mom.

"Not the happy reunion you were hoping for?" Bolton turned her so she could plant her face against his chest.

The tears turned to a horrible, nervous laughter. Nadia was pretty sure she had lost it, as she half laughed/half cried against his chest.

"Andra would be horrified at this display."

Nadia laughed harder as she clutched at his chest like a ninny. "I'm not hurting you, am I?" Bolton almost smiled. Shook his head.

Ben's phone beeped. Or she thought that's what it was until he lifted his wrist. "Will says turn on the TV."

They trailed into the room but steered to the side where the tiny TV sat high in a cabinet so the person in the bed, or whoever sat with them, could watch.

Nadia didn't look at her mom. She'd have seen the objection on her mom's face. Mom was going to have to get used to Nadia being there through Shadrach's recovery. And the armed guards Ben had called to watch the door. Whatever the woman had in her head that she couldn't manage to see a single bit of good in anything Nadia tried to do, she would likely fight when Nadia didn't leave before Shadrach said it was okay to.

Maybe she'd stay longer on principle.

Ben flipped on the TV. "...with the escape and continued evasion of federal prisoner and former DEA agent Dante Alvarez. This man is suspected of being an accomplice and in collusion with the crooked federal agent who was convicted of crimes too numerous for us to list in this short update. The man's name is unknown, though his picture is up now on the screen."

The newscaster disappeared, replaced with a mug shot of Bolton.

"Why are—"

Bolton didn't let her finish. He turned to Ben. "Dante knows where I am. This has to be Tristan."

Ben nodded. "He's trying to get ahead of Dante, to get word when someone finds either of you so he can control the fallout."

The newscaster spoke again, "He is to be considered armed and highly dangerous, and indications are that he is travelling with this woman."

The screen showed a grainy photo of Nadia exiting the salon where she had worked for weeks while she and Bolton had been hiding. Or at least, she'd thought they were hiding. He'd been in contact with Ben the whole time.

She whirled around. "I'm fine here, right? I'll be protected if I stay here, and you get those guards. Won't I?"

Ben didn't answer. Not a good sign. He clearly had an answer for her but wasn't about to give her one that she'd like.

"Shadrach's hurt. I'm not leaving."

"If you're in danger, then you can't stay." Her mom's voice cut through her. "If people are looking for you because this man—" She waved in Bolton's direction. "—is a criminal, then you'll bring danger to Shadrach when he can't defend himself."

Nadia wanted to wince…or cry. Whichever. But she didn't. Her eyes burned as she stared at Bolton.

"I'm sorr—"

She couldn't believe he was going to say that. "Don't apologize."

"I did drag you into this."

"It's not your fault Tristan is trying to flush you out so he's posting out pictures all over the news." She pointed at the screen. "This is local, right?"

Ben said, "Getting out of Denver would be a good plan. Before they leak this nationwide. They know you're here."

"But you guys are going to find—" Nadia cut herself off before she said it out loud. If their destination got leaked, it wouldn't be because of her. "The person you need to make sure is safe."

Bolton nodded. "Looks like you're coming with us."

"Um…pretty sure you can drop me off in the mountains of you-know-where on your way."

"There's no time," Ben said. "Not if we want as much chance as possible to get there ahead of Dante. I'll go tell them we've got an extra passenger, and then we'll figure out how to get you two out of the hospital." Ben strode out.

Nadia wanted to slam her foot down. "Is he always like that?"

Bolton said, "You've been in worse situations."

Nadia said, "Bye, Mom," and didn't wait for an answer. Remy would tell Shadrach what had happened when he woke up.

**

Nadia unbuckled her seatbelt and stretched. A ride in a cushy chair on a private plane had done her the world of good. It had been a long time since, and she'd thought it wasn't likely she'd ride chartered private ever again. Yet here she was.

Out the window, palm trees were silhouetted by runway lights, beyond which shone an array of night stars. She could hardly believe she was back in Hawaii again. That had been a fun vacation, not that she remembered much of it since she'd been so inebriated, but it was a great place. Nadia paused her thoughts. Why did she think that had been fun? Three minutes of familial harmony and a comforting hug from her mom had been more pleasant than spending a long weekend stumbling all over Oahu from club to club because she couldn't walk straight. Then, much like the hug, came the reckoning.

Yeah, so she'd just compared her relationship with her mom to getting drunk, but what else was she supposed to do? Process, and set it aside. Process, and set it aside. Her emotional outburst in the hall notwithstanding, the technique seemed to be working pretty well.

In the seat across from her, Bolton woke. Shot her a smile. He wasn't as relaxed as he projected. The man was wound tight and had probably slept fitfully.

Ben got up and crossed to the door, which he opened while Will sat in his chair typing. The tech guy was a one track mind if ever she'd seen one. He barely spoke. Maybe he was one of those people who conversed electronically more than they spoke out loud.

"So what island are we on?"

Ben turned at her question. "I guess that's valid, and it'd be hard to hide." He smiled. "Kauai."

"Oh, nice." Nadia looked outside again to see if her window was the ocean side of the airport, or the side where you could see the mountain peak. Sure enough, a huge towering hill poked up into the sky in an attempt to reach the beauty of the stars above.

"It's like a sauna out there." Bolton stood at the door. "Kind of reminds me of Miami."

Nadia didn't want to talk about places they'd been, or she'd have to admit she'd dismissed Kauai as being quiet, which equated to boring. If she'd met Bolton during that time both of their lives would have been remarkably different. She would never have gone to Sanctuary and never found faith in God.

Will spoke. "Dante and his pals seem to have chartered a plane of their own. Used a known front company. At least, known to us. Manifest says six people plus the pilot, and the flight plan has it headed to Phoenix."

"That makes no sense," Bolton said. "We know he's going to come here."

Ben paused in packing his arsenal of weapons into a black duffel type bag, one that looked like it was made of plastic, or rubber. Nadia had used a bag like that during a kayaking trip one of her friends had suggested. It kept her belongings dry. Was he going swimming?

"So he throws everyone off his trail and heads here anyway. Anyone looking wouldn't think twice. I figure he's far enough ahead of us that he's dreaming up ways to throw us off base. He's probably already here, though we have no way to verify if they've arrived." When he'd secured the top and clicked in the buckle, Ben turned to Will. "We're all set?"

Will clicked a series of keys and then leaned back, his laptop balanced on his knees. "You are now. Kikiaola harbor, one hour. He said you'll know where the keys are."

"And Grant?"

Will shrugged. "Not checking in probably means he went to dinner with the team and can't hear his phone."

Ben turned to Nadia. "Stay here with Will. Bolton and I will be back as soon as we can."

**

"What first?" Bolton glanced at Ben and his bag of tricks as they crossed to the hangar. Inside was a silver Taurus Bolton wouldn't have looked at twice back in the day. He'd driven a Camaro because he respected the classics. Thea had driven a Bentley since she was more about flash. Crime certainly did pay. That was why he was divorced, childless, injured, broke and homeless, hunted, and about to reunite with a woman who hated him.

Things were going real well.

Ben said, "Car to the marina. Boat is the only way to get close enough. Then we have to hike the rest of the way in. Usually they're brought in by helicopter, like one of those scenic tours that show you all the sights and the inaccessible part of the island. Grant explained it all."

Bolton buckled in. "So how do you hide people from nosy tourists with binoculars gaping out a helicopter window?"

"People see what they want to see. A beautiful waterfall, tree tops, and a canyon. Plenty of hiding spots if you can deliver supplies and the residents can adhere to the restrictions on beach visits. Though, it's nowhere near as big as Sanctuary. No sheriff, no mayor."

Bolton would've chosen it, too, if he'd known. "Wouldn't that be nice."

Ben smirked. "Yeah, the Sanctuary mayor is a piece of work. He wanted to arrest me. Apparently I 'assaulted' him."

"Did you?"

"Burden of proof lies on him. Not me." Ben drove the highway that snaked west around the island.

Dante was ahead of them, that was most likely true. Trying to get to Thea, like she needed him to hunt her down when she was busy hiding and being a mom. Bolton had worried more than once if she made a good mother. She wasn't exactly the nurturing type, and he didn't imagine there were many boutiques or salons in an inhospitable canyon. Maybe she'd have rather been in Idaho, in Sanctuary. Why had Grant offered them their respective towns? Bolton imagined the former director had his reasons, whatever they might have been.

Ben pulled into a parking space at the marina. "Time to swim."

"What?"

Ben pointed at a boat anchored off shore. The light on the deck illuminated it. Otherwise they'd never have known it was there. Which, Bolton supposed, was the whole point. "How's your back? Think you'll make it, or is it to be a watery grave for ye."

"Did you just talk like a pirate to me?"

Ben shrugged, and in the dim light, Bolton thought he might have seen a smirk. "Just tell me."

"I'm fine."

"Let's go then."

Shoes off. Ben stowed them in the bag, and they swam to the boat. On board, Ben opened the bag and emptied out all their weapons—dry as the inside of a gun.

Bolton pulled his shoes back on and tapped his earpiece. "We good, Will?"

"All set."

"And Nadia?"

**

Will's reply was immediate. "She's good."

Nadia sipped from the can of diet and stared out the window.

Will reached back for the gun he'd stashed under the tiny airplane pillow.

"Nadia's good."

Chapter 18

"I'm guessing you did a deal with some local, got them to turn a blind eye so you could hide people. The natives walk away with a bunch of the government's money and everyone is safe," Dante glanced back at Grant for a second. "Guess it didn't work." His white teeth flashed in the dark.

Grant trailed behind him, soaked, filthy, and tethered. If it wasn't for the honor guard of men who would shoot him if he even stumbled, he'd have had trouble walking straight. The drug they'd given him to get Grant to spill everything he knew about witness protection towns—which was a lot, though most of it they didn't care about thankfully—was wearing off, but he could still feel it crawling through his system like a thousand fire ants.

He'd lost feeling in his hands before they'd jumped from the boat into chest-height water. He'd never liked the ocean and appreciated it even less now that he'd gotten a wave to the face while his hands were tied together and someone pulled him along. Grant certainly had a greater appreciation now for his grandfather's experience on the beach at Normandy—not that this could be compared.

Give him his girls, his skis, and a black diamond any day. Sand got everywhere, and it wasn't helping the itching.

The barrel of a gun jabbed into his back. Grant stumbled but kept walking, a hike through mushy forest floor and dense trees. The air was thick like steam that left his skin damp and hot. His head swam, but Grant had to be able to think straight if he was going to effectively lead them on a wild Dodo chase through the island of Kauai.

When Dante realized he was stalling, Grant was a dead man. But he had little to lose, and Grant refused to tell them where Thea was.

He'd come to that realization fast, and there had been no question about what he intended to do. Grant knew too many secrets. If he lived, he would always and forever be Ben Mason's biggest weak spot. And his biggest headache. If he died—okay, so it wouldn't be fun. His girls would freak out, and he wouldn't be there to hug them. Grant could only hope their mom would get her head together enough to be a help. But if she couldn't, Grant's mom would. Grandma was one of their favorite people.

The rest of his family would go on without him. Grant only wished he'd had the chance to tell them goodbye.

Grant had "retired" from the US Marshals months ago now, giving this new life a real good try. But it hadn't worked. He simply wasn't built for freelance, and his head contained more secrets than one person should know in a lifetime. As much as it goaded him, Grant was basically a walking, talking threat to national security. It was a wonder he hadn't been locked up.

Since he'd walked out of the Marshals office for the last time, Grant had tried. He really had, but this new life wasn't him. He was supposed to have been a marshal until retirement. Grant's face, his whole life really, was too recognizable to be a help to anyone. Ben was going to have to save Thea and Javier and put right what Bolton and Dante had done. Ben was good at that.

Grant was even willing to pray if that got the job done and God was willing to aid either him or Ben. John was the spiritual one, and their other brother, Nate, called himself a Christian now. Grant had listened, because he was their big brother, but he hadn't understood what they were talking about. Not really.

"Which way?" Dante barked the question.

Grant surveyed the fork in the path. Who knew? He was basically guessing at this point. Not to mention also hoping some crazed local didn't come out with a machete and start a fight with a bunch of armed guys. He didn't need that kind of incident, even if it would solve most of his problems.

"Left." Closer to the interior of the island was better. Heading back to the beach wouldn't work, since that meant they couldn't walk in circles anymore.

They had to be headed somewhere. The beach was bare, and not a convincing hiding place.

It was a miracle he'd been able to regain enough lucidity to understand that he'd spilled the fact there was a second Sanctuary—though much smaller—in Hawaii. He'd thought all Dante knew was that Thea was in this state…until he realized he'd also told them what island the Hawaii Sanctuary was on.

Dante started down the left path, though he gave a long glance to the one on the right. Did he not believe Grant? Too bad. Grant was a marshal, and he would always be a marshal. With or without the badge, Dante was a fugitive. Capturing fugitives would always be Grant's business, and he wouldn't have chosen any other way to leave this world. But first, he needed to leave a warning for the locals.

Grant climbed behind Dante as the path rose in elevation. He scanned the ground with every step until he found what he was looking for—a plant with a leaf-edge that was razor sharp. Grant faked a misstep, stumbled and slipped his hand against the leaf as he went down on one knee.

Hands hauled him back up. Grant gritted his teeth as blood welled in his palm. The first step he took, Grant weaved to the right as though light-headed. Not too much of a stretch. He reached out his bound hands and swiped the bloody one against a tree trunk in the direction they were headed.

Was that the last good thing he would ever do?

**

Bolton skirted the No Trespassing sign and followed Ben between trees, up a hill. Was this even a path? It didn't look worn at all. How did Ben even know where he was going? The questions moved through his mind like an old accounting calculator where the receipt spilled out line after line of numbers. It was that or succumb to the fact that his spine felt like a razor under his skin, or a collection of razors brushing each other at the base of his back.

"We can rest."

Bolton didn't want to, but he nodded.

"Want me to look at it?"

"I'd rather you stuck a needle in there and plunged something numbing into me. Not sure what looking is going to do."

Ben didn't answer, he leaned around Bolton and lifted the back of his shirt. Bolton leaned forward a fraction. It was all he could do.

"I don't think you want to know what this looks like. Maybe you shouldn't be walking around."

"So I rest up, and Dante shoots my son. Great plan."

"You have no faith in me?" Ben stepped back, a wry look on his face. "I can make this work without you."

Bolton sighed. "Once I know they're safe I'll get off my feet."

"Fair enough."

What else was he going to do? Bolton should still be in a bed, recovering from the surgery that felt a lifetime ago now. Was it really only days?

Dante had forced his hand when he abducted Nadia. One of his men had shot Shadrach right in front of him. Now Dante was intent on destroying every other part of Bolton's life.

A rustle in the trees.

Ben whipped around, gun already up before Bolton could stand. The man who emerged from the trees looked like a bigger, younger version of Hal Leonard—all biker clothes, down to the chain that hung in a loop from his belt. A bandana had been tied around his head, disguising whether he had any hair or not. His gun was a gigantic revolver with a white grip.

Bolton reached for his weapon, but Ben put out his hand. "My name is Ben Mason."

"And I'm Michael Jackson. You're trespassing." Despite his joke, the man didn't show any signs of being amused. He was huge, taller than either Ben or Bolton and probably had more than fifty pounds on either of them. Bolton did not want to get punched by those ham-sized fists.

The man lifted a radio from his belt and brought it to his mouth. "Found something. Two somethings actually."

Ben said, "Are you in charge?"

"Of these trees?" The man's reaction didn't look fabricated but Bolton wondered. He was too smooth. He smirked then, but he wasn't the least bit amused. "Or is it the insects I'm to arrest for some infraction?" He spoke like a history teacher and looked like a biker who would ride his Harley into your drive, steal your sister while she smiled the whole time, and ride off never to be seen again.

Bolton didn't trust him at all. "We aren't going to get anywhere if none of us is going to say anything remotely true. So here goes. My name is Bolton Farrera, and I live in a town called Sanctuary."

That got him a reaction.

"If you're in charge here, I'm guessing you're a US marshal. Guarding this otherwise undetectable safe-haven hidden in a place no one would think to look beneath the surface."

"Call me Colt."

"Okay. Colt." Bolton waved toward Ben. "This is my friend, Ben Mason. His brother's name is Grant. Maybe you've heard of him before. He used to be the director of the US Marshals."

"I've heard of him. You too, but never had the pleasure before." The man didn't lower his gun, or move his aim from between the two of them—equal distance from either if they decided to make a move on him. Bolton didn't doubt he shot fast and with lethal accuracy. "So what are Bolton Farrera and Ben Mason doing on my island?"

Bolton couldn't imagine this man in a uniform, and he didn't wear a star badge on his belt. He looked like a normal…biker, out for a walk in the jungle.

Made total sense.

Ben spoke first. "Bringing a warning. If he's not here yet, Dante Alvarez is on his way."

"And why is that my problem? I could shoot both of you, bury you in this dirt, and do the same with this Dante when he gets here. Problem solved." He was so still he barely looked like he was even breathing. "Tell me why I need the two of you."

"You shouldn't underestimate him. He's not just here to visit, he wants to kill Thea Farrera."

"Should I know who that is?"

Bolton wasn't interested in denials. "We know she lives here. She and I…" That was way complicated, this guy would probably shoot them before Bolton was done with the story. "Let's just say she's in danger because of me."

"Then maybe I really should shoot you." The corners of his mouth turned up.

Bolton shrugged. "Go ahead. So long as you warn Thea that Dante is coming, so she can prepare for whatever onslaught he's going to bring."

He thought he caught something on the edge of his vision, a whisper of movement. If he had to guess, Bolton would say there were at least three people hiding in the bushes watching them. This "Colt" wasn't taking any chances. He had come out in force the same way the people of Sanctuary protected their own.

Bolton's town was surrounded by a ring of mountains. These people had water and the rough terrain of this part of Kauai, but they likely got wanderers in their vicinity from time to time. Was this how they dealt with them?

Bolton said, "I understand you want to protect your people, but we have no intention of intruding. And we don't want to know who lives here when it would put their lives in danger. We are bound by the same restrictions you are, though I can't say I wasn't surprised to hear there was another witness protection town. In my Sanctuary we don't ask where a person has come from. We accept them for who they are, and we live and work together to make our lives the best they can be."

Bolton realized that was exactly what Nadia had done with him. While he had kept himself locked safe behind a wall of secrets he didn't want to divulge, she had simply accepted him for the person he had been in Sanctuary. Whether that was the real him or not, he wasn't sure. But maybe he wanted to find out.

Maybe he wanted the chance to see if he could be a good man, one able to love a woman the way she needed to be loved. It was a heady thing. A tempting possibility it would be hard to walk away from. Nadia was a tempting possibility.

Colt nodded. "Pu'u honua is the same way."

"She may not be happy to see me, but please tell Thea that I'm here."

"First you tell me who she is to you."

Bolton nodded much the same as Colt had done. "She was my wife."

A man broke from the trees. On second glance Bolton saw it was a boy, a teen. The boy lifted a gun and fired. Ben's weight slammed into Bolton, and they hit the ground as the gun went off.

**

Will brushed past her chair. He'd put on his jacket, and now he went to the door with his cell phone in his hand. "I'm going out for a cigarette."

"Okay." What else was she supposed to say? It wasn't like he was confined to the plane the way she was.

He left the door open, and she heard his steps descend the metal stairs.

Nadia lifted up from her chair and peered over the back of the seat. The laptop faced her, screen on. Locked. She'd need his password to get on there. Or Remy to hack into it.

She wanted to ask Remy how her brother was doing. She wanted to call Bolton and make sure he was still okay.

Anything.

But she'd been benched, not that there was a whole lot she could do besides chase after them and try to catch up. If she had any idea where they'd gone.

Nadia got up and walked around just for the sake of stretching her legs. At least when this was over she'd be able to return to Sanctuary knowing it was done. She'd end up reading about it in some newspaper article weeks after the fact, instead of always wondering what had happened between Dante and Bolton.

Will stood at the bottom of the steps…but not smoking. He was on his phone, gesturing wildly. A hard look had settled on his face, so different from his usually unruffled demeanor. He paced two steps then back, and spoke into his phone. She couldn't hear the words, but they were bit out between gritted teeth.

He waved his arm, and she saw it. The flash of metal. A gun, tucked in his waistband. If it was to protect her, he certainly wasn't paying attention to her right now.

His face paled, and he lowered his phone to stare at the screen. A picture flashed there, and Will looked like he was going to be sick. He put the phone to his ear again and bit out more hard words she couldn't read off his lips.

He hung up then. Nadia stepped back so he didn't see her at the window. Why she felt the need to hide from him Nadia wasn't sure, but everything in her screamed retreat. She rushed to her bag and pulled out Shadrach's gun, the one he carried with him everywhere—except when he was injured in the hospital.

Nadia held it by her side, out of sight, while Will ascended the steps. His eyes were dark, and he looked on the verge of tears. "I'm really sorry about this Nadia." He started to reach for where the gun was. "I—"

Nadia aimed at his forehead. Shadrach had told her it was way scarier than aiming at someone's center mass. Let them think she had the skills to hit that spot between their eyes. He'd been smiling when he'd said it, but it was true. Shadrach was right. Maybe he'd always been right.

Will's eyes widened.

"Pull your gun out. Slowly. Drop it on the floor."

"Na—"

"I will kill you. Do not test me." Shadrach had taught her the scary voice, too. Authority, strength, and a don't-mess-with-me attitude. "Drop it, Will."

He lowered in a crouch and set the gun on the carpet.

"Your phone now. Drop it on the floor."

He tossed it on the floor even as fear flashed on his face. "Let me speak, please." Desperation laced his voice.

She could refuse, clock him over the head. Take his phone as she ran out. Or she could hear him out. "You have thirty seconds."

"You don't understand." He gasped.

Don't-mess-with-me Nadia would shoot him if he cried, she didn't do "emotions." But hopefully it wouldn't come to that. "Twenty seconds."

"There are things you don't know. Things going on that—"

The phone screen. The call he'd taken outside, and the way he'd looked. "Dante has something on you. Or someone."

Will nodded, frantic.

He'd been working behind the scenes for Dante the entire time. She could hardly believe there was a traitor so close to them, and Ben didn't even know. They'd never have left her here otherwise.

Puzzle pieces clicked in her head as she saw everything now in the light of this new information. "Are you the reason he knew exactly why I was in the bank before I'd even explained it all? You've been feeding him inside information this whole time. Admit it. It was how he got a man into the theater to shoot Shadrach, wasn't it?"

It was all so clear now.

Will said, "Your brother was the only one with no knowledge of Bolton's stash. Dante had to take out someone, and Shadrach was low on the totem pole. His plan is methodical to the point of exactitude. He intends to completely destroy everyone and everything in Bolton's life, and then take everything that he has left. After that he's going to kill him. You have no idea how ruthless this man is."

Nadia laughed, a sound completely devoid of humor. "I'm pretty sure I have an idea how evil he is."

"I'm sorry. I didn't know he'd try to *sell* you." Will said it like it was distasteful. At least he had some morals left.

Nadia didn't let the gun waver even an inch. "What does he hold over your head?"

Will swallowed. "He has my wife and daughter." When she said nothing, he motioned for his phone. "Can I show you?"

Nadia nodded. Would he do to them what he'd done to her? Will's wife, and a *child*. She wanted to be sick.

Will unlocked the phone and turned it so she could see it. "He took them two weeks ago. I had to tell him something so he'd stop threatening them, so I gave him your identity. From the minute you met with Ben and Shadrach at that house, Dante has known exactly who you are." Will pulled in a breath. "I'm the reason he went after your mother."

At least that had turned out in their favor. Though the only reason—again—was Shadrach's having taught both her, and apparently their mom, the skills they needed to save their lives.

"He said he was going to cut off my daughter's hand."

Nadia stared at the phone screen. The kid was cute, even scared like that. Probably around ten. She didn't need this affecting her young life in the way it was going to. "And you didn't tell Ben?"

"Dante was going to cut off. My. Daughter's. Hand."

"Call him."

"What?"

Nadia said, "Call Dante."

"What? Why? I'm only supposed to keep you here until" —he swallowed— "I'm supposed to make a video…of your death. So he can show it to Bolton when he finally gets the stash, and he's brought Bolton down as low as he's going to go."

"What is it with you people and videos?" Nadia said it under her breath, but Will heard.

"I'm not one of them!"

"Call Dante," she yelled back. "Tell him it's done. Tell him I'm dead."

Will shook his head. "What are you going to do?"

Nadia shoved past him and went to the door of the plane that he'd left open. "If I don't tell you then he can't torture it out of you, now, can he?"

Chapter 19

Gemma sat with her back to the wall, surrounded by a stack of papers. File after file had been locked away in a secret room in her father's radio station. He'd...

She could barely process all the things he'd done.

They began even before Vietnam, after a three-year stint in prison. Back when actual paper records were kept. He'd been released from prison in time to be drafted, according to the paperwork she'd read through. And yet, there was something so...sterile about this official documentation. Almost like it was only a label that indicated what had happened in very general terms.

A door being shut vibrated through the thin walls. Gemma had closed the door behind her and shut out the radio room. Like she could contain this big of a secret. It was probably Andra coming in to turn on the radio. Or to look around and remember Hal. Gemma didn't have any of those experiences.

She'd never been outside the mountains of Sanctuary, and her mom had told her that if she elected to leave—which meant she would never be able to return—she would be killed. So why go, even if she was curious enough to wonder about the outside world? The mystery of it all was what killed her. He'd lied to her for years, never once mentioning that they had any other connection than simply being residents of the same secret town. The *why*—that was what ate at her.

Hal Leonard had clearly done some...colorful things. Okay, so he'd killed people. In Vietnam some of his missions had involved delivering messages through enemy territory. She didn't understand half the military jargon, but some of it seemed to indicate he'd bought and sold weapons. Or been involved in it, or maybe found out who was doing it. Maybe he'd been some kind of investigator. Gemma couldn't make sense of the whole, only pieces.

Like who this missing person was they had so much paperwork on.

She blew out a breath and set the stack of papers on the floor by her hip. The mystery wouldn't be solved sitting here reading papers more than forty years old. She should go by her mom's house again, make her open the door this time.

Tap, tap. Pause. *Tap, tap.* Pause. *Tap, tap.*

The sound started in the corner to her right, moved all the way to her back, and then past her to the left corner. Someone was...

Looking for the room Gemma was in.

**

"You give me that gun now, son." Colt's voice didn't give the kid any option but to let go of the gun he'd just fired at Bolton.

His back on the ground, Bolton stared up at the boy. He had Thea's eyes. Bolton's heart clenched even as his stomach turned over. This was his son, and he'd just taken a shot at Bolton because of it.

Ben held out his hand, so Bolton grabbed it. He wasn't too proud to accept a hand to get up, but that didn't mean he wanted anyone to know how much it hurt. He'd landed funny on the ground, and his back felt like he was a hair from collapsing altogether.

Bolton hissed out a breath from between his teeth. "Javier?"

"Figures you know who I am." The kid spoke over Colt's arm, stretched across the front of his body, restraining his shoulders. "Are you here to kill me, too?" He struggled against Colt's arm. "Let me go, Colt. I have to warn her he's here. He's found us, and now he's going to kill us."

Colt started to argue, but the boy fought his way free and ran into the trees. He spun back, an accusatory stare in his eyes. "That true?"

"Would you believe me if I said no?" Bolton didn't even know how to answer. The kid was convinced he was here to kill him? "What has Thea told him about me that he thinks his own father is here to kill him?" He glanced at Ben, but got no answer there.

Colt's eyebrow rose—the one not pierced. "His father?"

Bolton sighed. "What now?"

"Neither of you step one foot into my town. Not when you're going to upset them."

"We have to make sure Dante doesn't get in."

Colt studied Bolton and Ben, as though he didn't know who the threat was: them or the man they claimed was coming. "Give me your guns and I'll take you there."

Ben didn't look impressed but handed over a Sig he'd had in a shoulder holster. Bolton gave Colt his gun, too. Colt checked each as it was handed to him and then stashed both in the back of his jeans.

"Let's go."

He waved them to go ahead of him, up a path through the trees. Colt's radio crackled. "Got a situation."

Bolton glanced back to see Colt lift his radio. "What is it?"

"Blood. A mile out, north-north-west on the Yancey fork."

"Any sign of anyone?" Colt sounded cautious but not worried. He projected total calm. The way John Mason did when crazy was breaking loose in Sanctuary—as though he could maintain order simply by projecting an air of being in control.

"Not yet. But Phil is checking it out. He thinks its Grant Mason."

"Shoulder height on a tree? Like he swiped his hand across it?"

"That's right. How'd you know that, Colt?"

"He's under duress. The swipe tells you which way he's going."

"But he's moving in the wrong direction if he's warning us that he's headed to town. He's going to pass right by us going that way."

"He might be under duress, but Grant isn't going to let them find us." Colt's eyes locked with Bolton's. "Alert everyone, we're under emergency protocols. I've got Ben Mason—correction, I *had* Ben Mason. He gave me the slip."

Bolton swung around. Sure enough, Ben had disappeared. Probably took the opportunity to skip out and help his brother while Colt was distracted. Leaving Bolton to deal with his family dysfunction all by himself. *Thanks a lot, brother.* So much for backup. If his son was willing to take a shot at him, who knew what Thea would do when he showed up?

"Guess it's just us."

Bolton started up walking again, though his gait had a hitch to it. He couldn't help it, there was no way to disguise the fact each step burned like fire in his back. Maybe, for the rest of his life, what Dante had done to him would be there with every movement of his body. A cloud of vengeance that never lifted. A poison that had saturated every part of him.

Nadia had told him one night, in their tiny apartment, that God had swept through her life and put everything right. But He wasn't going to fix Bolton's back. It wasn't like God would let him live pain free when it was Bolton's doing that he was injured this way in the first place. He had to live with the choices he'd made. Nadia had found peace living in Sanctuary. That town was the consequence of everyone's choice. She'd liked it, which meant Nadia deserved to live in a place where she was happy. But not Bolton.

Consequences were good or bad, depending on the person. And while clearly Nadia was a good person, the bad consequences she had suffered were because of her association with him. The quicker she got back to Sanctuary the better, as far as he was concerned. Then she'd be free of his influence. Because as much as Bolton might want to stay in her life, Nadia couldn't afford to have him stain everything she knew and everyone she loved with his influence.

He'd caused her pain for weeks, and he'd watched her diminish before his eyes. He'd been instrumental in the fact Dante captured her, and she'd nearly been taken into a life he didn't even want to think about.

Once this was done, they'd make sure she got back to Sanctuary where she was safe, where people loved her openly, where her life was happy. And Bolton would walk away.

He would cherish forever the memory of her smile, of her carefree nature that he'd experienced in Sanctuary. But he couldn't share that life with her. Ever since the medical center in town had exploded, things had been different. Neither of them had been able to ignore what was building between them. But it could never be. Bolton had to break it off, now that he knew she was safe. He had to walk away.

Because it was the only way Nadia would be really, truly happy.

**

"Thanks, Remy." Nadia hung up the payphone and strode immediately toward the marina, where boat after boat could be rented out. She walked past all the tourist boats, all the way to the end where an older man in a worn

T-shirt, denim shorts, and flip flops peered through his long hair at her as he sat in a deck chair, drinking from a long-necked bottle.

"How much for you to take me up the coast and drop me off?"

His chest jerked, but no sound emerged. The man's lips curled up as he took another sip. What was so funny?

He wiped his beard with the back of his hand. "Thirty thousand dollars."

"Ten."

He chuckled soundlessly once again. "I don't take credit cards."

Nadia slipped the backpack from her shoulder, unzipped it, and tossed it on the deck. Stacks of bills spilled out. "Good thing I made a withdrawal this morning."

That got the man's attention.

Sure, this tactic had bitten her once before. But now she had a gun. If the man tried anything, she'd just shoot him and take his boat anyway. And keep her money this time.

He unfolded his lanky body from the chair, lean for an old guy. Muscles toned from weathering big waves and his hands worn from the ropes onboard. Fishing nets. Poles. "Get aboard, woman. The meter's running."

Nadia smiled and hopped onto the deck.

Finally, things were going to plan. Thanks to Remy she knew exactly where everyone was. She had a new phone and internet. Weapons. Once she got to Pu'u honua she would be able to warn Ben and Bolton that Dante was already here—and that he had Grant. She could warn them Will had been feeding their enemy information for weeks.

Thank you, Lord. God had been protecting her, seeing her through this whole thing. And now he'd given her another opportunity to be there to help. Sure, she wasn't a trained agent, but neither was she the kind of woman who sat around. That had been proven.

Bolton seemed to think she was just going to go home, and that would be that. Like living in Sanctuary was the only solution. And not just that, but living there without him? Not her first choice. Somehow she had to convince him that it would only be worth going back there if he came with her. Because what was the point in her watching everything she'd ever wanted fly away in a helicopter and knowing she was never going to see him again?

Nadia gritted her teeth. Bolton was so set on living his own life, maybe he deserved to realize what being alone felt like.

Lord, help me keep loving him.

She wanted to know what connection felt like. John and Andra had it. Matthias and Frannie. Even Beth and Sam. Everything in Nadia *yearned* to know what it felt like, to belong to someone so completely that you were their whole world.

Why couldn't she have that?

Psalms said God would give her the desires of her heart, but she couldn't ask for this. It was too much, too selfish. Didn't those desires have to be pure in motive before God would give them to her? That seemed like it should be a thing, not using His power for her own gain. Sure, God wanted to bless her with good things, but she had to be wise with it, otherwise, she was only in this to have her own needs met. What about giving away the gift she'd been given, to other people, so that they were blessed by what God had done in her? It didn't seem right to get caught up in what she could get out of this relationship. That wasn't healthy.

Tell that to her heart.

Nadia gripped the edge of the boat as they motored out into open waters, and the owner kept them parallel to the shore. As they sailed north, she prayed harder than she ever had for strength.

**

Colt grabbed Bolton's arm and set him in a chair. Bolton couldn't quite silence the groan. The room was open, wood paneled walls, and shutters instead of glass. They probably barely kept the rain out. A bare bulb lit the room, a pull cord dangling down. It looked like a jungle interrogation room run by some local cartel, or a revolutionary force.

Colt looked like he was going to ask about Bolton's obvious pain, so he said, "Nice place." He couldn't figure out how people actually lived here. All there had been was one hut in the trees. Where did everyone else stay? How many people lived here? Were the houses underground?

Colt pulled out his radio. "We're clear."

"Understood." Thea.

Bolton sucked in a breath and turned his head to the door. "Is she coming in here? Are you going to let her shoot me, too?"

"That depends on Thea. Her son seemed to think you need to die."

My son. Bolton could hardly say it. Could hardly believe that years of knowing he'd never see his boy, but dreaming of it still, had culminated in the kid trying to shoot him.

"I don't know you." Colt folded his arms. "My town is under siege, and you likely have answers. So I guess we'll find out if Thea feels the need to take her vengeance on you." He shrugged. "One less thing for me to figure out."

He had to know what Thea was like. If Colt really was the person in charge around here—Bolton was beginning to doubt if he was a marshal—he had to know that Thea lied as easily as she breathed. That she complained about anything even remotely not to her satisfaction until Bolton had simply given in to get her to stop whining. How she'd survived here was a mystery, given it was pretty rustic.

She'd have driven everyone crazy in Sanctuary, too. That was certain. Wherever she went, Thea had left a trail of people who wanted nothing more than to get rid of her. Unless she'd simply fooled them all with that sickly sweet act that she'd used on Bolton. The one that wore off fast when he'd begun to have ideas about anything contrary to her opinion.

It had been a long three years, even though there were some good times. At least he thought he might have been able to remember some. Still, despite all the regret wrapped up in Javier, Bolton had honestly been a little relieved when she'd walked away.

The door opened, and Thea walked in. Silk blouse, cargo pants that hugged her figure like cling wrap, suede boots, and short hair that was spiked out in the back. She looked like Halle Berry. Her makeup was heavy but flawless. Bolton could count on one hand the times he'd seen her face clean of products. He stared at her, hardly even knowing what he was supposed to say.

Apparently she knew, because she set her hand on her hip and fired off a shot. "Are you here to kill us?"

"Why would I do that?"

"Why else would you show up, Bolton?"

"I'd have to actually hate you in order to want to kill you, Thea. And while you annoy me, tremendously, and there's a great deal of frustration wrapped up in there, I can't exactly say I hate you. Might be close, though, but Colt here took my gun."

Her head whipped to the other man in the room. "You can't give me privacy right now? You have to stick your nose in this, too?"

Colt sighed. The slight smile that had edged onto his lips while Bolton had spoken disappeared now. He glanced at Bolton. "Maybe I should be worried about her killing you."

Bolton shrugged. "If you could talk a person to death I'd be long gone already."

Colt chuckled. "I hear ya."

"Ex*cuse* me."

"No," Bolton said. "You know what, Thea? No. I came here because Dante is on his way. You aren't safe, and neither are these people. This town, if it even is a whole one, could be exposed."

She reacted. Spine straightening, lips thinning.

He turned to Colt. "Either you have defenses, in which case we employ them. Or we are the defense. In my town there's bunker where everyone was protected."

Colt nodded. "A cave."

"The alternative is we get everyone out of here. Now."

Colt lifted his radio. "All units, this is Colt. Get everyone to the south corner and wait for instructions."

"Copy."

"Copy."

"Copy."

The word came over his radio two more times. Colt clipped his radio back on his belt. "So what do we do while everyone hides?"

"Hides?" Thea set her hands on both hips. "We can't hide. He'll find us."

There was something off about how she said it, but Bolton couldn't nail down what it was. It had been too long since he'd seen her. His son had to be at least twelve. "You should get Javier to safety."

"Don't you say his name! You abandoned us," she hissed.

"You're the one who left." No one had whined at him for years, and he didn't miss it. But he had to focus. "Get your son to safety, and I'll make sure Dante doesn't get to you. That's why I came here." He paused. "Javier is—" He didn't even know how to answer that.

His voice had a hard edge to it, he heard it, and it was one she brought out in him. They'd never backed down, either of them, not once in a fight. That was why her divorcing him had made so little sense. He figured she'd rather have made his life miserable for eternity, the way he'd planned to do with her. Then a child came along, and she'd left. It still made no sense to him, no matter how long he thought about it.

"When this is done, you and I will have a conversation about how you kept my child from me and why the first time he saw me, that child tried to kill me." Bolton had to take a breath. "You took that from me, Thea. And I want an answer. When I'm satisfied, then I'll be leaving. But not before."

"You can't do this," she hissed.

"Go and protect your son."

He glanced away, dismissing her. If things went any further she'd know he couldn't get out of this chair. Bolton's legs had numbed to the point he wasn't convinced they would hold his weight.

Thea slammed the door behind her.

"You guys have a doctor?"

Colt lifted his chin. "What do you need?"

**

Ben crept through the trees. He shifted a giant leaf silently and peered through. Dante. Four men. Grant in the middle, hands tied. The path was a decent choke point if Ben could get ahead of them. He had enough guns he could take out maybe three before one got off a shot. Ben had no body armor, but he could get it off one of these guys after he killed them.

Men he'd hired to protect his brother. Men who had betrayed that trust and taken his brother right to the man he was trying to find.

Ben wasn't sure whether to shake their hands first before he killed them.

Grant stumbled. He was sweating pretty well, but he was in one piece. Ben had known he wasn't cut out for this life, but Grant hadn't been content being the corporate face of Ben's organization despite his extensive Washington contacts. The man had pull, that couldn't be denied. Field work had been about Ben making his brother feel useful, but hopefully Grant had that out of his system by now.

Ben lifted his hands to his mouth and sounded the call of a bird native to their home state.

Grant froze.

The man behind Grant shoved him forward. "Keep moving."

Ben set off through the trees.

Chapter 20

Ben readied himself. Grant wasn't going to last much longer before he either collapsed. Or snapped and forced Ben to move because he was tired of waiting.

Dante's phone rang.

"What?" Dante glanced up and stared at the sky. "She was supposed to be taken care of, and you tell me she's loose and ready to cause trouble? If she gets in the way, it's your family who will suffer. Understand me, Will?"

Ben took a breath to process the fact a man he trusted was being coerced into helping Dante. Dante had a man on the inside of Ben's organization for long enough Will could have done some serious damage. And Nadia was gone. He pulled out the burner phone Will had given him. Even if it was compromised, Ben didn't have much choice. Will had a family? Since when?

He sent a text to Remy and got a reply within seconds.

`She's fine. Boat ride to help you.`

One more player Ben needed to keep safe. His life was a chess board. King and pawns. Knights determined to help, who wound up getting in the way instead of being useful. All to protect a queen, one well and truly able to protect herself—and who wanted nothing to do with him.

Nadia fit in that mix somewhere, while Ben tried to move the pieces as much as he could control.

He texted her back about the town's emergency protocols.

`His name is Paul.`

He'd met Colt, but who was Paul?

Dante spoke into the phone. "Get me a location on this place I'm going. I want to know if the director is leading me the right way." He swung around and glared at Grant. "Great." Dante muttered, hung up, and stowed his phone away. When he turned back, Dante swung out with the butt of his gun and slammed it into Grant's temple.

Ben watched his brother slump onto the dirt and groan about a chocolate ice cream.

Dante leaned down. "What did you say?"

The smile curled Ben's lips nonetheless. *So impatient.* He readied both weapons and stepped out. Simultaneous shots took out the first two. Grant kicked out and swiped Dante's legs from under him. Three and four turned, and he put a bullet in both.

Dante moved to fire at Ben, but he fired first. Always quicker on the draw. Always. Ben shot the bullet maybe a hair from Dante's hand. He dropped the gun, eyes wide. "Ben Mason."

"You think I'd let you traipse out here with my brother and not come?"

"Oh no." Dante mock-gasped. "I *never* thought of that."

Ben kicked the weapon from each man, not that the four were getting up. It was the principle of disarming them. "I wonder how you managed to convince the DEA you were stable long enough to get through the hiring process." He kicked away Dante's gun and then cut Grant's bonds before he helped his brother to his feet.

"Looks like we found our prize." Grant smiled.

Ben wasn't so sure. "Any more of your men out here in this jungle?"

Dante lifted his eyebrows. "And if there were? You think I'd let them finish this when I could do it myself?"

Ben had to cover the variables fast, given the man looked that smug. "I think they'll bring Thea to you."

The man's eyes narrowed a fraction. "Interesting."

Ben hauled him up and patted him down before he secured the man's hands. "You might have escaped from federal prison but your fun is over. Time to go back."

"You think I'm going back there?" He barked a laugh. "Tristan will have me killed before I even get through the doors. He paid the Haitians to stab me at breakfast, and I barely got away. Wasn't gonna hang around for the next time."

"How did you escape?"

"Trade secret."

Ben had assumed he'd simply had friends on the outside who helped him. But not Tristan? The bug Ben planted in Tristan's house hadn't yielded as much as he'd hoped, but it appeared Dante and Tristan were at war.

"Is Tristan coming here?"

"Your man, Will, didn't know that. Didn't know much in fact. I'll have to let them know to kill his wife and daughter, so he knows exactly how helpful he was."

Ben shared a look with Grant and then pulled out his phone. He couldn't call Daire—the man was on personal time, and that meant no one could disturb him. It was the first rule of their company. The earth could be about to explode, but you didn't get a man off his vacation. Nothing was more important than leave.

Shadrach was in hospital. That only left outsourcing the search for Will's family for the time being. Ben called a man who worked in his field, a man whom Ben didn't know all that well except that Daire referred to him as "the boy scout." He was ex-Delta Force, freelance now. Rumor was he'd married a CIA double agent and settled down to a quiet life of private ops. Ben filled the man in and got an assurance he'd look into it.

Satisfied for the time being, he hung up and texted Remy to find out where Tristan was. If he was on the island, Ben wanted to know before he walked into the man's sights.

Grant subjected Dante to much the same treatment he'd received. They changed directions and headed down to the water. He didn't want Dante anywhere near the town or the people who lived there.

"If you want to check on the residents here, you're going the wrong way."

Ben shook his head as they walked. "You think I'm taking you there? You're crazy. Like I'd let you get anywhere near Bolton's ex-wife and his son? I'm not going to let you even see them, let alone hurt them just to get revenge on Bolton for testifying against you."

Dante trudged along in front. "You think that's why I'm here? To kill them." He barked a laugh. "You do. Oh, that's precious. Had you all fooled, but it looks like you're in for a surprise when you figure it out. Protecting people. You're so good at it, aren't you? The U.S. Marshals, oldest federal agency, all the good ole boys in their chaps with that star on their belt walking around like they're better than everyone else."

"We are." Grant's words echoed off into nothing.

"Not anymore you're not. You'll take anyone in, but do you know everything? No. The DEA is nothing but a bunch of cartel wannabe's to you. A bunch of dirty feds you wanna lock up, like you don't deserve the same for protecting murderers and thieves just for squealing for you."

"Thank you, for that completely insulting over-generalization of the good work the marshals' service does. And yes," Grant said, "the DEA is nothing but a bunch of cartel wannabe's. You know how I know that? Because of you. Lily white on the surface, flashing that badge everywhere you went. But underneath the table you're taking bribes, transporting drugs, and pocketing the profits."

"And Bolton? An FBI wannabe pretending to be a good guy while it's useful. The minute it doesn't go his way he's back to lying, stealing from me, and burying it in that stash."

**

They'd passed two sets of warning signs and gone through a gate that stretched across the river in a spot where it narrowed to less than eight feet. Nadia had thought it locked until the old man entered a code and clicked the padlock open.

"Kind of interesting," the older man said as he piloted the boat upriver between two fields of coconut palms, toward a dock. Nadia glanced at him. "You wanting to be brought to this exact spot when locals don't even know the dock exists. They've all heard the legends of the man-eating catfish that lives up here."

He grinned, which emphasized the lines around his eyes. This man had laughed often, and yet there was a darkness there now. "They say he protects a group of people who live in this 'uninhabited' portion of the island. Like some giant guardian…you know…*fish*."

Nadia wanted to laugh, but this guy might know something. He might be able to help her get to Bolton faster. "Aren't there helicopter tours? You'd think tourists would see someone on the ground as they were flying overhead."

"People see what they wanna see," he said. "The waterfall, the canyon. Tiny person in a sea of palms? Not so much."

Nadia folded her arms. "So there *are* people who live here secretly?"

He grinned and shook his head. "You're the one who wants to risk the wrath of the guardian and go looking."

"Question is, are you going to help me or stop me?"

"Depends on you, little lady."

She stared at him. "Who are you?"

"You mean, can you trust me?"

Nadia shrugged. "Kind of the same thing. Depending."

He navigated to the dock, jumped out, and then tied up the boat. A phone rang. The man reached in his pocket and pulled out a satellite phone.

Nadia stared. Should she make a run for it?

"Yep." His eyes narrowed on her as he listened. "I see. Thanks for the info." He locked the phone and tossed it on the dash. "Nadia Marie Carleigh. You wanna tell me how a resident of *not here* shows up at the wrong Sanctuary?"

How did he…

The man was working for, or with, someone who had access to information that was supposed to be buried. Someone like Remy. Or the federal government. She'd been so wrapped up in the adrenaline—about getting there to warn them Dante was here, how he'd been one step ahead of them—that she hadn't even noticed.

She said, "I'm here to warn them about the danger. Dante is here, on Kauai, and I don't know how you hide these people but they *can* be found. Nowhere is completely secure. We found that out when a rogue SEAL tried to blow up our town."

Crusty eyebrows rose. "I heard they made a lake out of the hole."

"They…what?" She shook her head. "What's important is that the people who live here are in danger, and I have information pertinent to helping them."

"You say Dante is already here?"

She nodded, suddenly wary. There were things he needed to know. But what if he was like Will, coerced into being on Dante's side? Or what if he worked for Tristan? There had been so many varying hues of gray in her formerly black and white world that she didn't even know where on the scale this man was going to fall. Right now she didn't even know where she fell. All she knew was that no one was totally innocent.

He opened a cabinet at the front of the ship, pulled out a shotgun, and then a handgun. He stowed the handgun in the back of his belt and switched out his flip flops for sneakers. As he stood, he pumped the barrel of the shotgun. "Let's go."

Nadia raced after him. "You're going to help me?"

"The day Dante Alvarez escaped from federal prison it hit the wires that certain people we protect could be in danger. That's why I was sent here." He glanced back with a neutral look on his face. *Just doing my job.* Probably with a *ma'am* at the end of it. "My job is to blend in, to watch the perimeter and keep an eye out for anyone coming and going. You're the first who showed up with a story and a good reason to make contact with Colt."

"Who is Colt?"

"Tried to make him the mayor, but he refused."

Nadia shuddered.

"Something personal you have against mayors?"

"The one in my town isn't so good."

"Colt is…well, he's just Colt, really. You either like him or you don't. Not that I've ever met the man, but I've seen his type plenty of times." He stopped, looked both ways, and then continued. "I read his file. Or at least, the parts I was allowed to read."

"If you haven't made contact, how do you know where they are?"

"I was read in on the town, along with a zillion page confidentiality agreement that's an addendum to the zillion page contract that gets signed when a marshal does anything with witness protection."

"So you are a marshal."

"I didn't say that?" He stopped and cocked his head to the side then stuck his hand out. "Deputy Inspector Paul Harrell."

"You already know my name."

"Know more than that." He blew out a breath and continued walking. "One thing you can say for this state, they certainly know how to make sure you get your ten thousand steps in."

Nadia smiled. She felt more at ease than she had in weeks, lost in the woods with a stranger. At least, she hoped they weren't lost. "It's nice to meet you, Paul."

He chuckled. "Come on then, girlie. You can help me bring Dante Alvarez in, and I'll split the glory with you. But the commendation I'm keeping for myself, you understand?"

"I totally understand."

"So tell me, who are we up against besides Dante. Any other players in this I should know about?"

"Sure." Nadia tried to breathe as she climbed the hill after him. She really was getting a work out, only the kind where sweat covered your whole body and fainting wasn't out of the question. "Well, a friend of mine, Bolton Farrera is here."

"Yep, got read up on him."

"And Ben Mason. Plus I think his brother Grant is missing, and Remy said he was here, too." Nadia glanced up a split second before she slammed into his back. He'd stopped. "What?"

"Ben and Grant Mason?" Paul's eyebrow rose. "Both of them?"

"I think so. Things have been squiffy since I got kidnapped, so it's hard to say. But Ben is here for sure."

"Well. Okay then." He swallowed. "Let's keep walking."

**

Bolton had six weapons hidden on his person. As he readied the seventh—a shotgun—a helicopter flew overhead of the cabin he'd been brought to.

"Not good."

He glanced at Colt, who frowned. "I take it the chopper isn't one of yours?"

Colt shook his head. "Not a scenic tour, either, flying low like that." He grabbed his radio. "Anyone got a '20' on that helicopter? I want eyes. Find out who it is."

Bolton waited until he was done barking orders. Whoever he was, Colt was clearly in charge. "Our Sanctuary, we get military deliveries each week. Supplies, mail, that kind of thing."

"No mail around here," Colt said. "No phones, no communication of any kind. We're totally cut off. Supplies and mail come in once a week, middle of the night. A ship off shore drops it over the side. Tide washes it in, done."

"All your food?"

"What we don't grow or catch, yeah." Colt shrugged like it was no big deal to be entirely and completely separated from the rest of the world. There could be people who lived here who didn't even know that 9/11 had happened, not unless they got the newspaper. It would be a particular kind of torture to receive no news from outside and then have to scour those columns of text to find out what was going on in the world.

Bolton tried to process why the marshal's service would feel the need to cut off these residents in that way. Were they dangerous or in danger? "Who do you have here?"

Colt didn't answer.

Bolton came at it from a different angle. "How many of you are there?"

"Fifteen. Give or take Chuck. He likes to roam the woods when he's in a mood, stays gone for days at a time usually."

"Fifteen." Bolton could hardly contemplate being forced to live in such a small community. Everyone already thought they knew his business in his town, but if there were only enough people to fill one large dining table the way his mom had forced them to on holidays, then everyone would know what he did every second of the day. Bolton was pretty sure he would be that guy who disappeared into the trees for days. It was that or, you know, *friendship*.

"More than that in your town?"

Bolton nodded. "We're bumping two hundred."

"Seriously?" Colt blew out a breath. "I didn't even know there were that many people in witness protection at any given time."

"That's only the ones who can't show their faces in any regular city, so they hide them in my town. I guess you got the ones that need even greater security than Sanctuary provides." Maybe they were a danger to anyone they came into contact with. Otherwise, why cut them off from communicating even when it might be completely benign?

Who was Colt?

"I guess so." The man gave absolutely nothing away. He could probably talk himself in or out of anything, while Bolton had been forced to learn how to do that.

Lucky for him, Ben had taught him how to lie his way out of a tight spot.

The radio crackled to life. "Colt."

He lifted it to his mouth. "Go ahead."

"Caught sight of the chopper after it hovered over the ridge. Six men, full tactical gear. Whoever's coming, they're here. Sent a team to do the job, and they mean business."

"Tell everyone to back off. Hole up in your spots."

"Copy."

Four more distinctive voices repeated the communication.

Colt stowed the radio on his belt. "Time to move." He was already out the door.

Bolton's back certainly had something to say about his sudden need to move around. The shot of adrenaline had gotten him up. Colt's poor excuse for a medic happened to have been an army ranger but knew nothing about complicated spinal procedures. Unfortunately. But Bolton wasn't exactly raring to go.

"I'm not going to let them get near Thea or Javier. If you tell me where my family is hiding I can guard them until Ben gets back. And one of those radios wouldn't go amiss."

Colt's mouth curled up. "Nice try, but you don't leave my sight. By my guess, Thea grabbed Javier, and she's long gone."

Bolton's middle turned to stone. He lifted a gun and pointed it directly at Colt. "You know this terrain. Which way did she go, and how far did she get?"

"Or you'll shoot me?" Colt didn't back down even an inch.

Neither did Bolton. "Tell me where to find her."

"Thea is no business of yours. Not anymore. But you're here, which means you get to assist in the protection of my town."

Bolton didn't lower his gun. "Did you have someone follow Ben?"

"You really think I'd let two strangers into my town and not enact every protective measure I have at my disposal? These aren't victims kept here." Colt let one eyebrow rise. "Now put the gun down before one of my men puts a bullet in your back. We have less than two minutes until either that tactical team gets here, or your friend gets back with his brother and the man they're escorting."

Bolton glanced over his shoulder and then the other. Two men flanked his back, weapons pointed at him. "Like I don't have enough back problems I need you to shoot me there, too?"

"You so much as move in a way I don't like." He waited for Bolton to lower his gun, then said, "Now we go hunting."

Colt set a punishing pace. They tore through trees and bushes in an arc until Colt gave the signal to hold. Two men caught up to crouch with them behind foliage. Rough men.

The tactical team strode down a winding path ten feet away. Machine guns. They looked like soldiers, probably hired guns. *Tristan.* He was in the center, men at his front and back. Cover against whoever they met with. Bolton had no way to get word to Ben. Brotherly loyalty just might be overriding everything at the moment, which didn't bode well for the rest of them.

He needed Ben on the big picture, not just out to save his brother. Bolton glanced at the men with him, they were not trained soldiers. Not that Bolton was, but he knew enough to spot one.

Colt whispered into his radio. "Get eyes on Mason."

"On it. They're just—"

The voice broke off with a crack of gunfire over the radio.

Chapter 21

Nadia's lungs burned from the exertion. Clearly Paul was in better shape than she was, though she wasn't about to admit it. After all, he hadn't had the week she'd had. There was no contest. Paul's stride slowed, and she came to a stop behind him.

A woman followed by a teen boy made their way at a fast clip down the path toward them. Both were carrying guns.

"Weapons down, people," Paul said.

The woman lifted her gun so fast Nadia hardly saw the movement with her eyes. She squeezed off one shot, and Paul spun. His body fell back into the brush.

"Why did you—" Nadia moved toward him. Was Paul dead? And who was this woman? It couldn't be Thea, could it?

She fired again, closer to Nadia but still at the ground.

Nadia froze. "You're going to shoot me, too? I don't even know who you are."

"Like that's a reason not to kill you?"

The boy stood beside her, a little back from—presumably, given the resemblance—his mom's shoulder. His eyes were blank. What had he gone through that he saw his mom shoot a man and didn't react at all?

"Gun on the ground."

Nadia crouched and laid Will's gun down. When she straightened, she lifted both hands palms out. "What now?"

"New plan." She pulled a phone from her pocket and stared at the screen. "Guess those blobs of heat signature weren't who I was looking for. So now we go that way." She waved her gun toward the trees. "Walk."

"At the risk of you shooting me, I'm going to venture a guess." Nadia trundled through the foliage. She didn't turn back but could hear the two of them walk behind her. Close enough it was a point blank shot to her back. No chance of survival. "You're Thea?" Nadia pointed behind her without looking. "And that's Javier?"

Paul's body disappearing into the brush replayed in her head until a lump settled into her throat.

"Mom, how does she know who we are?"

"Shut up, Javier. Be quiet until I tell you."

Nadia pressed her lips together. "What I don't get is why a supposedly innocent woman put in witness protection needs to murder a US marshal sent to protect this town, which includes you and your son."

"What I choose to do is my business."

Nadia wanted to go home now, more than ever. But could she go back to Sanctuary, knowing what the world had brought upon her? She didn't want to be scared, but what else was she supposed to be feeling? Bolton had protected her, until it had been beyond his control. She didn't want to be scared of him, but it was hard to separate in her head.

Bolton, Dante, and Earnest. Now Thea. All she'd seen was danger. Everything that had come at her since she'd climbed in that helicopter and flown out of town was peril. Fear had settled in her until it felt like her heart was a stone. Would it shatter before she managed to get home? Because, yes, Sanctuary was her safe haven. It always had been, and that was entirely the point of a town like that. The world wasn't a safe place. Nadia had been so blessed to be able to live a life there that was full of friendship, laughter. Blessings God had given her.

And yet, those things were still true out here where the danger was. God was still God, and He was good.

Even if she concluded that it was all Bolton's fault, she didn't blame him. There was too much feeling there for her to shovel condemnation on his head. It was complicated, and it felt like her insides were going to tear apart. Why couldn't things just go back to normal?

Nadia swiped the tear from her cheek. She wanted to curl up and cry, but there was no rest here. There had been no rest since she left Sanctuary. Safety was wrapped up in those Idaho mountains and, yes, still in Bolton to an extent. Nadia just had to finish this, and then she would be able to figure out where she was supposed to be. Surely Sanctuary could be her home still, even though she felt like the woman she had been in that town wasn't who she was anymore. Too much had happened, but her friends would still love her. They'd help her.

"Just up ahead. You should be able to see them."

Great. If they wanted to shoot, Nadia would be the one hit first. She was okay with that if it was her instead of the boy, but not if she was taking a bullet for Thea. No way.

But it was Ben. And Grant…

They didn't look good.

Nadia started to say, "What is…" Thea shoved her out of the way and ran past her…all the way past Grant and Ben, who Nadia now realized were tied up, to the man who stood behind them. Holding a gun on her friends.

Dante. And three of his friends, too, dressed in street clothes. Where had they all come from? She'd brought the only boat, and the helicopter had landed much farther away. She'd seen the men rope down. These weren't them. Had they hiked in, or did they have another boat at a different inlet?

"What happened?" Even as Nadia asked it, she reached Ben. Close enough to see the stain of blood that trailed from his shoulder to soak his black shirt. "He shot you?"

Ben gritted his teeth. "One of them got lucky. A couple of the residents here were following us, and decided to join Dante's cause. I don't like it when people shoot me."

Grant lifted his chin to her. "You okay?"

"Better than you guys by the looks of it." Both of them had their hands tied in front, and painfully by the way the ties cut into the skin of their wrists. Grant's bled, and it also trailed from his temple down the side of his face. She probably looked similar after Dante gave her to Earnest—or when her mom had freaked out in the hospital. He'd given Grant something, likely, to get all the info he'd needed on this Sanctuary.

Sucking noises caught her attention, and she glanced over as Ben and Grant turned. Thea was locked in a passionate embrace with Dante. The men watched, smirks on their faces.

Nadia couldn't believe it. "Okay, so I wasn't expecting that."

Thea leaned back, lifted her gun, and pointed it at them. "Which one do you want to kill first?"

Dante didn't even look at Javier, who stood to the side like he had no idea what to do or say. Nadia wanted to hold the kid's hand, but she'd probably get shot for it. Someone needed to support the boy. His whole world was crumbling.

Dante shoved the gun aside, and the force sent it dangerously close to being aimed at Javier. The boy's eyes widened, but Dante didn't even notice. "We're not killing them yet. We need Bolton, and they're the perfect bait for a trade."

Dante's eyes settled on Nadia for a second. "We meet again."

"Yeah, but I'm not tied to a chair this time. And I don't see any sex traffickers for you to give me to." Bravado probably wasn't a good plan, but she had nothing else. Where was Bolton? She didn't want him anywhere near this pair and whatever they were planning. He needed to get off this island. Thea didn't need protecting, and Javier probably only needed about thirty years of intensive therapy.

Dante sneered. "I'm sure we can work something out."

Ben didn't look happy at the exchange, but Nadia needed time to figure out how they were going to get out of this.

Dante turned to his guys. "Where's that radio?"

One of the men handed over the unit. Dante smirked and lifted it to his lips. "Bolton Farrera, you hear me?"

Silence.

Then, "Dante."

Bolton. Nadia's heart clenched, and Thea's eyes narrowed on her.

"Good. Everyone's here. Now listen up." Dante's eyes hardened as he spoke into the radio. "Thirty minutes on the beach at the bottom of the west fork. You for your two Mason buddies and this girl who keeps showing up every place I go. Don't show, I kill them. Come with me, and no one gets hurt." Dante lowered it.

"No one gets hurt?" Thea said. "I thought—"

Dante cut her off. "There's your problem." He slung his arm around her neck so fast she slammed into his side. "Let's go."

Nadia was sick of being marched all over the place. This whole thing was one giant mess, and super spy Ben Mason looked mad he'd been bested. He should be breaking free and fighting them all…and winning. Her brother would have done it. What was wrong with him that he looked like he was giving up? The only reason her brother would do that was…

She glanced at Ben.

He winked.

Dante thought he was going to trade their lives for Bolton. She hadn't considered that he'd really let them live, but neither did she want to be massacred in front of a boy already having a bad enough day.

"Are we at least going to kill Bolton when he gets to the beach?" Thea's voice had bled out its confidence. She sounded like a woman humiliated into taking the lower place when she'd considered herself Dante's equal. But Dante didn't answer. "I can't believe you really came here for me. I've been waiting for you all these years."

Did she really think romantic sentiments were going to work on a man like Dante? Nadia wasn't sure if the woman was delusional or just dumb.

"It sure has been a while," Dante said. "Lot of years in prison with no one to attend to my…needs."

Nadia nearly threw up in her mouth. It got worse when Thea giggled. She didn't want to know what was going on behind her, or what Thea had just whispered.

Bolton was going to have to see this. He was going to have to face the news that his ex-wife had been having an affair with his worst enemy. For how long? Nadia sucked in a breath and glanced at Javier, who looked at her with a question in his eyes. Was the boy even Bolton's son…or was he Dante's?

Nadia didn't know which would be worse.

**

Bolton and Colt walked through the clearing to where a patch of blood stained the grass.

"Someone's hurt." Bolton scanned the ground. Boot-prints in the soft mud made by big, heavy guys. Multiple sets.

Colt said, "Twenty-five minutes now. It takes ten to get to the beach if we run fast and cut through the trees, but it could be treacherous. We had some rain a couple of days ago, and I'm not in the mood to slide down the side of this mountain."

Bolton nodded. "Let's go, then."

The tactical team they'd seen headed to town had stopped long enough to laugh over the gunfire, and then continued on. Whatever had happened here, he didn't know who was dead or alive. Though Dante seemed to have emerged as the victor. Was it Ben and Grant? Bolton couldn't imagine them getting bested. But they weren't superheroes.

"What do you have that Dante wants?"

Bolton spoke as they walked. "I stole something from him. Insurance, you could call it. After I made it clear that I had it, the attacks stopped. But now Dante is out, and he wants it back. Well too bad. He thinks he can hurt the people I care about to get what he wants, but it doesn't work like that."

"Agreed." A man stepped out from the trees. Full tactical gear, but his face was in plain view.

"Tristan."

"Secure them." Armed men stepped out of the bushes on all sides. The team held their weapons on Bolton and Colt and the two men with them.

Bolton tried to resist. "We have to get to the beach. We can't let Dante hurt any of the people here."

"What do you think the plan is?" Tristan said. "Dante must be contained, and you're the reason he's loose. *You're* the reason he's traipsing all over the country hauling people from their lives and trying to kill them."

He gritted his teeth. "That's why I'm here, trying to stop him from getting to Thea and Javier, too."

Tristan almost smiled. Why would he— "Ah, yes. So innocent, and yet...perhaps not."

"What is that supposed to mean?"

Bolton was divested of his weapons, though they didn't find the knife in his boot, and then he was shoved with the barrel of the gun. Tristan said, "I guess you're going to find out."

Colt scanned the men with his gaze. Bolton could almost see the plan coalescing behind his eyes but gave him a short shake of his head. They didn't need anybody else here dying because of what Dante had done.

The whole plan had disintegrated into a heap of nothing. They were back to reacting instead of protecting this town from being overrun by men trying to kill or capture others. And where was the marshals' service? Surely these people weren't expected to take care of themselves. Not when armed men had amassed in the woods.

Grant, Ben, and Bolton should have been enough to take care of them. And Colt, along with his men. But things were getting worse and worse.

Dante had Ben and Grant. Was that even possible? He'd considered Ben some kind of larger-than-life superhero. Apparently he was only a man like the rest of them. Now Nadia was in danger, too. She was supposed to have been back at the plane with Will.

Dante had bested him.

Bolton glanced back. "How did he escape from prison?"

"He had help."

"Yeah, no kidding," Bolton clipped.

Tristan snorted. "If it was me then I've royally messed up, haven't I?" He paused. "Hmm…unless there's something Dante can do that no one else can. But what would that be?"

That was the question. Tristan was in no way above double crossing Dante, which meant if they were going to the beach he probably planned to screw Dante over. Tristan would probably put a bullet in Dante's head and then force Bolton to take him to the stash.

Like he'd tell either of them.

"I think you did set him loose. Or at least you allowed it to happen," Bolton said. "Does he still think you're loyal to him, even now? All that federal pull, a powerful thing. But you have to have come under scrutiny since your own partner is one of the dirtiest agents the DEA ever had." He blew out a breath in mock-empathy. "Can't have been easy, carrying on your good work with that scandal hanging over your head. You must have done an impeccable job of keeping your name out of the DEA's internal affairs files if no one ever connected you to Dante's operation."

Tristan shrugged one shoulder. "I'm good."

"I see that."

And yet there was no way the DEA wasn't at least watching Tristan Sanders. So far Ben had discovered bank accounts and that property on Bainbridge Island. He'd hidden them well, but not well enough that Remy couldn't trace the two back to Tristan.

His bosses at the DEA had to have done the same. So what were they doing about the fact yet another of their people was guilty of betraying their sworn oath? Had the DEA turned a blind eye out of embarrassment, or were they even now making a case against Tristan while trying to hide the fact Dante had escaped from federal prison.

Or was Tristan behind that, too?

Everyone wanted Bolton's stash, and if the risk was that it might wind up in someone else's hands, then he was entirely prepared to live without it. He'd find money somewhere else if it meant his insurance stayed contained.

Tristan grasped Bolton's collar and put a gun to his head. They emerged onto the beach like that. Nadia stood with Ben and Grant in a protective stance around her. Bolton could have kissed both men right then. She looked shaken but unharmed. At least physically. Her gaze flew to his, and she gasped loud enough it drew Javier's attention.

The boy stood to the side, and Dante was with Thea. Her face brightened in a way that made his insides cold. He'd seen it in her, years ago, but hadn't ever believed she would hit a point where she acted on the stripe of viciousness that lived in her. Apparently that day had come.

"Kill him," she yelled. "Do it now!"

Dante grabbed her arm and hauled her back to his side. To contain her as his prisoner, or to restrain her? The question was answered when Thea hugged Dante's side and gazed up at him the same way she'd once gazed up at Bolton. "Have your friend shoot him. For me."

Part of Bolton, deep down in his heart, was not surprised. Not in the slightest.

Bolton looked at Javier, who looked about to cry. Or run.

He should run, better than having to watch this. The boy's gaze locked with Bolton. Long enough Bolton sent the kid a short nod. He was old enough and smart enough to know when to cut and run and take care of himself. This was it.

He mouthed, *Go.*

The boy darted into the trees.

Gunshots rang out from beside him. One of the tactical team.

Bolton strained against Tristan's grip, while Ben grabbed Nadia and stopped her from going after the boy and getting killed. Dante fired once into the man of Tristan's who had been shooting at the fleeing boy. The man fell to the ground.

"What was that?" Tristan yelled. He fired at one of Dante's guys and the man dropped. "One for one, my friend."

"Like you didn't come here to kill me, Tristan? You think I'm crazy, but not so crazy I don't have a solid plan to get that flash drive."

Bolton gritted his teeth. "Too bad none of you are getting that flash drive, because I'm not giving up its location. Ever."

Dante turned to one of his men. "Get that boy." He straightened to stare at Bolton with intent in his eyes. "How about I shoot your kid if you don't tell me."

Okay, so that threat might work. Bolton prayed then, asking God to look out for his son. To help him get away. If God was going to aid anyone, it would be a kid whose life was in danger. Bolton didn't know much about God, but that seemed like it should be right.

"He's not..." Thea's voice trailed off.

"Spit it out, woman," Dante snapped. "I'm in the middle of something, and you aren't helping."

"Javier isn't Bolton's son. He's yours."

Nadia gasped loud enough to draw Thea's attention.

"I've had enough of you." Thea lifted her gun and fired.

Grant dove in front of Nadia, and they fell to the ground. Tristan's men opened fire. Dante's guys were blasted onto their backs, and even Ben took cover. Bolton covered his ears the sound was so loud. He glanced around and saw Colt on the ground. Ben was down. Were they dead? Was Nadia dead, or Grant?

God…

Tristan fired. A red stain erupted in the middle of Thea's chest. Her face flashed with surprise. As she fell, she fired off one shot. Bolton's leg went out from under him. The pain was like fire and raced all the way to his chest. His hip gave out, and he sank on his hands into the sand.

Dante strode forward. "Enough!"

Tristan hauled Bolton to his feet.

He gritted his teeth against the pain and managed to remain standing. Tristan otherwise ignored him, his focus on reaming Dante. "You want this to end, you end it. Nothing but grief you've given me. For *years*."

"Grief and a whole lot of money," Dante fired back.

"It doesn't count if I can't spend it. Internal Affairs is so far in my space I should charge them rent. This ends now, Dante." He shook Bolton with every word. As if any of this was his doing.

"Because you want the flash drive for yourself." Dante waved the gun around like he wasn't sure who to shoot first, Tristan or Bolton. "We get it. We split it. We go our separate ways."

Tristan was silent for a minute. Then he said, "Deal."

Chapter 22

With her face smashed against the ground, Nadia could only see Ben's shoes. Dante and Tristan were wrapped up in their conversation, so they didn't notice when Ben slipped away into the trees. Where was he going? The beach was littered with bodies, and Grant's was on top of hers.

Lord, please don't let him be dead. She liked her life, but it wasn't worth the former director of the Marshals. The world couldn't afford to lose a man capable of doing that much good for people who would never be safe apart from his help.

She tried to move, then, as Tristan and Dante yelled at each other. Making a deal over Bolton's stash.

"Stay still," Grant whispered in her ear.

Thank You, Lord. He wasn't dead, but Bolton was going to be by the sound of things. Tristan and Dante both wanted the stash, and he'd have to tell them. He couldn't hold out forever against whatever they would do to him. Then, when they had it, they would kill him. Everything she'd been trying to do so far—everything she had thought God put her with Bolton to do—would be for nothing. And so why would God do that? God didn't do pointless things.

Nadia held still while Dante and Tristan walked Bolton from one edge of her view to the other. They ignored everyone else. Their single minded pursuit, of whatever Bolton had hidden, ensured the fact no one else was going to get hurt here. At least she prayed they didn't plan to put a bullet in everyone before they left.

If they didn't care that anyone would follow or find them, then it meant they had extreme confidence that they would get what they were after. Nadia didn't know how they could have that much faith in their own abilities. She would make a lousy criminal, always second guessing herself and hesitating. She'd probably be dead before the end of the first week.

Out the corner of her eye, she saw when Bolton's leg give out. He moaned, and they hauled him back up to standing. He could barely walk. What had they done to him? Nadia rallied, praying harder than she'd ever prayed about anything. Bolton had been a huge part of her life for so long she couldn't imagine it without him. Or having to watch him suffer like this knowing it would grow much worse before it ended.

Their voices grew quieter until she couldn't hear them anymore. Nadia shifted. Grant let out a hiss. "Hold up." He rolled off her to the side and moaned.

Nadia lifted up and saw it then. "You were shot!"

She whipped off her jacket, balled it up, and pressed it to the wound high on Grant's chest. It was just under his shoulder blade. Half the blood on the back of her jacket was from where he'd lain on her.

"Grant." She breathed his name, not knowing the first thing about how she was going to help him. Was there even a doctor nearby? Could she call for a helicopter to stop at a place where there weren't supposed to be any people? Were there emergency protocols in place for this? He wasn't a resident, or a marshal. They weren't even supposed to be here.

Grant shifted. He lifted his phone up and ran his bloody thumb over the home button. The phone unlocked. He exhaled.

Was the injury in his lung? Was he having trouble breathing?

"Nadia."

She flicked her gaze up to his face.

"Dial six-four-seven." She fumbled the phone and got the numbers wrong twice. Grant set his hand over hers. "Relax, just breathe. Okay?"

She nodded and looked around. There was no one else here, no one but a bunch of bodies. With supreme effort she managed to dial the number. It was that or let Grant die.

"Go ahead."

"Um...hi. This is..." Should she even tell them? Who was this? "Maybe that's not important."

"Go ahead." The voice was impatient this time.

"Grant Mason has been shot."

"Understood." The line clicked off like a heavy textbook slammed closed in her face.

Nadia looked at the phone in her hand. "Who was that?"

"Help. That's all. Just help."

"It wasn't Remy."

"And Will has been compromised," Grant said. His face was pale, and he was sweating.

"Where's Ben?" She sucked in a breath and yelled, "BEN!"

"He'll show back up in a few. He does that."

"So we just wait? You're bleeding out. We need towels, and a Life Flight helicopter."

Grant had the audacity to smile.

"You could get an infection." She glanced around. "Maybe I should help you to the dock. We can take the boat." Even though she had no idea how to drive the thing. Or pilot it. Whatever you called it when it was marine stuff.

"Just keep pressure on," Grant said. He gritted his teeth together. Sweat beaded on his forehead.

"I don't want to be here, surrounded by a bunch of dead—"

A huge bear of a guy dressed like a biker sat up.

Nadia screamed.

Grant's chest shook. Was he laughing? "That's Colt."

The biker blinked, one hand on his chest as he breathed in and out. He moved it to a stripe of red across his side, and pulled it away with blood on his fingers.

"I don't have another jacket. You'll have to apply pressure yourself. The director is bleeding out."

"And you're freaking out." Colt's eyes narrowed as he got up and glanced around. "They took Bolton?"

Nadia nodded.

"And killed Thea."

Grant made a sound of disapproval with his throat.

Nadia said, "Who are you?"

The man didn't answer, he simply scanned the area.

Grant said, "Colt lives here. He was in charge of security."

Colt glanced over. "Was?"

"Your town was breached."

Nadia said, "That happened to us, too. They blew up the ranch and the side of the mountain. My friend Hal died." Tears filled her eyes. Was the same thing going to happen to Bolton? "Now—"

Colt lifted one hand. "You need to quit talking before we both get slapped with new gag orders. Got it?"

Nadia nodded. "What do we do?"

Colt came over and sank down onto his knees. His side was weeping blood, but it looked like a deep scratch. He moved the jacket from under her hands out of the way and stared at the entry wound. Then he replaced the jacket and rolled Grant to look at his back.

"What?" she said. "What is it?"

"Through and through."

"What does that mean?" It didn't sound good at all.

Colt moved his gaze from Grant to her. "It means we don't have to dig in there and get the bullet out."

Bile lifted to her throat, but Nadia swallowed it back down.

"Don't barf," Colt ordered.

She nodded, determined not to disappoint him.

"I'm a sympathy puker." The soft look disappeared so fast she wondered if he'd imagined it. "Gotta get you out of here, Director."

"I'm not the director anymore."

"Like that matters," Colt said.

"Reinforcements will be forthcoming."

"The call?" Nadia asked. When Grant nodded, she said, "And they'll get you to a hospital?"

"And maintain the integrity of this town."

Her next question, she asked Colt. "How many people live here?"

He glanced at the bodies on the beach. "Looks like we're down to somewhere near eleven. Twelve if we can find Javier."

"He ran off. And I'm so glad he did." Nadia took a breath and fought the nausea again. "He didn't have to watch them kill his mom."

"Yeah, cause she was Mom of the Year," Colt scoffed. "But finding the kid in the woods will be a pain. He knows these trees as well as any of us. I don't know if that brother of yours went after him, but he'll have a rough time following. Javier won't leave a trail. He's good."

"Ben will find him." Grant sounded so confident.

Nadia wanted to believe him. "I hope so."

Caught in the middle of all this, the kid didn't deserve the life he'd been given. If she could help somehow, Nadia would do whatever she could to make his life better.

"What about Bolton? We have to go after him. We have to figure out a way to help him." Even as she said it she thought through their options. Shadrach was in the hospital. Will had been compromised. Ben was in the woods looking for Javier, and Grant had been shot. "I need to find him. To help him. I don't know how, but I need to try."

Grant laid his hand over hers. "Remy might be able to figure out where they're taking him, but it's a needle in a stack of needles. You might have to face the fact he's gone. He wanted to find that stash he hid, and now he will. Dante and Tristan are Bolton's battle to fight. He wouldn't want you to get in the middle of it."

Grant waved his hand to encompass their immediate area. A deluge of bodies, the trail left in Dante's wake. Okay, so Nadia didn't want to be one more. But she needed to at least try and help him.

Colt sighed. "I'm not liking that look on your face at all."

**

Ben stopped. The rustle of leaves, tiny animals. Insects. Birds. He filtered the sounds to find what he was looking for.

The kid was good, but Ben had yet to find a man on earth he couldn't track.

Ben took two paces to the right and peered around a tree.

Javier looked up at him, wide eyed and trembling.

"Hi." Ben used the voice he used with Grant's daughters when they were upset. He lifted both hands so the kid knew he wasn't there to kill him—which seemed to be a genuine concern. Then he crouched. "I'm Ben."

"Javier." His voice shook, a boy on the cusp of becoming a man. A boy who's entire world had just shattered.

Ben's knees sank into the soft earth as he held out his hand. "Nice to meet you." They shook. "You know, this place is nice and all, but I think ants are crawling up my pants."

Javier's lips twitched.

"You think you could show me a spot that's not infested with bugs?"

"That's like the whole island."

"Hmm." Ben scratched his chin in an exaggerated move. "I see your problem."

He couldn't take the kid back to the beach where his mother lay dead in the sand. Or to his home, unless Javier was going to pack a bag so they could leave. But where could he take him? The kid needed protecting until this was over. Then, whether or not they conducted a paternity test, the kid would likely be parentless. And homeless.

Ben wanted to get him to the Idaho Sanctuary, where he would be safe and with people who would love him. Though Ben's mom's house was a close second. Either place Javier would be taken care of.

Despite the fact he was a child who would have little say over what happened to him, Ben wanted to give him the choice.

"I think we should get out of here. Do you have anything you need to grab?"

Javier got up. He strode to a nearby tree and reached into a hollowed out section. He pulled a backpack from inside and set it on his shoulder. Grasping the handle in front of him, the boy lifted his chin. "I'm ready to go."

**

Grant had been loaded on the boat by the time Ben showed up, followed closely by Javier. Nadia gasped. "I'm so glad you found him."

The kid looked at her like she was crazy. Colt looked up. When he saw who it was, he strode to Javier. He set his hand on the boy's shoulder and spoke low, face-to-face, until the boy nodded. The two of them strode to the boat.

Nadia smiled as he approached. "Javier, right?" He almost reminded her of Shadrach. Dark hair and eyes and that wiry body that would grow into a tall and lean man. He was going to be a handsome one, too. But where she looked for Bolton's features, she couldn't find any resemblance.

"Is Grant okay?" Javier's dark eyes stared at the former director.

Nadia nodded. "He will be once they get him to a hospital."

"Let's step back so these men can take Grant in." Ben led Javier away back from the edge where the boat bobbed against the dock.

Nadia looked at the uniformed men, whoever they were they looked official in all black gear. Though the sight of them was enough like Tristan's team that she'd been taken aback when they'd first arrived. Grant seemed to know them, even if they didn't appear to be part of any law enforcement agency she knew of.

Grant's gaze snagged hers. "Stay with Ben." He was her best option for finding Bolton. But Grant would be the first back in civilization.

"Back up, Nadia." It was tempting to simply jump on board the boat. Until Ben pulled her back by her arm.

"Fine. I was coming."

The boat engine revved, and it sped away. Paul's boat was still docked beside where Grant's boat had been. "Let's take the other boat. Get out of here." She looked at Colt. "Are you coming or staying?"

"None of you are going anywhere." Paul strode out of the trees, gun trained on them.

Ben shoved Javier behind him and stood in front of Nadia. She peered around both of them. Paul didn't look like he would kill them here. He looked...like he was doing his job. "What are your orders, Paul?" He was here in a professional capacity. "What do you need?"

The marshal's aim loosened, and he let the gun drop enough she relaxed. Though, Ben didn't.

Paul said, "I'm taking charge of Pu'u honua." He lifted his chin to Colt. "With respect, Mr. Thompson, your services here are no longer required. Though you'll need to call in. Get a reassignment."

Colt shrugged. "Fine by me."

"Good. Javier?"

The boy didn't move. "I'm fine."

Paul glanced at Ben. "I trust you'll venture down the correct channels as you transport a federally protected minor across state lines."

"Of course I will." Ben folded his arms. It sounded like he was smiling. Apparently Paul knew Ben, or *of him*.

Colt turned to her and asked in a low voice, "Do you ever feel like you've woken up in some freaky dream, and you have no idea what is going on?"

She wanted to smile. She really did. "All the time." She touched Ben's sleeve. "But we have to go. They took Bolton, and we have to get to Will before that."

Ben looked at her. Not acquiescence. What was written on his face was more like a grave kind of sympathy. "Let's head out."

"What about—" Javier didn't finish his question.

Ben turned to the boy and said in a soft voice, "What do you want to do with the body?"

Javier's gaze flickered.

After a minute, Paul said, "There's a team of Marshals headed here. They will process the crime scene, and I can contact you when your mother's remains are ready for burial."

What did a twelve year old boy do with his mother's body when he had no money to pay for a funeral? Or maybe he was loaded. Nadia didn't know anything about him, or even who he had thought his father was all these years.

Nadia slipped her hand into the boy's. They were about the same size. "You can call me," she told Paul. "I'll help Javier figure out what to do."

The squeeze of his hand was almost unnoticeable, but it was there.

Paul nodded.

They climbed onto the boat, and Paul watched as Colt piloted away from the Hawaii Sanctuary. Nadia hadn't even seen the town. She could try and look at it on Google earth later, but it was probably just trees. The government was good at blind spots used to hide what was really underneath.

She glanced at Colt then at Javier, who sat at the back of the boat. "What are we going to do? I want to find Bolton. Should I call Remy and see if she can track them?"

"That's your best bet," Ben said. "We'll find him."

"Hopefully not too late, or he'll be dead. You know they'll kill him once they get what they want. I'm not going back to Sanctuary until I know if he's okay."

"And if he chooses to take his money and walk away, then what?"

Nadia blew out a breath. "He has this crazy idea that the stash will solve all his problems, when the reality is that he's just searching for freedom. For a future of his own making. I wanted that, too. A long time ago. But do you know what I discovered?"

Ben shook his head.

"The future God had planned for me was far better than anything I could have come up with. He gave me a home and a family. Bolton didn't see it that way, but it was a blessing to me, and he was part of that, the gift God gave me. I need to tell him that."

Ben stared for a second. "And if you do, if he knows what he means to you, and he still walks away..." Ben shrugged, like *what then?*

"It'll hurt, but he has the right to make his own choice. I'll go back to Sanctuary either way."

"Because you aren't willing to live his life with him, your only answer is that he lives your life with you?"

Nadia had an answer on the tip of her tongue, but it evaporated. God had placed her in Sanctuary to gift her with a peaceful life. Surely Bolton's presence there had been the same, not the prison he had seen it as. But if he returned, would he see it the way she saw it?

Had God only given her Sanctuary for a season, and now he had removed her from that place for a different reason? Maybe God might want her to walk Bolton's path with him now, instead of going back. She'd assumed it was him who had to make the choice. What if God wanted her to pick a life outside Sanctuary? The threat to her had passed. If Bolton survived this, and he and Ben cleaned up the mess, the threat to him would be over as well.

Could they live a life outside Sanctuary, together?

Did she want that?

God, have I been selfish this whole time? Have I assumed I'm fine, and that Bolton was the one who needed to change? He needs to find You, to find faith. It will bring him the peace he needs, but will it change the direction he's walking in? Should I be going with him, to the end? Whether it ends in disaster or not, is that my path?

Nadia glanced at the horizon, and the sun now peeking up from its watery slumber to wash the sky in orange.

Make it clear, Lord.

So long as he lived, did it matter where that was? Bolton's life had to come first. His salvation. Whether or not he felt about her the way she felt about him, Nadia had to trust God on the outcome. Her heart was so tied up in him it was difficult to think she might not see him again. That she could lose him the way Javier had lost his mother.

She could live, Lord willing. She would return to Sanctuary one way or another, whether that was only to gather her belongings and leave witness protection. But first, she had to find Bolton so Nadia could tell him she'd been in love with him for years.

After that it would be up to him.

Chapter 23

Bolton ripped the packet open and pressed the gauze onto the wound on his leg. He rummaged in the first aid kit and found a bandage. It took some doing, with his hands tied, but he managed to get a loose wrap that he tied and pulled as tight as possible with his teeth. Bolton leaned back against the wall of the airplane and shut his eyes. He sucked in some deep breaths to push down the nausea.

Dante's feet came into view. "A first aid kit?" He chuckled. "Like that's going to help you with what's coming."

Bolton didn't look up. He didn't want to engage Dante when that would only incur his wrath. Sitting still and saying nothing would incur his wrath as well, so Bolton figured he'd save his energy either way.

Dante slammed his foot down on Bolton's leg. The pain flashed white spots across his vision. He leaned to the side and vomited.

"Gross." Dante backed up. "Tell me where the stash is, and I make the pain stop."

Because Bolton would be dead.

Not telling Dante what he'd been asking for since they left Kauai was keeping Bolton alive. He wasn't going to give up the only thing he had left.

Ever since he'd left Sanctuary, Bolton had only made the situation worse and worse. After the helicopter exploded he should have left Nadia in that pastor's house and gone by himself. But no, he'd selfishly dragged her with him, into his troubles. And she'd been damaged because of it. Not that she wasn't strong. She was so strong. Probably stronger than Bolton, given she'd stuck with him and held tight this whole time. She'd pulled through all this in one piece.

At any moment she could have walked away. She could have left him and gone back to Sanctuary, to her life. Yet Nadia had chosen to stick with him. He knew she believed God allowed her to be in every situation. Not that He would knowingly put her in danger, but that He had a purpose in whatever He led her to. She'd told him that.

She'd told him a lot of things.

Like the fact Bolton didn't have to be defined by who other people thought he was. Or by his mistakes. That God had called him by a different name. That God loved him, and all about what He had done for Bolton. He'd listened, but figured he'd had better things to do than talk to someone who was invisible. God was God, and Bolton hadn't given it much more thought than that, even though he'd attended a Bible study in Sanctuary with Matthias a few times. They'd been friends, and he'd figured that's what friends did. Plus it got Matthias to quit asking him over and over again to go.

Still, it hadn't fully hit him what an immense thing God had done. The idea had crept up on him in increments. Until now. The open invitation to the peace and hope Nadia had that kept her with him this whole time.

What if Bolton did get killed here? What if Dante walked up to him the next time, decided Bolton wasn't going to tell him where the stash was, and then put a bullet in Bolton's brain?

Nadia had told him—straight up—that just being a good person wouldn't get him to heaven. He figured he'd never really been a good person. More like just a chump. Or some guy who followed whatever path was in front of him and wound up in witness protection with a target on his back.

She said God had given her a new start and a new identity. Bolton didn't need either at this point, considering the span of his life could be measured in hours at this point. But he didn't want to spend eternity in hell if he could avoid it. So what did he have to lose?

Bolton sat on the floor of a private airplane, bleeding onto the carpet, and asked God if he could be part of His family. Not because of anything Bolton had done, because he had nothing to bring to a Father God who, if Nadia was right, had done more for him than he could ever repay. Because of Jesus.

"Is he dead?"

Dante snorted at Tristan's question. "He better not be. We need the location of the stash."

Bolton opened his eyes. He didn't feel different. Was he supposed to? He looked up at the two men who stood over him. "Are we just going to fly around the US in big circles until we run out of fuel?"

Dante lifted a gun and pointed it at Bolton's face. "Tell me where you hid it."

Bolton sighed. "I'm not sure I can remember. Maybe you should threaten to kill me some more. Or maybe there's a spot where I don't already have a bruise, and you can give me a fresh one."

Tristan snorted. "He ain't gonna tell you."

"That's why we're headed to Miami."

Bolton reacted. He had to. He had no reserves to cover any kind of response, and there was so much in him that was tied to that city he couldn't help it.

"Bingo."

Of course, Dante would think that.

Miami was...well, it had been home, and Bolton had loved it there. Made his home in Sanctuary look like a shanty town in comparison, given how much he'd poured into that property trying to satisfy Thea's wants. The rooms he'd decorated for himself, the ones she'd rarely ventured into—the media room and the garage—were the only places on earth he'd ever felt even a modicum of peace.

Tristan strode away. "I'll inform the pilot."

Dante's mouth curled up. "You're a dead man."

"Ditto," Bolton said. "You drugged Nadia and then gave her to that guy. You think I'm gonna let that slide?"

"What are you going to do? Bleed to death all over me?" Dante shrugged. "I got life in a federal prison because of you, and everything I had earned and spent *decades* building up was destroyed. Now, not even Tristan trusts me. I have to look over my shoulder every single day to see which of my men is going to stab me in the back next."

"We make our own beds."

"So you're just going to play the noble card, is that it? You'll die on that little hill of your own truth and goodness." Dante crouched, bringing the gun within Bolton's reach. If he was fast enough. Then maybe—

Dante said, "You were nothing when those feebs found you, got you to spy on me so they could double cross me."

"That was your dangerous game. I only got caught in the middle. And for what? So you could sleep with my wife?"

"Please." Dante snorted. "That was all Thea's doing. Guess you weren't all that, since she jumped at the chance to get in bed with me." He paused. "Though, if I recall, there wasn't a bed involved. It was more…spur of the moment than that."

Bolton tried to be surprised, but what was the point in lying to himself. "What about Javier? Did you ever stop to think about him?"

"Like that scrawny little thing belongs to me? You saw him run away."

Right before Dante put a bullet in Thea. Bolton was glad Javier had run instead of being forced to watch his mother be killed. Bolton's mom hadn't been a part of his life for years, and when she had, it had been clear she was under his father's thumb. Yet another reason a relationship with Nadia would be impossible. He didn't even know what a healthy, loving, respectful relationship looked like.

The possibility that Thea had been lying, and that Javier might really be his child, hadn't left Bolton. But he would never know. Dante would kill him before he got the chance to find out.

"I won't ever tell you where the stash is."

He knew it was a death sentence, but neither Dante nor Tristan could ever get their hands on what he'd hidden with the money and supplies. If Dante killed Bolton, the location of the stash would be sent to Ben. Only Ben. He was the one person Bolton trusted to do the right thing—destroy it.

"Three hours," Tristan announced as he strode back over. "Good. You didn't kill him yet." He motioned for Dante to move the aim of his gun away. "You realize it's a three acre estate with a five thousand square foot house, right? I'm not searching that whole place—it'll take forever. And if you kill him, that's exactly what we'll have to do."

Dante turned to his partner. "Do you have any idea how sick I am of you ordering me around?"

"Probably about as sick as I am of having to try and control you," Tristan fired back. "How many times was our entire operation almost exposed because of you? I was constantly trying to reign you in because you are so crazy you had no fear. Dealing with the FBI, pulling in gangsters. Making deals with the cartels. You didn't exclude anyone. You let the whole world know you were dirty, and you had your finger in all their operations because it was never enough. If I had to control you, it's because you weren't satisfied, and you weren't going to be until you got us all caught or killed."

"So you let Bolton survive long enough I was convicted, and you walked away with control of the operation." Dante's voice was deadly serious.

"I scaled it back. We make a mint—"

"Which I can't spend in prison."

"Who told you Bolton was out?"

Dante's gun hand clenched on the grip. "If you hadn't, it would've looked mighty suspicious. That's you. Still playing everyone." He studied Tristan, then said, "So what's your play here? Think you can use me to find the stash then turn around and bring me in? The loyal DEA agent, just doing his job."

"D. That's not what this—"

Bolton saw Dante's intention a split second before he moved. Tristan didn't have time to react. Dante slammed the butt of his gun into Tristan's forehead. He dropped to the floor of the plane, so Bolton could only see his legs. Prone. Dante pointed his gun and fired one shot into Tristan.

Dante leaned down. When he straightened, he slipped Tristan's badge onto his belt and then turned to Bolton. "Guess it's just you and me. For now."

**

It felt like hours before they made it to the plane. Days since they'd arrived with Will on the island of Kauai.

Nadia turned in a circle as they walked to the plane, which had the stairs down and the door open. The mountain peaks loomed like lush, green monuments. A breeze coming from the sea, while palm trees stood like sentries over the land.

Night was ready to fall.

"Will we ever come back here?"

They turned at the same time. Ben, Nadia, and Colt stood around Javier. Colt set his hand on the boy's shoulder. "Whatever happens I'll make sure we end up in the same place. Deal?"

Did he have the power to make that statement? Nadia had no idea who Colt was. He was no marshal even if the town's security and safety had apparently been under his purview. He'd been kicked out, but Javier simply had no reason to stay.

Nadia stepped closer to him. "Do you want to stay, Javier?"

He shook his head. "I can't be here. Not anymore." His eyes filled with tears. "What happened to that man, the one Dante took?"

"The one you tried to shoot?" Ben's voice was clipped, and he showed no concern for Javier's reaction. "First time I saw you, you heard his name and you pointed your shotgun at him. If Colt hadn't stopped you, you'd have shot him."

"Bolton Farrera destroyed my family. He ruined our lives."

"How?" Ben folded his arms.

The boy opened his mouth. Hesitated.

"Your mom tell about him?"

Nadia stepped between them. "Leave him alone, Ben. He's just a kid." One who'd just lost his mom. "He doesn't need the third degree."

Ben turned to her. "You want me to place him in Sanctuary, where he can decide he doesn't like someone else, and then shoot him? How about Pat? Or Andra?"

Nadia's best friend. And she'd seen how he was with his nephew. Of course, they were his priorities. "Isn't that a risk with anyone? Do you really ever know who you're letting in?" She folded her arms. "Why is it your decision anyway?"

"There's no way this kid is going anywhere near my family without me at least asking a few questions."

"Are you the vetting process? Is that how the system works now that it's privately run?"

Ben shot her a look, like *maybe*. Nadia rolled her eyes and faced Javier. "Don't worry about him." She jabbed her thumb in the air, in Ben's direction. "He gets paid to be like that. All you need to worry about is being a kid. We're going to make sure you stay safe, and I just want you to let us take care of the details of where you'll end up. Can you do that?"

Colt shook Javier's shoulder a fraction in a move of solidarity. "My man here and I will work on that. But we need details." He flicked his gaze to the side to include Ben. "Trust goes both ways."

"Agreed."

Ben's expression didn't change. They probably paid him for that, too. "Let's board the plane." He pulled a gun.

"What's that for?" Nadia trailed after him with the other two behind her.

"We don't know if Will is still here or not."

"You know Dante kidnapped his family."

"So he says." Ben glanced back over his shoulder for a second. "I didn't even know he had a family."

Nadia blinked. She followed him upstairs. Will hadn't told Ben about his family? She knew he hadn't shared about the kidnapping, but— "I saw it. The photo Dante sent. I saw them on his phone."

Will appeared in the doorway. "I can show you." He looked terrible—hair disheveled. He might even have been crying.

"We should get in the air," Nadia suggested. "Head back to the mainland. Will, you could ride in the cockpit with Ben."

Ben whirled around to face her. "You want a man coerced into betraying my organization to ride up front by the instruments? He could sabotage the plane and kill us all. How do you know he isn't still under orders from Dante?"

Nadia couldn't look at Will. She didn't want to know how Ben's words sliced through him, not more than what she saw out the corner of her eye. "Talk to him, Ben. I'll call Remy to see if she can find out where Dante and Tristan took Bolton."

Ben opened his mouth, but it was Will who spoke. "They have him?" Will's eyes widened.

Nadia glanced at him then. "Any chance you can call him and find out where they're going?"

He shook his head, a man with no hope and nothing left to lose. "They don't trust me, and I have no leverage. My family is probably dead already."

She touched his arm. "We don't know that."

Ben said, "We'll find out."

Nadia nodded. "Do you have people who can get on that while we search for Bolton?"

"Hmm. Let me see." Ben's tone was the epitome of sarcasm. "I'm here, Grant is headed for the hospital, Shadrach is already *in* the hospital, and Daire is on vacation."

"So call Daire off his vacation."

"I already called a third party."

"Remind me to say no if you ever offer me a job." Nadia jerked her head side-to-side. "We have to find Bolton, and whoever you called has to save Will's family. But first, we have to get back to the mainland."

Ben snapped into a salute. "Yes, Captain." But he didn't move.

"Why are you not so fired up to go find Bolton? Don't you care at all? I thought he was your friend. You're just going to let him…" It dawned on her. "No. You wouldn't do that. Not even you."

"The most heartless person you know?"

She wouldn't have said it like that. "But you don't care if he dies." Nadia's brain spun as she processed it. "Is Bolton worth more to you dead? Or the same. There has to be a reason you're not jumping at this, rushing off to save him. I'm trying to get to him and you don't even care."

"I know you want to save him, Nadia. But life is more complicated than just one person's emotions." He said it without inflection or expression. She'd seen him with his family. He cared. It just didn't look like any expression of care that she'd ever seen before. "This whole situation is more complicated than you know."

"And you're just going to wait it out? See how the chips fall?" She took a step back, unable to decide whether she wanted to hear the answer or run so far she couldn't hear it.

"Bolton can take care of himself."

"Because you've decided that? He's injured, and they'll kill him."

"They need him alive to tell them where the stash is."

"And then you swoop in, is that it? Apparently not, because you're here." She shook her head. This was unbelievable. "You get what you want, no matter what happens to anyone else?"

"Nadia—"

"Don't bother." She stepped back. "I think I understand you perfectly." She turned to Will. "Do you have a clean phone I can use?"

Will nodded.

When she had the phone, and the plane engines had been turned on, Nadia dialed Remy's number. Colt and Javier were talking. Will was up front with Ben, who had better get them there in one piece.

Nadia swiped at the wetness on her face. Why had Grant told her to stay with Ben? He had to have known this would happen. He'd have been able to get her to Bolton faster, surely. She wouldn't have had anyone to help her, but she didn't care at this point. No help would have been better than Ben's lackadaisical attitude.

"This better be important."

"Remy?" Her voice cracked.

"Nadia. What is it?"

"Is everything okay? Shadrach isn't..."

"He's okay," Remy said. "Well, as okay as he can be. They're doing some tests now to make sure everything's healing properly."

Nadia blew out a choppy breath. She explained to Remy everything that had happened since their last call.

"I wasn't sure about Paul, but I had a hunch. I'm glad you're okay." Nadia heard the click of keys. "I'm running a search right now. There's only one airport on Kauai, so it shouldn't be hard to check their cameras to find Dante and Tristan loading Bolton onto a…" Her voice trailed off. "How can that—it's an off-books federal plane. In fact, it's one Grant has used before, and it only ever files a dummy flight plan. Why tell the FAA where you *aren't* going, why not just tell them to butt out of your business because it's private."

"Rem."

"That's what they're taking, and not to the west coast. They'd have landed already. Looks like they're headed southeast. Following that course, if they're not headed to Atlanta, I'm going to guess Miami."

"Bolton used to live there."

"Would he have hidden something important in his hometown?"

"Maybe. He'd know the area really well."

"I'll keep on top of it, let you know when they land and where exactly they're headed."

"Thanks Remy." She made her way to the cockpit. Will and Ben quit their conversation, a tense one by the look of it. She told them the direction, and Ben just nodded.

Nadia trailed back to her seat. They knew where to go now, but why did that leave her with the taste of dissatisfaction in her mouth? *God, I don't want to lose him.* When she helped him get out of this alive, Nadia was going to have to tell him why she cared so much. If he even got out of this alive.

Ben's help or not, Nadia faced again a man who'd already brought her low. He intended to kill Bolton and steal from him. She didn't know what Ben wanted, but Nadia cared more about Bolton's safety than anything he had hidden.

Was that why God had placed her here?

Chapter 24

"DEA! Open up!" Dante fired one shot into the key hole. He dragged Bolton by the arm, toward the door, and slammed his boot beside the handle. Bolton took the moment to drop Tristan's badge on the ground outside the door. Dante was distracted enough he didn't notice, just as he hadn't seen Bolton take it from the dead DEA agent on the plane.

The door swung open and a woman inside screamed. She huddled with a man, both dressed like they'd spent a day at the country club. The man cowered, like he was trying to hide behind the woman instead of protecting her. "What are you—"

Dante shot both of them.

"Your stay here is over." He pulled Bolton past the current owners of Bolton's house, stepping over the prone bodies. "Now tell me where you hid the stash."

Bolton glanced over his shoulder and saw the man's eyes were still open. Blood was smeared low across his chest. He wasn't dead, but a gut wound was never a good thing. He let the man see all the terror that had settled in his gut. Dying by Dante's hand wasn't supposed to be part of the plan. Not for Bolton, and not for these people, either.

The man started to reach for a cell phone that had fallen on the tile as his gaze darted around, still feeling the surprise of having been shot. Bolton sent up a prayer that the phone wasn't broken. That the man wasn't hurt too badly, that he could call and get help in there.

Cops.

Bolton had never wanted to see a police officer so badly in his life. He could have cried aloud for it. The pain in his body eclipsed almost everything else, and every step was agony.

Dante twisted around and fired one shot. The home owner's hand slumped and the phone clattered on the tile again. The screen was illuminated, but before he could read it, Dante shook him, his face right in Bolton's. "Where?"

Bolton blinked. "Give me a second." He was ready to throw up. His back and leg hurt so badly. Had the owner's call connected? Were the police on the open line—were they coming?

Dante let go, and Bolton hung his head. "There's a basement. Off the hall between the garage and the laundry room." Not that it was where he hid the stash, but it gave him the chance to stall until the owner's call got the cops there. If it connected. *Please, God.*

He wanted to lie down, but hours sitting still on the plane hadn't helped. Bolton needed a hospital, but he had no ID, no insurance, and no way to contact the marshals. What he needed to do was kill Dante before or at the point that Dante killed him. That was the only way out of this. Problem solved. Too bad Dante had the only gun.

"Open it."

Bolton grasped the door. Blood on his fingers left a sticky mess on the handle, but he got it open. He needed to wipe that off if he got the chance to leave here, right? Too many questions would be asked if his fingerprints or DNA were run. He wasn't supposed to show up back at his house. Bolton's head spun with the possible outcomes and what he'd have to do to contain this as much as possible. He'd managed to keep a low profile so far, but Tristan leaking his identity to the press hadn't helped. Not if there was a chance he might live and need to disappear.

The stairs had been repaired, the wood now bare pine where before it had been painted because, despite never once venturing down here, Thea had insisted they keep up appearances. Dante shoved one hand against the middle of Bolton's back.

The stairs rushed up and hit him in the face.

Bolton tumbled, side over side, until he hit the concrete floor at the bottom of the steps. The next thing he knew, Dante stepped on his back. Bolton's yell echoed in the cavernous, empty basement.

"Get up!"

Bolton couldn't move. Unconsciousness teased the edges of his world like a black hole about to suck him into the abyss of nothing. It would be easier. Just surrender to it and leave Dante to his fruitless search. At least Bolton wouldn't be hurting anymore, because he wouldn't feel anything at all when the final bullet came.

Dante pulled on Bolton's arm until he sat upright, then he let him slump against the stairs. "Seriously? It's one shot to the leg. I always knew you were worthless. If you worked for me I'd have killed you by now for being a waste of perfectly good air."

Bolton wasn't going to explain that Dante's last attempt to kill him before Sanctuary had put him in the hospital with a spinal injury or that the surgery from days ago hadn't healed. Or that Bolton was having trouble moving his toes. His legs were cocked at a funny angle in front of him. Bolton stared at them, as though the force of his will could make his legs move.

Finally, he managed to get his shoe to twitch.

Bolton pushed out a breath. He hated even the idea of being helpless. Facing down Dante while essentially paralyzed wasn't going to be a good idea. He didn't need to give Dante that much of an edge. The man couldn't know that Bolton could barely walk. At best.

Sweat ran down his face to sting his eyes. He lifted a leaden hand to wipe it away and felt the grit on his skin.

"Where is it?" Dante stood over him, gun aimed straight at Bolton's head. He may as well have put the thing away, for all the effect it had.

There weren't a whole lot of hiding spaces down here. Should he tell Dante he'd buried it under the floor? He'd have to go steal a jackhammer and break up the concrete. That would take a while. The other alternatives were less destructive.

"I can't see. It's dark down here."

Dante shone his cell phone around until he found the switch. Fluorescent lights washed the room in light, bleaching out everything. Bolton squeezed his eyes shut for a second while his brain processed the stabbing sensation of so much light at once.

He squinted at the room and saw the air vent panel in the corner. "Got a screw driver?" He motioned toward it. That was a logical hiding place, right?

Tucked away in the basement, hidden even when Bolton left the real world to hide out in a secret witness protection town.

Dante circled the room, found a tool box, and rummaged for a screw driver. He left his gun on the bench beside the dryer. Did he know Bolton couldn't get it? When he strode to the vent, Dante sent him a smirk. A dare to go for it or be a coward who couldn't fight back. All Dante did was challenge people, it was a wonder he'd survived prison for as long as he had.

Bolton glanced back at the top of the stairs.

The clock was ticking on his life. There were only seconds until Dante found nothing behind that vent.

Dante tossed it to the side. It clanged on the floor and the sound echoed at a deafening level. Hand in. Reaching around.

He pulled out a stuffed manila envelope Bolton had never seen before. "It better all be here." Dante up-ended the envelope. Two bundles of money and a passport. Dante looked at the picture. "This is for Thea."

Dante stormed over and threw it in Bolton's face—the reality that his wife had forged a new identity for herself so that she could finally betray him one last time. Instead she'd left him and gotten herself a place to live in Hawaii, while Javier grew up to hate him. Bolton would never know if the boy was his son or not, and maybe he didn't want the chance to be disappointed. She'd twisted his emotions against Bolton regardless of who his father was.

He punched Bolton over and over in the face, and then he spat on him. "You're not even worth the bullet it would take to kill you. Nothin' but a cheat and a liar who thinks he can win when I'm the one who calls the shots. Always." He knelt beside Bolton, grabbed his hair, and shoved the gun under his chin. "No one would miss you. Not your wife, not that little Jesus-lover girl. The kid isn't even yours. Marshals can't help you now. There's no one to cry to, Farrera. It's just you and me."

He moved the gun, pressed it into Bolton's left shoulder, and adjusted his grip, ready to fire.

The doorbell rang. Someone pounded on the door.

Then the doorbell rang again.

Dante raced up the stairs. Bolton leaned his head back on the steps and tried to breathe. Tried to muster the strength to get up, to get away from Dante.

"DEA Agent Tristan Sanders?"

"Sure am," Dante's reply was chipper.

"I'm Officer Michaels, this is Officer Sands. Is everything okay?"

"Got an unruly suspect in here. You'll have to excuse the mess I'm in. Not my best day." His laugh echoed all the way to the basement.

"Need any help? My partner and I can back you up if you're having some trouble."

"I got it. Everything's cool." Just another day on the job. Didn't these guys recognize his face? He had to be famous. Dante's picture should be all over every news agency, except he was the DEA's biggest disappointment. Keeping the story of his escape under wraps was probably a full time job for someone high up, someone who didn't want to answer a whole lot of uncomfortable questions about why Dante had ever been hired in the first place. Tristan, probably. But the man was dead now.

"You're sure?"

Bolton lost the next couple of exchanges. He tried to rally against the pain, but it was getting harder. Any second now Dante would shut the door on those two cops, and they would never know he was down here. They'd never know there was a dead couple laying on the floor right behind the door.

Bang.

Bang.

Boot-steps. The stairs shook with each pounding footfall. "Stupid cops can't mind their own business."

Bolton's only way out. His rescue.

And Dante had killed them.

**

"Thanks." Ben hung up the phone. He'd landed the plane in Miami, and was the only one who hadn't slept. But if he was tired it didn't show.

Nadia had hoped his mood would have improved having spent enough time with Will during the flight that he might have some closure. Or at least a decent plan that didn't feature "wait and see" as the main element. But she was disappointed. "The marshals are waiting for you and Javier," he said to Colt. "They'll explain what's going to happen to you next. Let you weigh your options."

Colt nodded.

Ben turned to Will. "Stay with the plane and call Remy. See if she can help you get a location from the photo or any of the calls back and forth with Dante."

"Dante was never with them. They originated from a third party."

Nadia prayed for him. Dante had bigger things to worry about now, and he didn't need Will's family, which meant they could very well be dead. Or he'd done to them what he had done to Nadia. Either way, it was up to computer-genius Will to look for them. And this mysterious "contact." With God's help the impossible became possible. She'd seen that happen before, and it could again.

She'd seen an assassin find forgiveness and freedom. She'd seen traumatized people find peace. She'd felt the condemnation, of the things she had done and the choices she had made, disappear in the light of God's grace and His love for her.

What Nadia didn't understand at all was a man who could be all torn up and then just give up. So it was hard. Wasn't everything in life? At least the parts that were worth fighting for. Which made her wonder again about the woman who had bought her back from Earnest. What was her connection to Ben? Was she the woman he had given up on ever having, the way Will seemed to have lost faith in getting his family back?

"Let's go."

Nadia nodded and followed Ben. The marshals shook hands with Colt and Javier. They would be okay, or safe at least.

A driver was parked beyond the marshals' vehicles. A black town car, the older man dressed in a suit and black cap with driving gloves on looked like Bruce Wayne's guardian. Nadia could have smirked.

Ben put his hand on the small of her back, and the driver opened the rear door as they approached. "Alan."

"Good afternoon, sir."

Nadia climbed in and didn't wait for Ben to buckle up before she said, "Please tell me we're going to Bolton's house."

"What do you expect to be able to do when you get there?"

"That's why you're coming," she said. "I don't want to face Dante again, not after the last time. But I can't just sit around and do nothing when Bolton's life is in danger. Once Dante gets the stash, he'll kill him."

"Or he'll kill him because it's not at Bolton's house." Ben's expression didn't change. It was like he was discussing the weather. "He's not dumb enough to hide it at home."

"Then why are they there?"

"I don't know, but Bolton is probably stalling in the hopes rescue will come."

"So let's go!"

Ben said, "That's why I'm not letting you go by yourself. This is dangerous stuff, Nadia. Rushing in won't serve the situation well. It will only cause more problems."

"And Bolton being dead because we took too long won't be a problem?"

"I know you want to save him, but a grown man must face the consequences of his actions. He has to see this through, or he'll never be able to move on." He stared at her with that infuriating knowing look. When did he decide he knew everything? "Nadia, if you rush in and rescue him then you rob Bolton of the chance to end this himself. You can't fight his battle for him. I know you understand what I'm talking about."

"It doesn't mean I agree with it."

She'd felt the need to contact Dante and make a deal, but it hadn't helped. She'd only made things worse. So why was she doing the same thing now? Rushing in and saving the day wasn't exactly what she was trying to do. She couldn't fight Dante for Bolton's life. But neither could she sit around and wait for Bolton to call because it was over. Or not. God had put her here to *do something*. Not nothing.

Was it just to pray?

She looked at Ben and frowned. "All those skills and abilities, and you won't use them to save a man who is supposed to be your friend?"

"Sometimes even I can't save someone. Not when they don't want to be saved." He sounded so lost Nadia might have cried. "Bolton has to make that choice for himself, otherwise his life means nothing."

Nadia shook her head. She didn't even want to think about that. Bolton had allowed her to be part of what was happening to him, but he'd never said he wanted her there with him. He hadn't asked for her or pursued her. Nadia had been the one who stayed in his life of her own choice. And even tried to help him.

In return, he'd been there for her some. He'd cared, but Bolton had never indicated it was anything more than that for him. A couple of stolen kisses that maybe didn't mean more than the fact he'd gotten caught up in the heat of whatever moment they'd had. Maybe he didn't even want to be with someone forever. Perhaps Thea had killed that desire for him when she betrayed him so thoroughly.

Nadia didn't know what it was like to be that closed off to the beauty of what this life could hold. If all she ever saw was the darkness—the life Earnest had tried to place her in, or the pain she saw around her and in the people she cared about—then there would never be light. But she'd found a light to look to in the Lord.

Bolton was still in darkness.

The car pulled over, outside a mansion with a giant circular driveway filled with vehicles, news vans, and a SWAT truck. A couple of helicopters even circled overhead.

"What on earth?" She got out, and Ben followed, looking grim.

"Seems like they've attracted some attention." Ben knocked on the trunk. His driver, Alan, opened it remotely from the front. Ben rummaged in a duffel bag and slipped a black wallet into his pocket before he shut the trunk again.

Alan drove away.

"He's leaving us here?"

"He won't go far. If we need a ride, I'll call him back."

"Oh." That life, the one where other people were payed to be at her beck and call, was a million years ago now.

"Come on, partner." Before she could ask what that meant, Ben strode to the nearest official looking person and pulled out the wallet. He flashed a gold shield at the uniformed police sergeant. "Special Agent Woodrow Barton, FBI. What's happening here?"

The sergeant frowned. "Four people dead, the homeowners—" He looked down at his notepad. "Tilly and Barrett Freese, as well as the two officers who first responded to the 9-1-1 call. Came from Barrett Freese's phone, and what we think was the kill shot was recorded. Then he killed the two officers who showed up to investigate. Now the killer is inside, and he isn't responding to our attempts to make contact."

The front windows of the house had been shot out, but Nadia couldn't see anyone on the ground floor. Where was Dante? "Just one man in there, the killer?" There should be two others.

"No. And it's interesting that you ask that." The sergeant cocked his head to the side. "What did you say your name was?"

"She didn't. She's with me." Ben paused for a second. "Special consultant to the FBI."

The sergeant glanced at Ben. "I'm supposed to believe that? The FBI is already here. Now you know only what the media knows. Except for this, after which you will tell me everything you know, and not just what you think might be helpful."

Ben didn't nod or give any other sign he agreed.

"Please tell us." The desperation was there in her voice, but Nadia didn't have anything else other than the need to know if Bolton was okay.

The sergeant looked at her. "A man we believe to be a crooked federal agent, an extremely dangerous fugitive the DEA has been hunting for years, is holding one of their agents, Tristan Sanders, hostage inside that house. A house which used to belong to him."

Bolton wasn't the fugitive. If he was in there, he was the hostage. Who was in there with them? And who had been left behind?

Nadia opened her mouth, but Ben put a restraining hand on her arm. She shrugged him off. "Where is Bolton Farrera?"

The sergeant frowned. "Who?"

Chapter 25

"What are we going to do?" Nadia hissed her question at Ben. The sergeant had been called away, with the promise he'd need to ask them more questions. People kept showing up at the house, filling the drive with yet more uniformed officers of whatever law branch they represented. "They've got the completely wrong impression of who is in there, and why."

"I don't know what to tell you, Nadia. We can play it out, let the cops breach with their SWAT team and get the 'hostage' to safety, but we have no idea who it is. Dante or Tristan could swing this whatever way they want and get Bolton killed in the crossfire."

"But Dante's an escaped fugitive! They can't just let him walk away from this."

"The DEA kept this so far under wraps that Tristan's people can spin this whichever way they want. They can blame the whole thing on Bolton and claim he's Dante long enough for him to get locked up in place of Dante." Ben fell silent for a second. "It's actually kind of clever."

"Well then we need to be cleverer than they are!" She wanted to scream but was instead forced to yell in a whisper, so that no one overheard their conversation. "We need to get in there first and help him."

Ben's eyebrow rose as he stared at her. They were nearly eye-to-eye. Why hadn't she noticed that before? Ben blended in so completely it was hard to discern much about his physical stature. He probably disappeared underneath people's noses all the time.

"Fine." Nadia sighed. "*You* need to get in there. I'll, you know, hold down the fort out here."

His lips twitched.

"But you have to *promise* me you'll save Bolton."

"Some things are beyond even me, Nadia." He followed that awesome statement with, "But I'll do my best."

Nadia felt better enough she leaned over and kissed him lightly on the cheek. "Thank you."

Ben stared at her for a second. He glanced aside with only his eyes and then disappeared into the crowd while Nadia stood there. So she did what everyone else in the world did when they have nothing else to do—she pulled out her phone. Staring at the screen and ignoring everyone around them seemed to be what these people did best. When she went back to Sanctuary she'd have to surrender the electronic tether to virtual reality, and there wouldn't be one day in the rest of her life she'd miss this thing. All she would miss was the opportunity to do what she was doing right now whenever she wanted.

The phone rang, and she put it to her ear.

"Nadia?"

"Remy." She exhaled. "How is he?"

"Awake." Remy's voice reverberated with emotion. "He's awake. I'll put him on." There was a rustle over the line. "It's Nadia." Then more clearly, Remy said, "Just talk. He can hear you."

"Shadrach?" Tears filled her eyes. "Shadrach, I'm so glad you're awake. I was so worried, and then I would remember how much you've survived so far I couldn't believe I was doubting you'd pull through this. I just had to pray, because I don't ever want to lose you." Nadia stepped aside, wanting privacy as she blubbered into her brother's ear. "I don't think I could handle losing you, or anyone I love."

"Nadia…" he said her name on a slur, low and slow. Like he was halfway between narcotics and a nap. "Strawberries are ripe now."

She laughed. "Okay, brother. Let's go get some."

"Yum."

In the background, she could hear Remy's amusement too. "I love you, Shadrach."

"Mmm, love too. Nads."

Remy came back on the line. "Aaaaand he's out again."

Nadia chuckled. "I can't thank you enough, Remy. That was exactly the thing I needed."

"You're the one with the good timing, girl." It was the Lord's timing. *Thank You.* Remy said, "How are things there? Did you find Bolton?"

Nadia filled her in.

"Ben will figure it out." She sounded so sure. "He'll make sure nothing happens to Bolton that he doesn't want to happen."

That Ben didn't want, or that Bolton didn't want? That was the question. At this point, it was kind of hazy what side Ben was on. Or even if he was on any side. So he wasn't working for Tristan or Dante, but he certainly had his own interests and those interests might outweigh Bolton's ability to have a free and happy future.

"Take care of my brother, Remy."

"You know I will."

Nadia did. Despite whatever awkwardness she'd seen between them, or how they were coping after Remy's ordeal. She knew that Remy wouldn't desert her brother. It was the reason she'd been able to leave, knowing Remy would be there. Otherwise she'd have made things worse for Shadrach, trying to contend with her mother, day after day, in that hospital room.

"You have a green light! Go!"

She hung up and watched as the SWAT team raced toward the house so synchronized it was clear they'd done it many times before. Four men ran in the front door, fully decked out in their uniforms with huge guns and helmets that covered their faces. Others went around the outside of the house to the back.

Nadia clutched the phone to her chest and prayed Ben was among them somehow. That he'd gotten inside so that he could assist the outcome. If anyone could, it was him.

An ambulance pulled in front of her, red and blue lights flashing as people parted. Did they anticipate casualties? Preparedness was one thing, but was this SWAT team good enough to diffuse the situation without casualties?

The ambulance stopped.

Nadia took one look at the driver and blinked. He had the uniform, complete with a ball cap that looked so out of place it was almost comical.

Ben's driver glanced at her then motioned to the back of his bus with one jerk of his head.

Nadia ran around and climbed in the back. Clothes had been tossed on the stretcher.

"Put the uniform on." He pulled the door across, blocking her from view.

**

Dante punched Bolton across the face. Hard.

His boots pounded the stairs and Bolton was left with only the sound of blood rushing through his ears. The room stretched and contracted like a rubber band pulled taut and then released. How could he get out of there if he couldn't even see, let alone walk?

He'd done what he had come there to do. Stalled long enough for the cops to show up and take Dante back to jail. Held his secret in, despite the pressure Dante had put on him. The stash was safe, and it was going to stay that way until Bolton—and only Bolton—unearthed it. Otherwise, what was the point in hiding resources and insurance in the first place unless it was secure from his enemies?

"Is he dead?"

Boots vibrated the stairs under his head. Bolton wanted to swat away the intrusion. He'd been feeling kind of peaceful until they disturbed him.

"Lemme check."

Two fingers pushed in the side of his neck. Bolton lifted his hand and swiped aside the forearm with his hand with barely enough strength to push the guy away.

"Whoa. Got a live one."

Bolton blinked until the man's face came into view. Black helmet. SWAT, probably. The man crouched and grabbed Bolton's hand. He pressed his finger on to the scanner of a handheld device, waited a second and then shook his head.

"Bolton Farrera?" He glanced at his buddy. "I didn't believe it, but this thing don't lie."

"Right? I'd figure he was smoking something if I didn't see it with my own eyes."

The first man stowed the handheld fingerprint scanner in the thigh pocket of his cargo pants and pulled out a pistol.

"Lights out."

**

Ben's gun smoked, and the shot rang in his ears. He ducked back behind the wall and turned, not waiting to see Dante fall or the surprise on those SWAT guys' faces who'd been about to approach him.

He raced down the hall to the basement, where they would likely already have Bolton secured.

Ben's back hit the wall, and he glanced around the corner.

Maybe the plan was "dead" not "secured."

**

A shot rang out. Then another immediately after it. The SWAT guy dropped, and whoever had stood on the stairs behind Bolton tumbled down over the top of him to lie by his buddy.

"Time to go."

"Ben?" His face appeared in front of Bolton in time for him to brace as Ben hauled him up over his shoulder.

Ben grunted and started up the stairs. "Have you thought about Weight Watchers?"

Bolton didn't have the energy to laugh.

"Time to make our strategic exit, before someone else trying to kill you can aim a gun your way. I don't have a free hand to deal with it."

Hallway floor.

Dead owners.

Fresh air.

"Can I get some help?!" Ben's call erupted into a bustle of noise. Hands grasped Bolton, and he was laid on a stretcher. "He's bleeding pretty bad. I don't know how long that guy had him in there or what they did. But he's pretty messed up."

A man in a sergeant's uniform stared down at Bolton with too much knowing in his eyes. Where was Ben? Had he evaporated into the crowd and just left Bolton there?

The sergeant lifted his chin. "Somewhere between here and the hospital, find out who this guy is."

"Will do, Sergeant."

The gurney was pushed until an ambulance ceiling floated into view above his head. "I'll take it from here, boys."

Soft hands touched his arm, and she gave his hand a squeeze.

Who—

"Easy now." She pressed his shoulder back down. "We'll get you fixed up in no time."

The ambulance doors shut, and they started moving.

"Bolton." Nadia's face was in his. "What did he do?" Tears pooled in her eyes.

He shut his eyes and shook his head. She didn't want to know about his business with Dante. "Did they catch him?"

"You were the first one brought out." She touched his face, and her eyes softened. "I didn't see Dante, or Tristan."

Dante had killed Tristan on the plane. That couple, and the cops.

He'd run out of the basement. Where had he gone? And who were those guys that tried to kill him? They must have been DEA, pretending to be SWAT. The whole situation had been crazy, and where was Ben?

Bolton's brain spun. A door slid open, and Ben said, "Above your head. Get one of those packets, rip it open, and hold it on that. I'll get this side."

Pressure. Nadia applied it like a champ, and he almost managed to contain his reaction.

"Sorry. I'm sorry."

Ben said, "Ignore him. It hurts, and he's feeling it." Ben grabbed something in his teeth and tore it open.

"Uh-uh." Bolton didn't like the look of that needle one bit.

Apparently Ben didn't care. "Don't be a baby."

"What are you going to—" Nadia was too late. Ben jabbed the needle into Bolton's arm and pushed down the plunger.

"Why does that hurt more than being shot?" It made no sense, but the sting didn't leave after the needle was drawn out. He'd never liked needles. "I'm guessing no hospital."

Ben shot him a look and donned gloves.

Nadia gasped. "You're going to stitch him up?"

"It's that or he bleeds to death."

He didn't have to talk to her like that. Bolton reached for her, but she had both arms straight pushing on his leg. "It's okay, Nadia."

"Okay? None of this is okay." She looked at Ben. "Where's Dante?"

"Dead."

Bolton whipped his head around. "He's gone?"

Ben nodded, his gaze concentrated on Bolton's wound. "I took care of it before he could escape by the men breaching the house, or before he could pretend to be the victim." He snipped with scissors. "One down, three to go."

Nadia blew out a breath. "Where are we going? Home?"

Was he going to take Bolton back to Sanctuary? Ben wanted the stash, probably as much as Dante and Tristan had.

Ben said, "One more stop before we figure out who goes where." He pulled out his phone. "Yeah, Remy. This is Dante's phone. Call the Boy Scout, get me a location on Will's family, will you?" Pause. "Thanks."

He looked at the screen and scrolled. Punched in a series of digits. The phone chimed, it increased in tone, and then chirped.

"You're helping Will?"

Ben shrugged in answer to Nadia's question.

"I knew you were a good guy."

Ben set the phone aside and sighed down at Bolton. "He really did a number on you, didn't he?"

"Doesn't matter." Bolton didn't look at Nadia, then. She was determined to see the good in every situation, and he didn't want to see her face. "They'll heal." He had more serious problems that likely weren't going to get better like the couple gunshot wounds and the other more minor injuries. Ones that weren't going to heal for the rest of his life.

"Seriously, Bolton. He's right." Her voice was incredulous. "How are you even still conscious with these wounds?"

Ben's face was grim and didn't leave Bolton's gaze when he said, "Because he can't feel his legs."

**

Nadia stared at him. "Were you going to say anything?"

Bolton's dark eyes didn't chance. No remorse. No regret. "What is there to say?" He blinked and looked away.

Ben continued to sew him up. Nadia couldn't look at those wounds. She didn't want to think about all the ways Dante had hurt him.

She looked up at Ben's head, bent down to his task. "Is Dante really dead?"

His eyes lifted. "He's gone, Nadia."

She needed a week just to get used to the idea.

"Tristan, too," Bolton said. "Dante shot him on the airplane and took his ID. That's why he had Tristan's badge and wallet at the house."

"He would have pretended to be DEA while you were killed in his place. He'd have made it work so that you couldn't talk," Ben said. "And since no one knows who he was, he'd have gotten away with it. Free and clear, but hunted for the rest of his life. He'd have disappeared so thoroughly I doubt they'd ever have found him." Ben's voice had a hard edge that made Nadia wonder if he would have personally seen to it Dante was brought in. "But now he can't hurt anyone else ever again."

Nadia didn't know what to do with the swell of relief from just contemplating that, while Ben seemed to draw comfort from the fact he had drawn the situation to a close. "So it's really over?"

Bolton said, "Once I get to the stash, it will be." He and Ben locked eyes for a second, and something passed unspoken between them. Nadia wasn't even sure she wanted to know what secrets they kept.

"Then it's back to Sanctuary for me." She bit her lip, determined not to let it get to her. Bolton had to make his own choice. If that wasn't her, she needed to go back to Sanctuary in one piece. She couldn't let it affect her, otherwise she would drown in it. Instead, she focused on the need of another person. "If Javier and Colt end up there, they'll need help settling in."

"Colt?" Bolton's stare hit her like a blow.

"He could get transferred there. But it's more about Javier." Didn't he know that? Colt was just some guy who'd been evicted. She didn't know the first thing about him. "The boy just lost everything. He's going to need people around him who are prepared to love him."

Bolton nodded slowly. "Sanctuary will be good medicine."

But it wasn't good for Bolton? The man who only needed his "stash" and nothing else. No *one* else. It was infuriating. If he hadn't been shot multiple times and pretty much tortured, she would have kicked him. Nadia looked at Ben instead of acting on her impulses. "Can you find out if they go to Sanctuary, and let me know?"

He nodded. "Sure. I'll do that."

"And you'll make sure Will's family is safe?"

"Nadia—"

She shook her head. "I know it's a long shot that Dante didn't already order them killed, like hours ago. But you have to at least try." She blew out a breath. "Just...don't tell me. If it doesn't work out, I don't want to know. Tell me if they're fine. If not... Well, I'll just know, won't I?"

Ben stared at her until Nadia looked away.

She leaned back against the wall of the ambulance and closed her eyes. Bolton was still determined to go his own way, to live his new life the way he wanted to. Didn't he even care whether the boy was his son or not? Did it matter, when he'd been protecting the kid this whole time? Even if Javier had been Dante's, he'd been nothing more than the son of Bolton's heart. Now he had no one. Javier was facing years in a new town he might not like. People would take care of him, but that wasn't like having a real family. Who would he live with? Colt hadn't seemed like the foster father type, but Nadia couldn't tell. Maybe he would rise to the occasion.

Bolton apparently didn't even care. He was going to get his things and be gone, leaving everyone else to pick up the pieces of his mess.

They'd shared something, but apparently that had meant as little to him as it did to his son. Maybe Bolton wasn't capable of loving someone. Maybe Thea had messed him up too much for him to have a real, loving, normal relationship with a parent. Nadia didn't want something that would turn out to be a disaster, and she didn't want him to live in a place where he'd be unhappy, but all relationships took work. It was never a fairytale, just real life.

So she was going home.

And she wasn't going to ask him to come with her.

"For what it's worth," she waited until his gaze caught hers, and then she said, "I am sorry." Nadia took a fortifying breath. "I thought I was supposed to help you become the man you were in Sanctuary. Someone…better, the way we all want to be better people."

Except he had no intention of changing. "I guess I was wrong to think that. Or to expect something you weren't willing to give. I was supposed to love you anyway, no matter what you decided to do. And it was really hard, but it's done now. You have your life to live, and I have mine to get back to."

It was the hardest thing God had ever asked of her. But now it was done.

**

"Do I want to know where you got a wheelchair from?" Bolton looked back over his shoulder at Ben, who stood behind him in the hangar. "Maybe I should just ask you how you plan to get me up the stairs and into the plane." This was going to be fun. And completely dignified.

Bolton wanted to roll his eyes, but that was lame. Never mind, this whole situation was lame. Bolton was pretty sure the surgery had failed—whether it had been destined to anyway, or he'd forced the outcome because of his circumstances.

"I have things to do."

Still, Ben stared at the plane door where Nadia had disappeared in a mood. She'd retreated into herself and hadn't spoken to him after she'd announced she was going back to Sanctuary for Javier's sake.

Bolton said, "I know you do, Will."

His feelings for a man who would betray his boss—his friends—wasn't hidden from his voice. The wife and daughter were innocents. Will held all the blame on this one for not adequately protecting his family.

Alan slammed the ambulance door and strode over. "Ready to load the cargo?"

Bolton didn't laugh. The man had the worst sense of humor. He was having trouble believing Dante was really dead and the threat was over. Is this what Nadia had felt when she'd been told that the man trying to kill her was dead? And yet, she'd chosen to stay in Sanctuary. She could have gone anywhere. Lived any life. She had money, the means to do whatever she wanted. And yet, she'd stayed.

For him.

Because she'd found something there she wasn't prepared to give up, not for the whole world.

Nadia strode out of the plane and down the stairs, slinging a backpack over her shoulder. She lifted a phone and waved it at Ben. "I'm borrowing this."

He didn't even have time to respond before she swept past them.

"Where are you going?" Bolton yelled after her.

She turned around and walked backwards for a few steps. "Home, Bolton. Like I said, I'm going home." She moved her gaze to Ben. "Find Will's family."

Ben nodded.

Bolton didn't even know what to say or do. She was *leaving*? Just like that, making her own way back to Sanctuary. She'd probably have to call for assistance for the final leg of the journey, but she walked with supreme confidence.

Like she didn't have a care in the world. Like she wasn't striding away, taking his heart with her. It was more painful than any of his wounds, watching her leave. He could almost hear the rip of her walking away with his heart in her hands.

"Ready to go?" Ben asked.

Bolton turned away. Was he ready?

Chapter 26

The unmarked silver car had been parked at the side of the road. Ben pulled over behind it and Will climbed out of the SUV without a word.

Night was coming fast, and the light would evaporate with the day. They'd be blind without flashlights to announce their presence to anyone who cared to look.

Ben left the keys in the ignition, shut the driver's door, and crept to the car. No one inside. The hood was still warm. "They aren't far ahead of us."

The most he could figure was that the men who'd had Will's wife and child hadn't heard from Dante. He'd kept them going with texts from Dante's phone, but they'd grown suspicious.

How the DEA expected to completely cover up the truth was anyone's guess. Ben would've leaked the whole thing to the media if he cared enough to meddle. But exposing lies wasn't worth the energy it took to pull all the evidence together. Injustice was everywhere. Liars filled every sector of society. Changing policy or fighting the roaring juggernaut of government, or some organization with their oversight, wasn't nearly the same as meeting someone in need, face-to-face, and saving their life.

Besides, Ben hardly needed another target on his back, and neither did Bolton. The DEA would eventually figure out what he had been doing and come calling…to put a bullet in his brain. He had enough enemies.

He followed Will down the path. His voice echoed back to Ben. No waiting, Will had charged in. The sight of his family too much to bear thirty seconds of waiting.

Bang.

The first man went down. Will's gun pointed at him, smoked in the chilled air. The second aimed at Will, but Will hadn't noticed yet.

Ben fired one shot, and he went down.

Will jumped and spun around.

Ben didn't come out of the shadows.

"Daddy!"

"Will!"

They slammed into him. Will went to his knees and hugged his family to his chest. Sobs echoed from them.

Ben stared at the family. Little girl arms tight around her daddy's waist. Will's fingers on his wife's face as they shared a desperate kiss of two people who hadn't known if they'd ever see each other again.

The feel of her breath on his face as he pulled her close. The way the world melted away, and nothing else seemed to matter about that. Right then and there. Him, and her. It was like there was no one else in the world.

Ben slid the phone from his pocket as he walked back to the car. Typed in her number. His thumb hovered over the button, so close to dialing.

Ben flipped the phone over and pulled out the sim card. The minute he hit blacktop Ben dropped it on the ground and destroyed it with the heel of his boot. He threw the rest of the phone across the street, into the trees.

Alan turned the corner and pulled up.

Ben got in, and they drove away.

**

Bolton pushed on the wheels and huffed until the wheelchair was at the top of the long ramp. *Disabled access.* Back then he never would have dreamed he'd even need it one day, let alone that he'd actually be here. The button stood on a post, that disabled sign jeering at him. The surgery had been pointless, he might as well have not spent the money.

A little girl slammed her palm on the button and hopped from one foot to the other while the door to the Payton County Library slid open. The minute the crack was big enough she could fit through, the little girl darted inside.

Pennsylvania. Maybe while he was here he could find someone to talk to about this whole "God" thing that wasn't letting up. Sure, he'd talked to the big man in the heat of the moment when he'd been sure he was going to die, but did it have to be a constant now he was free to live his life? It almost felt like God didn't want to let go of *him*.

"So this is where you hid it."

Bolton couldn't turn around. He glanced over his shoulder, and Ben came to stand beside him. Aside from his neck, he could barely move at all. Remy had said that he'd be able to bend and twist when everything finally healed—as much as it would heal—but he would probably never be able to walk.

He should have stolen a horse instead of using this chair. Then he'd have been looking down on Ben, not the other way around. Though, that might draw unwanted attention.

Bolton wheeled through the entrance. He'd hidden the stash here a long time ago, under the cover that he'd been on a binge weekend. Instead, he'd used a fake ID to travel halfway across the country to a tiny town with an even smaller library where he'd stashed the metal cash box.

"I gotta use the bathroom." He didn't look aside at Ben.

"I'll go with you."

"Because we're girls, so you gotta go with me?"

Ben didn't laugh. What was his problem anyway? The man had a serious humor deficiency.

"I know you're only here to get the flash drive."

Ben held the bathroom door open. "You know that's not all of it."

"Don't try to convince me letting Nadia go was the wrong thing." He didn't need Ben to say anything about that. After weeks and weeks of having her there with him, and before that living in a town where neither of them could leave, now she was gone. Bolton didn't know if he would ever get used to it.

"What about the boy?"

Bolton didn't know what he was supposed to think about Javier, either. "He isn't my kid. Thea said he was Dante's."

"He's dead, she's dead. You're the closest thing that boy has to family left on this planet."

"Except his grandfather." Not to mention the kid had tried to kill him. Bolton's heart was so mixed up about the kid, he didn't know what to think about Javier.

"He tried to shoot Grant. He's currently incarcerated." Ben shot him a look. "You really think Thea's father is the answer?"

A suited man at the sink pulled two paper towels and wiped his hands. He blinked at the sight of Bolton and then scurried out.

Yeah, so he looked like he'd been in a warzone. What else was new? "Anything else you haven't told me?"

"I've barely gotten started."

Bolton turned the chair so he could face Ben. "I used to think we were friends."

Ben made a face. "You think I have friends?"

"When they suit your purposes." Ben reacted, but Bolton didn't let that bother him. "You're so good at lying I wonder if you even know what the truth is anymore."

Ben motioned to the bathroom. "Just get the stash."

Bolton folded his arms. "Maybe I really did need to take a leak." He wheeled into the larger stall at the end and slid the lock home. "You know there are plenty of people in Sanctuary who would love to take an orphaned boy under their wing. I could spend ten minutes listing off names."

Bolton pulled the chisel from his backpack and counted tiles.

"And you'd be smug the whole time. Because you've convinced yourself that means Javier doesn't need you for anything."

"When he'd only try and shoot me again?"

"That was a different set of circumstances."

"So you want me to go back to Sanctuary to be a father to a kid who already tried to kill me, and probably is the child of my greatest enemy." Bolton shook his head and worked the chisel behind the tile. "Sounds like a win-win."

The tile fell to the floor and smashed.

It was almost tempting to go back there and pretend like everything hadn't changed now that Nadia knew who he was and what he'd done. Not to mention how he felt. At least about almost everything—he hadn't ever told her how he really felt about her.

Maybe he should have. Maybe then she'd have come with him, left everyone she knew and everything she loved to live a life of anonymity with him.

Even now he had to stay under the radar, wear a disguise. He'd be condemning her to always looking over her shoulder unless he lived in Sanctuary, where they would both always be safe. At least that was the idea. It had been a haven for him, more than just a place he could lick his wounds and plan his next move. Nadia's presence there had made it a home.

The hole for an old ventilation system sat behind the tiles. Bolton reached in and grasped the cash box. There was no key, there never had been. It was why he'd picked this one.

He let himself out of the stall, the box on his lap. "We'll have to cut it open."

Ben pulled a pouch from his pocket. "Set it on the counter." He picked the lock on the cash box. "You do the honors."

Inside was a passport, a clean pistol, fifty thousand dollars, and the flash drive.

"Seems kind of anticlimactic, given all the fuss."

Bolton shook his head and lifted out the flash drive. "That's because you don't know what's on this." He handed it over. "It's in your hands now. I know you'll do what's right with it."

Ben nodded.

Bolton pocketed the rest of the stuff. "Guess this is my cue to leave."

"What's your plan?" Ben looked like he wanted to sigh. "Where are you going to go?"

"I'm going to find myself a new home." He grinned but didn't feel it. "Do they have disabled accessible beaches?"

Ben was silent for a minute. Disapproval flooded from him in waves. "I know of a home that might be good for you. It blew up a couple of months ago, but maybe your friends rebuilt it."

"I told Matthias to wait."

"Then you get to redesign it yourself. Maybe with room for a wife and a son."

Bolton set his hands over his pockets, the contents of which had always been his ticket to a new life. He'd been so focused on finding the stash and securing his future that he hadn't had time for other dreams. "You want me to be confined to one town for the rest of my life?"

"Only when everything you've ever wanted but were too scared to dream of is right there in Sanctuary."

I'm not scared.

Ben was already gone, the door swished shut, and Bolton was left in the library bathroom by himself.

It wasn't fear. That wasn't it. He wasn't afraid of Sanctuary or afraid of being happy. Thea had cured him forever of the need to trust someone else with his future, his peace and happiness being so dependent on everything they said and did.

He didn't want that life.

Bolton wheeled to the front door. He hit the button and left the library.

Outside the sky was bright, too bright to look at. The air crisp and cold, made his aches and pains hurt all the more. He would find somewhere to live; he'd be happy.

He just didn't know where to start looking.

**

Nadia saw her mom outside her brother's hospital room, and her steps faltered. Her mom looked up.

No going back now.

Nadia strode forward. "I came to say goodbye to Shadrach, I won't be staying long." She turned to the door.

"Nadia." Her mom sounded almost…nervous.

She looked back.

"Remy explained a few things to me."

Nadia wasn't sure if she even wanted to know what Remy had told her mom.

"I didn't mean to blame you." She hesitated. "Okay, I did mean it. I wanted to blame you. But not because of anything you'd done. It was just easier than acknowledging that my life wasn't what I thought it should be. You were so talented and so wild. Shadrach was the only person that calmed you. I couldn't even do that. Your own mother."

Nadia sighed. "Mom—"

"Then all that danger, and you disappeared. I didn't know if you were dead or alive until Shadrach filled me in." She paused. "Witness protection…" She breathed the words like they were both fantastic and terrible. "And I still blamed you. Because it was easier."

"And now?" She had someone special in her life. She'd survived a terrible threat of her own and come through victorious.

"You should count your blessings that you survived so much, considering you were determined to destroy yourself."

"I do count them. Every day. Even more than you'll ever know."

Her mom almost smiled. "It was nice to see you, Nadia."

She let herself into Shadrach's room, wondering if she could say the same. The past few weeks had been so chaotic Nadia didn't know when she'd feel like things had gone back to normal.

Normal would feel really good right about now.

Shadrach looked so bad she nearly said a word she wasn't supposed to. But that wouldn't help anything, and it would hardly make her feel better. Though the struggle with her tongue was about as close to normal as she could have gotten right then. *Thank You, Lord.* He'd given her what she'd asked for by reminding her of that constant struggle against her flesh. His Spirit in her would see her through this, not her frail human reactions.

So help me with the Bolton thing, too. God would, she knew that. He wasn't the kind of father who up and left one day because he was tired. God was going to support her, and even though things hadn't gone the way she had thought, Nadia would still find her strength in trusting Him.

"Hey."

She smiled at the slur in her brother's voice. When she opened her mouth to speak, a sob was the only thing she could give him. Shadrach flicked his fingers toward himself. Nadia held her brother as well as she could without hurting him, and cried.

Two days later Nadia sat in a helicopter as the mountains of Idaho rushed under them like a river in spring. They flew over the farm, over Main Street, and the rows of houses that flanked it. Her salon. The bakery, and the sheriff's office. The medical center that had been rebuilt. At the far end was the ranch, cows dotting the landscape beside a lake. The town sat like a bowl within a ring of mountains designated as a no-fly-zone except for authorized aircraft—like the one Grant had arranged for her.

No longer a federally owned and operated town, Nadia had essentially bought her way back in. She'd gladly transferred a portion of her money to a charity that provided assistance for veterans, and the rest she'd used to secure her place as a board member of the private entity who now owned the town. She'd have a say in its upkeep and help decide who got to live here from the referrals they were given by the US marshals. People who desperately needed Sanctuary.

"So this is it, huh?"

She glanced at Javier and spoke through her headset. "Not quite Hawaii, but I like it."

He gave her a tentative smile. "I'm sure it'll grow on me."

She laughed. Since she'd met up with him in Seattle for the trip to Sanctuary, he'd started to come out of his shell. Colt had to stay in Washington State for longer, so his paperwork could be processed. He would be joining them in a week or so.

Nadia prayed both of them would settle well and find safety here.

The helicopter set down on the blacktop, the road that should have led to the ranch house. Instead there was little more than a hole in the ground now full of water. A dock.

The house and all its debris had been cleared away. The barn still stood, like a bomb hadn't exploded under the mountain and cracked the ground open in places.

Hal had died here. Now that Bolton wasn't coming back, would it ever get rebuilt?

"Thanks for the lift."

"No problem, ma'am."

Nadia removed the headset and climbed out. A Jeep marked with the emblem SHERIFF drove toward her. Then it blurred in a wash of salty tears. She'd hardly dared to believe she'd make it back home.

The door flung open before it even stopped, and her *very pregnant* friend jumped out. How someone that huge could be so agile was a mystery. Nadia laughed. "Andra!"

John got out the driver's side. "Andra!"

She waved him off, her black hair flying behind her. Except for the roots, which were not black.

Nadia laughed again. "Looks like your hair needs some work." She had a job to get back to, along with her life and her new position on the board.

Andra didn't say anything. She simply collided with Nadia and wrapped her arms around Nadia to squeeze the breath out of her. Then she groaned and leaned back to put two hands on her beach-ball sized tummy. "I can't do anything with this thing sticking out of me. Halfway through this pregnancy and I'm already huge."

Nadia didn't know which question to ask first.

"It's a girl. We're going to call her Marie." Andra groaned again. "You're going to cry more now."

Nadia nodded while the tears streamed down her face.

Andra sighed and pulled her in again.

"I'm so happy for you."

When she leaned back, John caught them both in a hug. "You look like you needed another."

Nadia nodded.

His brow crinkled. "Where's Bolton? I was surprised to hear he wasn't coming with you."

Nadia shrugged. She really didn't want to cry again. She was done crying about Bolton. She glanced at where his house had stood.

"Was he really a criminal?" John said. "I'm having trouble with that one."

Nadia shrugged. "He..." Her voice broke. Where did she even start?

"Tell us later," Andra said. "When you're ready."

Nadia glanced aside at her.

"What? I'm pregnant. Apparently hormones make you sympathetic. Go figure."

Nadia felt her lips curl up in a smile. "I have someone for you to meet." She waved the teen over, as he'd been hanging back. He stepped closer and even took her hand. "This is Javier."

John shook his hand and introduced Andra. "I already alerted the welcoming committee that you were coming."

Nadia leaned her head closer to Javier's. "That means you have to shake a lot of hands on Friday night, but there'll be cake."

He smiled. "I like cake."

Andra laughed. Nadia walked with them to the Jeep, and climbed in. She wanted to get back to her salon, to start up her life here again, and see how Javier fit into it. He'd be living with a family who had teens so that he had parents, and kids his own age, but she'd be able to see him all the time. Maybe he'd even let her cut his hair.

The town was the same, except for the damage to the ranch. It was Nadia that was different. Maybe that was why things felt strange. She'd find her footing and settle back in. Go to church. Maybe date someone...not yet, but a ways down the road when her emotions weren't still tied up in a man who had chosen his own path.

She sighed and leaned forward to squeeze Andra's shoulder. "So what's new?"

"Hmm," Andra said. "Well, we have a new doctor, and he's smitten with Shelby. The mayor is still acting weird. That whole thing is bizarre. Olympia is still the same, and unfortunately so is Maria. But Antonia is her usual crazy self—though her hair needs doing. Basically everyone's hair needs doing." Andra laughed. "Oh, and Gemma."

John's head whipped around. "What about Gemma?"

Andra shook her head, her gaze on her husband. "I don't know, that's the point."

"Something's up with Gemma?" Nadia had always thought the girl was pretty settled, almost like nothing could ruffle her.

"She's been acting weird for *days.* Get this, Hal was her father."

"No way."

"But she's not upset. She's like, hiding. And no one knows why."

Andra might think no one knew why, but Nadia was pretty sure John had an answer.

**

Ben waited all day for his mom to step out for a cup of coffee before he strode into the hospital room where his brother was staying.

Grant looked up. "I'm so glad it's you. Can you tell mom she needs to—"

"No." Ben didn't move. "I got the flash drive."

"That's good, right?" Grant didn't look nervous. He should have.

"Explain Pu'u honua to me, one more time. I'm not sure I quite understood what that was. Fifteen people living in the Hawaiian jungle..."

"More like ten now."

"Grant."

His brother blew out a breath, and Ben waited for an explanation.

The real story.

Epilogue

One month later

Nadia stepped back and eyed her work. "So, I'm basically an *artiste.* You know that, right?"

The client smiled. "You really are."

They laughed, though Nadia's amusement sounded hollow even to her own ears. She turned away before the client could see it. She didn't know the woman well and didn't need a dissatisfied client. Not when her customer base was limited to the two hundred people who lived in town.

The client charged the cut and color to her account, and Nadia glanced around her empty salon. The familiar smell wasn't as comforting as it had been before she left. She almost wondered what *he* was doing, but had decided not even thinking his name was best. Who cared what he was doing? It wasn't like she'd ever see him—

The bell over the door clanged and then got stuck as it was wedged wide, and *he* rolled in with a wheelchair.

Nadia stumbled back. She clipped the edge of the chair and it spun. Hit her in the hip. She didn't move. "You can't be..."

The cords of his throat moved as he swallowed. "Nadia."

She didn't want comfort or smooth words. Nadia steeled herself against all the feeling that rushed through her and folded her arms. Just so he was clear, she also lifted her chin. "You hated it here."

Why was he back? He looked tanned. Almost at peace. Okay, so he looked good but she didn't want to notice. This wasn't a place you just visited. It was a witness protection town, and he didn't live here anymore.

Bolton stared at her for a moment. Why did he look at her like she was some kind of apparition? "I tried to. Seems like I tried to convince myself of a lot of things. Most especially things about you."

She didn't even… "How did you get here?"

"Grant. He's doing fine now, recovered and everything. I saw Shadrach, too. He's good. Remy's taking care of him."

"You saw Shadrach?"

"I needed some advice." His white teeth flashed at her. "He gave me a black eye." Bolton pointed at his left eye. Sure enough, there was an edging of blue shadow against his skin. "He wants to Skype with you. John is going to set it up."

"John knows you're here?"

Bolton nodded. Of course. Incoming aircraft couldn't be a secret in this town. That meant he'd known Bolton had been coming, probably days ago. He hadn't said anything at dinner the night before, but she had left early. It hurt too much to be around happy, in love people. Even if they were her best friends.

Nadia couldn't make sense of any of this. "Why are you here?"

"That depends on you." He grasped the wheels of his chair and came closer.

"Why are you in that thing?"

"The surgery, or me not resting, didn't work. Whatever the reason I can't walk, and I haven't been able to since Dante had me in that house."

"Your house."

He nodded. "That was a long time ago, Nadia. In another life. I've had a lot of time to think the past few weeks. Time to figure out where I want to be, and what I want to do now. Enough time that I realized I left something here, something I need if I'm going to be happy."

"And what is that?"

"It's you, Nadia."

She didn't move. "You'd subject yourself to a life of misery stuck in this town just to be with me?"

"Yes, I would."

"I don't believe you. What's changed?" He hadn't wanted her more than the stash. "Did you blow through the money already? New life wasn't what you thought it would be."

He sighed. "I found a hotel, and I tried to decide where to go. Met with a doctor, and had some tests run. They ended up admitting me until the swelling went down. I had more surgery, and the prognosis isn't good. I won't ever walk again, but maybe a few steps. I can't do manual labor, so I have no idea how I'm going to work. I had to face a lot of things, not the least of which was that the one person I wanted to be there with me, holding my hand while I heard that news, wasn't there."

Nadia bit her lips together so she didn't say something out of frustration and make him leave. She could be all strong, independent woman, but she also wanted to be needed.

"It's not an easy life I'm offering you. You know what it's like to live with me when I'm like this." He gave her a small smile. "But I'm hoping that if we tell each other the truth, things will go a lot better this time."

"And what truth is that?"

"I love you, Nadia Marie Carleigh. Even if your brother hates my guts, I still love you. I want a life with you, a family, if we can."

"What if I say no?"

"Then I'll find a place here, and spend every day for the rest of our lives trying to convince you to take a chance on me."

"Bolton—" Her heart squeezed in her chest, and tears filled her eyes. "Everything I ever wanted is right here."

He smiled wide. "Yeah?" The word was tentative still.

Nadia nodded. "I always loved you." She laughed and ran a hand through her hair. "It's been frustrating, painful, and heart-wrenching, but I wouldn't trade that for anything. I wanted to leave with you, and I would have if you'd asked me to. But if we could stay here, I would be the happiest woman in the world."

"I think I could love anywhere, if you were there." He held out his hand. "I want to kiss you, but you're going to have to come down here."

Nadia set her hand in his and smiled. "What if we took things slow?"

Bolton stared at her hand in his with disbelief. He rubbed his thumb back and forth over her hand then brought it to his lips. "It would be my pleasure. How about, for starters, we go get some lunch at—"

Javier strode in with a grin on his face. "She had the roast beef." He held the white bag of sandwiches up. They'd shared lunch regularly the past four weeks.

His face fell as he looked at her and Bolton. His father. "What is he doing here?"

Bolton turned the wheelchair. "Hello, Javier."

The teen turned to Nadia. "What is he doing here?"

She gave him a small smile. "Bolton has decided to move back home."

Bolton started, "Jav—"

"No." He tossed the bag on a chair. "I'll see you later, Nadia."

Her heart sank. "I'm sorry. He's had a hard time adjusting to being here, with everyone wanting to talk about you."

"He seems fine with you."

"We're friends."

Bolton hadn't let go of her hand. He lifted it again to his lips. "Thank you for that."

"He'll get used to you being here."

"And you?"

She smiled. "I'll muddle through it." Nadia leaned down and kissed him on the cheek. "I'm glad you're home."

Thank you for reading Sanctuary Deceived!

If you enjoyed this novel,
please leave a review online
where you made your purchase.

Thank you!
Lisa

Find out more at

www.authorlisaphillips.com

Where you can sign up for Lisa's newsletter and be the first to know about new books!

Made in the USA
Monee, IL
26 May 2022

97098433R00152